White Roses Calling

Dakota Hudson

*Quest Books
by Regal Crest*

Texas

Copyright © 2014 by Dakota Hudson

All rights reserved. No part of this publication may be reproduced, transmitted in any form or by any means, electronic or mechanical, including photocopy, recording, or any information storage and retrieval system, without permission in writing from the publisher. The characters, incidents and dialogue herein are fictional and any resemblance to actual events or persons, living or dead, is purely coincidental.

ISBN 978-1-61929-170-6

First Printing 2014

9 8 7 6 5 4 3 2 1

Original cover design by Donna Pawlowski
Final cover design by AcornGraphics

Published by:

Regal Crest Enterprises, LLC
229 Sheridan Loop
Belton, Texas 76513

Find us on the World Wide Web at
http://www.regalcrest.biz

Published in the United States of America

Acknowledgments

Many thanks to the ladies at Regal Crest for being willing to take a chance on a novice author. A very special expression of appreciation to Verda, who proved herself to be an editor of unbelievable patience while working with me!

Kudos also to my very first beta readers: Kasie (who was there from the beginning and helped break the ice on the first attempts at the more intimate story moments) and Corina (because having a straight-girl beta reader is just fun and leads to very interesting late night conversations when mixed with adult beverages).

Finally, thanks to all the fine officers who I have had the privilege of working with over my two decades plus of police work. The work we've done and the adventures we've had together have provided the foundation for this fictional work.

Dedication

This, my very first published work, is dedicated to my wonderful wife – who even after fifteen years still hasn't quite caught on to the fact that I rule with an iron fist. I have confidence that she'll accept that fact eventually. Until then I guess I'll just keep doing what she tells me to do.

Author's Notes

Obviously, the Los Angeles Police Department is a real agency. I have tried to do justice to my Department and the organizational references, policies, ranks and various commands are accurate. The task force in downtown Los Angeles, to which the fictional Sergeant Alexandria Chambers is assigned, does exist, though it goes by a different name than the one utilized here. Similarly, the Office of the Los Angeles District Attorney exists and, as depicted here, their flagship office is located within the top floors of the Central Courts Building in downtown Los Angeles. I have tried to accurately reflect the rank structure and organization of the District Attorney's Office, though I have likely erred in some respects. Any such mistakes or inaccuracies are mine alone and no disrespect is intended.

The general geographical references are accurate within the context of the sprawling 465 square miles that make up the City of Los Angeles, especially the descriptions of the downtown region. Runyon Canyon, where Sydney Rutledge's home is, does exist within the hills above Hollywood, though I have taken some artistic liberties with the actual surrounding geography and environment.

Chapter One

SERGEANT ALEXANDRIA CHAMBERS refused to give up. Both predator and prey dodged pedestrians and cars as she chased the man down the sidewalk, then across the busy street. A large delivery van came to a sudden halt as Alex ran diagonally in front of it. When she crossed into the next lane a small compact car, obviously irritated with the stalled progress, pulled into the center lane to go around the truck. The car accelerated right at her with its horn blaring. With no time to fully dodge the vehicle, she launched herself up and over the corner of the hood, sliding across the smooth metal, somehow keeping her feet below her as she hit the pavement on the other side. She regained her balance and continued running, noticing she had lost ground on her suspect. Her long strides continued to close the distance as she reached for her radio and tried to put out a clear and concise broadcast as the chase continued.

"One-zebra-twenty, foot pursuit of one-eighty-seven suspect, southbound Alameda from Fourth Street. Male white, brown jacket and black pants." The dispatcher placed the frequency on a standby, leaving it free for her further broadcast. She knew without hearing that every available officer in the immediate vicinity was en route to assist her as she gave chase to an individual she believed to be a vicious serial killer.

They ran down a lengthy block, bordered on each side by warehouses. A black and white police car with overhead lights flashing suddenly turned onto the street a few blocks in front of them. Alex was breathing hard as she closed the distance between them. Sweat slid down her back beneath her bullet proof vest. The suspect also seemed to be tiring. He suddenly changed direction and headed down a narrow alley. Alex followed without hesitation.

She updated her direction of travel over the radio, identifying that she was now westbound in the alleyway. She was only about twenty feet behind him when another black and white crossed the other end of the alley. The suspect stopped when he saw the police car screech to a halt and begin to back up to maneuver into the thin passageway. With his avenue of escape now blocked, he turned back toward Alex. Sweat dripped down his face and his lips curled in a strange snarling smile.

Alex's senses became hyper-sensitive, preparing for the confrontation she knew was inevitable. Her hand dropped to her holster but the suspect appeared unarmed. He was advancing as if he intended to engage her physically, so she chose to leave her weapon holstered. In the background she heard the police car begin to accelerate toward them, tires squealing. Then, with an almost feral growl, he charged the last ten feet, head and shoulders down in an effort to steamroll past her.

Alex waited until he was mere steps away, then shifted slightly to one side, avoiding his upper body as he barreled partially past her. She reached out and grasped him about the waist, allowing him to move onward as her arms circled his hips then moved down to wrap around his knees. Unable to run further as she tightened her grip, he tripped and fell forward to the ground. Her elbows and forearms scraped painfully across the asphalt, trapped beneath his legs. As they both hit the ground her grip jarred loose and he kicked partially out of her grasp, freeing one leg as he turned onto his back to face her. His knee came into her ribs as she rose to her knees and launched herself at him again, trying to keep him from getting to his feet. She could still hear the police car coming up the alley, but the two seconds that had passed felt like minutes as the struggle continued. She landed on his torso and straddled his waist, grasping the front of his jacket to control his movement. He grabbed her throat and began to squeeze, but she knocked the hand away then delivered a quick punch to his face. He was stunned briefly by the punch and Alex was able to grab his shoulder and jacket sleeve, forcing him onto his stomach. Two officers bailed from their police car after screeching to a halt nearby. The fight was quickly brought to a halt as the three officers were able to overpower the struggling suspect.

Minutes later, Alex was talking with her fellow task force sergeant, and good friend, Sal Donatelli. The suspect glared at her as the fire department paramedics wiped the blood from his face. Alex smiled as he flinched in pain. The paramedics weren't being terribly tender in their treatment.

"It's definitely him," Sal said. "Drivers license in his pocket reads Matthew Sinclair and matches the wanted bulletins." Alex simply nodded, as she leaned casually on Sal's black and white.

"You owe me a cup of coffee, Alex," Sal said with a shake of his head. "This is another use of force report I've gotta write for you." Alex smiled at Sal then glanced over to where her arrestee was being loaded into the back seat of a police car. "So, his nose is broken and what else?" Sal asked.

"I think some chipped teeth," Alex replied. "And the medics said he'd probably need some stitches for that cut over his eyebrow." She bent her elbow to look at her bloodied forearm, now cleaned and wrapped in gauze, compliments of the fire department paramedics who had been called to the scene.

"And you?" Sal asked, looking her up and down. "You okay?"

"I'm good," she said. "It's gonna sting a little in the shower, but I'll survive. I'm more upset about the uniform." She looked down in disgust at the rip in her pants. She pushed off the car. "Hey, I've got a hunch I wanna follow up on. Have you got this, Sal?" She indicated the scene in the alley.

"Uh-huh," he said. "What do I tell the R.H.D. guys when they get here?" he asked, referring to the Robbery Homicide Division detectives who were en route.

"Just call me when they get here," Alex said. She turned to make her way back to her own police car, left parked several blocks away. "I'll be on my cell."

ALEX PICKED UP her vehicle then drove to the storage unit rental facility just a couple blocks from where she had sighted Sinclair. She parked and made her way into the rental office.

"Hi," she said to the teenage clerk behind the counter. "I was wondering if you recognize this gentleman?" She placed Sinclair's photo in front of him. The bulletin had been carefully folded to hide the large title declaring that he was, "Wanted for Murder."

"Yeah," the clerk said without hesitation. "He's got a unit in here. Always walks in through the gate." He indicated the small pedestrian gate immediately outside the glass windows of the office. "I've never seen him drive in. He was just here about an hour ago."

"I saw your video cameras outside," Alex said as she folded the bulletin up and put it back in her pocket. "Do they record?"

"Yeah, but I can't pull the recordings, only my boss can."

"Okay, you're going to want to call your boss and tell him it's a police emergency and we need him to come in and pull some video for us. And we're going to need him to pull some rental records for us. If he asks, you can tell him we'll have a search warrant by the time he gets here." Alex pulled her cell phone out and called Sal as she watched the clerk's eyes get big. He quickly reached for his own phone and began frantically dialing.

Several hours later, an unmarked Ford Crown Victoria pulled up to the rental facility and made its way down the first aisle to where Alex waited, guarding a padlocked single garage-sized unit. Detective Chuck Severs got out of the car with a grim look of satisfaction on his face. Chuck was a former partner of Alex's from almost fifteen years prior, when Alex was a rookie officer herself. He was now a seasoned homicide detective assigned to the Robbery Homicide Division, and was one of the primary investigators on the White Rose case.

"Got it?" Alex asked.

"Yep." Chuck's partner held up a stack of several papers, indicating the warrant had been approved and they were ready to move forward. Over the last several hours Alex and the detectives had identified the specific unit Sinclair was utilizing and had now obtained the warrant needed to enter the facility. "We've also got a set of keys Sinclair had on him when you caught him. One of them looks like it may go to the padlock on the unit door. The brand is the same at least."

Chuck's partner, Detective Kim, singled out a key on the ring and slid it easily into the padlock. It turned smoothly and the lock clicked open. Kim slid the door up and open to reveal the contents of the unit. They found the unit empty with the exception of a lone storage trunk sitting in the middle of the floor. They glanced at it, then all three sets of eyes turned to focus on one side of the unit where multiple newspaper articles had been cut out and taped on the wall.

"Ho-ly shit," Chuck muttered.

After spending several minutes looking over the display of articles, they turned and gathered around the chest. Chuck bent to the padlock.

"Are we good with the search warrant for opening this?" Alex asked.

"Yep. We included all locked articles within the unit," Chuck said as he tested several keys on the ring. One finally slid in and turned. Chuck removed the padlock and opened the lid of the trunk.

He reached a gloved hand into the trunk, removing a shoe box and opening it. Inside were several pieces of jewelry, including necklaces, earrings and watches. He handed the shoe box to his partner and reached back into the trunk, removing a manila envelope. Chuck opened the envelope and tipped it up, allowing several photographs to slide into his hand. He shuffled through the photographs and Alex recognized several of the White Rose murder victims caught in everyday activities, walking to and from their cars, several in public areas and restaurants, and even a few that appeared to be taken through windows, catching the victim's inside their own residences.

Alex noticed something in one of the photographs. "Wait. Go back to that one you just passed." Chuck moved a photo back to the top of the stack. It appeared to be taken with a telephoto lens and showed a young lady sitting in the open patio area of a restaurant. "Look at her bracelet," she said, pointing to a large bangle style bracelet clearly revealed in the photo. Alex then pointed into the shoe box and Detective Kim removed a similar bracelet.

They went through the photos more slowly, paying closer attention to the items of jewelry shown in the pictures. They quickly identified several more items of jewelry in the box that were shown in the pictures being worn by the victims.

"Well, now we know for sure that he stalked them before he killed them," Chuck said. "And he kept trophies."

SIX MONTHS LATER, Alex found herself sitting with the R.H.D. case detectives in a District Attorney's conference room on the eighteenth floor of the Central Courts Building in downtown Los Angeles. They had all been summoned for a pre-trial conference and were awaiting the arrival of the assigned DAs. As she waited, Alex thought over the crimes ultimately tied to Sinclair.

The White Rose Murders began four years prior. By the time the perpetrator was identified and apprehended, twelve women in and around Los Angeles had been kidnapped, viciously beaten, tortured, raped, and then murdered by strangulation. The bodies were dumped in secluded areas of the city, sometimes a considerable distance from where they were kidnapped. The coroner's reports indicated the beatings and torture were significant and occurred over several hours. Ligature marks from the murder weapon, believed to be some kind of leather belt, were consistent on the neck of each victim.

The nature of the victims, all attractive and successful professional women, had led to the presumption the suspect moved in the same professional circles. In addition, it was determined that prior to each victim's disappearance, and ultimate murder, she had been the recipient of a delivery of a dozen white roses. When this fact was revealed in the course of his eventual trial, the press had dubbed him "The White Rose Killer."

Alex looked up as the conference room door was pushed open. Her interest was piqued by the entrance of a slim and attractive woman carrying a thick case file. Her eyes followed the woman, noting her trim build and shoulder length wavy brown hair with natural auburn highlights. Her chestnut eyes met Alex's momentarily and they exchanged a brief smile.

"Good morning everyone," the Assistant District Attorney said. "I'm Sydney Rutledge and I'll be handling the Sinclair prosecution. I recognize a few faces in here." Alex noted nods from a few of the detectives, including Chuck and his partner, Robert Kim.

"Thanks everyone for being here this morning. I know we've got several weeks before hearings begin, but I wanted to get a solid feel for this as early as possible," Sydney continued. "How about we go around the table and have some introductions before we get started?"

Each of the attendees introduced themselves as Sydney cross-noted their names on a legal pad. They then began a review of the case with Detective Severs providing an overview of the exhaustive three year investigation that had led to the identification of Matthew James Sinclair as the White Rose Killer.

"Tell me about Sinclair, Chuck," Sydney asked the detective. "What's his background?"

"He's a trust fund baby. He was actually adopted at a young age by the Sinclair family and as a result is the only child in a very wealthy family. His parents died about five years ago, making him a very rich man."

Sydney nodded. "I've already received notice from his attorneys. They're from a very high dollar private firm."

"Yeah," Chuck continued. "That money also let him play the part of the wealthy entrepreneur and philanthropist. It seems that's how he was able to establish relationships with the victims. He would use different names with each victim and always insisted on private meetings with his victims. From our interviews with family and friends, it appears he would tell the victims that he was a very private person and wished to keep his business investments or charitable pursuits confidential. In most cases his victims, all professional women themselves, were involved in charity work or looking to establish a new business. For the most part they kept their association with him to themselves because he made that a condition of his investment in their business or his donation to their charity."

"And our first break was when he was finally caught on video camera at one of the victim's condos?" Sydney asked.

"Yep. We got real lucky there. Unfortunately that didn't happen until the eleventh victim, and then it took a while to find what we needed on the footage. We knew on several occasions he picked the victims up from their residences or places of employment. We were checking the footage off every security camera in the vicinity of every victim. In this case, the camera covering the entrance to an adjacent property had been knocked off its normal field of vision and was recording the curb-line in front of the property, including several parked cars. We had it enhanced to obtain colors, makes and models of each of the cars and even several full and partial license plates. Fortunately most of them belonged to residents on the street. It took us several days of leg work, but we were eventually able to track down the owner of each of the cars and determine their legitimate business on the street. All except one, that is."

"Sinclair's." It was not a question, but a statement by the attractive female DA.

"Right," Chuck said. "One silver seven series BMW we tracked down to a high end leasing company. After repeated questioning, the female clerk finally admitted she'd taken cash from an honest looking wealthy gentleman, her words not mine, and loaned him the vehicle off the record. He evidently told her his wallet had been stolen and he had no credit cards or identification, but he needed the vehicle for an extremely important executive meeting. She insisted he was well dressed and charming, that he didn't look like anyone she should be concerned about. He filled out the paperwork, which she accepted with no ID but never processed in the company's system. He returned the vehicle first thing the following day and no one else ever knew about it. Of course the name he gave was completely fabricated.

"But..." Sydney left the sentence hanging and Chuck smiled.

"The vehicle had not been rented or driven since its return two days prior and it appeared to have been wiped clean by our suspect. But we got lucky. We pulled one partial print off the back of the rearview mirror. That partial matched up to Matthew Sinclair."

Sydney shuffled some paperwork which she looked over.

"And Sinclair's prints were in the system because of his prior rape arrest," she said as she reviewed the copy of the prior case. "He was arrested for the rape of another co-ed when he was in college. The charge was later dropped when the victim declined to cooperate with the prosecution." She looked up. "According to the DA up in the Bay Area where he went to school, they have always thought the Sinclairs paid her family off for her silence." She took a deep breath. "Okay, so the clerk identified Sinclair out of a photo line-up?"

"Yeah, I did the follow-up and she identified him without hesitation." This came from Robert Kim, Chuck Severs's partner at R.H.D.

"And she's available and willing to testify?" asked Sydney. Both detectives nodded. "Okay. Next we've got the phone trace?"

"Right," continued Kim, taking over the narrative. "The name Sinclair gave on the paperwork was of course fictitious. But the clerk did one thing right. She confirmed the cell phone number he gave by dialing it as he was in the office, making sure it actually rang before she gave him the keys. The number was to a throw away phone, one of those pre-paid ones you can pick up at any electronics store. But at least we had a witness who put it in his possession. We obtained a warrant and traced the phone history and found out that the night of the murder a call was made from that phone and relayed off a cell tower in the area of the victim's condominium. The time of the call was very close to when she was picked up. And the clincher, the number it called was the victim's."

"Okay. No forensic evidence was found that tied the victim directly to the car, right?" asked Sydney.

"Right," replied Kim.

"But," she said. "We have the vehicle on film at the victim's condo at the time she was picked up and last seen. We have him identified as the renter of that vehicle in that time frame of the kidnapping and murder. We have him in possession of a throw away phone which made a call to the victim from the victim's neighborhood at the time she was last seen." The two detectives nodded in confirmation. "And that is how we got a warrant for his arrest and a search warrant for his property in Ranchos Palos Verdes." They nodded again. "But he wasn't there when you served it and no evidence was found at his house." This time the detectives shook their heads.

"So we continued to track the phone, just in case he used it again," said Detective Kim.

"Yes," Sydney shuffled papers back to the detectives' report. "You pinged the phone." Sydney was referring to the ability to track a cell phone by the calls made or received, or to even send covert signals out of the phone to determine its general location.

"Right. He only had the phone on occasionally and for brief periods of time. But we were able to determine he was frequently in the area of the east side of downtown L.A., in the industrial neighborhoods near the Los Angeles River. Then the phone went silent. We figure he destroyed it."

The chestnut eyes finally turned to Alex.

"And this is where you enter the picture, correct Sergeant Chambers?"

"Yes, ma'am," Alex replied. "My task force received the information on the suspect and that he was suspected of possibly being in the area."

"You're a supervisor with Central Division's Violent Crime Task Force?" Sydney was again reading from her own notes.

"Yes, ma'am," Alex said again.

"And you were driving down the street, minding your own business when Mr. Sinclair happened to wander into view?" Alex found humor emanating from the chestnut eyes that captured her own as the question was asked.

"Something like that," Alex said with her own slight smile.

"Uh-huh." Sydney looked back to her notes. "Tell me about how you determined Sinclair was likely in the area you found him."

Alex nodded and took a deep breath. "My squad was working the day R.H.D. provided us with the wanted bulletin and their belief that he was possibly in the Skid Row or Central City East area. I happened to concentrate my efforts in the far eastern sector of Skid Row, the warehouse district near the railroad tracks and the riverbed. I'd worked the area a long time and have a pretty good relationship with a lot of the business owners there." The attorney nodded in acknowledgment and Alex continued.

"One of the property owners thought he might've seen Sinclair in the area. He said he stuck out a little because he was usually well dressed and appeared clean cut and wealthy. He was always walking, which attracted my informant's attention, because he didn't seem like the kind of person that would take the bus or anything into that area. He thought the guy was maybe delivering dope because he sometimes had a bag or backpack with him. After seeing him several times, he watched a little more closely and saw him go into the storage facility a couple of blocks away."

"And?" Sydney asked.

"I asked him to call me the next time he saw him." Alex replied and watched a slight smile grace the attorney's expression. Sydney raised an eyebrow in question, an expression Alex took to silently infer the unasked yet obvious follow-up question.

"And he did," Alex quickly added with a slight smile of her own. "So I responded to the area and took a position of observation just in time to see him walking down the sidewalk. He saw me and then tried to flee."

"Did you see him go into or come out of the storage facility?" Sydney asked.

"No."

"But you thought that was a possibility?"

"Yes, based on what was reported as his prior routes of travel in the area, that seemed a likely destination," Alex said.

"So he ran and you chased him?"

"And I caught him," Alex added with a nod. She was enjoying the back and forth with the attorney, who she found refreshingly straightforward.

"Then you returned to the storage facility and determined Sinclair did have a unit rented there?"

"Yes. Right after Sinclair was caught, while waiting for R.H.D. to respond, I went to the storage facility and the clerk identified Sinclair's photo from the wanted bulletin. He said he was a renter who had just been there. I determined there was video on the facility that we could access and had the clerk contact his manager and begin pulling rental records. Then I waited for Chuck and Bob to arrive and take over."

"Where were you when you first saw Mr. Sinclair?"

"I was in a raised position of observation with a clear and unobstructed view of the street and sidewalk." Alex gave the answer just as she had countless times in prior court hearings when she intended to maintain the confidentiality of her source or location.

"And where exactly was that?" the attorney pressed.

"Ma'am, my informant is a business owner in the area. His business is the only source of income for his family and is putting two of his children through college. He's cooperated with too many police investigations for me to even count. He's provided information from his own observations and never denied us access to his property so we could make our own observations of the surrounding area. He's done all this with the understanding that we do not identify him or his business. His assistance has led to countless arrests and successful prosecutions. Revealing the location of his property could jeopardize future investigations. More importantly, revealing his involvement could jeopardize his safety or the safety of his family and the viability of his business. I've personally promised him confidentiality in return for his assistance." Alex paused and took a breath. "With due respect, ma'am, I can't go back on that promise. His circumstance is exactly why Section 1040 exists." Alex referred to the section of the California Evidence Code which allowed law enforcement to maintain the confidentiality of locations or informants who assisted law enforcement but feared for their safety should that cooperation be revealed.

Alex was aware of Chuck, who was seated beside her, shuffling nervously in his seat. She watched as the attorney paused and looked at her as if she was contemplating another question. Then Sydney turned to the detectives again.

"You were able to pull the tapes and rental records for the storage unit?"

"Yep," Chuck said. "The rental contract was in the same name he used with the vehicle leasing clerk, Matthew Brooks. He had paid in cash in advance each month.

"The surveillance video over-writes the recording every seventy-two hours, so we couldn't go back more than that. But the tape from that day clearly shows Sinclair going into the facility to his unit, then exiting. He is shown wearing the same clothes Alex arrested him in that afternoon, so he clearly had just left the facility."

"So you secured the unit and obtained a search warrant?" Sydney prompted.

"Correct. We figured out a key in Sinclair's pocket opened the padlock on the unit as well as the trunk inside. When the warrant arrived we entered the unit and found the newspaper articles, the photographs showing he had stalked most of the victims and the collection of trophies from all twelve homicides."

"But no murder weapon," said Sydney.

"Correct," said Chuck. "It's never been found. The coroner opined that is likely a belt or some kind of leather strap with a distinctive stitch pattern."

Chapter Two

Four months later...

"YOUR HONOR, THIS defense motion is a waste of the court's time." Assistant District Attorney Sydney Rutledge stood before the judge making her point. "The Evidence Code clearly allows for law enforcement to maintain the confidentiality of property owners and locations utilized for surveillance as an effort to protect the safety of the property owners who fear retaliation, and to maintain the resource for use in ongoing or future investigations. The property owner in question is not a material witness in this case, he simply provided the vantage point from which the observations were made."

"Your Honor," Sinclair's attorney interjected. "The Evidence Code sections cited by my esteemed counterpart are utilized primarily for narcotics investigations. This is far more serious. My client is charged with the most serious of charges, and the prosecution has stated their intent to pursue the death penalty. As such, all witnesses may be material to our case. The defendant must be afforded the opportunity to directly question all witnesses and challenge all evidence against him."

Sydney stood to give her response. "Your Honor, the intent of Section 1040 and 1041 is to acknowledge the risk and maintain the confidentiality and trust of those who willingly cooperate with law enforcement. According to the defense's argument, that trust, that willingness, should only be fostered on those less serious offenses, and should not be applied in law enforcement's efforts to pursue the most serious of predators. Sergeant Chambers has clearly articulated the history of cooperation this property owner has provided. This individual did so with the understanding their address and identity would never be revealed. That is precisely the purpose of 1040 and 1041. To violate that trust now would be immoral and illegal, and would have widespread ramifications on public trust and the sanctity of investigations statewide."

"But, Your Honor," Sinclair's attorney addressed the judge once again. "Failure to force Sergeant Chambers to produce this witness leaves open the possibility she fabricated and framed my client." Alex hid the smile when the attractive prosecutor leapt to her feet to defend her, or at least that's the way Alex liked to think of it.

"If you have evidence of police misconduct, bring it forward, counselor," Sydney challenged. "If your best defense is baseless innuendo and insinuations, then I'll start working on my sentencing arguments now."

"That's enough, Ms. Rutledge." The voice came from the judge's bench. He turned to the defense. "Mr. Bristow, you can present your theory to the jury who can make their own determinations on the credibility of witnesses and evidence. That is, after all, their job. I find the owner of the property from which Sergeant Chambers made her observations is not a material witness and is protected by Evidence Code Sections 1040 and 1041, and am denying your motion to compel the prosecution to present Sergeant Chambers's citizen source." At hearing this Alex silently clenched her fist in victory as the judge continued.

"Does the defense have anything further for purposes of this preliminary hearing?"

"Motion to dismiss the charges, Your Honor, based on insufficiency of the evidence."

"That motion is also denied," the judge said. "I find there to be sufficient evidence to hold the defendant over for trial."

The procedure in the courtroom continued as a few more brief arguments were made over bail before the judge continued Sinclair's incarceration without bail pending the trial.

The courtroom emptied, and Sydney gathered her paperwork.

"Nice job, Ms. Rutledge," Alex said.

"It's not over by a long shot, Sergeant," Sydney said as they made their way through the courtroom. "Remember, this is Los Angeles. Home of the jury that couldn't convict O.J. Simpson."

"Yeah." Alex placed her hand on Sydney's arm. "I know you were under a lot of pressure from your office to just produce my source. I'm truly sorry to put you in that position." Alex shrugged and her shoulders dropped, "I just —"

"I understand." Sydney smiled reassuringly at Alex when their eyes met again. "Really, I respect what you did. And it's all worked out so far, right? But we know the defense is going to make this an issue for the jury. Are you ready for their attacks?"

"I'm thinking you're gonna make sure I am, right?"

Sydney smiled and nodded as Alex pushed the door open, allowing Sydney to precede her into the third floor hallway of the court building. Sydney was experiencing the same feeling she'd had numerous times in the past during meetings with Sergeant Chambers. She silently wished for the contact to be prolonged as they continued down the hallway toward the elevator lobby.

"So, your office decided to make it a capital case, huh?" Alex asked as they waited for an elevator.

"Yes. We filed the notice of intent to seek the death penalty this morning."

Alex nodded. "Couldn't happen to a nicer guy."

Sydney glanced up to watch the numbers above the elevator doors count down and then gave in to a spur of the moment impulse. "I'd kill for a cup of coffee. Join me?" she asked Alex as the elevator doors opened.

"Sure," Alex said.

They stepped into the elevator and Sydney wondered why the sergeant's acceptance of the invitation gave her such a warm feeling and brought a smile to her lips.

Four weeks later...

THE DEFENSE COUNSEL stood at the podium and shuffled his papers. He was one of the panel of high priced attorneys afforded Sinclair by his multi-million dollar trust fund. Sydney glanced away from him to Sergeant Chambers seated patiently on the witness stand. Sydney's direct examination of the sergeant had taken all morning and cross examination was now set to commence after the court's lunch recess.

Sydney knew this was likely going to be a grueling experience for the sergeant and had done her best to prepare the woman. They knew the defense needed only to plant a kernel of doubt in one juror's mind regarding the case against Sinclair. The arguments made in the preliminary hearing, as well as a variety of motions to suppress the evidence found in the storage locker, made it very clear the defense intended to provide that reasonable doubt by attacking the police sergeant's integrity and motives. Defending Chambers against the accusation was made more difficult by the fact that the officer steadfastly refused to provide the identification of her source. He was the only uninvolved witness who could put Sinclair going in and out of the facility with regularity and could validate the foundation of Chambers's discovery. Sydney knew Chambers had faced pressure from her own chain of command, and even other members of the D.A.'s office, many of whom felt she should not hesitate to provide the identity of the source. Their paramount, and only, concern was solely a successful prosecution in the highly publicized trial.

Moments later, after making a written notation on a paper in front of him, David Bristow began his questions.

"Sergeant Chambers, Detective Chuck Severs, one of the primary investigators on this case, is a close personal friend of yours, isn't he?"

"I wouldn't say that. We aren't really social away from work or anything," Alex responded.

"But he was your training officer when you first came on the job?"

"Yes."

"So you worked closely together early in your career?"

"Yes."

"Would you say he's been influential in your career?"

"I would say he's one of many competent officers who I deeply respect and who have been influential."

"Uh-huh. And he approached you some time ago and provided you with a wanted bulletin containing my client's photograph, is that correct?"

"Yes, sir."

"And when was that?"

"As I recall, it was two days prior to your client's arrest."

"You're sure the two of you had no discussions about Mr. Sinclair prior to that?"

"I'm quite sure."

"You did not discuss with Detective Severs the fact that Mr. Sinclair had been accused, falsely, I might add, of a sexual assault while in college and that he would make a good suspect for this murder spree?"

Sydney jumped to her feet before Alex could even begin to respond.

"Objection, Your Honor. If counsel has some evidence of such a conversation he needs to bring it forth immediately. It is improper for him to launch blatantly unfounded allegations of some far-fetched conspiracy."

"Your Honor, I am merely presenting the defense theory of the case, which we believe will establish reasonable doubt."

"I'll allow it. The objection is denied. But tread carefully here, Mr. Bristow," the judge said.

The defense attorney nodded as Sydney took her seat. She looked over at Alex and gave her a reassuring nod as Bristow resumed the questioning.

"Detective Severs had to be under a lot of pressure to make an arrest in this case. There was significant political pressure, was there not?"

"I don't know if I would characterize it as political pressure. Twelve murdered women in a community is something that reaches beyond politics."

"So the public was pressuring for an arrest."

"No, sir. The public was hoping to feel safe. They were scared. Our job was to make them safe again." Sydney gave the sergeant a slight smile as she listened to Alex give cogent answers to the questions. Alex wasn't allowing herself to be backed into providing the wording Bristow was looking for. She had clearly clued in that the defense was looking for an admission, or an avenue to imply, that there was political pressure to make an arrest, any arrest, in the case.

"The capture of a supposed murderer is quite the feather in your cap, isn't it, Sergeant?"

"I'm not quite sure what you mean, sir."

"I mean that you, a mere patrol sergeant, supposedly single-handedly captured a wanted murder suspect. That's going to reflect well for you, professionally. Perhaps, if it leads ultimately to a successful prosecution, it'll result in commendations, accolades, maybe a promotion for you?"

Sydney recognized the slight smile that curled the sergeant's lips and was happy that Alex wasn't responding to the degrading reference.

"I like to think, as a mere patrol sergeant, I will simply be seen as having done my job. What the taxpayers of the city pay me for, sir. I also think you'll find that mere patrol personnel in my department capture wanted violent predators on a fairly regular basis. What I did is not that unusual, sir."

Sydney had to look down at the notes on the table in front of her to hide her own smile now. Out of the corner of her eye she noticed the defense attorney again shuffling his paperwork. His first attempts at confusing and antagonizing the sergeant and trying to put her on the defensive having obviously failed. He looked back up at the uniformed sergeant.

"So, you make reference to this all-knowing citizen who magically recalled seeing Mr. Sinclair coming and going from the storage facility. Who is this individual, Sergeant?"

"As I stated previously, sir, that citizen spoke to me in confidence, on the condition of anonymity. They fear for their safety and the safety of their family, not to mention the viability of their business, if it becomes known they gave information to the police or cooperated with us in any way. This is an individual who has provided information in the past that led to significant arrests. I was ultimately able to independently corroborate the information they provided through my own observations."

"Yes, that's all very convenient for you, isn't it?"

"Your Honor!" Sydney was once again on her feet contesting the antagonizing question.

"I withdraw the question," Bristow said with a wave of his hand as if he was implying the answer was obvious and therefore unimportant.

"When Detective Severs approached you with the information on his suspect," Bristow motioned with his fingers to imply quotes around the word. "Didn't you two discuss the fact that the department needed a quick arrest in this case?"

"No."

"Didn't the detective tell you he had the evidence, but simply needed to tie it to my client somehow?" Bristow's voice began to rise in an accusatory fashion.

"No."

"Detective Severs focused on Mr. Sinclair as his suspect from the beginning and the two of you conspired to plant the evidence in his storage facility, didn't you?"

"Absolutely not," Alex said calmly.

"And didn't you manufacture the existence of this anonymous citizen, creating the avenue that would lead you directly to my client, his locker and this overwhelming physical evidence? This citizen informant doesn't even exist, does he, Sergeant?"

"I assure you, sir, he exists."

"Objection, Your Honor, he's badgering the witness." Sydney leapt to her feet, trying to stem the verbal attack. But Bristow was on a roll and continued before the judge could intervene. He leveled an accusatory finger at Alex and practically screamed the accusation.

"You and Detective Severs framed my client, an innocent man, didn't you, Sergeant?" The courtroom went absolutely silent. Even the judge seemed shocked into inaction, failing to address Sydney's objection before the officer's strong and confident voice was heard.

"If your client is innocent, Mr. Bristow," Alex calmly responded. "Then why did the murders stop as soon as he was arrested?"

Sydney glanced over at the jury and saw a couple of them give slight nods while several others raised their eyebrows. Every juror looked back at the defense attorney, clearly waiting for his response. Bristow stood frozen and Sydney recognized a fleeting look of panic pass across his eyes. Then he recovered and addressed the judge.

"Your Honor, I request the witness be instructed not to editorialize and to simply answer the question posed to her."

"First, I believe Ms. Rutledge has an objection on the record," the judge said.

"I withdraw my objection, Your Honor," Sydney said, somewhat smugly. She gave Alex a quick wink and a small smile as she sat back down. Sydney had a feeling the defense line of questioning had possibly done more damage than good to Sinclair's case. The sergeant was doing just fine on her own and her quick thinking had turned Bristow's questions right back at him. Sydney was curious to see how much further the defense would try and take this line of questioning.

"Very well," the judge said, then he turned to Alex on the witness stand. "Sergeant Chambers, you're advised to respond only to those questions posed to you."

"Yes, Your Honor, my apologies." She turned back to the attorney. "In answer to your question, sir, no. I can assure I did not frame your client. There was absolutely no need."

Bristow initially looked as if he would continue his questioning, then gathered his notes and looked up at the judge. "I have no more questions at this time, Your Honor. But we may have need to recall this witness at a later time."

"That will be it for today, Sergeant Chambers. You are excused but are subject to recall." He turned back to the District Attorney's table. "Is the prosecution prepared to have your next witness ready first thing in the morning, Ms. Rutledge?"

"Yes, Your Honor. Our forensic expert is prepared to take the stand in the morning and we estimate our direct examination will take us at least to the lunch break." The judge nodded then raised his gavel.

"Very well. This court stands in recess until nine tomorrow morning." The gavel dropped and the occupants of the courtroom stood as the judge retreated to his chambers.

As soon as the door to the judge's chambers closed, Alex made her way down from the raised witness stand to the prosecution's table. Sydney noted her approach as she gathered her notepads and references.

"If you have a few minutes, Sergeant? I'd like to discuss your testimony." Sydney's statement was clipped and official sounding.

"Um, yeah. Sure."

Sydney noted Alex's concerned, almost uncertain tone and realized it was due to her very officious sounding approach. She glanced at Alex and then looked directly at the retreating jury, the last of whom were standing only a few feet away in the jury box gathering their own notepads, purses and jackets. Sydney was trying to send the signal that she needed to remain professional and reserved in front of them. She watched as Alex followed her look to the jury and recognition dawned. Alex turned back toward her.

"Need any help with anything?" Alex asked, indicating the various folders Sydney was now placing in the file box attached to a small rolling dolly.

"That's okay. I'll meet you outside."

Several minutes later, Sydney exited the courtroom to find Alex waiting in the hallway. "Walk with me, Sergeant," she said and continued toward the elevators. She remained silent when she noticed the defense team and several jurors gathered outside the elevators. When the doors to the elevator opened, she gently grabbed Alex's wrist to hold her back from entering with the others. When the doors closed the two were left alone in the hallway. Sydney immediately turned to Alex.

"That, Sergeant Chambers, was fantastic. You completely turned that questioning around. No one could possibly have handled that any better." She leaned into Alex as she laughed.

"I'm glad it worked out," Alex said, and smiled.

Sydney suddenly realized she was leaning somewhat intimately into the sergeant, with one hand grasping Alex's arm and the other her hand. She slowly straightened up and began to back away, but felt Alex's fingers give hers a slight squeeze before letting go.

"It better than worked out," Sydney said as she reached once again for her rolling files. "Did you see Bristow's face when you pointed out the murders had stopped? And the jury's response? You can't un-ring that bell." The doors on a nearby elevator car opened with the arrow illuminated to indicate it was continuing up. Sydney moved toward the open doors. "Well done, Sergeant." She turned in the car to face the still open doors. "Shall I keep you posted?"

"Absolutely," Alex said as she held her hand in the open doorway to keep it from closing. "Let me know how things go. Good luck with the rest of the trial." She waved as she stepped back.

"Stay safe," Sydney said as the doors began to close and Alex disappeared from view. She leaned back against the wall as the car moved upwards and her mind went back to the feeling in her fingers when they had been held by Alex, and the look they had exchanged when Sydney had realized their closeness. She shook away the dreamy feeling when the doors opened again on the eighteenth floor and she made her way to her office. Allowing for pointless daydreaming was not going to get her prepared for the next day in the courtroom.

Two weeks later...

"THE DEFENDANT WILL rise," the judge ordered. "The jury foreperson may read the verdict."

"We the jury, in the above entitled action, find the defendant, Matthew James Sinclair, guilty of the murder of Michelle Bethany Moore, a violation of section one-eight-seven, subsection A of the penal code of the state of California, as charged in count one of the information. We, the jury, further find that the murder of Michelle Bethany Moore was committed willfully, deliberately and with premeditation, within the meaning of penal code section one-eight-nine, and is a serious and violent felony pursuant to penal code sections one-one-nine-two-point-seven, subsection C, as charged in count one of the information."

The foreperson read on, twelve counts in all. He was found guilty on all twelve counts of first-degree murder. All of the counts included findings for the existence of special circumstances, which left the potential for a verdict involving either the death penalty or life imprisonment with no possibility of parole. The reading of the verdicts continued on for almost forty minutes during which time Alex noted Sinclair showed absolutely no emotion, except for a slight smile when the last name was read.

At the conclusion the judge questioned the jury as to the unanimous nature of their findings, formally accepted the verdict for the record, then thanked the jury for their diligence. He then turned and looked at the prosecution and defense tables before looking down at his calendar.

"Now as to the sentencing hearing, any particular time frame good or bad? Ms. Rutledge, will you have victim impact statements?"

Sydney stood and turned a page on her legal pad. "Yes, Your Honor," she glanced down quickly at her notes. "I have four written statements to include with the sentencing recommendation and five family members wish to address the court." The judge nodded as he noted the request in his notes.

"Anything else?" he asked. Both attorneys shook their head in the negative. "Very well. Sentencing recommendations to me by August tenth, hearing will be August twenty-fifth. See you all next month. This court is in recess." With a bang of his gavel, he stood and exited the courtroom.

Sydney began gathering her paperwork the moment the judge left his bench. She was vaguely aware of Alex as the sergeant rose from her seat in the first row of the gallery immediately behind her.

As if she finally sensed the intense gaze, Sydney looked up from her files and her eyes met Sinclair's. His sinister smile engendered a startlingly vivid sense of dread, his eyes seeming to trap and hold hers. Her breath caught and an irrepressible shiver ran through her body in response to the predator's intense scrutiny.

"I look forward to seeing you again very soon, Ms. Rutledge. I'd love to spend some time alone with you," Sinclair said as the bailiffs pulled him away from the defense table and toward the door leading to the court detention cells.

His eyes didn't leave hers and Sydney couldn't look away as he pursed his lips and sent a leering kiss in her direction. The terrifying connection was finally broken when a broad uniformed figure stepped between them. The sergeant maintained her position, standing tall with her arms crossed, essentially facing down Sinclair as he was led from the room. He cackled an evil laugh and kept looking past Alex toward Sydney as the bailiffs forcibly pulled him from the courtroom.

When the door finally closed behind him, Alex turned around to face Sydney with a concerned look, touching Sydney's elbow gently.

"Are you okay, Ms. Rutledge?"

Sydney tried to shake off her fear and smiled weakly. "I'm okay," she said, more in an effort to convince herself. After all, it wasn't as if Sinclair would ever be able to follow through on his threats. Alex pulled her hand away and again assumed a look of courteous professionalism.

"Well done, counselor," Alex said. "Chalk one up for the good guys."

Sydney's smile warmed slightly and become more genuine.

"Yeah," she replied. "Like you said, couldn't happen to a nicer guy." Sydney continued placing the paperwork into her soft-sided briefcase.

"Your office still intends to pursue the death penalty?" Alex asked. She lifted Sydney's additional file box of materials and led Sydney through the now empty courtroom.

"Yep," Sydney followed, smiling slightly yet internally puzzled by the butterflies in her stomach brought on by the officer's gallant gesture.

"Outstanding. Like we keep saying, couldn't happen to a nicer guy."

Alex pushed open the heavy door leading out into the hallway, holding it open as Sydney passed through. As they walked down the hallway toward the elevators, Sydney's cell phone vibrated in her hand.

She looked down at the caller I.D. then put the phone to her ear as she moved against the wall out of foot traffic, looking up and apologizing to Alex with her eyes.

"Hey, Stan," she said. "That's right...on all counts and all special circumstances...uh-huh...sentencing will be August twenty-fifth...okay...I'm coming back to the office then I'm taking the rest of the day off...thanks, Stan. See you Monday."

Sydney looked back at Alex as she slipped the phone into a side pocket on her briefcase.

"Sorry about that," she said. "It was the boss."

"No problem," Alex said. "Calling with appropriate congratulations, I take it?" They continued toward the elevators.

"Yeah. So will you be here for sentencing?" Sydney asked, hoping to hear a positive answer.

"I'll certainly try, as long as I don't get tied up in the field."

August twenty-fifth...

"HAS THE JURY arrived at a verdict with respect to the penalty in this case?" The question from the judge was directed at the jury foreperson, standing once again before a packed court.

"We have, Your Honor."

"Please read the verdict."

"We, the jury, in the above entitled action, having found Matthew James Sinclair guilty of first degree murder in count one, and having found the special circumstances to be true, fix the penalty at death."

The jury foreperson paused before continuing. Alex glanced away from him to Sydney. She watched as her shoulder's seemed to relax just barely, though her eyes never left the jury.

"We the jury, in the above entitled action, having found Matthew James Sinclair guilty of first degree murder in count two, and having found the special circumstances to be true, fix the penalty at death."

Once again the verdicts went on, twelve counts, twelve death penalties. When the foreman finished the judge thanked the jury for their service and excused them.

Two weeks later they were all back in court again for the formal sentencing hearing. The judge wasted no time in announcing his determination.

"Mr. Sinclair, it is my considered judgment that not only is the death penalty appropriate, but it is almost compelled by the circumstances. I must agree with the prosecutor that if this is not a proper case for the death penalty, then there likely never will be."

Shortly thereafter the gavel sounded and the judge moved to exit the courtroom as the bailiffs moved forward to escort Sinclair back to his cell to await final transportation to Death Row at the California State

Prison at San Quentin. Once again his eyes were fixed to Sydney as he was pulled from the room, the unwavering sinister look locked onto hers and refused to release her until, once again, the broad uniformed presence of Sergeant Chambers stepped between them, breaking the connection.

Chapter Three

SYDNEY SAT AT her desk just a couple of days after the conclusion of the trial, her mind drifting back again to that day in court immediately after the judge read the sentence, when she looked over at Sinclair and discovered him staring back at her across the twelve-foot distance. Even now she shivered as she remembered the sickening smile and sadistically lustful look in his eyes. She could still hear him laughing until he finally faded out of earshot in the cells to the rear of the courtroom.

She found Sinclair's attention and statements frightening, and the trial had been exhausting and disturbing. It was the most difficult of her career. The one positive thing that came out of the experience was her introduction to Sergeant Alexandria Chambers. They had spent several "working lunches" together both before and during the trial.

Her mind effortlessly formed a picture of Sergeant Chambers. She was five-foot-nine, with short light brown hair and hazel eyes, and an athletic, muscular build. Even out of uniform, some might find Sergeant Chambers intimidating or imposing. As time had gone on Sydney developed a clear understanding of how this officer had been capable of subduing the fleeing serial murderer.

Sydney was impressed by Sergeant Chambers's confidence, strength and professionalism during the trial. Chambers, a seasoned officer of fifteen years, remained calm, clear and concise in her testimony and lengthy cross-examination.

Even under these challenging circumstances, Sydney had to admit the officer had not required anywhere near the amount of trial "prep" she had given her. Sydney had looked forward to their time together, and even manufactured the necessity or opportunity to meet. This confused her, as she had never had an issue with maintaining a professional distance. There were times when not only co-workers but also victims and witnesses had extended overtures toward her. She had never responded nor invited that kind of attention, had never felt the impulse to.

Sydney's thoughts returned to her current circumstances and she made a concerted effort to clear her mind and return to the work at hand. But later that same day she turned to her best friend to bounce her feelings off him. Tyler Houston was also an assistant district attorney working in the same downtown office. The two had met in college at the University of Southern California. Within weeks they were virtually inseparable, their bond soon growing to the point where Tyler revealed that he was gay. They had partied together, studied together, graduated together and then moved on to USC Law School. They later graduated then passed the bar together. Then both joined the ranks of the District Attorney's Office despite both receiving lucrative offers from high level private firms. They had turned to each other and shared everything for almost their entire adult life.

As they sat in the empty office spaces later that evening, Sydney relayed to him what had happened in the courtroom after the sentencing hearing. Without realizing the wistful nature of her voice, she revealed to him how she had been somehow comforted by the presence of the sergeant.

"It was nice to have her there, even though he was in chains. She's so obviously capable," she said. "And fearless."

Tyler seemed to read more into it. "And attractive?" he asked.

"What on earth are you talking about?" Sydney said, flustered, turning away from Tyler and busying her hands by moving paper around her desk.

"I couldn't help but notice you guys spent a lot of time together during the trial," he said. "You seemed to, what's the word I'm looking for? Bond? Yes, bond, quite quickly. You know she's a lesbian, right?"

"Please. We were together for trial prep and we caught a couple lunches during testimony because we had to discuss the progress of the case. And yes, I had presumed she was a lesbian. But it's not as if I am."

"Really? I always thought you were an open spirit, just looking for your soul mate," he said with a smile. "It certainly doesn't surprise me that your soul mate could be a woman. Don't forget, I was at that homecoming party back in college. You know the one I'm talking about."

Sydney did remember exactly what he was talking about. That specific party she had attended with her boyfriend at the time. For reasons Sydney no longer remembered, they had not been getting along too well. Midway through the party they had a heated argument that ended when Sydney stormed out to the secluded back porch of the residence. There a woman she had never seen before approached her. The two women struck up a conversation and it soon became apparent the woman was a lesbian and was interested in Sydney. Shortly afterwards, when Sydney saw her boyfriend watching through a nearby window, she decided to play into the flirtatious banter, then allowed it to go further as they had embraced passionately and kissed.

Unbeknownst to Sydney at the time, Tyler had also gone in search of her and observed the intimate interaction on the porch, a fact he revealed to her later with significant glee.

Sydney never saw the woman again after the party. She later thought she had engaged in the encounter out of spite and anger, in an effort to make her boyfriend jealous, assisted by the fact she had way too much to drink that night. The truth was she hadn't been drinking that heavily. She had found the woman attractive and couldn't deny she enjoyed the physical experience. It felt somehow right. But afterwards she returned to her normal dating pattern, succumbing to social expectations.

Sydney was an exceptionally attractive woman who was never short of attention from the men around her. She had certainly been active in the dating scene throughout her thirty-five years. She'd been sexually attracted to, and sexually active with, several men over the years and had partaken in a few moderate length committed and monogamous relationships. She'd even flirted with marriage once, but broke the engagement after deciding the relationship lacked that "real spark."

Sydney wondered if this was what that "real spark" felt like. What exactly was it she was feeling toward this handsome and commanding woman? If she was, why had she never been attracted to, much less felt this way, about any other woman? Of course, she'd never felt this way so quickly about a man, either. Sydney shook her head, now more confused by her attraction to Sergeant Chambers.

A WEEK AFTER the trial and formal sentencing concluded, Sydney was attempting to put Sinclair's acts, and the disturbing veiled threat behind her. She was forced to revisit the unsettling discomfort one morning when a dozen white roses arrived for her at the office. She returned from a hearing to find them sitting on her desk. When she opened the card it read almost the same as his statement to her that day.

```
Looking forward to spending some time alone with you.
```

There was no name or signature, but there was no doubt in her mind who the flowers were from. Cold fear washed over her and she backed away from the desk. She exited her office, leaving the roses sitting untouched, and quickly walked down the hall to Tyler's office. He looked up as she entered.

"Syd, what's wrong?"

"I just got a flower delivery, white roses, and this." She handed him the card that arrived with the roses. He read the note, then re-read it before looking up at her.

"Isn't that—," he began, then stopped when she nodded.

"Yep, it's exactly what he said to me in the courtroom. Word for word."

"We need to call someone. Who's the detective who handled the case? The primary investigator?"

"Chuck Severs. His partner was Robert Kim, Robbery Homicide Division. His number is in my cell, which is in my bag, in my office." Sydney looked up at Tyler. "I don't really want to go back in there right now with those..."

"Don't worry about it. I can track him down." He leaned forward and began flicking through his rolodex. He found the number he was looking for and dialed.

"Marla? It's Tyler. Listen, sweetheart, I need you track down one of your detectives over there. I don't have his cell number...yes, Chuck Severs. Can you tell him it's regarding the Sinclair-White Roses case and it's urgent...yes, give him my direct office line...thanks, hon. We'll be waiting for his call." He hung up and looked up at Sydney with a smile. "You don't need to know anyone else when you have an in with the commanding officer's secretary," he said with a wink.

Tyler's phone rang less than five minutes later. "Tyler Houston. Yes, detective, thank you for returning my call so quickly. There's been an incident here at the D.A.'s office."

Tyler looked over at Sydney and raised an eyebrow in question. She nodded her head to indicate she would speak to the detective as Tyler continued. "Yes, we think it's related. It involves Sydney Rutledge, the D.A. who handled the case...yes, she's right here, hold on." He handed the phone across the desk.

"Hello, detective."

"Ms. Rutledge. What's going on? Are you okay?"

"I'm fine, I guess. I returned from court this morning to find a dozen roses had been delivered to me. White roses, and there was a card attached. The note on the card is a direct quote of something Sinclair said to me in the courtroom at the end of the trial."

"Is it a threat?"

"Yes. Well, maybe not exactly. I don't know I guess. It felt like one at the time, and now..." Sydney took a deep breath.

"No problem, Sydney," Chuck said in an understanding voice. "What does it say exactly?" Sydney glanced at the card sitting on the desk in front of Tyler. She didn't have to read it to remember the statement Sinclair had made.

"It says, looking forward to spending some time alone with you. Those were his exact words that day. I remember them distinctly."

"Yeah, I remember that as well. Do you know what company delivered the flowers? Does the card say?" Sydney reached over the desk and retrieved the card, looking at it then turning it over.

"Yes, it says here on the back of the card, Spring Street Flowers."

"Okay. Hang tight. Let me grab my partner and one of us will come to you now, and we'll also check on the flower delivery to see what we can figure out."

"Thank you, detective." Sydney hung up and looked up at Tyler. "They're on their way."

"I better let Stan know," Tyler said. "I'll also let Cathy at the front desk know to send them back here to my office first." He walked around his desk toward the door, giving her shoulder a gentle squeeze as he passed by. "You and I are going to dinner tonight. I don't want to hear any argument from you."

Sydney couldn't help but smile at his gentle demand. She was thankful for his mothering. She definitely didn't want to spend the evening alone. She let her head fall back against the chair, suddenly feeling drained. A collage of images went through her mind, consisting of crime scene photos, autopsy details, and a replay of Sinclair's eyes fixed on her as he was dragged from the courtroom. She had no doubt the creepy veiled threat, accompanied by her intimate knowledge of the torture, rape and murder case, would keep her awake for many nights to come.

TWO DAYS LATER Sydney was walking in the hallway between court rooms, her attention focused on the files she was shuffling in her arms when a familiar voice caught her attention. She turned to see Sergeant Chambers approaching.

"Good morning, Sergeant Chambers."

"Hi. Uh, how're you doing?"

Sydney thought she picked up on a slight nervousness in the sergeant's demeanor, but immediately discounted it as her imagination.

"I'm okay," she replied. "Getting back in the swing of daily prelims now that the trial's over." Sydney indicated the stack of case files in her arms.

"I ran into Detective Severs yesterday. He mentioned the roses. Are you, uh, I mean, is everything okay?"

Sydney's heart skipped a beat at her obvious concern. "Yeah, I think I'm okay," she replied. "It was a little creepy, I have to admit. Did the detective tell you about the aunt?"

"Oh, yeah," Alex nodded and rolled her eyes. "It always helps to have an evangelical aunt with a slight case of dementia. He convinced her he'd found God in prison and needed to make his apologies to those he'd offended."

"I guess so," Sydney said. "The detective told me he convinced her to pass along the request to some friend of his. He gave her the phone number to call and the message to deliver. They were able to track the number, but it's one of those pre-paid throw away cell phones. So we'll never know who helped him."

"Well, you know the crazy fan club members that serial killers always pick up. And despite the system they always find a way to make contact with these psychos. They're freaks, but more often than not they're harmless. And they've restricted Sinclair's contact with anyone except his attorneys now, so I don't think you'll have any more issues with him."

Sydney appreciated Sergeant Chambers's attempts to make her feel better about the incident. A smile graced her lips at Sergeant Chambers's reassuring words. She lost herself looking into the hazel eyes of the woman standing before her and was unsure exactly how long the pause in the conversation lasted when she saw those same eyes blink and look down at the floor.

Was the tall sergeant nervous? Sydney discounted that thought as impossible. Surely she was reading way too much into her body language. And why was she doing that? Why was she reacting this way? As the sergeant asked her which court she was heading to next then began walking with her in that direction, Sydney wondered why she once again found herself searching for excuses to prolong the conversation.

THE NEXT DAY, back in Los Angeles, Sydney made her way toward her car at the end of a hectic day in and out of various court hearings. As she walked through the garage beneath the courts building she noted an object on the front windshield of her car. When she recognized the object she stopped short. Propped against her windshield was a single white rose, starkly noticeable against the dark background of her graphite black Mercedes Benz SL500 convertible.

Sydney looked at the rose from several feet away for a few seconds, then took a deep breath, willing herself to calm and pushing the tingle of fear aside. She straightened her shoulders, then walked up to her vehicle and removed the rose, walking to a trashcan several parking spaces away and throwing it unceremoniously in the receptacle. She quickly returned to her vehicle, entered and drove from the garage. On her way home she alternately cursed herself for her sudden stab of fear and then the person who put the rose there in the first place. By the time she arrived home she'd convinced herself it was a vicious and cruel joke, likely perpetrated by some other employee within the criminal courts building.

For the life of her, however, she couldn't think of a likely offender. She was determined not to allow it to bother her or to give anyone the satisfaction of seeing a reaction.

Chapter Four

A COUPLE OF weeks later, on a late afternoon midway through the court week, Sydney made her way through the crowded fifteenth floor hallway of the courthouse, having been held late in court on an evidentiary suppression hearing. As she made her way toward the central elevators, she was suddenly aware of a commotion within one of the courtrooms. The yelling and profanity could be heard through the double doors and over the usual noise of the busy outer hallway. Male voices were raised in anger, followed by what sounded like a violent physical altercation. Sydney began to back away from the doors in question when suddenly they crashed open and several bodies came barreling out into the hallway.

Two medium built Hispanic men, their gang affiliation obvious due to their dress and display of various tattoos, were locked in combat. They were followed by several additional friends and family, many of them displaying signs of their respective gang affiliations, as well as two sheriff's department bailiffs who were attempting to bring about some sense of order to the chaos.

As Sydney sidestepped the mass of bodies that hurtled toward her, she glanced up at the remaining crowd of people against the opposite wall by the bank of elevators. Several of the bystanders were pushing their way into the single set of open elevator doors, hoping to escape the violence unfolding before them. As additional battles broke out amongst the other gang members, Sydney began to cycle her eyes back to the melee and backed toward her own avenue of escape. Then her eyes were for some reason drawn to those of a tall figure standing against the rear wall of the open elevator and she froze.

Despite the fast moving violence breaking out all around her, Sydney stood frozen, unable to move as an unstoppable spike of terror went through her. Though the figure was wearing dark sunglasses, strange within the interior confines of the courthouse and the elevator, Sydney believed she recognized the unmistakable face of Matthew Sinclair.

ALEX WAS RETURNING from the restroom, taking a break from sitting in a nearby courtroom waiting for her case to be called. A gang dispute had turned violent and war had broken out in the halls of the courthouse. She saw Sydney at the very edge of the quickly expanding altercation. Her attention didn't seem focused on the increasing violence, instead directed toward something or someone behind the closing door of one of the elevators.

Two of the combatants suddenly lurched toward Sydney. Without conscious thought Alex threw herself at the two, successfully intercepting them on their collision course and sending both sprawling to the floor along with Alex herself.

After they all hit the ground Alex straddled one of the gangsters, as he lay on his back and continued to struggle against her. She turned briefly back to Sydney.

"Ms. Rutledge, get back!" she yelled, diverting her focus then taking a fist to the side of her head for her inattention. She quickly recovered and delivered an elbow strike to his face, stunning him sufficiently to allow her to force him onto his stomach in an effort to handcuff him. She then noticed the other gang member had regained his footing and was coming toward her with his hands clenched.

"Back off!" Her attention split as she fought to pull the first offender's hands behind his back and keep an eye on Sydney, still standing unmoving nearby.

"Fuck you, bitch!" was the gangster's only reply as he continued to advance, bringing a booted foot back and coming forward in a vicious kick aimed at Alex's exposed ribcage. She attempted to twist away from it and brought one arm up to deflect the incoming kick, but it still connected partially. At that moment one of the bailiffs tackled him before he could deliver another blow to Alex.

The suspect Alex was struggling with used the opportunity, and the now free arm, to drive his elbow up and back, connecting with her face. Alex was dizzied by the combination of blows but delivered her own combination of punches to the suspect's kidney area then the side of his head. He stopped resisting and she was able to finish handcuffing him. At that moment the cavalry arrived as several additional sheriff's deputies came pouring out of nearby courtrooms, the elevator and stairwell.

Alex jumped up and moved to Sydney's side, positioning herself between Sydney and the combatants. The scene became momentarily more chaotic as the dozen or so officers forcefully regained control. Alex grasped Sydney by the shoulders, gently moving her against the wall. Sydney collapsed into her body, Sydney's forehead against her chest. Alex felt a shudder go through Sydney's body as she stood protectively between her and the gradually receding violence. The scene was brought under control and Alex turned her attention to fully focus on the woman in her arms.

Sydney took a deep breath and straightened her posture. Alex was suddenly aware of the somewhat intimate embrace in which she held Sydney. She loosened her grasp and took a partial step back, giving Sydney her personal space, yet remaining close enough to lend support if needed.

"Hey, are you okay?"

Sydney finally seemed to focus on the activity around her. "Um.

Yeah," Sydney said with not much conviction. She seemed slow to collect herself and Alex couldn't help but notice her eyes drift repeatedly to the elevators. When one of them let out a loud "ding" and the doors began to open, Sydney's eyes flashed with terror. Alex glanced over at the same doors and watched them open. None of the current occupants exited, all apparently following the afternoon exit pattern and intent on riding the car to the ground floor. Many of those uninvolved in the now ended hallway altercation jockeyed for position in the car.

When Alex turned back to Sydney, the woman seemed to have collected herself and was straightening out the files she was carrying, which now threatened to fall. Alex reached over and kept some of the files from falling as Sydney repositioned the shoulder strap of her leather satchel briefcase.

"Thanks," Sydney said with a quick smile of gratitude as she continued to organize her files. Alex was pondering asking Sydney about her look of fear when the vibration emanating from her uniform pocket sidetracked her. She gave Sydney an apologetic look then stepped aside to answer the cell phone.

"Hey, Sal," she said, having noted the caller I.D. "What's up?"

"We just had a back-up request put out by the sheriffs in the courthouse, fifteenth floor. It's code-four now."

This indicated that the situation was under control and no further assistance was needed.

"Tell me you're not in the middle of this?"

"Uh, well, now that you mention it—"

"Shit, Alex," Sal said. "Say no more. I'm just about to get on the elevator."

"Thanks, buddy," Alex said and laughed. "I'll be waiting on fifteen."

SYDNEY WATCHED ALEX tuck the phone away in a pocket and turn back toward her. For the first time she noted the side of her face was bloodied, coming from a gash near one eyebrow. She saw Alex reach up and run her fingers along the cut, then appear more frustrated than hurt. Sydney watched as Alex walked a short distance then paused as a stocky male sergeant, who had just stepped off the elevator, met her. The new arrival seemed to joke with her about something as they spoke briefly and he took some notes.

When Alex walked away and entered the nearby ladies' room, Sydney handed her briefcase to Tyler, who had joined her in the hallway.

"I'm going to make a quick bathroom stop, Ty." He took the briefcase and files from her and she noticed the mischievous glint in his eye. She rolled her eyes."I'm just using the facilities, Tyler. Control your imagination." But she couldn't keep a slight smile from her own lips as she turned away and headed to the ladies' room.

She entered the restroom and saw Alex leaning over the sink splashing water onto her face, washing away the blood. When Alex straightened up a trickle of red could be seen still coming from her eyebrow.

Alex looked into the mirror and their eyes met for a moment. She appeared shocked by Sydney's entrance.

Sydney moved to the paper towel dispenser. "You're bleeding," she said as she tore off a section and held it out to Alex. "Are you okay?"

Alex took the paper towel and smiled her thanks at Sydney through the mirrored reflection. "It's just a scratch. No big deal," she said as she wiped her face. "How are you?" she asked.

"I'm fine," Sydney said, though her eyes drifted away in evasion as she said it.

Alex leaned back on the sink as she held the towel to her eyebrow. "You sure about that?" she asked quietly. "It seemed like something had you a bit...startled. Something different than the chaos in the hallway."

"I, uh, just thought I saw someone I recognized in the elevator," Sydney said nervously. "Someone I'd really rather not see."

"I could tell you weren't really focused on what was going on around you," Alex said. "I'm sorry if I startled you by jerking you around. It looked like a couple of those guys were going to steamroll over the top of you and I didn't want you getting hurt."

Sydney's stomach fluttered pleasantly when she saw the look of concern on Alex's face. She was again thrown off by the feeling, by her own reaction to being in this woman's presence. Flustered, she turned to the sink herself, washing her hands as she attempted to figure out what to say next. Alex made no move to leave, wiping her own hands dry then returning the favor as she handed Sydney some paper towels to dry her hands.

"Not at all," Sydney said. "I appreciate you looking out for me. You seem to do that quite a bit with me," she added. She thought she saw Alex smile somewhat nervously in response.

"Uh, if you wouldn't mind talking to the other sergeant about what you saw that would be a big help," Alex said. "He's got to write a use of force report on me and needs any witnesses who saw what happened."

Sydney nodded. She was familiar with the L.A.P.D.'s administrative use of force reports as they sometimes came into play in cases she handled that involved resisting arrest charges or assaults on police officers.

"As you noticed, I kind of zoned out there for a few moments," Sydney said somewhat sheepishly. "But I'll certainly share what I do remember seeing."

"Hey, you help put a lot of the worst of the worst away. It's perfectly understandable if you're thrown off a little when you run into one of them, or their family members, in the open hallway." Alex held the door open for Sydney and they exited the bathroom back into the hallway.

Sydney realized Sergeant Chambers believed she'd run into someone she'd previously prosecuted. She was relieved not to have to explain any further and tucked the experience away as a symptom of being tired and somewhat stressed. Clearly she had allowed her imagination to get the better of her common sense.

"This is Sydney Rutledge, she's an A.D.A. She was in the hallway and saw most of what happened. Ms. Rutledge, this is Sergeant Sal Donatelli." They shook hands and smiled in greeting to one another.

"I can make this real quick," Sal said as he pulled out a small notepad and wrote Sydney's name on it. Then he looked back at Alex. "Give me a minute to get a quick statement then I'll take you to Good Samaritan Hospital to get your face looked at."

"No rush," Alex said. "Probably don't need the hospital. We can swing by the fire station and I'll just get an ice pack or something." She wandered across the hallway to lean on the wall with her arms crossed.

"She really should get some ice on that as soon as possible," Sydney said quietly to no one in particular. "And she may need some stitches." Sydney looked across the hall at Alex, who was leaned back against the wall, eyes closed.

"Uh-huh," Sal said. "But Alex can be a little pigheaded at times."

Sydney continued gazing at Alex and almost missed the next quiet comment that Sal added.

"And like Alex always says, chicks dig scars."

Sydney turned back to Sal, who appeared to be innocently looking in his notebook as he wrote something. She then looked at Tyler, who wore his smirk plastered on his face. She glared briefly at him and he almost laughed out loud as he turned to a nearby drinking fountain. She glanced again at Alex and Sal, and wondered if either of them had noticed how long she had been gazing at the attractive female sergeant.

"So," Sal interrupted her thoughts and looked up with no expression. "Can you just tell me where you were in the hallway and exactly what you saw?"

"ISN'T THAT THE A.D.A. from your White Rose case?" Sal asked ten minutes later as he and Alex were riding the elevator down to the ground floor.

"Uh-huh," Alex said casually.

"I think she's interested in you."

Alex turned toward him. "You're smokin' your socks, Sal."

"Nope...she's definitely interested in you."

"She's straight, Sal. I'm telling you there's no way."

"And I'm telling you she's interested, or at least curious. Trust me."

Alex rolled her eyes. "You're nuts." She got into the passenger side of the black and white. But inside she wondered if there was any chance Sal could be correct. Could she be interested? Even a little?

"What makes you think she's interested?" Alex asked as they drove from the scene.

SYDNEY AND TYLER returned to their offices on the eighteenth floor. Sydney was unusually quiet during their journey up from the courtroom hallway on the lower floor. She had to admit to herself that the disturbing gift left on her car was playing havoc with her mind. She'd been having trouble sleeping, her dreams riddled with disturbing images from the crime scene photographs during the Sinclair trial. She considered what she had imagined in the elevator lobby. It was just her imagination, wasn't it?

"You okay, Syd?" Tyler sat down in the chair on the other side of her desk, putting down one of the cups of coffee he'd just picked up from the break room. Sydney looked at him for a few moments, contemplating her reply.

"Someone's played a messed up joke on me," she finally said. "And I think it's making my imagination over-react a little bit." Tyler only lifted his eyebrow and waited for her to continue as he sipped at his own coffee. "Someone left a rose on my windshield a couple weeks ago."

"You have a secret admirer?" he asked, though the slight smile disappeared at Sydney's next comment.

"It was a white rose," she said simply.

"What kind of fucked up—"

"Yeah, I told myself it was just some messed up, vicious game being played by someone and tried to ignore it. But I think it got my imagination going a bit, because then today I imagined seeing Sinclair in one of the elevators just as the fight broke out."

"Imagined?" Tyler asked. Sydney nodded then leaned back and looked up at the ceiling.

"I froze. I could swear it was him. But we all know he's in prison. He's on death row, for Christ's sake."

THE NEXT EVENING Sydney made her way across the garage toward her car. Her head was down and her eyes were tied to her cell phone scrolling through several emails. She looked up as she put her phone away and stopped short. A white rose had, once again, been placed against the windshield of her car. Sydney looked around, feeling extremely exposed and very alone. She backed away from her car, then turned and bolted for the elevator. The doors opened immediately after she pressed the call button and she was thankful the elevator had not yet left the subterranean level. She pressed the button several times, willing the doors to close more quickly.

Sydney rode the elevator to the eighteenth floor. She was unsure of what she intended to do, she only knew she couldn't remain alone in the darkened garage. The elevator traveled directly to the upper floor, the late hour reducing demand on it with most riders on the way down and out of the building. The doors opened onto the lobby and Sydney hurriedly exited, practically running into Tyler, who was waiting to leave.

"Hey, what's the rush, Syd?" he asked with a smile. He stopped their collision with outstretched arms.

"Tyler!" Sydney grasped his hand and closed her eyes in relief, then took a deep breath to calm herself.

"Syd, what the heck is going on? What's wrong?" He guided her to a nearby lobby chair and sat next to her. "What happened? You just left a few minutes ago."

The more she calmed, the more Sydney began to feel a little silly. She shook her head. Maybe she was making a bigger deal out of this than she should? Tyler waited patiently until she finally answered.

"Ty, it happened again."

Tyler remained silent and simply raised his eyebrows in question.

"Another white rose on my windshield."

"Somebody," Tyler said quietly, "is being an asshole. Was there a note or anything?"

Sydney shook her head. "I didn't see one."

They sat for a couple more minutes, Tyler simply rubbing Sydney's back in comfort. Then Sydney mentally ordered herself to get a grip.

"Okay, this is ridiculous. It's just a stupid sick joke and I shouldn't give anyone the satisfaction of seeing more of a reaction." She stood and slung the strap to her satchel over her shoulder, acting with more confidence than she actually felt. "Walk down with me?" she said with a somewhat sheepish look on her face.

"You're sure you don't want to make a formal report or anything?" Tyler asked as he stood.

"I'm sure. It's nothing. If I ignore it, hopefully they'll move on to harass someone else with their immature crap."

"Okay." Tyler moved with her to the elevator doors and pressed the button to recall the elevator. "Let's walk you to your car and I'll take care of it. But I want you to promise me you'll tell me if anything else happens."

A COUPLE OF weeks, later Alex ran into Sydney once again in the hallway on one of the courthouse floors.

"I see you're none the worse for wear," Sydney said. "Did

you end up with stitches?"

Alex rolled her eyes to indicate how she felt about the required medical treatment. "Yeah. Just a few."

Sydney leaned forward, reaching up to Alex's chin and turning her face to get a look at the injured eyebrow.

"Looks good," she said. "You almost can't see the scar, even knowing it's there." Alex felt Sydney's fingers linger momentarily, maintaining their contact with her skin. Alex's eyes closed and she shuddered slightly at the contact. When she opened her eyes moments later their eyes met and neither moved or spoke for a moment. Then Sydney pulled her hand back and looked away, leaving Alex somewhat embarrassed at her own reactions. She wondered how much Sydney had noticed, or if Sydney had felt anything herself.

Alex cleared her throat and then explained she was in one of the courts for a preliminary hearing on another narcotics case.

"My case has trailed until after the lunch break," Alex said, and then paused, gathering the courage to continue. "You interested in grabbing a quick bite?"

Sydney smiled "I'd love to."

Alex was relieved to see that she didn't seem uncomfortable with what had occurred between them. "Pete's Café okay?" she asked.

"Sounds good."

They walked to a small restaurant across from the courthouse. There they talked over salads, sticking primarily to current events at each of their jobs and cases they were engaged in. Then Alex decided she'd branch out and steer the questions to more personal details.

"So, Ms. Rutledge, tell me about your family. Where are you from?"

"Well, I'm originally from the raging metropolis that is Duluth, Minnesota," Sydney said with a smile. "My dad was a very successful attorney, primarily dealing with large company corporate law and international contracts. My sister and I did most of our growing up in Duluth, but we did travel quite a bit. We both couldn't wait to get out and experience the big city. Fortunately our parents could afford to support us through college. She went east and I went west. She ended up in medical school on the east coast and now practices in New York. I ended up at the University of Southern California for undergrad and law."

"Ah, a Trojan, outstanding," Alex said, her eyes shining.

"Are you a Trojan?"

"Nah," Alex said with a shake of her head. "I was too dumb and too poor to get into USC. But you know, you grow up in the LA area and you're either a USC Trojans fan or a UCLA Bruins fan. I don't see how you can take a football team seriously when they wear powder blue and have a teddy bear as a mascot," she added with a shrug.

"Excellent." Sydney laughed. "I'm quite the rabid Trojan football fan myself. So what about you, Alex? Where did you grow up and go to college? Major?" The questions were rattled off.

"What makes you so sure I went to college?"

"You forget, I've read your reports. I know you write quite well. And I've seen you on the stand being challenged by high dollar and very aggressive defense attorneys. If you didn't go to college, you should have. Shoot, you should've gone to law school. You'd be better than a lot of attorneys out there right now."

Alex smiled at Sydney's response and briefly debated on how much detail to provide on her less than ideal family history. But before she could answer, her thoughts were interrupted by an emergency transmission on her radio. A somewhat breathless officer was requesting back-up, clearly chasing a suspect on foot. Then she caught the location.

"That's just down the street," she said as she rose, pulling money from her pocket and placing it on the table. "I've gotta run."

"That's too much," Sydney said. "You're part is probably half that."

"Then you can pay me back next time," Alex said as she hurriedly backed toward the door. She smiled when she heard Sydney's response.

"I'm going to hold you to that," Sydney said. "Be careful."

ON FRIDAY AT the end of that same week, Sydney discussed the Sergeant Chambers situation with Tyler again as they sat in her den drinking wine after sharing a meal. He brought the subject up first.

"So," he said. "I've been doing some investigating on your sergeant friend."

"What?" Sydney almost choked on her wine. "What do you mean investigating?"

"Well, I saw you two sitting in Pete's together at lunch the other day."

"Have you been spying on me or her?"

"Neither. I was picking up a sandwich next door and happened to see you two sitting in there. You both looked quite...what's the word? Engaged? Singularly focused on one another."

Sydney rolled her eyes in feigned irritation. "Alex asked if I had plans for lunch because she was stuck having to come back and testify afterwards. I'm sure she was just bored and looking for any company she happened to come across."

"I don't know about that," Tyler said. "She doesn't look like she lacks the confidence to do anything alone. And, according to my contacts, word in the lesbian world is she doesn't have to fear being alone if she is in need or want of company. I have it on good authority if she expresses a desire there are those who are standing in line to fulfill it."

For some reason Sydney felt a certain sense of discomfort at the last comment. But she immediately gave herself a mental kick. She was surprised at the sense of jealousy she felt toward these unknown women who may be keeping Alex company.

"Okay," she finally said, curiosity getting the better of her. "What have you found out?"

Tyler leaned forward with a smile.

"As we both knew," he paused and looked critically at her, "well, as I certainly knew, she is a lesbian. She has a reputation for being quite competent and popular both to her officers and her superiors. Though she's a bit of a maverick at times and this has pissed off some of the more politically correct of the department's command staff." He then took a deep breath.

"She's single." At that Sydney looked up sharply, having been staring at her wine glass as she listened. Tyler winked at her and smiled. "Uh-huh, very single. She was involved with someone outside the department and evidently that ended abruptly. That was about a year ago from what I'm hearing. She's not overly social, very committed to her work. She's occasionally seen at some of the bars and clubs, occasionally accompanied by a date, though rarely the same one more than once from what I hear. And quoting one of my sources, who goes to the same gym as she does and tends to be attracted to the tall, muscular, slightly butch type, she has a body to die for."

The last part Tyler added with a feigned, overly dramatic and very feminine swoon. He then popped up and looked at Sydney expectantly and she couldn't help but laugh.

"Please tell me no one knows you've been conducting this exhaustive background investigation on my behalf?"

"Oh, no." he said. "Your name never came up. As it turns out, Cindy, the secretary in the gang unit, has had the hots for your sergeant for over a year. There's also a Vicky-something, one of the third year law students clerking part time in the Domestic Violence unit, who's been after her. Between the two of them they've evidently compiled quite the dossier on Sergeant Chambers."

"First of all she's not 'my sergeant'." Sydney emphasized the title. "And second, she has no interest outside our professional capacity. And I don't even understand what I'm thinking here." She shook her head in exasperation. "I just know when I spend time with her, I kind of don't want it to end."

"You have to explore that feeling," Tyler said. "That's the only way you're going to figure it out."

Chapter Five

SYDNEY SAT AT her desk trying once again to complete the closing arguments for her current home invasion robbery trial. She'd been at it off and on for several hours, but the interruptions never seemed to end in the busy downtown Los Angeles D.A.'s office.

She had to admit the most recent distractions were more of her own making. Her eyes drifted once again to the folded newspaper sitting on the edge of her desk. The front-page headline announced in bold letters:

`Third Murder Points to Possible 'White Rose' Copycat.`

The article described a string of three homicides that had occurred in Las Vegas, Nevada, Barstow, California, and then Ontario, California, just the day before. All eerily similar to the murders of the now infamous, and currently incarcerated, Matthew Sinclair, the "White Rose Killer."

The case was the most disturbing Sydney had ever handled. She couldn't escape the fact it brought her in contact with Alex. In the past several weeks she had run into her several more times around the court building. They had smiled and exchanged pleasantries, and each time they parted Sydney couldn't fight the feeling she would've liked it to continue. She frequently found Alex prominent in her mind for a long period afterwards.

Just yesterday they had run into each other during the lunch court recess. It was the first time she'd seen Alex in a couple of weeks. This time Sydney took the initiative and asked if she would care for some company at lunch. Alex at first seemed startled by the invitation and Sydney feared she'd made a mistake. Alex recovered quickly and accepted her offer. They had agreed on a sandwich shop down the street. Once again Sydney was engrossed in the conversation, enjoying Alex's company and wanting it very much to continue, hoping to learn more about this intriguing woman.

Sitting at her desk the day after the encounter, she caught herself daydreaming again and kicked herself mentally for letting her mind wander. The fact that her mind was constantly being drawn to this woman was exceptionally frustrating. Sydney had never allowed personal feelings to interrupt her work. Never before developed feelings for a woman either, which was somewhat startling, yet not entirely uncomfortable, as she pondered it for the umpteenth time.

Sydney shook her head. This was ridiculous. What was it about that woman that did this to her? Maybe she should just avoid her. After all, there was work to do. Sydney put pen to paper once again and tried to refocus on the partially written closing argument. But before she could continue there was a light knocking on her open door and she looked up to see Tyler standing in the doorway with a big grin on his face.

"Hey, Ty. What's up?" she asked, frustration evident in her voice.

"I found someone wandering the halls here on the eighteenth floor and thought you might want to say hi." He stepped aside. Sydney's breath caught as the source of many of her daydreams appeared in her doorway.

"Hi," Alex said with an element of shyness.

Sydney's frustration and irritation boiled momentarily to the surface as the cause of all of her confusion appeared in the doorway to her office. Before she could stop herself, the words escaped her in a less than hospitable tone.

"What are you doing here?"

ALEX WAS SOMEWHAT confused by her own reactions over the past several weeks. She wasn't one to find herself swept away like this. For many years she'd been perfectly content to slip from one short term relationship to another, never willing to commit, to open herself up to anything deeper than satisfying lustful and erotic urges. Her last lengthy relationship ended in disaster, and she knew most of the fault lay squarely in her lap. The relationship with Regina Carlisle, the dedicated social worker who was several years her junior, was casual and comfortable for Alex, but nothing more. It had been far more serious for Regina. Alex admitted she let the vibrant and passionate young woman think she was taking the level of commitment far more seriously than she actually was.

It all came to a head when Alex hedged Regina's invitation to move in together. They'd been exclusive and monogamous for over a year by that time, and "domestic unification," as Regina called it, was the next logical step. But Alex was unable to take that next step, couldn't bring herself to commit at that level. Regina threatened to end the relationship if Alex refused. She was shocked when Alex let her go without a fight.

There was a reason for her inability to commit, to bond at that level. That reason reached back well into Alex's relationship past. It was an experience that Alex shared with only one other person in her life. After the disaster with Regina, she gave up attempting to engage in any substantial or meaningful relationships. The past year had been filled with sporadic short term dating forays, interspersed with occasionally seducing, or allowing herself to be seduced by, nameless one night stands. So why did she have the urge to approach this woman? This straight woman of all people? Especially after what happened so many years ago?

These were the thoughts that raced through Alex's mind just five minutes earlier as she rode the elevator up to the D.A.'s offices on the eighteenth floor of the court building, only to remain inside the car and ride it right back down again. Why was she doing this?

She had spent the last several weeks making up excuses for running into Sydney, which primarily consisted of taking every opportunity to coincidentally find herself near the right courtrooms during the lunch break. Why? All the information she could surreptitiously gather indicated fairly clearly Sydney Rutledge was quite straight. She had very briefly discussed the issue with Sal as they worked together on New Year's Eve, ending the conversation by again reiterating it was pointless pining on her part. Yet Alex couldn't help but feel some portion of the attraction she felt toward Sydney was being reciprocated.

The elevator doors opened again on the ground floor lobby. Alex remained unmoving in the elevator a second time, then finally pressed the button for the eighteenth floor once more. As she rode the elevator up again she tried to think of an excuse for being there after business hours. What reason would she have for being here on one of the D.A.'s office floors rather than on one of the lower courtroom floors? What rationale could she have for wandering around the eighteenth floor?

Before she could come up with something the slightest bit believable the doors opened onto the eighteenth floor reception lobby. Alex stepped out into an empty waiting area. She presumed the receptionist, who usually sat behind the glass partition, had already gone home. Alex was standing in the empty lobby contemplating whether this was just a bad idea, or perhaps a really bad idea, when a door at one end of the lobby opened. A gentleman stepped through it with an armload of case files. She recognized him as Sydney's friend.

Tyler looked up as he came through the door and seemed to notice Alex and smiled.

"Hi. How ya doin'?" he said. "I hope you haven't been waiting long. Cathy took off early for a long weekend." He nodded toward the empty reception desk. "Who are you here to see?"

"Uh, I was around the building so I thought I'd swing by and see Ms. Rutledge."

Tyler's smile grew wider and his eyes seemed to sparkle. Alex got the distinct impression he found this scenario somehow amusing.

"Oh, great," he said with enthusiasm. "She's been shut inside that office all day working. She'll be thrilled for an excuse to take a break."

Alex willingly followed as he took off across the lobby and led her through the secured doors on the other side. He dropped the files on a desk as he passed it, then turned and waved for Alex to keep following him. She noted the smile once again as she followed and wondered what exactly was so amusing.

They approached Sydney's office and Tyler stopped in the doorway and knocked politely. A slightly tired sounding female voice that Alex immediately recognized said, "Hey, Ty. What's up?"

Alex had a momentary feeling of anxiety, then just as quickly Tyler stepped out of the doorway to make room for her, indicating that she should enter. She responded automatically, stepping past him into the office. And there was Sydney Rutledge, looking somewhat tired but still so very gorgeous in Alex's eyes.

"Hi," Alex stammered.

Alex knew immediately how lame she must sound and struggled to think of something to add. The look she saw on Sydney's face when she looked up solidified in her mind that this visit was a very bad idea. Sydney was clearly irritated by her interruption.

"What are you doing here?" Sydney said with an exasperated sigh.

"I was, uh, in the building for a meeting and thought I'd stop by. Hey, bad timing on my part. You're obviously busy," Alex said. "Sorry for the interruption." Alex retreated from the office and started down the hall back toward the elevator lobby.

"Alex, wait!" Sydney called and Alex paused and turned back. "I'm sorry," Sydney said as she drew near. "It's been a long, frustrating day and I was at my wits end. I shouldn't have taken it out on you. I could really use a break and a few minutes of distraction. Please don't go."

Alex believed Sydney was honestly regretful and sincere in her invitation. She nodded her assent. "No problem," she said. "We all have those days sometimes."

As they re-entered the office and Sydney returned to her seat behind her desk, Alex saw the newspaper sitting on the edge of the desk and jumped at the opportunity for an excuse to keep the visit and conversation going. "I was wondering what you thought about all this," she said, stepping forward and tapping the article on the killer.

Sydney leaned back in her chair and pointed at the chair across the desk from her. "Please, have a seat," she said. Alex sat down, working hard to keep her face neutral and not reveal how thrilled she was that the effort to extend the stay had been successful.

"That's the creepiest thing," Sydney said. "This copycat is right on the mark. I'm not sure how much detail was in the papers during the trial. I was a little too busy to pay attention to the media, but whoever's doing this must have studied every detail."

Alex nodded in agreement. She picked up the newspaper and glanced at the article she had read earlier that day. "Yeah, that's certainly the way the article makes it sound. And it's almost as if he's making his way toward L.A. First Vegas, then Barstow, now Ontario. All tortured, raped, strangled."

The conversation continued for several minutes as they talked over the facts laid out in the various recent newspaper articles. When the conversation eventually petered out Alex grasped for an excuse to return to Sydney's office in the near future.

"You know, this has really got me curious. I'm going to check with the guys from R.H.D. and see what they can tell me. They have to have had calls from Vegas P.D. and the others. I'll see what I can find out tomorrow morning." Alex let the idea hang between them for a moment until Sydney replied.

"I'll be tied up in court all day tomorrow. I have closing arguments then jury instruction on this robbery trial. But it's Friday and I'm not going to want to wait all weekend wondering if you found out anything interesting. I don't suppose you'd be willing to brief me tomorrow at the end of the court day?"

"Sure, I can swing by tomorrow afternoon." Alex tried to say it as nonchalantly as she could. Although she was sure the invitation was simply the result of what Sydney saw as a shared professional interest, Alex was thrilled by the prospect of seeing Sydney again so soon.

Alex's heart nearly skipped a beat when Sydney added with a smile, "Great. I'll treat for coffee," she said, nodding toward a coffee maker in the corner of a nearby bookshelf.

Alex smiled. "Sounds good. I'll let you get back to work. Best of luck in court tomorrow. I'm sure you'll be great."

She gave a brief wave as she made her way out of the office and down the hall. She smiled as she walked out of the court building to her black and white at the curb. Then the pessimist in her took over. What the hell was she doing? Falling for a straight chick? Wasn't it clear that Sydney's interest was purely professional? Or was it? Why did Alex continue to feel as if some of her personal interest was being reciprocated? Was she imagining that? Or was that electricity really flowing both ways? Maybe she was about to find out.

SYDNEY WAS LEANING back in her chair staring at the ceiling when Tyler jumped through her doorway.

"Coffee? That was the best you could do? On a Friday evening you talk about coffee in your office?" he said with exasperation.

"What?" she said. "It's not supposed to be a date. I really do want to know about the case, and you know I'm in court all day tomorrow."

"And you and I both know you really do want to spend more time with her." Tyler replied. "This was your perfect opportunity to propose something that could, you know, go either way. Start as a work meeting and transition into something better. But I assure you bathroom water coffee in your office will not afford you that transitional opportunity. What on earth am I gonna do with you?"

"Oh please." Sydney was half frustrated and half giggling at Tyler's melodrama. "I have no idea what I was thinking. Besides, it's not as if she's the slightest bit interested in anything but official business. She was here in the building for another meeting and stopped in to talk about the White Roses case." Sydney waved the newspaper at him.

"And that, my dear, would be where you're so badly mistaken," Tyler said with a huge grin as he fell into the seat across the desk from her.

"What are you talking about?"

"I was coming back through the employee entrance after picking up some files I needed from the archived files downstairs. I saw her pull up out front and go into the elevator lobby. By the time I dropped something off in the records unit and came up the elevator she was outside in reception. She didn't have any meeting. That was just her cover story." He leaned forward and said quietly, "She came here to see you."

SEVERAL HOURS LATER Sydney made her way down the elevator to the subterranean garage. As the car descended her mind replayed the earlier conversation with Alex. Her appearance in the doorway, just as she was mentally dealing with the frustrations and questions about her own feelings for the woman, had shocked her. She remembered being horrified by her own reaction and leaping to her feet to stop Alex from retreating further down the hallway. She couldn't help but think she'd seen a look of disappointment cross the sergeant's face when she at first implied she would be unavailable all day Friday. As the elevator came to a halt she pushed the thought out of her mind as some kind of wishful thinking.

It was nearing nine p.m. and her car was one of only a few remaining in the facility. As she exited the elevator she had a clear view of her black two seat Mercedes. Her breath caught in her throat as she saw the single white rose once again lying across the windshield. She turned immediately, caught the automatic doors before they closed, and re-entered the elevator. She frantically pushed the buttons for the doors to close and for the main floor lobby. She hoped against the odds that a security officer or sheriff's bailiff was still sitting there near the entry doors. When the doors opened again and she hurriedly exited into the lobby, she found, to her fear, that she was alone. She reached for her cell phone and frantically pulled up a number, pressing the button for the call to connect.

ALEX DROVE THROUGH the streets in her black and white, passing slowly by in search of anything interesting or out of place. It had been a relatively slow evening, probably owing to the cooler late evening winter temperatures, which seemed to have driven most of the predators into whatever holes they had. She reached for her phone as she felt it vibrate in her chest pocket, thinking perhaps Sal was also bored and was calling for a coffee meeting. She was surprised when the number was identified as belonging to Assistant District Attorney Sydney Rutledge. Alex was unsure exactly how to handle this, so she fell back on her official persona.

"Chambers," she said.

"Sergeant Chambers, are you still on duty?"

"Yeah, what can I do for you, Ms. Rutledge?" Sensing something was wrong, Alex made a U-turn and began heading toward the courthouse less than a mile north of her.

"I think maybe...I don't know...maybe someone's stalking me." Alex was startled by the panicked edge to Sydney's voice. Her foot pressed down harder on the accelerator as Sydney went on. "I found something on my car in the garage and, well, I think I might be the last one left in the building. I can't even find any security officers."

Alex reached down and hit the lights and siren. "I'm just a few blocks away. Stay on the phone with me," she said. "Where are you in the building right now?"

"I'm in the lobby on the main floor. Do you want me to come outside?"

"No, stay inside. I'll come to you. I'm just coming north up Broadway right now. I'm going to pull 'round to the main doors on Temple Street."

The lobby had two main sets of doors into the facility. The door on the south side overlooked a recently constructed public park. The other one on the north side faced Temple Street, one of the main thoroughfares through downtown.

"I'm pulling up in front now." Alex pulled to a stop in front of the doors and extinguished the emergency lights and exited the vehicle.

"I see you," Sydney said. "I'll come out."

The two women met on the sidewalk.

"Are you okay?" Alex barely stopped herself from putting her arms around Sydney in an effort to comfort the obviously flustered woman.

"Yes," Sydney replied. "I'm a little embarrassed. I think I'm probably blowing this out of proportion. I'm sorry to drag you out here. I freaked out a little and wasn't sure who else to call who might be nearby."

"Don't worry about it. I'm happy to help." Alex noticed Sydney shiver slightly and realized she was probably chilly in her business skirt suit with no jacket. "Come on," she said, taking the leather satchel off Sydney's shoulder. "Sit down in the car where we can warm you up and you can tell me what's going on." She led Sydney to her nearby vehicle and opened the door for her, putting the satchel in the back of the car then walking around to the driver's seat. She started the engine and turned up the heat.

"All right. Why do you think someone's stalking you?" she asked quietly.

"I've had roses left on my car by someone," Sydney said as she gazed out the window in front of her. "They're leaving them on my windshield. No note or anything. They're just waiting for me when I get off work."

"How many times has this happened?"

"Tonight was the third one. All single roses." Sydney looked over at Alex. "White roses." She shook her head and closed her eyes, leaning back against the headrest. "I'm sure it's nothing. Just a sick joke," she said.

Alex could hear in Sydney's voice that the statement was as much an effort to convince herself as anything else.

"You have no idea who?" Alex asked.

"No. But we have all kinds in the D.A.'s office, just like I'm sure you do in the police department. There's no shortage at any time of someone who may have a personal grudge or feel slighted against a supervisor or someone they think shouldn't have gotten a promotion over them. You know how it is."

"True. But it never hurts to be careful," Alex said.

"No. I'm being silly," Sydney said forcefully. "It's a flower, for Christ's sake." She shook her head again and gave a nervous laugh. "Please, can we just pretend this never happened, that I never panicked?"

Alex smiled at her reassuringly when she looked up. "You didn't panic. You responded reasonably and rationally," she said. "But if it makes you feel better I won't tell anyone. I will, however, log that you spoke to me about the occurrences. Just so it's documented. You never know, even if it does turn out to be another employee in your office, it might be beneficial to have it documented." Sydney nodded in understanding. "Now," Alex continued. "How about you give me your keys, then you wait here and I'll go down and bring your car around? What kind of car do you drive?"

"It's a black Mercedes SL500. But—"

"Nope," Alex said. "Either I go down and get your car or I go down with you, in which case I have to walk back up again. By that time you'll be driving away and I won't have the keys to come back through the building and I'll get hopelessly lost in some stairwell with no way out."

"I'll give you a ride back up here to your car," Sydney said as she started to reach for the door.

"Nope," Alex said again, putting a soft restraining hand on her arm. "You're not dressed to be running around in the cold anyway. And it's not like I get a chance to drive a car like that very often. Please?" She turned her hand over, palm up, and wiggled her fingers in a "give me" motion.

Sydney smiled in response, then explained the keys Alex would need.

"Main doors," Sydney held up a key and pointed back to the court house doors behind Alex. When you get into the elevator put the same key in the space marked for employees and turn it before you press P3 for the employee parking level." Alex nodded. "Obviously this is the key fob, just deactivate the alarm by pressing the unlock button."

"Got it. Back in a flash." Alex gave her a smile then exited the police car, leaving the heat on and the engine running, locking the doors and looking around her as she made her way into the courthouse lobby and down the elevator.

As soon as she exited the elevator she glanced around the almost empty garage, seeing no one else. Her eyes came to rest on the lone black sports car with the white rose prominent on its windshield. After looking around for anything else out of place she discarded the flower in a nearby trashcan then entered the vehicle and drove it out of the garage, exiting onto one of the side streets and driving around the block to Temple Street. She pulled up behind her own black and white and met Sydney at the passenger side as Sydney stepped out. She retrieved Sydney's satchel from the back seat and walked with her to the Mercedes, opening the driver door for her and handing her the keys.

"You'll need to move the seat forward some," Alex said as Sydney got into the driver's seat.

"Yes, I see."

"I didn't mess with the mirrors though," Alex said somewhat sheepishly as she held out the satchel. "Are you okay to get home? Want me to follow you to the freeway or anything?"

"No, really," Sydney said. "I feel foolish. I'm sorry to have bothered you with something so silly."

"Don't feel that way," Alex said. "I'm glad you called." They looked at each other for several moments then Alex finally stepped away from the open window. "Drive home safe," she said. "I'll see you tomorrow afternoon?"

"Yes, I'll see you then."

Chapter Six

ALEX AWOKE THE next morning in her small two-bedroom bungalow in the Burbank foothills and began her normal routine for a day off. A long workout at the gym, a good run and some cleaning around the house. By mid-morning she decided she'd better do some of that research she'd promised Sydney. She made a phone call to Chuck Severs, her old partner and one of the detectives on the original White Rose case.

As she had assumed, the police departments in Las Vegas, Barstow and Ontario had been in direct contact with each other as well as R.H.D. The victims in the three new cases did match the patterns of the White Rose Murders. The victims were all kidnapped, tortured, raped and strangled in the same fashion as those in the original case. All three were the recipient of white roses immediately prior to their disappearance.

"The new murders are very similar, Alex. Even for a copycat they're too close. We're actually conducting a study of all the details that were publicly released. You know, what was in the media. Whoever's doing the new murders studied the case and knows the intimate details. We're not even sure at this point if some of the similarities were ever publicly released or revealed in court."

Alex could sense the frustration in the detective's voice.

"We've checked the visitor records at the prison. It doesn't look like Sinclair could've talked to anyone. We've even checked the records to see who may have ordered court transcripts," Chuck continued. "But nothing unusual is showing up. But that doesn't eliminate the possibility some nut-job actually sat in court each day and took notes. I mean, the court was full but not overflowing. Pretty much everyone who showed an interest in watching it in person was able to get a seat. So if anyone can find a witness on any of these new murders who can describe a possible suspect, you can bet they're going to be asked to scrutinize every frame of still photo or video footage taken in and around the courtroom." Alex felt her breath catch as Chuck gave the next piece of information.

"In the original case all the victims were young professionals of some kind or another," he said. "CEOs, financial officers, doctors, etc. All three of these victims were attorneys."

"Chuck," Alex finally said after absorbing this information. "I need to fill you in on something to do with Sydney Rutledge. She's been getting white roses left on her car by an unknown individual. Three of them in the past few weeks." She heard Chuck exhale and he paused for a moment before speaking.

"So a bouquet of roses delivered to her office with a note matching Sinclair's comments to her, and now roses being left on her car?"

"Yep. The last one was last night."

"The night after the latest murder victim was found?"

"Uh-huh."

"Can you find out the dates of the other two?"

Alex immediately caught on to what Chuck was getting at. "Shit! I can't believe I didn't think of that. I should've asked her last night when she told me. You want to compare them to the dates of the murders, don't you?"

"It might be nothing, Alex. But we should check. It could just be some infatuated admirer who remembers her handling that case. It could be someone competing with her at work who's trying to throw her off her game. Hell, it could be the family member of some asshole she's prosecuting right now. She does work Major Crimes after all."

"Yeah, that's what she's trying to convince herself of as well. But you're right, we need to check. I'll talk to her today and see if she can back track the other dates. Listen, Chuck, can you keep me in the loop on this one?"

"Sure thing, Alex."

"Thanks, buddy. Talk to you later."

Alex spent the rest of the day washing her truck and running some errands. By four p.m. She was showered and stood in her closet paying more attention than usual to her wardrobe selection. She finally settled on a white button down shirt with black jeans and a leather jacket. By four-thirty she was making the thirty-minute drive from Burbank to downtown. The security officer at the entrance to the juror and employee subterranean parking garage let her in when she showed her badge. And just that quickly she entered the elevator and was on her way up to the eighteenth floor. She gave herself a once over inspection in the reflective elevator walls then looked at her watch. It read five-fifteen p.m. Most people should be gone for the day on a Friday. Maybe she and Sydney would have some privacy. Then she kicked herself for thinking that.

"This is a just a business meeting," she said to herself. "With a straight chick," she added. "Get a grip."

When Alex got to the reception area she was surprised to find Tyler sitting at the receptionist's desk behind the glass partition. He looked as if he'd been waiting for her, waving immediately and getting up to open the door.

"Wow. You're here kinda late for a Friday," Alex said.

"Syd mentioned you were coming," he said as he led her back the now familiar path to Sydney's office. "I knew the staff would be pretty much gone and I didn't want you stranded in the lobby. So I told Syd I'd stick around. I'll be heading home now."

By that time they had reached the open door to Sydney's office and

Tyler stood aside to let Alex enter.

SYDNEY'S BREATH CAUGHT when Alex appeared in the doorway. She knew Alex had a fit and athletic body, but she'd never seen her out of uniform. The uniform didn't do that body justice. She suddenly realized she'd been staring at Alex for a moment, her eyes roving from Alex's boots and working upward. She noted Tyler standing behind Alex with a huge Cheshire cat grin on his face.

"Hey, no uniform," she finally said. "Did you get off early?"

"Nah. I was off today."

Sydney's heart did a small somersault as she realized what that seemed to indicate. The meaning clearly was not lost on Tyler, either. She watched his grin grow even larger as he gestured behind Alex, pointing at himself then back at Sydney as he silently but emphatically mouthed "I-told-you-so."

Alex seemed to become aware of motion behind her and turned. Tyler immediately transitioned his gesturing into a casual wave as he assumed a serene look of innocence.

"Time for me to leave. You two have a nice evening," he said then retreated down the hallway.

Sydney picked up her leather soft-sided briefcase from the floor and began placing various files and a laptop computer in it.

"I was actually thinking it might be nice to get out of the office," she said as she gathered items together. "If you give me a minute to pack some stuff up here, maybe we can go across the street to Starbucks instead?"

"Actually," Alex said, "I had kind of an early lunch and I'm really famished. Would you be up to grabbing some dinner instead?" Sydney stopped packing her bag and looked up. "I mean," Alex added quickly, "unless you've already got plans. That's cool, we can just grab a quick cup and I'll fill you in on what I know."

"No, I have absolutely no plans. Dinner would be great." Sydney put the last file in her satchel then grabbed her purse. "Give me two minutes in the ladies' room then we can be on our way."

Sydney had no need to use the restroom. She stood in front of the mirror and tried to collect herself. As she brushed her hair, refreshed her make-up and removed otherwise invisible lint from her suit jacket, she attempted to calm her excitement. She'd been trying to think of a casual way to make this more than just a quick cup of coffee and now it was.

Is this a date? She wondered as she removed her suit jacket, analyzed the look in the mirror, then put the jacket back on and re-assessed the look. She thought about what Tyler had said about the visit the day before. Now here Alex was, on a day off, asking Sydney to join her for dinner. It sounded kind of like a date. Sydney undid the top button on her blouse. No, too much. After all, maybe it was exactly what Alex had implied. Maybe she was just hungry and felt like a meal was a better use of time than coffee as they discussed the case. Sydney certainly hoped that wasn't it.

Sydney visualized Alex, imagining the toned body concealed beneath the leather jacket and jeans that hugged in just the right places. She couldn't deny the physical attraction she felt. But was that feeling the slightest bit mutual? There was only one way to find out. She finally settled on no suit jacket and removed it and carried it over her arm, but she left the blouse fully buttoned except for the top one.

"All right, Sergeant," Sydney said as she re-entered the office and picked up her satchel. "Ready to go?"

Alex turned from where she had been looking at the various diplomas and legal certificates on the wall.

"Sure," she said. "There's just one thing." Alex paused and Sydney looked at her with questioning eyes. "I think you should call me Alex, you know. We run into each other so much I really think we're a little more familiar with one another."

"Sounds good, Alex. And you can call me Sydney." Sydney smiled. "Or Syd." Then she led the way out the door, pausing and trying to find the keys in her purse in order to lock the door. Alex reached out and grasped the shoulder strap to her satchel.

"Here, let me hold this for you." She took the bag as Sydney smiled her thanks, her hands now free to manipulate purse and keys. She locked the door and they continued down the hallway. Alex made no move to return the satchel, clearly intending to carry it to her car for her. As Sydney led the way down the hallway she smiled to herself, silently placing one more point in the—it might be a date—column.

"So, any idea where you'd like to go?" Alex asked as they rode the elevator down.

"I'm up for just about anything."

"How do you feel about Mexican?"

"I absolutely love Mexican."

"Outstanding." Alex grinned. "How about El Cholo? Ever been there?"

"Went there once on an office luncheon and loved it. I've heard the original on Western is better, though."

"The original is usually the best. But the one on Flower Street is still really good. Does that sound okay?"

"Sure, sounds great. Shall we take separate cars to avoid having to come back this way?" They exited the elevator and Alex walked Sydney to her car. She placed Sydney's bag in the trunk then pointed to her Dodge truck parked a few rows away, one of the few cars remaining in the subterranean garage.

"That's me over there," she said. "I'll follow you."

ALEX SMILED TO herself as she followed close behind Sydney on the drive to the restaurant. She'd noticed Sydney had touched up her makeup when she retreated briefly to the bathroom. Not that she needed to, Alex thought to herself. Sydney was stunning regardless. Alex couldn't help but think that was a positive sign. But then that nagging doubt hit her again. Perhaps that was just what most heterosexual women do when they go out in public in general?

"Stop it." she scolded herself as they pulled into the restaurant parking lot. "Just go with the flow."

They ended up at a booth in a quiet corner of one of the smaller dining rooms, far from the noisier bar and boisterous large groups. Alex was thrilled with the arrangement and when she looked at Sydney as they sat down she noted Sydney certainly didn't look uncomfortable with the somewhat intimate environment.

Their waitress appeared and asked if they would like drinks as they looked at the menu.

"I would love a margarita," Sydney said, looking somewhat guilty. Alex was thrilled at this development and looked up from her menu.

"How about nachos?" she asked. "They say El Cholo invented nachos." Sydney nodded with enthusiasm and Alex ordered nachos and her favorite light beer.

After their drinks were delivered, Alex asked how the day in court had been.

"Well, we had closing arguments today, and by the time jury instructions were given, it was already well into the afternoon session. The judge decided to release the jury for the weekend. They'll begin deliberation on Monday. I'm pretty confident in the case we presented, but it was somewhat convoluted, so anything could happen. There were multiple defendants. All gang members. Each defendant had their own public defender, and faced multiple charges. Robbery, false imprisonment, aggravated assault and conspiracy. I requested gang enhancements for every one of them."

"Do you expect a quick verdict?" Alex asked.

"Just the number of charges alone will take the jury an entire day to get through one at a time, and that's if they all agree on the verdict on each charge from the start. If there's any real deliberation it's going to go into at least day two."

"You know, I had an amusing experience in a prelim this week," Alex said after taking a sip of her beer. "It was a robbery caper. The suspect walked into the liquor store with a gun and did your standard stick up then ran out with the bag of money and the gun. One of my units saw him take off down an alley and when we caught him on the next block he'd ditched the bag and the gun. We went back and found it in the trash bin in the alley. He was doing the classic defense of mistaken identity. You know the story, he was never there, and we can't prove anything since we didn't catch him with the money and the gun on him. And to be honest, it was a little shaky because the clerk couldn't I.D. afterwards. He was so scared all he remembered was the red sweatshirt and the gun in his face. So, the clerk was on the stand and testified that the suspect walked in, pointed the gun at him, and ordered him to empty the cash register or he'd — put a cap in his ass —." Alex raised two fingers on each hand to indicate quotation marks around the final statement. "Well, the defendant jumps out of his seat and screams — That's not what I said."

"Oh my God. That was your case?" Sydney asked through her laughter. "Everyone heard about that case. It was the biggest courthouse story this week."

The conversation paused momentarily as the waitress brought their nachos and took their dinner order. The waitress had been gone a few minutes and both had enjoyed several bites from the nachos before Sydney broke the comfortable silence.

"So, while I'd much rather talk about more pleasant things this evening, I have to ask. Were you able to find out anything on this copycat?"

Alex relayed everything she had learned earlier that day.

"According to Detective Severs, they may actually turn to scrutinizing old video footage and photographs from the press conferences and trial to see who, other than the media, was consistently present and possibly a little too interested," Alex said. She wiped her hands on her napkin, partially as a delaying tactic, as she looked at her dinner companion and tried to figure out the best way to broach the next question.

"Listen, Sydney," Alex said. "About the roses left on your car. Do you think you can recall the dates of the other two? I want to document that, just to be safe and thorough."

Sydney's eyes widened slightly. Alex could see the gears working in her mind as Sydney thought through the question. Sydney was a criminal prosecutor who dealt with clues, patterns and circumstantial evidence. She was more than capable of connecting the dots. It was apparent moments later that she had done just that.

"You think the dates may be linked to the new murders?" As much as she tried to make the question sound routine she couldn't quite keep the concern out of her voice.

"Hey," Alex said. "We don't know anything yet. There's probably no connection and it's someone trying to throw you off your game." But Alex knew Sydney didn't believe that any more than she did.

They remained quiet for several minutes as Sydney had a slightly faraway look in her eyes. Alex saw her shiver slightly and fought the urge to move next to Sydney and hold her. When Sydney looked up and saw Alex gazing at her she blushed noticeably.

"You okay?" Alex asked.

"I know, it's stupid and crazy," Sydney said. "It's just been in the press so much with this new guy out their replicating the murders. It's just...creepy. I even imagined I saw him one day."

"Sinclair?" Alex asked.

Sydney nodded. "Do you remember the day there was that gang fight in the hallway at the courthouse?"

"Yeah, I remember."

"I saw someone in the elevator I thought looked like Sinclair. That's why I froze." Sydney looked down at her plate. "I know, he's in prison. It's crazy."

Alex shook her head. "It's not stupid and it's not crazy," she said. "It's perfectly understandable. The guy is an animal and you had to study all the terrible details about what he did. It would be crazy if you didn't react somehow, especially considering what happened at the end of the trial, with what he said to you. I was there. And then there were the roses. Yeah, it's entirely natural for you to respond this way. Just keep reminding yourself this is someone totally different, some psycho who watched too much TV and read too many newspaper articles. Even if Sinclair manages to avoid the needle, he'll still never get out of prison. You've got nothing to worry about from him."

Sydney smiled weakly and nodded in agreement. Then she took a large swig of her margarita, her second margarita actually, and leaned forward looking into Alex's eyes.

"And besides," Sydney said with a coy smile. "You wouldn't let anything happen to me, right?"

Alex paused momentarily with her beer to her lips, then continued drinking in order to give her an extra moment to digest what Sydney just said, and what it indicated. Was she flirting?

"Of course I wouldn't," Alex said quietly, gazing into Sydney's eyes and matching her shy smile. Sydney blushed, finally breaking eye contact as the waitress showed up with their dinner entrées.

The rest of the evening went by in a blur as they discussed their respective jobs, office politics, interesting cases and incompetent bosses. Too soon they were sipping coffee and the waitress was placing the bill on their table. The conversation lulled for several moments as neither of them spoke. Instead they simply looked at one another. Both aware of something intangible passing between them. Alex cleared her throat and broke the silence.

"Thank you for humoring me and joining me for dinner," she said and reached for the bill. "And it's on me, by the way." Sydney reached out quickly and grasped Alex's hand, not allowing her to pull the check away. Both women were aware of the tingle that erupted from the contact. Alex smiled and tugged gently only to have Sydney's hand squeeze more tightly. "Really," Alex said. "I insist, it's on me."

"On one condition," Sydney said after a moment. "You have to come to my place and let me cook you dinner."

Alex's smile grew. "Okay," she said. "When?"

"Sunday," Sydney replied firmly and with certainty. "Sunday at six." Alex could only grin and nod.

Sydney reached into her purse for pen and paper and wrote her address and phone number while Alex settled the bill and left a tip. Then they walked out in companionable silence to Sydney's car. As they approached, she used the remote to unlock the vehicle and Alex reached out to open the door for her. Sydney handed Alex the paper with her address.

"Can you find it?" she asked.

Alex's eyebrows rose when she noted the address in the hills above Hollywood. "I can find it."

Sydney leaned closer and pointed out the phone numbers. "I added my home number and the office number for my task force, just in case."

"Got it. Just in case," Alex repeated.

They stood there in the dim light with only the door between them, looking at one another, saying nothing. Just as Alex was contemplating leaning in to kiss her, Sydney lowered herself into the car and slid behind the wheel.

"I'll see you Sunday," she said and grinned.

"See you then," Alex said as she closed the door for her. She watched as Sydney pulled out of the parking lot and drove out of sight.

Part of Alex could've kicked herself for not kissing Sydney when she had the chance. She felt pretty sure Sydney was sending the signal that she would welcome a kiss. But then, on second thought, she wondered if Sydney was even aware she was sending the signal. Maybe it was best Alex hadn't kissed her. She didn't want to scare Sydney away.

WHY DIDN'T SHE kiss me? Sydney wondered as she drove from the parking lot. I lingered. I sent all the signals. Wait. Maybe the signals are different for women?

Her mind drifted back to the first few minutes at the table, right after their drinks arrived. Alex had taken her jacket off, revealing toned and muscular shoulders underneath the slightly snug white button down shirt. Sydney had never been so physically attracted to another woman. She couldn't remember being instantly attracted to anyone in the way she was to Alex. She found her unbelievably sexy. But it was more than that. The emotional strength and confidence, the humor, the way she expressed herself, the compassionate soft side Sydney could tell was hidden beneath. They seemed to click and it just felt right to be with her.

Sydney drove up the 101 Freeway and then east along Mulholland Drive virtually on autopilot. Her mind returned to the vision of Alex sitting across from her at the table, looking into her eyes and smiling. She thought again of how it would feel to have those arms around her, to have Alex's hands slipping under the bottom of her blouse and up toward her...

"Oh, geez," Sydney gasped quietly.

She wasn't sure how long she'd been sitting in her car, parked in her own garage. She shook her head and scolded herself, then went inside and took a cold shower despite the cool January weather. Even then she had a hard time falling asleep.

SYDNEY WAS AWOKEN around seven the next morning by the ringing telephone. She rolled over and grabbed the phone. Tyler didn't even wait for her to say hello.

"So," he said in a mock conspiratorial whisper. "Are you alone?"

Sydney couldn't help but giggle. "Yes, silly. I'm alone."

"Oh," he said raising his voice. "Well. That's boring."

"Please. What kind of girl do you think I am?"

Tyler laughed. "So, tell me everything."

Sydney giggled again, and proceeded to share all the details of the evening, including the conversation that led to Sunday's dinner date. This seemed to thrill Tyler. When Sydney talked about her doubt as to whether Alex had wanted to kiss her at the end of evening Tyler reassured her.

"She doesn't want to move too fast and scare you off. Trust me, she wants to kiss you."

"How can you know that?"

"Please, girlfriend," he said. "She made up a corny excuse just to stop by your office then essentially tricked you into a dinner date. She wants to do way more than kiss you."

Sydney still wasn't sure but didn't argue the point. The two agreed to meet for lunch later to discuss menu options for Sunday evening. Sydney's face held an exasperated smile as she hung up on Tyler in mid-sentence as he began listing every culinary aphrodisiac he could apparently think of.

Chapter Seven

ALEX SPENT MOST of Saturday helping her best friend Sal, and his girlfriend, paint the interior of their new house. Sal and Alex had been friends since being partnered together in their early careers, and now were both assigned as supervisors on the Violent Crime Task Force. Sal's girlfriend, Tiffany Pierce, was an emergency room nurse at a local hospital. The two of them met years earlier when Sal had ended up in the emergency room after a particularly violent arrest resulted in several stitches to his forehead. He'd been immediately enamored with the attractive ER nurse and after several bouquets of flowers were delivered, Tiffany had relented to a date. They'd been inseparable ever since. They had recently purchased a town home in Glendale, just a few miles from Alex's.

As they worked Alex casually brought up the subject of Sydney. "Do you remember that Assistant D.A. I told you about? The one from the White Rose case?"

"You mean the one you thought was incredibly sexy?" Sal replied. "The one you keep coming up with bullshit excuses to bump into? That one? Yeah, she sounds vaguely familiar to me. In fact, I seem to recall telling you she was interested."

"Yeah. Well, we kind of had dinner together last night."

"What?" Sal popped up from where he had been dipping a paintbrush. Fortunately he had laid down old sheets to protect the floor, as drops of paint went flying from the sudden movement.

A similar exclamation was heard from the kitchen where Tiffany was making turkey sandwiches for their lunch. Alex and Sal heard a knife crash to the kitchen counter as Tiffany abandoned her task.

"Stop. Not another word until I get in there. I've got to hear this." Tiffany appeared in the doorway a moment later wiping her hands on a towel. "Okay," she said. "You may now continue." When Alex didn't start talking quickly enough Tiffany prompted her. "I thought you told me she was straight?" Tiffany said to Sal.

"Wait a minute. You guys have talked about this?" Alex looked from Tiffany to Sal.

"Well of course we have." Tiffany said. "You didn't think we both have an active interest in your love life?"

"Yeah," Sal said. "You come to me gushing about this incredibly gorgeous, incredibly sexy, incredibly smart A.D.A. Of course I'm gonna come home and talk about it. Including the part where you also implied she was incredibly straight."

"Well, I guess maybe she's not. I think I'm maybe picking up some signs."

"Oh really?" Sal said. "So I wasn't smokin' my socks when I told you she was interested?" He was now standing with paint dripping down his arm from the still suspended paintbrush. "Is she bi or something?" he asked.

Alex shrugged as she tried to play it off like it wasn't a big deal and continued painting.

"Maybe. I guess," she said. "It's not like it was even a date, really. But—"

"But what?" This prompt came from Tiffany.

"But we're seeing each other again tomorrow night. She's cooking me dinner at her place," Alex said with a smile.

"Holy shit," Sal said. "You sure this is a good idea?"

"Stop that." Tiffany flicked the towel at him. "You two get to work and finish that painting. Then we'll have lunch and I'll discuss with you what you need to do to woo a lady."

As Tiffany retreated back into the kitchen and Alex and Sal resumed painting, Sal repeated once more, quietly, "Be careful my friend. You've been here before with a straight girl. You don't deserve that again."

SUNDAY AT A few minutes before six p.m. found Alex pulling into Sydney's driveway. Her house was located about twenty-five minutes from downtown, on a secluded street off Mulholland Drive near the crest of the Santa Monica Mountains. She stood in the driveway for a moment and admired the surroundings. The house itself was reminiscent of a ski lodge you would find in the mountains of Vail. Surrounded by what was essentially forest land, it was hard to believe that just a few miles down the road at the bottom of the mountain was the sprawling Los Angeles metropolis.

Alex made her way to the front door, admiring the large bay windows in what she believed had to be the master bedroom on the second floor. She didn't see Sydney's car but figured it was likely parked inside the attached three-car garage.

Alex knocked on the door then turned to admire the view again. It was a cool, clear January evening and the sun had set an hour before. Alex could just make out the glow of what she assumed was city lights from below, though at tree level she couldn't be sure. There wasn't another house in sight, yet she knew there were other homes along the canyon road she had traveled. The view from the porch was impressive, so it must be amazing from the upper floors.

She turned when she heard the door open behind her and the bottle of wine she'd brought almost slipped from her hand. Alex had never seen Sydney away from work and so was accustomed to the skirt and pant suits, which were the prescribed court uniform for the Assistant D.A. And while Sydney wore those suits very well, that didn't hold a candle to the vision Alex now saw before her.

"Hi," Sydney said quietly when Alex didn't say anything.

Alex's mouth went dry. "Hi," she managed to get out. "Uh, wow...you look incredible." Then she looked down at herself. She was wearing a somewhat snug black pullover sweater, black jeans and boots and black leather jacket. "I'm beginning to think I'm under-dressed."

"Nonsense," Sydney said. "You're perfectly dressed. Come on in."

Alex entered into a hardwood entry hall and noted a formal living room off to her right and a wooden staircase to her left extending up to the second floor.

"Let me take your jacket," Sydney said as she opened a closet beneath the staircase.

Alex realized she was still holding the wine.

"Oh, yeah. This is for you," she said, handing it to Sydney. "You mentioned on Friday how much you enjoy a good glass of Chardonnay at the end of a day. I don't know anything about wines, but the guy at the shop said that was a good one."

"I'm impressed you remembered that little detail. Someone was paying attention on Friday." Sydney put the bottle down on an entry table and reached to take Alex's jacket.

As Sydney turned and reached for a hanger, Alex's eyes wandered from her slim back, with a hint of camisole just barely visible beneath the slightly sheer cream silk, down her trim waist to her incredibly firm buttocks and shapely legs, all visible as Sydney reached upwards to grasp and then replace the hanger.

Alex had an incredible urge to wrap her arms around that waist from behind and pull Sydney to her. She imagined what it would be like to gently sweep the shoulder length hair away, exposing the back of Sydney's neck. She would begin kissing and caressing her neck as she reached to the front of Sydney's blouse and then began opening the buttons. Alex would gradually work the kisses down her neck to her shoulder as more of it was exposed. Her hands would reach within the front of the now unbuttoned blouse—

The closet door closed with an audible thump and Sydney turned back to her. Alex, now back in reality, reached into her rear waistband and removed her off duty weapon, a small Glock handgun.

"Is there somewhere you'd feel comfortable with me putting this?" she asked.

Sydney paused. "Oh, sure. You can leave it here if that's okay with you." Sydney opened a small drawer in the entryway table as she picked the wine up. "Come on into the kitchen and I'll get us some drinks."

Alex followed Sydney to the kitchen. Sydney put the wine on the counter, pulled a single wine glass from a cupboard and a wine opener from a drawer, and then paused. She looked up at Alex as she slid the paper across the counter.

"Just to get this out of the way," she said. "Here are the dates for the other roses that were left on my car. I tracked them down by the court cases I remember handling on those two days." Alex took the paper and looked up at Sydney without even glancing at what was written on it. Her eyes met Sydney's.

"In case you're wondering, I already checked," Sydney said quietly. "They're both exactly one day after the discovery of the other two murder victims."

"Syd—"

Sydney shook her head. "Let's not talk about it, please?" she said. "You do what you need to do with those." She pointed at the paper in Alex's hand. "I'll talk to my boss about it tomorrow and I'll just deal with it. It is what it is. But please let's enjoy this evening. I've been looking forward to this."

Alex heard the plea in Sydney's voice and couldn't help but surrender to it. She smiled as she replied, "I've been looking forward to this as well."

Sydney smiled at Alex as she turned toward the refrigerator. "Good. I'm going to have a glass of this wonderful wine you brought." She reached into the fridge. "But I get the distinct feeling you're not a wine person, so I thought you might prefer this." Sydney removed a bottle of Sam Adams light beer, popped the lid and handed it to a smiling Alex. Clearly she hadn't been the only one paying attention to such details on Friday. Sydney uncorked the wine and poured her glass, then raised it to touch Alex's bottle.

"Cheers," she said, then added quietly, "To what I expect will be a wonderful evening." Their eyes met as they each sipped their drinks and Sydney blushed slightly.

"Please make yourself at home. Take a look around. I've got to get a few things ready on the stove and then I'll give you a tour of the rest of the house if you'd like."

Alex wandered throughout the first floor as she sipped her beer. The kitchen was along the back of the house. She looked out a large bay window and even in the dark she could see a large rear wood deck extending into an unfenced backyard, which went to the dense tree line of the forest. There was a formal dining room in the back left corner of the house adjacent to the kitchen. The table looked as if it could easily seat ten people. A smaller, more intimate dining area, what some would call a breakfast nook, was located off the other side of the kitchen. Alex noted that smaller table set for two with candles.

Beyond that was a comfortable den with a fireplace and walls lined with built in bookshelves holding all manner of books. Through the den she circled back to the front formal living room adjacent to the entryway. Every room had large expansive windows out the front to the woodland area to the rear of the house, or looking out onto the cityscape below the hills. Both the formal dining area and den had

French doors leading out onto the rear deck. Between the kitchen and den Alex saw a small spiral staircase leading up to the second floor. She noted it was situated on almost the opposite side of the house as the entry staircase, providing two separate convenient avenues to the upper, presumably more private, living quarters.

The front of the house consisted of the formal family room, the entryway and staircase. A door adjoining the entryway led to the attached garage. Again, the living room had similar large windows along the front and side of the house. Finally, there was a guest bedroom and full bathroom located off the short hallway between the entry and the kitchen.

Alex wandered back into the kitchen just as Sydney appeared to finish readying various pans on the stove.

"We'll eat in about ten minutes," Sydney said. "Want to see the rest of the place?"

"Absolutely, lead on."

Sydney led the way into the comfortable den and library covering the back right third of the first floor. It had plush couches and recliners, a large screen television, fireplace and large bay windows providing views out three sides of the house. One portion of the room, furthest from the fireplace, held a large executive desk and custom built-in bookshelves.

"This is one of my favorite rooms to hang out in," Sydney said. She pointed at the spiral staircase at one corner of the room. "That leads up to the master bedroom, so I can come here with a cup of hot chocolate in the winter and sit in front of the fire until I'm tired, then head right up to bed."

Sydney then led Alex back through the living room to the primary staircase and up to the second floor landing, which looked down to the entryway and looked out on the vaulted windows at the front of the house. The second floor consisted of two additional spacious bedrooms and a full bathroom as well as the master suite. Alex noted both bedrooms had large windows with views either out the rear or front of the house.

Sydney then walked her across the landing to the open doors of the master suite. As Alex walked in she was struck by the size. The bedroom was huge, running the depth of the house from front to back and along one side wall. The walls essentially consisted of windows. The half of the room that overlooked the backyard was a comfortable sitting area situated around a fireplace. The top of the spiral staircase could be seen in that portion of the room. Glass French doors led out to a private balcony overlooking the backyard. The bathroom was enormous, and included both a shower and a Jacuzzi tub. The sleeping area was in the forward part of the room, surrounded by windows. Alex walked to the windows and could see the lights of Los Angeles far below. She then scanned the tree top horizon.

SYDNEY STUDIED ALEX as she looked out through the window at the panorama of lights below them. Sydney couldn't help but notice how the black sweater was just snug enough to show off the strong arms and broad shoulders that tapered to a trim waist, all complimented by the small yet shapely feminine breasts. She admitted to herself that a portion of the feelings she was experiencing had to do with a sexual attraction. She couldn't keep herself from wondering what it would feel like to have those arms around her, to feel Alex's breasts pressed against hers. Her breath sucked in at the thought and she finally broke the silence, partially in an effort to hide her own flustered reaction to the thoughts.

"I know what you're wondering," Sydney said. "But contrary to what you may think, it's really quite private. They designed the building plans up here to stagger the houses, so you really can't see each other even though the houses are sometimes just a few acres apart. Of course the trees help. All in all, it would be quite a challenge to spy into someone's bedroom without a helicopter and a zoom lens." She moved up beside Alex, leaning past her to a small panel in the wall beside the bed.

"And I do have window coverings. There's a panel like this near the spiral staircase and the door from the landing. They open and close the drapes." She pressed one of the buttons on the panel and the room grew gradually darker. "And controls the lights," she added.

Sydney straightened up and gazed out the window. With the room darker the crisp lights of the city below were more pronounced.

"The windows throughout the house are what I really love about this place. On a clear day you can see the ocean from up here. And on a clear night the moon and stars are incredible." She turned back to Alex after gazing at the skyline for a moment. She found Alex watching her rather than looking out the window. As their eyes met she became very aware of how close together they stood, of how the moonlight provided an intimate glow around them.

She was vaguely aware of Alex's hand softly grasping her elbow, gently pulling her, and she willingly moved closer. Their bodies were only inches apart and Sydney was immediately tense with desire. The emotions Alex seemed capable of stirring inside her were incredibly intense. She looked up into Alex's face and knew she read the same desire there. As Alex's face tipped toward her she closed her eyes and barely parted her lips in anticipation of the kiss.

Then suddenly a faint ringing could be heard from downstairs. Sydney's eyes popped open and Alex straightened up as she released Sydney's elbow.

"Oh geez," Sydney whispered. "That's the oven timer. I guess dinner's about ready."

Alex seemed surprised and a little embarrassed. "I guess we had better go get it then."

She stepped back to allow Sydney to lead the way downstairs. Sydney took them down two floors through the spiral staircase and they were quickly in the kitchen again. She busied herself stirring the contents of several pots on the stove and removing a large clay pot from the oven then a salad from the fridge.

"Can I help with anything?" Alex asked.

"Sure," Sydney said, then retrieved a frosted pint glass from the freezer, a bottle opener and another beer and handed Alex a pack of matches. "Pour me another glass of wine and yourself a fresh beer, then take them to the table and light the candles. I'll be in there in a moment."

Alex did as she was told and was just finishing lighting the candles and sitting down when Sydney came in with two salads. She put them down then went to a nearby wall panel and lowered the lights. When Sydney sat down their eyes met once again.

"What?" Sydney asked. "Is everything okay?" She scrutinized the table as if something could be missing.

"Everything is perfect." Alex raised her glass, tapping Sydney's wine glass. "To a wonderful evening."

Time went by quickly over dinner, pausing momentarily as Sydney cleared salad plates and returned with a perfectly cooked roasted chicken over rice. Alex complimented her numerous times throughout the meal as they discussed friends, family and various personal interests.

"So it occurred to me, Alex, you never did answer my question about where you grew up and went to college."

"Well," Alex stammered slightly. "I grew up in Torrance just south of LA. I enrolled at Cal State Long Beach out of high school. I got an athletic scholarship for softball. But during my sophomore year there were some financial issues. My scholarship only covered tuition and books, not dorm fees or anything. So I couldn't afford school anymore. I dropped out and joined the Marines."

"What about your parents. They couldn't help out to get you through college?"

"They were at first. I was still living at home while I went to school." Alex paused and took a sip of her beer.

It appeared to Sydney that Alex was taking a moment to collect her thoughts. She had the feeling this was not something Alex was entirely comfortable talking about and thought she may have pushed too much. Then Alex continued.

"They kicked me out when they found out I was a lesbian. Evidently my dear brother discovered that fact and gleefully educated them." She shrugged. "It was kind of sudden. A big screaming match one evening and I was on the street that night with orders not to come back. I stayed with friends until the end of the semester, but there was no way I could keep doing that. So at the end of the school year I enlisted. I got picked up by the LAPD after my four years of active duty time."

Sydney reached across the table and grasped Alex's hand. "I'm sorry about your family. That must've been incredibly difficult. How old were you when they kicked you out?"

"I was nineteen," she said. "But in answer to your original question, I did end up completing my degree. Went back part time and got it from Cal State LA, in Criminal Justice. It took me a few extra years after I was hired, but I got it done. So do you get back to Duluth very often?" Alex asked.

Sydney was aware of the subject change and accepted it easily, silently thankful Alex had revealed a little bit of her private self.

"No, not really. Neither Jen nor I are very interested in going back. I guess the big city life is more our speed. My dad made good money so we were fortunate enough to travel a lot. We owned property on both coasts as well as the house in Duluth. When our parents were killed ten years ago, she ended up with the New York apartment and I ended up with this house. It was my dad's dream house. It had just been completed when the accident happened. They hadn't even moved any furniture in."

Their hands were still clasped on the table and Alex gave Sydney's fingers a gentle squeeze.

"I'm sorry. They died in a traffic accident?"

"Yeah. In the snow. A big rig lost control on black ice and jackknifed."

"Are you and your sister close?" Alex asked.

"Oh, yeah," Sydney said. "Jen and I are about as close as you can be while living three thousand miles apart."

"Who's the oldest?"

"I'm the baby. Only by a couple of years but Jen makes the most of it and never fails to remind me."

"Do you get to see her that often?"

"We visit as often as we can. She's a fairly well respected surgeon, so she tends to travel around a bit. I try to catch up to her whenever I'm able. We find ourselves meeting in Chicago a lot. It's a city we both like to visit and it's kind of in the middle for each of us."

After several more minutes of pleasant conversation there was a pause. Sydney stood and started clearing dishes and Alex jumped up to help, following her into the kitchen. "You can put those dirties down next to the sink. I'll take care of them later."

"Dinner was delicious," Alex said as she put down the dishes as directed then leaned with her back to the edge of the counter.

"I'm glad you liked it," Sydney said. "How about some coffee or hot chocolate?"

Alex smiled. "Sure, whatever you're having."

"Good. Why don't you go into the den." Sydney pointed to the archway leading into the den. "See if you can get the fire started. I'll join you in just a moment."

ALEX HEADED INTO the den. It took her a couple minutes to find matches on the mantel, turn on the gas and get the fire started. She then moved to the wall panel, and after a moment or two of analysis and testing a couple buttons figured out how the light adjustments worked. She dimmed the lights to a setting she thought was appropriate.

Alex was gazing out the window over the back deck below and into the dark forest when she thought she saw movement and wondered what animal was out there at the tree line. She heard Sydney enter the room and turned to see her put a tray with two mugs and a plate of homemade chocolate chip cookies on the coffee table in front of the fire.

They sat next to each other on the couch in front of the fireplace.

"So how long were you in the Marines?" Sydney asked.

Alex took a sip of her hot chocolate. "Twelve years altogether. The first four years of active duty and then eight more in the reserves."

"Did you get sent to Iraq or Afghanistan?"

Alex nodded and took another sip. "Yeah, I was recalled to active duty in 2002 and was gone almost two years. I traveled around quite a bit at times." She reached for another cookie. "Mind if I take the last one?" she asked, then received a nod.

When Sydney rose to take the now empty plates into the kitchen, she stopped Alex, who also stood up to help.

"Don't worry about these," she said. "I'll be right back."

Alex glanced up at the clock on the mantel and was shocked to find it was past eleven o'clock. She stood and walked the length of the den and into the adjacent living room to the stand at the window, nervously wiping her hands on her pant legs as she contemplated what she should say next. She contemplated what had occurred in the bedroom before dinner and found herself strangely nervous, or anxious, in a way she had never been on any previous date.

When Sydney returned from the kitchen Alex watched her reflection in the window as Sydney's eyes searched the now empty den, then finally came to rest on her. They had left the lights in the room dimmed, the fireplace providing the majority of the illumination, so the adjoined room was dark.

"Is everything okay?" Sydney finally asked, breaking the silence as she slowly approached Alex, stopping to lean on the back of chair in the middle of the room.

Alex turned away from the window and faced Sydney, leaning back and resting her hands on the windowsill on either side of her. She finally cleared her throat and spoke quietly.

"It's getting late. I know you have to be at work in the morning. I really shouldn't have kept you up so long." She wondered if Sydney felt the sense of unspoken expectation hovering between them.

"It's quite all right," Sydney said. "I've really enjoyed you being here." There was a long pause as they stood looking at one another in the darkened room.

"I have a confession to make," Alex finally said, still speaking in a quiet voice. "I didn't have a meeting in your building last week. You know, on Thursday? I just wanted to see you again. And I really wanted to spend some time with you, like this."

Sydney took several more steps toward her, closing the distance between them to just a couple of feet.

"Why, Sergeant Chambers, do you mean to tell me this is...a date?" Sydney asked with a coy smile.

"Would you like it to be?" Alex asked after a brief pause.

Sydney also paused momentarily, then replied, "Yes. Yes, I think I very much would." She spoke with quiet sincerity. "But there's something you should probably know," she added, looking down at the space between them then back up into Alex's eyes. "I've never...ummm...been...never dated—"

"You've never dated a woman?" Alex completed her faltering statement. Sydney simply nodded. "Are you sure you're okay with it?" Alex felt her insides screaming for them to move closer. She silently battled her own urge to create the physical contact her body was craving.

Sydney looked away momentarily, and then took a breath before she looked back into Alex's eyes.

"Yes," she replied in a whisper. "I'm quite okay with it." Alex smiled upon hearing that answer. "Everything about you, about us, seems okay," Sydney, said as she moved still closer to Alex, who was still stationary against the window. Sydney stopped a mere foot away appearing hesitant to invade Alex's personal space. "Would you be willing to let me cook for you again?"

"Absolutely," Alex said, still trying to resist the urge to reach out for the woman standing before her in the semi-darkness. "But there's one other thing." she said, finally giving in to that urge and leaning forward slightly. Alex rested her hands on either side of Sydney's waist and pulled the woman those last few inches to her.

Sydney had slipped off her heals earlier while sitting in front of the fire and so was once again several inches shorter. She stood looking up into Alex's eyes. "What's that?" she asked, matching Alex's sultry whisper.

"I've been wanting to kiss you all night. So I'm going to do just that unless you tell me to stop." Alex searched Sydney's face for any sign of fear, hesitancy or intimidation, but found only the same desire she was feeling.

"I'm not going to tell you to stop."

Alex leaned down and felt Sydney tilting her head so their lips could meet.

Alex was momentarily struck by how soft and tender Sydney's lips were as they met, but that thought was quickly lost as she was carried away by the moment. She finally moved her hand up to caress Sydney's cheek, and then pulled her lips away gently. Sydney opened her eyes and the two women stood looking at one another. Alex's warm palm was stationary against Sydney's cheek and she gently rubbed her thumb across Sydney's lips.

Then Alex pulled away and silently took Sydney's hand, leading her to the front entryway, only letting go when they reached the door. Sydney retrieved Alex's coat from the adjacent closet and Alex shrugged into it. She collected her weapon from the drawer nearby and reached back, lifting her jacket to put it into her rear waistband, a carry position the holster was designed for. As Alex repositioned the jacket over the handgun, Sydney stepped forward and reached up to grasp the front zippered edges of the jacket at Alex's chest, pulling it snug around her. Alex's body was again on fire and she concentrated hard to keep from continuing the previous intimacy.

"All right, Sergeant Chambers," Sydney said quietly. "You drive home safely."

"I will," Alex said in a hoarse whisper. Sydney nodded. Alex brought her hand up and caressed Sydney's neck and cheek once again with her palm, then leaned down and kissed her once more, very gently, lingering for just a moment.

"I'll call you," she whispered. "Thank you for dinner." She opened the door and backed away.

Sydney nodded again, then leaned on the open door, apparently oblivious to the cold night as she watched Alex walk to her truck. Alex turned and waved before getting in and starting the engine. She was aware of Sydney watching from the doorway until she exited the end of the driveway and turned for home.

Chapter Eight

OVER THE NEXT two days Alex tried hard to follow her normal routine, heading directly to the gym each morning for a solid workout before burying herself in work. However hard she tried she could not seem to fall into her usual "zone" at either work or the gym, which usually provided the escape from outside thoughts and influences. She quite simply couldn't get her mind off Sydney. The thoughts followed her home on Monday night and were prominent on her mind throughout Tuesday morning. She wondered how long she should to wait to call Sydney to avoid coming off as too desperate. She fought the urge through the early Tuesday afternoon, finally deciding around three p.m. she'd waited long enough.

"Hey, you," came Sydney's voice over the phone before the second ring, surprising Alex and making her think Sydney had perhaps mistaken her for someone else she was expecting a call from.

"Uh, hi. It's Alex."

"I know that, silly," Sydney said. When Alex paused Sydney seemed to sense her confusion. "I still have your number in my cell so I saw the caller I.D. I guess I never bothered to erase it after the trial was over."

"Uh-huh." Alex smiled at that revelation. "Well, I wanted to call and say thanks for dinner Sunday night. I really enjoyed the evening."

"Good. So did I." Alex seemed to sense more meaning in Sydney's simple reply and so she plunged ahead.

"I'm, um, not sure where the line is drawn these days. You know, how much time should pass before its acceptable to express genuine interest versus..." Alex paused, uncertain how to go on.

"Versus what?" Sydney interjected into Alex's lengthy hesitation. Alex now clearly heard the smile in her voice.

"Versus just looking like a crazy stalker, I guess."

"Sergeant Chambers, are you saying you've been sitting around stalling a call to me for fear of looking like a stalker?"

"Something like that, yeah." Alex was emboldened by the soft snicker she heard from the other woman. "So, at the risk of sounding even more like a stalker," her voice dropped an octave. "When can I see you again?"

"Like a second date?" The smile was still evident in Sydney's voice and Alex's heart nearly skipped a beat.

"Yes, Ms. Rutledge, I'd like to take you on a date, if you're comfortable with that."

"I think I'd be very comfortable with that. I'd really like to see you again as well, Alex. I've been, well, I was really hoping you'd call today, or stop by."

Alex silently released the breath she'd been holding. "Really? I thought about stopping by your office to see you, instead of calling. But I thought it might be too—"

"Stalker-ish?" Sydney finished the sentence with a tease in her voice.

"Exactly," Alex said. "So once again, at the risk of sounding stalker-ish, are you free tomorrow for dinner?"

"Absolutely. What time?"

"How about I pick you up at six?"

"Okay. Any dress code?"

"Not formal, but a little dressy. Is that okay?"

"Got it." Alex heard a buzz in the background. "Hold on a second, Alex." Alex heard Sydney activate her office phone on speaker.

"Yeah, Stan?"

"Syd, can we meet in my office for a few minutes? I want to talk to you about some cases that came in over the weekend."

"Sure thing. Give me a second and I'll be right there." Alex heard Sydney disconnect the call then her voice came back over the line.

"Sorry, Alex. That was my boss."

"No problem. I'll let you go. I'll see you tomorrow at six."

"I'm looking forward to it." Sydney's voice then lowered an octave. "And, Sergeant Chambers?"

"Yes?"

"You can stalk me anytime you like."

The phone went dead before Alex's brain could format a response, much less tell her lips to vocalize it. She was left staring at her own cell phone, wondering if she'd imagined the bold statement.

ALEX WAS BACK on the third floor of the downtown court building Wednesday morning. A couple of weeks earlier, two of her younger officers had made an impressive narcotics arrest. Possession of crack cocaine for sale. Neither of them had previously testified as court qualified experts on possession for sales, so the assistant district attorney handling the preliminary hearing requested the seasoned sergeant to provide that expert testimony.

The case was one of the first called and Alex walked through her expertise then provided an opinion based on the amount of product in the defendant's possession, the packaging, and the amount of money he was also taken into custody with. Several minutes later she was heading out of the courtroom with the defendant having been held to answer on the narcotics violation. She met the arresting officers in the hallway outside and gave them the good news.

She was still loitering and talking with several officers about various cases when a young brunette approached them, professionally attired and carrying several files.

"Sergeant Chambers, good to see you again," the young woman said as she stopped beside Alex. Alex recognized her as one of the law clerks from the district attorney's office whom she occasionally had contact with. They'd also run into each other several times at the gym Alex frequented near her home. It was not lost on Alex that the woman had occasionally engaged in just slightly veiled flirting with her.

"Hi. How are you doing?" she replied.

"Hey, Sarg, we're gonna head back out," one of the officers said as they backed away, heading for the elevators.

"Sounds good, guys. See you out there." Alex didn't miss the slight smile on both of their faces. They seemed to know exactly what was going on and apparently felt it appropriate to leave their sergeant to work her mojo. Alex turned back to the younger woman.

"It's Vicky, right?" she asked in an effort to be polite.

"Yep," the woman said and smiled at Alex. "I've missed you at the gym lately. Don't you come in the mornings anymore?"

Alex shrugged in response to the clerk's inquiry. "The work hours are a little sporadic," she said. "You know, with court and everything. I end up working out at the station or the academy a lot these days."

"Well, you're obviously still getting your workouts in." Vicky ran a hand up Alex's arm. "You look great."

Alex almost flinched at the touch, then became aware of someone standing nearby. She turned to see Sydney, apparently watching the exchange, and was thankful for the interruption. Alex smiled, then noticed a strange look on Sydney's face as she looked at the clerk then stepped between them.

"Good morning, Sergeant Chambers," she said. Alex turned to Sydney and her eyes sparkled. She watched as Sydney gave Vicky an icy smile and a nod. "Good morning," she added in her direction.

"Morning," Vicky replied, pulling her hand slowly back from Alex's arm as Alex focused on Sydney.

An odd thrill went through Alex's body at Sydney's unexpected arrival. A smile crossed her face containing far more warmth than the polite expression she had worn for Vicky. "Good morning, Ms. Rutledge."

Alex and Sydney looked at one another for a few brief moments, saying nothing. Alex analyzed the body language displayed by both women and couldn't help but be a little fascinated by what she saw. Was Sydney really jealous?

"I'd like to speak to you about one of your cases if you have a few minutes," Sydney finally said to Alex.

"Uh, sure."

"Would you excuse us?" Sydney said to Vicky. Alex could have sworn she saw a look of resentment cross Vicky's face, but it passed quickly.

"Sure thing," Vicky said, and then turned dismissively away from Sydney and focused her attention once again on Alex. She pulled out a small pad of paper and began writing on it. Then she looked up at Alex with another seductive smile. "Well, I've missed you. Since I don't see you at the gym enough anymore, we'll have to arrange something else," she said as she tore the slip of paper from the notepad and slipped it into Alex's hand. "Call me. We'll get together sometime." Alex watched as Vicky's eyes raked across Sydney, carrying an almost blatant look of challenge as she pivoted and walked away, turning once to smile back at Alex as she entered a nearby courtroom.

Alex turned back to Sydney, who appeared to be shooting daggers with her eyes at the departing figure. "Uh-oh." She glanced down at the paper in her hand and crumpled it within her clenched fingers.

"What's up?" Alex asked, unsure exactly what to do with the paper in her hand. "I didn't know I had any pending cases. I don't think I've been served any other subpoenas."

Sydney shook her head and a slightly amused exasperation covered her face. "You're right, you don't. I just wanted to get you alone to talk about tonight."

"Oh..."

Sydney grinned and Alex was relieved to see she appeared more amused than irritated with her.

"I'm looking forward to it," Alex finally said in a rush, and then a moment of uncertainty passed through her mind. "Are we still on? I mean, you're okay with it?" she asked. "I understand if something's come up," she added, hoping that wasn't the case.

"Absolutely," Sydney said. She reached between them and gave Alex's wrist a reassuring squeeze. "You can't possibly think I was canceling on you?"

Alex glanced away with a shy shrug, concealing her overwhelming sense of relief.

Alex noticed as Sydney's attention as caught by another assistant D.A. poking his head out of a courtroom door some distance away. His eyes locked on Sydney and his eyebrows raised in a question. Sydney waved and lifted one of the files she was carrying, silently indicating to her protégé she was en route to deliver it to him.

"Hey, I'll let you get back to work," Alex said, picking up on the communication.

"So, I'll see you at six, right?" Sydney said as she began to drift down the hall, walking backwards so she could continue facing Alex.

"You bet," Alex said.

Sydney nodded and then glanced down at the paper still in Alex's hand.

"Hey," Alex said. "Can you do me a favor?" She took several steps toward Sydney then held her hand out. "Throw this away for me?"

Sydney smiled broadly as she took the crumpled paper from Alex.

"My pleasure," she said, and then gave a wave as Alex headed for the elevators.

ALEX KNOCKED ON Sydney's door that evening promptly at six and it was opened almost without delay. Sydney smiled and moved aside to allow Alex to move past her into the entryway.

"Wow," Alex said, as she entered, taking two steps through the doorway then turning and watching Sydney close the door. She admired the slightly tight dark blue cocktail style dress, which came to just above Sydney's knees, the top plunging suggestively toward her cleavage. When Sydney turned away from the door she stumbled into Alex who immediately caught her around the waist.

"You look fantastic," Alex said.

"You're looking pretty sharp yourself, Sergeant," Sydney said. Her eyes tracked down Alex's silk shirt and cashmere slacks.

Alex didn't miss Sydney's gaze drift back up to her lips, and took this as a subtle invitation. She leaned forward and gave her a gentle kiss. The kiss lasted longer than Alex had intended as Sydney leaned into her and caressed the back of her neck.

"You ready to go?" Alex said when they finally pulled away from the kiss and looked at one another.

"Yeah," Sydney said, making no move. They remained standing in each other's arms for several moments until Sydney finally pulled away.

"Let me get my purse and, you know, do that last minute check in the mirror."

"You don't need any last mirror check," Alex said. "Like I said before, you look great."

Several minutes later Alex held the passenger door to her truck open and helped Sydney in. Sydney smiled her thanks and they were on their way.

"So where are we off to?" Sydney asked as they pulled onto the freeway heading west. Alex glanced over at her and smiled.

"I just thought we could have a nice quiet dinner. Maybe a view, some candles, you know..."

"Something romantic?"

"Yes, exactly."

Alex rested her elbow on the center armrest between them, turning her hand over palm up as a subtle invitation. She was silently gratified when she felt Sydney's hand rest in hers and their fingers entwined. They traveled west on Sunset Boulevard then turned southbound and drove down to Santa Monica Boulevard. Neither felt they needed to interrupt the comfortable silence as Alex felt Sydney's thumb slowly massage the top of her hand.

They soon pulled into a parking lot and stopped adjacent to a valet booth, both doors opened simultaneously by the red vested staffers. Alex handed over the keys and they made their way to the door.

"Café La Boheme," Sydney said as they entered.

"Yes, have you been here?" Alex asked, relieved when Sydney shook her head.

"No, but I've heard about it." She turned to smile at Alex. "You must've read my mind. I've been wanting to come here."

"I have a reservation for Chambers," Alex said to the maître d', who nodded and welcomed them to the restaurant then led them upstairs to a dim booth on the second level. Sydney's eyes continued to look around her, finally taking in their own private candle lit setting. Her eyes came to rest on Alex who was sitting, simply gazing at her. Their knees made contact softly beneath the table and Sydney smiled as their eyes met.

After the meal they shared a crème brûlée and coffee, talking about anything and everything as they virtually lost themselves in one another, completely losing track of time. Alex left a generous tip for the waiter as they had occupied his table for most of the evening and prevented him from serving other parties.

The evening was crisp but dry and so at Alex's suggestion they walked through the heart of West Hollywood. As the night cooled Alex removed her jacket and gently placed it over Sydney's shoulders. Sydney gave Alex a smile of appreciation and reached out to take Alex's hand, giving it a gentle squeeze and then not letting it go. They walked hand in hand as they meandered slowly through the commercial heart of West Hollywood.

"Have you spent much time in WeHo?" Alex asked.

"Oh, I've come here quite a bit with Tyler," Sydney said. Alex nodded thinking that was why she was comfortable with the public display of hand holding. Sydney clearly was familiar with WeHo being the gay mecca of the Southern California region.

"Thank you again for a wonderful dinner," Sydney said later that evening as Alex walked her to her door. It was almost eleven o'clock when they returned to the home in the Hollywood Hills. Sydney opened the door and stepped inside, Alex holding it open for her.

"Can I interest you in a nightcap?" Sydney asked as she let the jacket slide from her shoulders. She turned to find Alex standing there, looking at her, making no move to enter the house.

"I think I should let you get to sleep. You do have closing arguments tomorrow in your jury trial," Alex said, though her inner voice was screaming that yes, of course she would love to stay a while. Sydney, however, moved closer, clearly reading her hesitation.

"Sergeant Chambers, are you making excuses to not be alone with me?" Sydney rested a hand on Alex's shoulder and another around her neck as Alex, almost on autopilot, wrapped her arms around Sydney.

The kiss that followed was passionate and lengthy, taking the breath from both of them. Their lips parted and tongues probed. Alex pulled Sydney toward her, their chests and hips meetings, locking them in a strong embrace.

ALEX'S LIPS traveled down Sydney's neck to the silk collar of her blouse. Sydney's arms moved naturally around Alex's neck. She moaned and arched her body against Alex then ran her fingers through Alex's hair as Alex's lips again found hers, kissing her deeply. The kiss ended the way it had begun, with hesitancy and tenderness.

When their lips finally parted Sydney recognized the incendiary look of what was undeniable sexual desire consuming Alex's expression. They were both breathing rapidly and Sydney was thankful for Alex's strength. She felt dizzy and short of breath, as if she would have slid to the floor if she didn't have Alex's strong arms around her.

Alex closed her eyes as if willing herself to remain calm and in control. It was clear to Sydney that Alex was hesitant to allow herself to move quickly. She silently wondered what inner battle might be raging inside Alex's head. They stood for a moment together, embracing, foreheads touching. Sydney was smiling gently when Alex finally opened her eyes and looked at her.

"We really have to stop this here," Alex whispered. "Because in a little while I might not be able to stop at all."

"Would that really be wrong?" Sydney asked.

"It wouldn't be right," Alex said. "One of these days, when you're absolutely sure you're ready, and it's what you want, then you ask me to stay. Okay?" Sydney could only nod as they stood simply holding one another. Sydney's arms were still around Alex's neck, her fingers playing gently with the hair at the back of her head.

"I'm going to miss you this weekend," Sydney said in a quiet voice after several moments. Alex's eyes showed momentary confusion, then she appeared to remember.

"That's right. You're meeting your sister in Chicago. Jen, right?" Sydney nodded. "Just through Sunday?"

"Yes. I'll just be staying Friday and Saturday night, then fly home late Sunday. I was supposed to leave tomorrow, but with this jury trial the plans had to change and the trip shortened by a day. Will I see you tomorrow?" Sydney asked.

Alex gave a regretful shake of her head. "I don't think so. I've gotta work late tomorrow, Friday and Saturday."

"Damn the L.A.P.D.," Sydney said in mock annoyance. "Are you sure you won't stay, just for a while—

Alex stilled her mouth with a gentle finger. "I will not be responsible for the County of Los Angeles losing this case. It's already late." She leaned down once more and their lips caressed. "You're gonna be great tomorrow. Call me when you're out?" Sydney agreed and they kissed once more, just briefly, before Alex finally retreated out the door. Sydney once again watched Alex's truck until it turned out of sight at the base of the driveway.

THURSDAY AFTERNOON FOUND Sydney out of court and back in her office. The closing argument went well, with both the defense and prosecution summarizing their cases for the jury prior to the lunch break. They returned to court afterwards and the judge read his jury instructions, then handed the case off to the jury to begin their deliberation. Sydney called Alex as soon as she returned to her office.

"You done?" Alex asked, though she sounded like she was on the move.

"Yeah. I think it went okay. You sound busy."

"We're just about to go into roll call. Can I call you later this evening?"

"Sure. Go to work. We'll talk tonight."

Sydney reviewed case files for upcoming trials and smiled when her eye ran down a list of witnesses and arresting officers and a particular name caught her attention. She was interrupted when Cathy came into her office carrying a dozen red roses in a glass vase.

"Look who got a delivery," Cathy said with a smile. She placed them on Sydney's desk, gave Sydney a wink, and then left, only to be very quickly replaced by Tyler.

"Well, someone had a good date," Tyler said. He reached over and pulled the small card from the bouquet of flowers and began opening the envelope.

"Hey!" Sydney stood and reached over her desk and grabbed the card before he could read it. She turned away and finished opening the envelope.

> Thank you for a wonderful evening. I hope you enjoyed it as much as I did. A.

"So?" Tyler closed the door to her office. "Tell me everything."

"I can't. Not here. Let's go for dinner after work and I'll tell you about it. But I have work to do now and you need to get out."

"All right, all right. But at least tell me if you got to, oh I don't know, second base?"

"Get out!"

But Sydney's blushing face and the way she held the card close against her chest told him all he needed to know. "I knew it! I just knew it!"

Sydney chased him out of the office, slamming her door in mock frustration.

ALEX HAD JUST finished supervising the scene of a moderately sized narcotics sales arrest by a couple of her officers and was standing in the street leaning on her black and white when her cell phone rang. She answered it and found Sydney on the other end of the phone.

"I got the roses," Sydney said. "They're lovely."

"Are you sure they're okay?" Alex asked. "I mean, right after I had them sent I was kind of kicking myself. You know, roses, with everything that's going on. But they're red, so I thought it was kind of traditional."

"They're beautiful. And yes, red is traditional. So you're a romantic at heart, Sergeant Chambers."

"Well, I don't know about that. Don't get your expectations up too high. But I'm glad you like them. I really did have a wonderful time," Alex said. "How has your day been?"

"It's been okay. It's much better now that I have something beautiful in my office to look at." Alex smiled at Sydney's appreciation of the flowers. "I might have trouble concentrating now, though, with that constant reminder of someone more pleasant to think about."

Alex was silent, unsure exactly what to say in response. She looked around as if checking to see who else could be listening, despite the fact she was alone on the street. Sydney's voice was quiet when she spoke again seconds later. "I'm almost regretting my trip this weekend. I think I miss you already," she said.

"Well, I've been thinking about that," Alex said. "Why don't I give you a ride to the airport tomorrow and pick you up on Sunday evening? It'll save you the hassle of parking and stuff."

"What about your work schedule?" Sydney asked. "You're working late tonight and I leave very early tomorrow."

"Don't worry about it, I can work it out. I'll go back home afterwards and take a nap before work. Besides," Alex's voice dropped lower this time. "This way I can give you a proper goodbye kiss at least."

"That's nice, but I think I'll definitely be looking forward to the hello kiss more."

"Good, it's settled."

ALEX ARRIVED AT Sydney's doorstep the next morning before six. When Sydney answered she stepped in to find Sydney's suitcase sitting inside the door. She looked at the full sized suitcase then back at Sydney. "You are just going for the weekend, right? Just two nights?" She looked back at the suitcase with raised eyebrows.

Sydney slapped her shoulder lightly. "Yes, Sergeant Smartass," she said. "I'm just going for the weekend. But you know us girly-girls, we have stuff we have to take."

"Stuff?"

"Yes, stuff," Sydney said, putting her arms around Alex's neck. Alex leaned down and met her lips as they kissed. When they finally broke apart Sydney looked up at Alex and fondled the hair at the back of her neck. "How is it I already know I'm going to miss you so much?" she asked. "We've only had a few dates. Does this make me a stalker?"

"You can stalk me anytime," Alex said with a smile. She brought Sydney closer into her embrace in a tight hug. "And I'm going to miss you, too." Sydney looked up at her and Alex met her lips in a passionate kiss once again.

"I guess we should be on our way," Sydney said when they separated once more. Alex gave her one last embrace and a smile then moved to the suitcase.

"All right. I've got your, uh, *weekend* bag," she said as they moved to the door.

The drive to the Burbank Airport was brief with almost no traffic in the early morning hours. Part way there Alex was aware of Sydney reaching over to run her fingers down Alex's arm then settle comfortably in Alex's hand.

"You know," Alex said. "It's kind of funny you should mention we've only had a few dates." Alex was aware of Sydney looking at her from the seat next to her. "Do you feel as if we have a little more of a connection than you'd normally feel after three dates?"

"Yes," Sydney replied without hesitation.

"Well, I have a confession to make."

"If it's anything like your last confession, I'm sure I'll like it." Sydney gave Alex's hand a squeeze.

"Well, the last couple months, uh, I might not have had court as many times as you might have been led to believe." Alex looked over at Sydney and found nothing but a slightly amused and curious look on her face. She plunged on with her explanation.

"I was just really interested in seeing you again, so I may have, uh, embellished the demand on my court appearances."

"You embellished the need for you to be in court?" Sydney asked. "You hadn't really been subpoenaed to appear?"

"I had subpoenas some of the time. But, yeah, something like that."

"Because you wanted to see me again?"

Alex smiled. "Yeah, then again, and again..."

"So it's not really as if we've only had three dates, then. Right? I mean some of those lunches and coffees weren't really just coincidence to kill time between court appearances because you had nothing better to do. You were actually there because you wanted to see me?" Alex nodded as Sydney spoke.

"Well, I certainly can't think of anything better I could have been doing." This time Alex squeezed Sydney's hand and then brought it to her lips for a brief kiss. "And yes, I can honestly say I was there a lot of the time just because I was hoping we'd run into each other. I wasn't completely avoiding my duty. I do, after all, work Central Division, which includes the courthouse. I was technically just providing some extra patrol there." Alex shrugged. "But I guess after all this I really am a stalker."

By this time they were pulling into the airport terminal area.

"Well, you may not find you need to make those excuses too much anymore, because an above average number of cases you're involved in may have somehow, coincidentally, found their way onto my desk," Sydney said with a smile. "And I'll say it once again, Sergeant Chambers, you can be my stalker anytime." Sydney gave her hand one last squeeze as they pulled to the curb before she opened the door to get out.

"Call me if you have a chance?" Alex asked a minute later as she gave Sydney a final hug at the curb in front of the terminal.

"Absolutely," Sydney said without hesitation. She surreptitiously kissed Alex's cheek before releasing her and taking the handle of her wheeling suitcase. They exchanged waves and Alex watched as Sydney made her way to the terminal doors, turning once more to wave before entering and proceeding out of view.

SYDNEY HAD AN enjoyable visit with her sister in Chicago. They met at the hotel Friday evening when Sydney arrived and after Jen finished the week long conference that had brought her to the city. They spent Saturday walking through downtown Chicago, window shopping on the Miracle Mile and visiting the Navy Pier. That evening found them seeking refuge from the cold in Lou Malnati's, the famous pizza establishment.

"God, Alex would probably kill for this pizza," Sydney said after several bites of the deep dish Chicago style pie. The exclamation came almost without thought. She looked up to find Jen looking at her with a smile on her face and sparkle in her eye.

"So, Alex is it? Is that who I heard you making sexy talk with on the cell while I was trying on that dress this afternoon?" she asked.

Sydney rolled her eyes but couldn't keep the blush from rising. "It wasn't sexy talk. We were just talking."

"Uh-huh," Jen said, still with a playful smile. "So, you mentioned when you came for Christmas that you had your eye on someone. And then in our call earlier this week that you were seeing someone with possibilities. Is Alex the guy you were talking about?"

"Alex is someone I'm seeing," Sydney said. A part of her wondered how close she was to being outright dishonest with her sister and how long she could carry it off. The interrogation continued.

"So, tell me what kind of guy is this Alex? What does he do?"

"Alex is..." Sydney resigned herself to playing it safe. She wasn't ready to be entirely forthcoming with Jen yet, despite the slight discomfort she felt for misleading her. "A sergeant with the L.A.P.D. We met during a trial." Sydney spoke to Jen on the telephone at least once a week and shared pretty much everything. She was sure she had mentioned the talented female sergeant during the course of the White Rose trial, probably by name. She hoped Jen wouldn't make the connection. Not yet at least.

"And what does Alex look like? Got a picture?"

"About five foot nine, light brown hair, hazel eyes, nice build. You know, athletic." Sydney tactfully avoided the question about a photograph, of which she had several on her cell phone.

"Sexy?"

"God, yes," Sydney replied.

"Slept with him yet?"

Sydney rolled her eyes. "Jen."

"What? It's a reasonable question and you've never refused to answer it before. So how's the sex?"

"Well, we haven't, uh–"

"Wait a minute." Jen put the slice of pizza she was about to bite into back on her plate. "How long have you two been seeing each other?"

"Well, we've only been really dating a little over a week." Sydney thought back to Alex's confession on the way to the airport and smiled. "But we've been running into each other quite a bit over the last few months. You know, around the courthouse. Alex confessed those weren't entirely coincidental. And I might have somehow ended up with some of h...some particular cases that weren't entirely assigned to me by chance." She saw Jen's eyebrows raise in question. "Hey, prerogative of seniority. Stan likes me to help figure out case assignments sometimes." Sydney silently hoped it was not her slip in almost referring to Alex as "her" that had raised Jen's curiosity. "So I sometimes take the cases that interest me—for one reason or another."

"Uh-huh." Jen nodded, apparently having missed Sydney's almost misspoken pronoun. "So you two have been flirting with each other, creating excuses to run into one another, for the past several months and you finally started actually dating when?"

"Last Friday."

"How many dates?"

"Three."

"In one week? Have plans for the next one yet?"

"I'm being picked up from the airport Sunday."

"But you haven't slept together?"

"Geez, Jen. We're taking it slow. Letting the relationship develop before we jump into bed together. I just, well, I guess I really don't want to screw this up."

"Okay. So you're saying this may have serious potential, huh?" Sydney nodded and Jen reached across the table to squeeze her hand.

"Then I hope it all works out. And I expect introductions to this wonderful man of yours in the very near future." Jen picked up the slice of pizza to resume eating. "But, Syd, seriously, tell me you've at least had some touchy-feely time? I mean three dates has got to earn something."

The sparkle in Sydney's eye and the slight blush to her face was the only response Jen got to that particular question.

"Uh-huh. Good kisser?"

"Oh my God, Jen. You have no idea."

IT WAS ALMOST eight p.m. on Sunday when Sydney entered the baggage claim area of Burbank Airport. Her eyes immediately settled on Alex as she stood off to the side. A warm feeling overcame her as she saw the look of pleasure take over Alex's face when their eyes met. They hugged briefly, aware of the very public surroundings. Both women looked at the other with eyes that communicated far more. They spent the drive to Sydney's talking about her trip and her sister and making other small talk.

When they arrived Alex carried Sydney's bag into the house, up the stairs and into the master bedroom. Alex quickly exited the bedroom and led the way back to the main stairs. Alex's virtual rush from the bedroom did not go unnoticed by Sydney.

"Sergeant Chambers." Sydney reached out and grabbed Alex, turning her and looking up into her face. "Are you trying to escape?" Sydney leaned up and kissed Alex's neck.

"No. I—"

"Then why the rush?"

"I was just..." Alex paused and Sydney noticed her nervous glance toward the bedroom door. When Alex looked back down at her Sydney gave her a reassuring smile, clearly communicating she was aware of the cause for Alex's trepidation. Alex pulled her closer and returned the smile. "God, I missed you."

"Come sit with me a while." Sydney took Alex's hand and led her downstairs to the den. "You want to turn on the fire?" she asked as she made her way into the kitchen to make hot chocolate.

As she prepared the chocolaty drinks her mind returned to the conversation she'd had with herself on the flight home. Sydney knew Alex was self-conscious about her lack of experience with women, and was therefore hesitant to be too aggressive in her affections. She also knew it was likely on her shoulders to push their relationship to the next level and she was determined to make it very clear to Alex that she was serious about them. As she stirred in the miniature marshmallows she decided she would begin sending that message tonight.

Sydney returned minutes later and handed Alex one of the mugs then sat down next to her, leaning into her. Alex responded by looping an arm around Sydney's shoulders. They sat together like that for a while, discussing each of their weekends as they sipped from their mugs. The conversation eventually tapered off and they cuddled in comfortable silence and watched the flames for several minutes.

"I probably shouldn't stay too long," Alex said, breaking the silence. "I know you've got to be up for work tomorrow and it's probably been a couple of long days for you with the travel back and forth?"

"Not so fast, Sergeant. I love my sister and I enjoyed the trip, but I've really been looking forward to some time alone with you. So don't be in such a hurry to leave." Sydney removed the mug from Alex's hand, placing both mugs on the coffee table, then snuggled back into Alex, partially facing her. She caressed Alex's cheek, slowly drawing her fingers down Alex's neck, letting her hand come to rest against Alex's chest. Sydney looked up into Alex's eyes then leaned closer into her embrace.

"Syd..." Alex whispered.

"Shh." Sydney covered Alex's lips with her fingers, as Alex had so often done with her at this point. Then she smiled seductively. "Please, Alex. Don't over think it."

Sydney pulled Alex down to meet her. Their lips met and Sydney was swept away, a sense of warmth rushing through her body, starting from somewhere deep inside. Alex wrapped her arm around Sydney, drawing their bodies closer together.

Their breasts crushed together, and she felt as much as heard her own groan of passion.

Moments later Sydney gently broke the kiss. Alex opened her eyes and looked at her in concern.

"Are you —"

Sydney interrupted her inquiry with another delicate kiss. "Relax," she whispered.

Her eyes stayed locked on Alex's as she grabbed the front of her shirt, pulling her down. Sydney leaned back onto the length of the couch with Alex poised provocatively over her, chests mere inches apart. Alex leaned on her arms, apparently hesitant to allow her full weight to come to rest on Sydney.

Sydney couldn't help but smile. "Alex, I'm good. I want this. I want us like this."

"I don't want you to feel —"

"I know. I'll let you know when I'm ready for the rest. But right now, this is good. This is perfect." Sydney pulled Alex down, starting again where they'd left off. Their lips met in a gentle kiss that built gradually in intensity. Moments later she felt Alex allow the rest of her body to surrender. With a half sigh, half groan, Alex lowered onto Sydney's body.

The intensity and passion was overwhelming and Sydney lost track of all time and sense of location. Alex's hips moved between her legs, and Sydney welcomed the sensation. She moved her legs to allow Alex to nestle deeply into her, looping an ankle over the top of Alex's leg. Just as Sydney felt the need to perhaps bring the tempo back to something controllable, Alex drew back slowly, breaking the kiss. Alex remained absolutely still and looked deep into Sydney's eyes as their foreheads rested against each other. Sydney saw the same passion and longing radiating out from them, though tempered with a touch of nervousness and uncertainty that Sydney found so endearing.

Alex closed her eyes and Sydney smiled as the woman clearly concentrated on regaining full control of her body and mind. When Alex opened her eyes, Sydney was still smiling. Sydney reached up and brushed the hair back off Alex's forehead. They lay like that, in each other's embrace, forehead to forehead, for several more minutes.

"I really should be going," Alex finally whispered, breaking the spell.

"I know. This is just really comfortable. Here, with you. Just being together like this." Alex nodded and gave her a gentle peck on the lips before she rose to stand and then helped Sydney to her feet.

"We'll have much more time to spend like this in the future," Alex said, hugging Sydney and kissing the top of her head.

Sydney returned the hug, resting her head against Alex's chest. "You promise?"

"Yes. As long as you'll have me."

They held hands on the walk to the front entryway and Sydney waited as Alex put on her jacket, then she once again moved into her embrace for a final hug.

"Thank you again for the ride, and another wonderful evening," Sydney said.

"Thank you for spending it with me." Alex put her fingers to Sydney's chin and raised it gently. Their lips met in a final tender kiss. "Sleep well," Alex said as she backed out of the door. As was now her habit, Sydney stood in the open doorway and watched until Alex's truck made the turn onto the street below.

Chapter Nine

SYDNEY'S MONDAY WAS busy, like most Mondays at the district attorney's office. She had just finished a meeting with a more junior attorney who had been assigned to second chair an upcoming attempted murder trial. She was still waiting for the jury to return on her previous week's trial and was now sitting at her desk reviewing other case files. Cathy, the receptionist, appeared in her doorway with a bouquet of white roses and a smile on her face.

"This is beginning to take on a pleasant pattern," Cathy said as she put the vase down on Sydney's desk, winked at her, then left the office.

Sydney hesitated, shocked at the appearance of the white flowers before her. She sat still for several seconds, finally mustering courage to reach for the prominently mounted envelope amongst the green stems. She was just pulling the attached card from its small envelope as Tyler came to her doorway. Sydney sank slowly into her chair, holding the card in a shaking hand.

ALEX MANAGED TO get off duty a little early and decided to stop by and see Sydney. She was just walking down the hallway toward Sydney's open door when she heard Tyler's exclamation.

"Syd! What is it? What's wrong?" The alarm in his voice made Alex hurry the last few steps. She came through the door and saw Sydney sitting in her chair, one hand to her mouth, another holding a small card in front of her on the desk. Tyler was kneeling beside her looking concerned. On the desk was a large vase containing a dozen white roses.

Sydney looked up at Alex as she approached, then wordlessly passed the card to her. Alex saw the inscriptions on the card and knew immediately the cause of Sydney's distress.

```
Still looking forward to spending time alone with
you.
```

There was no name.

"I'm calling security and getting Stan," Tyler said as he gently grabbed Sydney's shoulders and looked into her eyes. "You're safe, Syd. You're gonna be fine." She nodded and he was out the door moments later.

Alex moved to her side, kneeling down and taking Sydney's hands in hers as Sydney looked at her, fear in her eyes.

"How?" Sydney asked quietly.

"The news of the original flowers was in the media," Alex said.

"It's probably the same wack-job playing a cruel, sick joke." She tried to sound reassuring, though inside she was far from feeling that way.

"But the message? It's exactly the same. That was never publicized. How could they know?"

Alex had no answer and could only shake her head. At that moment Tyler returned, followed by Stan. Alex was torn, not knowing what affection she should show in front of Sydney's boss and peers. She wanted so badly to reach out and take Sydney in her arms, to comfort her, promise to protect her and not allow anything to happen.

Instead, she took Sydney's hand, squeezing it gently. "Syd, I'm going to step out and make a couple of phone calls. I'll just be in the hallway and I'll be right back." Sydney nodded.

"Please," Sydney said as Alex turned toward to the door. "Take those with you." She nodded to the large bouquet of roses still sitting inches away on her desk.

Alex grabbed the vase, then more carefully the card, and stepped out into the hallway where she put them down on a desk in an empty cubicle. She doubted there would be fingerprints or DNA evidence at this point, but she was careful to handle the card and envelope along the edges just in case. Then she called Chuck Severs from R.H.D. and relayed to him what happened. He said he would make the appropriate department notifications and be there immediately. True to his promise, Chuck arrived shortly thereafter with his partner, Detective Robert Kim, a department photographer and an evidence technician. Alex explained everything she knew and Chuck's partner went off to gather preliminary information from Cathy regarding the delivery service.

OVER AN HOUR later the R.H.D. detectives were concluding their on-scene investigation. Alex left them in the hallway and re-entered Sydney's office. Sydney was alone, still seated in the chair behind her desk, head leaning back and eyes closed. She looked exhausted. Alex walked around and leaned back against the desk. She bent slightly and placed one hand on the arm of Sydney's chair. "How are you doing?"

Sydney opened her eyes and took a deep breath. "I'm doing okay, I guess."

Alex took Sydney's hand in hers, rubbing her thumb gently across Sydney's knuckles. "Chuck and his people are very good at what they do. They'll figure this out."

Sydney's attention focused on something behind Alex and Alex followed her gaze. Lieutenant John Ramos stood in the open doorway. She turned toward Ramos, giving Sydney's hand one more squeeze and then releasing it.

Alex saw Ramos's eyes descend just as she let Sydney's hand go. He rolled his eyes and said, "Oh, brother," just loud enough for her to hear, then turned and walked from the doorway out of sight.

"God dammit! What the fuck is he doing here?"

Sydney leaned forward, took Alex's hand once again and turned Alex toward her. "Who is he?"

"No one you need to worry about," Alex said. She squeezed Sydney's hand and then released it. "I'll be back in a minute," she said, then walked out of the office. Alex turned in the direction Ramos had walked and saw him standing down the hallway speaking to Chuck. Ramos's back was to Alex and he was unaware of her approaching. As she drew closer she overheard part of what he was saying to Chuck.

"...is probably a bunch of bull. You know that's how it is with these queers. This is all probably a byproduct of some deviant relationship."

"You son of a bitch!" She rapidly covered the remaining space between them. Ramos turned to her as she came face-to-face with him. They stood toe-to-toe and nose-to-nose, their heights relatively equal. "You goddamn son of a bitch!" Alex repeated. "Don't even think about trying to downplay this!"

Chuck stepped between them, turning his back on Ramos and physically restraining Alex. "It's not worth it, Alex. Don't worry. It's R.H.D.'s case, not his."

"I'm the commanding officer of Central Detectives," Ramos said with a sneer. "I have every authority to insist on being kept in the loop on this. It occurred in my division." He then lowered his voice. "And if I think department assets are being wasted on this case, then it's my responsibility to communicate with the C.O. of R.H.D. and make a suggestion that this case be de-prioritized in favor of other more pressing and valid concerns."

The comment nearly sent Alex over the edge as she pushed against Chuck, not quite sure what she would do, but wanting desperately to get her hands on Ramos.

"You wanna play in a man's world, Chambers?" Ramos said, as if egging Alex on, trying to provoke a violent response. "You better learn how to play the game right."

"It's not a game, you homophobic asshole," Alex said quietly, with deadly steel in her voice. "And don't even think about getting anywhere near this case, Ramos."

"Or what, Chambers?" Ramos brushed past Chuck and walked down the hallway and out of sight.

"Alex, don't worry," Chuck said. "The whole Department knows he's an asshole." He spoke a few more words of reassurance, never giving any indication he knew the nature of Alex and Sydney's relationship, or that it mattered. Alex knew her sexuality was no secret around the department. Chuck, for his part, seemed to simply respect that Sydney was someone significant to Alex and extended every professional courtesy. He assured Alex that Ramos would have no influence on the case and that it would have R.H.D.'s full attention. Chuck and his team departed minutes later, promising to keep Alex in the loop on anything they discovered.

HAVING HEARD THE commotion and raised voices outside her office, Sydney walked to the door and looked out. She saw Alex standing with her fists clenched at her sides as if she was barely controlling a violent outburst. Chuck was standing between Alex and Ramos as Ramos continued talking in a low voice.

Ramos walked away and Alex made her way back down the hall to Sydney.

"Who was that?" Sydney asked again as Alex entered her office.

"He's the commanding officer of Central Detectives," Alex said. "He and I have had issues in the past. But don't worry." Alex reached out and rubbed each of Sydney's arms. "He has no influence on this case. R.H.D. will be handling it and like I said, Chuck and his people are the best."

Sydney moved almost unconsciously into Alex's arms, feeling the need to be in her embrace. She felt the tension in Alex's back and shoulders and wished she could relieve her anger and concern. Alex folded her arms around Sydney and Sydney melted against her, both of them taking solace in the bond. Sydney finally took a deep breath and stepped back.

"Come on," Alex said. "Let's get whatever you need and I'll drive you home. We'll figure out how to get your car home later." Sydney nodded and silently placed some items in her bag, then the two left the building. Sydney's hand found Alex's as they rode down in the elevator to the subterranean garage and Alex led Sydney to her truck. As they drove out of the garage onto the street in the evening darkness, Sydney's hand once again sought Alex's. They drove the twenty minutes to Sydney's house in companionable silence.

After Alex parked in the driveway, Sydney led the way to the porch, unlocking the front door and letting Alex follow her in. Alex put Sydney's satchel briefcase down on the entry table and turned to Sydney.

"I want you to wait here while I take a look around, all right?"

Sydney's eyes grew round in shock as she realized the implication of what Alex was saying.

"It's just a precaution," Alex said. "Give me a few minutes. I'll be right back."

Sydney could only nod in silence. Then she watched as Alex made her way through the entryway and disappeared to the rear of the house through the kitchen and dining areas. Sydney noticed the way Alex's hand hovered near the weapon in her waistband.

Several minutes later Alex came down the main stairs to the entryway. She had obviously used the rear spiral staircase to access the upper floor. Sydney felt momentary relief and turned to lock the deadbolt, then leaned against the door. Tears brimmed in her eyes and Alex moved to her, pulling Sydney into her arms. Sydney sank into

Alex's embrace.

"My God," Alex said. "You're shaking."

"I'm sorry," Sydney said, her face pressed to Alex's shirt. "I know I should be handling this better."

"Don't be silly, you're handling it fine." Alex said, "Anyone would be freaked out by this." They stood like that for several minutes until Sydney collected herself and pulled away, looking up into Alex's face. She reached up and pulled Alex's head down, kissing her gently.

"Thank you," she said. "What would I do without you?"

"We should have some dinner," Sydney said a moment later, making an effort to add some normalcy to the situation. "I've got some leftover chicken I can throw in a salad if that's okay."

"Sounds great. Listen, I'm just gonna take a quick look around outside before we eat." Sydney looked at her questioningly. "Just to get the lay of the land. It'll only take a few minutes." Alex gave Sydney another reassuring hug. "Okay?" Sydney nodded and Alex opened the door. "I'll be right back."

ALEX HAD RETURNED and was analyzing a lighted panel near the front door when Sydney came from the kitchen into the entry.

"This is an alarm panel, isn't it?" Alex asked.

"Yeah, but I haven't always been as strict about using it as I probably should be," Sydney replied. "I guess it would be smart to be more disciplined with that."

"If you've already got one, it's better to be safe than sorry, even on a normal day." Alex said with a reassuring smile. "Come on, show me how this thing works."

Sydney entered the code and they watched the digital screen flash to "Armed." Alex nodded in satisfaction then removed her jacket, which Sydney took and hung in the closet, though she noted Alex left her weapon tucked securely in her rear waistband rather than removing it as she had in the past.

After dinner the two retired to the den, once again with hot chocolate. They sat together on the couch in front of the fire and made small talk. Alex sat reclined at one end and Sydney was facing Alex sideways on the middle cushion with her legs curled up to her chest.

"You should get to bed," Alex said, "You've had a hell of a day and you look exhausted."

Sydney looked over at her, and then reached out to where Alex's hand was resting between them on the couch. She traced Alex's fingers with her own, slowly and gently.

"Thank you for everything today. I don't know what I would've done if you hadn't been there. I'm not going to lie, I was afraid to be alone this evening. I still am."

"Not a problem," Alex said. "We've got to get you downtown to pick up your car at some point tomorrow anyway. Why don't I just crash here," Alex patted the couch cushion, "and we'll figure it out in the morning."

"You'd do that for me?"

Alex nodded.

"You know, I have four bedrooms in this house, I'm sure we can arrange an actual bed for you, Sergeant Chambers."

"Nah. The couch will do. There's a blanket here. I'll be fine." Alex indicated to the spiral stairs just a few feet away. "And this way I'm just a yell away if you need anything," she added with a smile.

"Are you sure I can't get you anything else?" Alex shook her head in response.

"I've got a bag in my truck that I keep for emergencies at work. It's got some toiletries and a change of clothes. I'll be good."

"As long as you're sure." Sydney yawned and stretched, then stood. Alex stood with her and they found themselves looking at each other, almost touching.

Alex took Sydney's hands in hers and brought them to her lips, kissing the backs. "Sweet dreams," she said. "I'm right here if you need anything."

Sydney smiled as she went up the spiral stairs to her bedroom above.

ALEX WENT OUT to her truck to retrieve her emergency "go bag," carefully deactivating, then reactivating, the house alarm. Inside was a change of underwear, jeans, a t-shirt and sweatshirt, a towel and toiletries, some granola bars and extra ammunition. Everything she needed to get through any critical circumstance that could keep her away from home for an extended period of time.

When she returned to the den she flicked through the contacts list in her cell phone, hesitating after locating the number she was looking for. For not the first time in the last several hours she contemplated whether the call she was about to make was a good idea. She glanced at the nearby spiral staircase that led to Sydney's room then moved toward the front of the house. As she stood looking out the front window overlooking the driveway, she took a deep breath then pushed the send button.

"Hello, Alex," the smiling voice answered after only two rings, obviously having noticed the caller I.D.

"Hey, Reg," Alex said to the ex-girlfriend she hadn't spoken to in over a year. "How're you doing?"

"I'm okay," Regina said simply. When an uncomfortable pause followed, Alex decided she had better cut to the chase.

"Listen, I'm hoping you can help me out with something. It's a work thing."

"Isn't it kind of late to be making an official business call?" Regina said, but from what Alex could tell from her tone she didn't sound upset.

"I'm sorry. It's sort of off the books. A friend is really in need of a favor."

"Is this a female friend?"

"Reg, I—"

"No, don't answer that," Regina said. "It's none of my business. What do you need?"

"I've got a suspect who I need some background on. I know he was adopted, that came out during the investigation. But I was hoping you know someone in the foster system who can figure out this guy's history, how he ended up in the system, some information on his real family, that sort of thing."

"What's his name and date of birth?" Regina asked. Alex provided it from memory, having reviewed several official reports over the last couple of days.

"We're not talking about a kid here, Alex," Regina said. "How long ago was he in the system?"

"I'm not sure. I don't know how old he was when he was adopted. I'm assuming he was a kid. And I'm assuming they changed his name, at least his last name since he ended up with the adopted family name. I've got to assume the adoption took place about thirty-five years ago."

"Sinclair," Regina said thoughtfully. Alex held her breath while she waited for Regina to make the connection. "Wait a minute, Matthew Sinclair is the White Rose Killer. Alex, he was convicted and is on death row. Why on earth do you need to know about him?"

"Listen, Reg. This needs to be kept between us. There's a copycat out there and he knows way too much." Alex paused. "He's targeted someone I know. Someone I care about. There's got to be a connection with Sinclair and I need to know what it is."

"Hmm. Nobody's seen you in the clubs for a while," Regina said. "Tell me, is this friend you care about the reason why?"

Alex sighed. "Yes," was all she said. There was a long pause, as if Regina was waiting for Alex to say something more. She didn't.

"Okay, Alex. I'll look into it," Regina finally said. "It'll probably take a while. These are going to be old records, probably locked away in archives in hard copy. I imagine this adoption possibly occurred before anything was computerized. I'm going to have to be careful also, since this isn't exactly official."

"Thanks, Reg. I really appreciate it." Again the conversation reached an awkward pause. "How are you doing, Reg? Are you seeing anyone special?"

"No, Alex. There hasn't been anyone special since you."

Alex immediately regretted asking the question.

"I'm sorry. I never meant to hurt you, Reg."

"I'll call you when I find anything out," was all Regina said then she abruptly hung up, leaving Alex to say goodbye to a dead line.

Alex made her way back to the couch. She debated on whether it had been a smart call to make, or if she had just opened old wounds that should have remained untouched. She'd meant it when she told Regina she never meant to hurt her. Regina had been looking for something Alex couldn't provide. Had that changed? Was she in a different place now? The questions rolled through Alex's mind as she sat for several minutes, unmoving. She finally took off her boots, removed her weapon and placed it beside her phone on the nearby coffee table. Then she settled in, eventually falling into a restless sleep.

ALEX WAS AWAKENED several hours later by a noise she first could not identify. She lay unmoving for several moments until she heard it again, a muffled scream from the room above. She leapt from the couch and grasped her Glock then raced for the spiral stairs. She hit the top of the stairs half expecting to see an intruder, but none was there. In the moonlight pouring in through the windows Alex could see Sydney. Her head and arms were thrashing about as if she were struggling with an unseen attacker, gasping and yelling. Her eyes were clenched shut but tears were streaming down her cheeks as she cried out in obvious terror.

Alex moved to the bed and, after placing her handgun on the nightstand, grasped Sydney by her shoulders to stop her thrashing.

"Syd, wake up!" she said. "It's okay. It's just a dream. You're okay."

Sydney began sobbing and Alex took her in her arms as she cried.

"It was him. I dreamt of him. I knew it was him and I knew what he was going to do to me...what those women went through...before he..."

Alex held Sydney as she burrowed into her shoulder, sobbing. After several minutes the crying diminished and Alex thought Sydney had fallen back to sleep. She lowered her to the pillow and began to stand when Sydney took hold of her hand.

"Please don't go," Sydney said, half asleep. Alex sat back down on the edge of the bed and gazed down at her. "Please stay. I don't want to be alone. I just want you to hold me." Sydney moved to the middle of the bed, making room for Alex, who silently lay down next to her. Sydney moved into her in a spoon position, pulling Alex's arm around her waist and clasping one hand against her chest.

Alex could tell by Sydney's breathing that she was almost asleep. Feeling strangely comfortable and content, Alex followed not very far behind.

WHEN SYDNEY AWOKE alone in her bed the next morning she wondered exactly which portions of the previous night she had imagined. Had Alex actually been in her bed? Held her? She had vivid memories of the nightmare, but questioned the rest of her recollection. She put on a robe and slippers over her nightshirt and briefs and headed downstairs to the kitchen. At first she didn't see Alex and wondered if she had left, then noticed her standing outside on the rear deck. Alex turned when she heard the sliding glass door open.

"Hey there, sleepy head," Alex said with a smile as Sydney approached, and then a look of concern crossed her face. "How are you? That was quite a nightmare last night."

"I'm okay." She moved up to the railing beside Alex. "I'm sorry. You must think me terribly pathetic and dependent."

"Nonsense," Alex said. "You've been through a lot in the last twelve hours or so. Your reactions are human."

Sydney moved into her arms without hesitation and hugged Alex around the waist. Alex pulled her close and they stood together like that for several minutes, with Alex providing the comfort and support she needed.

Sydney finally broke the silence. "Would you like some breakfast and coffee? Then maybe I can beg you for a ride to work?"

"Work? Or just to get your car?"

"Work," Sydney said with a note of conviction as she slowly pulled away. "I've got to keep going. Last night was bad enough, but I'm not going to let this ruin my life. For all we know this is just a sick joke by someone taking advantage of the copycat killings. They knew about the original flowers and decided to build on that. Besides, this doesn't even follow the M.O. of the original murders. He never threatened his other victims. It just doesn't follow the pattern."

"Are you absolutely sure?" Alex asked.

"Yes, I have to keep going. I won't let this rule me. Besides, my jury should return today. So come on. I'll make us some breakfast then take a shower and have you drop me off at the courthouse."

"I don't need anything big. Just some toast and some caffeine. I'm going to head to the gym after I drop you off," Alex said.

"Toast and caffeine it is then," Sydney said. She took Alex's hand and pulled her toward the kitchen.

By nine a.m. Alex was pulling up on Broadway in front of the courthouse building.

"You're sure this is what you want?" Alex asked for probably the tenth time as Sydney opened the door to exit.

Sydney smiled back at her. "Yes," she said. "I'm absolutely sure."

"You'll call, right?" Sydney nodded in response. "Just be sure you call me if you need anything," Alex added.

"I will. Be safe at work." Sydney shut the door and waved as she turned to enter the building.

AFTER DROPPING SYDNEY at the court building, Alex went home

and put herself through a rigorous workout. This was often her escape when things were hectic or she needed to think things through. Her mind kept returning to Sydney and the circumstances of the day before. She was startled by her own reaction to what had happened. She felt a deep need to protect Sydney. An urge that went beyond the professional concern she would usually profess. She was taking this personally. She would trust no one else's efforts at protecting Sydney.

Later that day while at work, Alex fought the constant urge to call Sydney and check on her. She'd called once in the morning shortly after dropping Sydney off and finally gave in to the urge again at mid-day. The office secretary told her that the jury on Sydney's case had returned and she was in court. Alex waited another hour then called Sydney's cell.

"Hi, you," Sydney answered, sounding a little tired.

"How are you doing?"

Sydney took a deep breath. "I'm doing well, actually. It's been a refreshingly normal, uneventful day. Thank you again for last night."

"Sure," Alex replied. "The jury came back with a guilty verdict, I presume?" The conversation continued for several more minutes.

"You'll call me tonight?" Alex asked.

"Yes. I'll call you after I'm home and getting ready for bed."

"And you'll be sure to set the alarm?"

"Yes, I promise to set the alarm."

"And you'll call if you need anything? Or if you just want to talk? If I'm tied up on something I may not be able to answer right away, but I promise I'll get back to you soon as I can."

"Alex, don't worry. I'll call if I need anything." Alex could hear the smile in her voice. "Thank you," Sydney said in a quiet and sincere voice.

"You're welcome," she replied. "I'll talk to you later tonight."

LATER THAT EVENING Sydney followed through on the promise.

"All right, Sergeant Chambers, I'm home safe. The doors are locked and the alarm is set."

"You sure you feel okay? You don't need anything?" Alex asked Sydney for probably the third time that day.

"Yes, I'm sure." Sydney knew deep down inside she would love nothing more than to have Alex in her home again. She knew it would bring her an added sense of safety and security. Not to mention she just enjoyed being around Alex and having her close. But she refused to be that needy.

"I'm sure I could slide out of here if necessary," Alex added.

"Alex, as much as I'd love to see you, I can't have you leaving work every time I feel the slightest bit insecure," she said. "I have to work through this."

"But you will call me if you need anything? And you know I'm going to be checking on you."

"I look forward to that," Sydney said with a genuine smile. The two talked of random things for several minutes before wishing each other a pleasant night.

Sydney couldn't help but smile at the gentle watchdogging Alex had engaged in since the flower delivery. Her frequent phone calls and texts were endearing and comforting for Sydney. By mid-week she found the fear ebbing as she once again began to believe the flowers had been nothing more than a sick joke.

Chapter Ten

THE MIDAFTERNOON HOURS on Wednesday found Alex carrying a cardboard tray with two cups of still steaming coffee. She was smiling as she made her way to Sydney's office. Cathy, the gatekeeper at the lobby door, hadn't even bothered to call back to Sydney's office before buzzing Alex through.

"Good morning, Sergeant," she said with a smile as she reached for the toggle button just under the edge of her desk, behind the large bank teller style window. A loud click was heard as the door lock released.

As Alex pulled the door open she wondered if her presence was becoming that routine around the eighteenth floor of the criminal courts building.

She turned and paused in the open doorway to Sydney's office, initially unnoticed. Sydney sat with both elbows on the desk and her head in her hands as she leaned over, studying the contents of the case file lying open on her desk. Alex stood silently for more than a minute watching Sydney. The woman's facial expression and body language displayed a sense of frustration, but it occurred to Alex she looked quite stunning, in a slightly frazzled yet intense way.

Sydney lifted her head and reached down to turn the page and noticed Alex in her doorway. A smile transformed her face. She was on her feet in an instant, moving toward Alex. Without a word, she grasped the front of Alex's duty belt and pulled her from the doorway into the office, reaching past her with her other hand to push the office door closed. The latch caught with a resounding click. Sydney took the beverage tray out of Alex's hands and placed it on her desk. She turned back to Alex. Still without speaking a word, she put her arms around Alex's neck, pulling her head down and into a kiss. Although initially caught off guard by Sydney's aggressiveness, Alex recovered and wrapped her arms around Sydney's waist. The kiss became deep and passionate. Lips parted and tongues probed.

The kiss ended and both stood slightly glassy eyed in each other's arms, catching their collective breaths. Alex realized that in the course of the kiss one of her hands had drifted south and now rested gently on Sydney's ass. She slowly repositioned that hand as a roguish smile formed on her lips.

"Wow," Alex said with a husky voice that trembled ever so slightly. "Uh, can I take from that you're at least a little happy to see me?"

Sydney laughed in response. "You have no idea," she said, the sexual tension evident in her voice.

"How are you doing?" Alex asked.

"I'm good," Sydney rested a hand on Alex's chest. "Really. I'm good." She leaned up and kissed Alex again.

Alex shrugged helplessly, smiling as Sydney gazed up into her hazel eyes. She finally leaned down to kiss the top of Sydney's head, then turned her toward the desk. She removed one of the coffees from the tray and handed it to Sydney. "Tell me if I got it right."

Sydney took a sip and her eyes grew wide. "My café con leche. How did you know?"

"Two sugars, right?"

"Yes, it's perfect." Sydney circled her desk to sit down at the high backed executive chair, taking another sip and leaning back as she gave an appreciative sigh. "How did you know?" she asked again.

"I remembered when you had someone pick one up on a particularly challenging day during the trial," Alex said, referring to the White Rose trial. "You sent them to the Cuban coffee place down on Olympic Boulevard. I remember you mentioned then it was your favorite coffee." Sydney looked at Alex in wonder.

"You remembered from that one occasion? That was months ago. And you even remembered I take two sugars?"

"You said it was your favorite, and I am a trained observer, and, uh..."

"And you were already stalking me?"

Alex cringed inside with Sydney's use of the term, but then she noted Sydney seemed okay with it.

"Well, I was at least thinking about stalking you, I guess."

They continued to gaze at one another in companionable silence for several more moments as they sipped from their cups.

"I should be going," Alex finally said, breaking the silence. She motioned toward the still open file on Sydney's desk. "You looked like you were intensely engaged in your work when I arrived. I should let you continue."

"Yeah," Sydney said. "I guess I should get back to reviewing these case files." Yet neither of them moved for several seconds.

Sydney finally stood and walked around the desk. Alex came to her feet as Sydney stopped before her, only inches away. Again, the sexual tension existed almost as a physical presence sparking between them. Alex reached up to Sydney's cheek and guided their lips together in a sensuous kiss.

"Come to me tonight," Sydney said when their lips parted. "To my house...after..." Sydney didn't even open her eyes as the words came out almost in a gasp.

Alex nodded. "Okay," she whispered, before crushing their lips together once again. She let the hand on Sydney's cheek drift down her shoulder then her arm, grasping Sydney's fingers just as the kiss ended. Alex took half a step back. She drew Sydney's hand up to her lips. "Until tonight," she said, still whispering, then kissed the back of

Sydney's knuckles before opening the door and stepping through it.

SYDNEY HAD BEEN home for only about fifteen minutes when the knock came at the door. She could tell from the tempo it was Alex. She had that distinct "cop knock," short and powerful. Sydney almost ran to the door in her excitement, throwing it open to reveal the woman who had been captivating her mind almost non-stop for the past twenty-four hours.

The two stood there staring into each other's eyes, Sydney feeling as if the rest of the world just fell away around them. Alex stepped through the doorway and pulled Sydney into an embrace. Sydney had decided she would have to make her intentions very clear to Alex. She leaned her smaller frame into the woman, pushing her against the now closed door, bringing their hips together. The forceful move obviously surprised Alex and she exhaled sharply. Sydney watched as Alex's eyes grew darker with desire.

Alex leaned down, kissing Sydney's neck then pausing, resting her head briefly on Sydney's shoulder. Sydney now recognized her body language. Alex was clearly attempting to rein in her desire. Her shaky voice soon made that admission.

"God, Syd," she said in a ragged breath. "You're making this really difficult to keep my hands off you. You keep this up and I'm liable to completely lose control here."

"Good. I'm hoping that's exactly what you do." Without hesitation Sydney grabbed Alex by the hand and led her up the staircase toward her bedroom. She felt Alex stiffen as they made their way up the stairs.

Alex stopped them mid-stride at the top of the stairs and pulled Sydney's hand, bringing Sydney into her arms once again. Hesitation was written plainly on her face as she looked into Sydney's eyes.

"Syd, I want you so bad it hurts. But more than anything I respect you and want to make sure this is okay and right for you. I don't want this to be because you feel..." Alex took a deep breath. "Because of what happened, the roses, everything. I want it to be because this is what you want. What you would want even if none of that had happened."

Sydney leaned forward and kissed Alex in a tender but firm kiss.

"Yes," Sydney whispered. "This is what I want. I've wanted you, us, for a long time. This has nothing to do with anything except the two of us." She turned and led Alex by the hand, finding Alex no longer offered any resistance. Sydney let go of Alex for a brief moment to light a single candle near the bed and pull the covers back. Alex was immediately beside her, cupping her face with both hands and guiding their lips together. As the kiss grew stronger Alex guided Sydney to a seated position at the edge of the bed then knelt between Sydney's thighs, leaning into her.

Sydney ran her hands up Alex's shirt and felt the woman tremble as her nails ran across Alex's muscular back. Alex leaned into her, working kisses down her jaw to her neck. Alex lifted Sydney and climbed onto the bed. Without breaking contact she lowered them both to the soft surface, covering Sydney's body with her own. Alex continued to gently touch and kiss Sydney, seducing her body and making her acutely aware of the clothes that were getting in the way.

Alex pulled Sydney up into a sitting position, as she knelt before her, kissing Sydney deeply. Sydney's world narrowed to just the two of them and how Alex made her feel. She kissed Alex back and both refused to break the intense contact for several moments.

Sydney felt the heat rising within her. There was no hesitation, no confusion. She knew exactly where this moment was going and she embraced it without pause. She pulled away from the kiss and reached down, grasping the hem of her shirt and lifting it over her head.

Alex leaned back and watched Sydney, saying nothing. Sydney reached behind her toward her own bra clasp, but Alex leaned forward and caught her hand, stopping her.

"Let me, please," she said as she worked her hands around to the clasp at Sydney's back, unhooking it then pulling the garment slowly away. "Beautiful," she whispered. Alex lowered Sydney to the bed, her kisses working down Sydney's neck to her collarbone, then nuzzling the tops of Alex's breasts. Sydney's arms went around Alex's shoulders as her breasts were caressed.

Alex was still fully clothed and Sydney pulled at Alex's shirt, sending a silent message. Alex quickly moved to help, pulling first her shirt up and over her head and then taking off her bra, throwing them to the floor beside the bed.

Sydney's breath caught when their bare skin made contact. She closed her eyes and threw her head back, lost in the sensations that were overwhelming her senses. She sucked in a sudden breath when Alex ran the tip of her tongue in a tiny circle around the nipple of her breast and massaged it with her tongue as her fingers applied light pressure to its twin. Alex sucked, gradually increasing the pressure on her nipple. Just as Sydney felt she couldn't take the barrage any longer, Alex gave a gentle kiss to her breast then looked up at her, one last question in her eyes. Her hand came to rest at Sydney's waist, one finger running along the inside of her waistband. Sydney reached up to Alex's cheek and guided their lips together in a kiss.

When they pulled away she looked into Alex's eyes and whispered one word. "Yes."

Alex brought their lips together again and moved her hand down between them, unfastening Sydney's jeans. Alex pulled away slightly, then dragged kisses down Sydney's chest and across her stomach as she worked fingers under the waistband of the pants, slowly lowering them. Sydney lifted her hips just barely, allowing the pants to slide off. Sydney was amazed as this strong woman used the gentlest of hands as she touched her.

Alex shed the rest of her own clothes then lay down once again. The sight of Alex's naked body was magnificent. She gazed at the toned and muscular form and again wondered how this powerful woman could be so tender and gentle. Sydney's attention was diverted as Alex looked into her eyes. Her hand rested on Sydney's stomach, then moved slowly downward to Sydney's black thong. As she paused momentarily with her hand at the edge of the lace, Sydney gave a small smile and a nod.

Alex slipped her finger in the waistband and pulled it down slightly. She leaned in and kissed Sydney's flat stomach, starting from her belly button and working her way to the spot she gradually exposed below the edge of the silk. She ran her tongue the length of the thong's waistline and Sydney gasped. Her heart pounded as the last of her clothing dropped to the floor.

Alex kissed her way back up Sydney's body. Soon Sydney was aware of nothing but Alex's hand and lips, which felt as if they were everywhere on her skin. The sensations traveling through her body gradually drove her to a breathless ecstasy.

THEY LAY FOR several moments with their foreheads together and eyes closed. Sydney's body shuddered as Alex seemed to move away, but then pulled her almost limp body on top of Alex, Sydney's head resting on Alex's chest. They remained unmoving like that for quite a while, just feeling the closeness between them as their bodies relaxed.

"That was wonderful. It was amazing," Sydney said quietly when she was able to speak. Then she paused, unsure of her next words. "I don't really know how to say this. I want to touch you. To make you feel as good as you made me feel. But I don't know what to do. Alex, I've never, well, I mean, I've never been with a woman before."

"Syd, just touching you, it's everything I dreamt of. Just being here with you is incredible." Alex gave a shy smile. "I practically, you know, just touching you, watching you. God, you are so incredibly sexy. Just being close to you pretty much puts me over the edge."

Sydney leaned up and kissed Alex, gently at first, then with building passion. When the kiss ended she looked deeply into Alex's eyes.

"I want to touch you," she whispered. "I want—"

Alex leaned up and kissed her. "Relax," she whispered. She took Sydney's hand and laced their fingers together, moving their joined hands across her own breast. Alex's eyes fluttered closed momentarily and she audibly moaned.

Watching the effect the touching was having on Alex sent Sydney's blood surging once again, and she knew what Alex meant—she could feel her own body responding just from this contact.

Alex continued to guide Sydney's hand across her body, all the while looking into her eyes, letting her know how good it felt. Sydney leaned down and kissed Alex as their hands moved together. She found all her fears and nervousness gradually replaced with pure desire. Alex moved their hands lower and the contact felt so good, Sydney was finding it difficult to breathe. She moved her lips to one of Alex's breasts, sucking gently on the hardened nipple. Alex arched beneath her, resting her hand on the back of Sydney's head.

Alex guided their joined hands lower then let go.

Sydney heard Alex's sharp intake of breath as her fingers worked their way freely over Alex's body.

"Oh, God, Syd," Alex gasped, her eyes drooping closed. This was all the reassurance Sydney needed as instinct and desire took over.

Their bodies found a natural rhythm as though they had been lovers for years, moving together until they collapsed into each other's arms once again.

They spent the next several hours exploring each other's bodies, and it was well after midnight when physical exhaustion finally brought the passionate adventure to an end. Sydney lay sprawled across Alex's body as their hearts slowed and their breathing returned to normal. They shared a final kiss, then fell asleep with their naked bodies intertwined. The candle eventually burned out and plunged them into darkness and a deep satisfying slumber.

SYDNEY'S EYES OPENED as the early morning sunrise started to creep into the room. Her gaze fell upon the woman sleeping beside her and she smiled with the realization that the previous night had not been just a wonderful and erotic dream.

She moved closer to Alex, snuggling into her side and placing her head on Alex's chest. Alex stirred and Sydney felt an arm go around her shoulders.

A bashful smile took over Alex's lips as she opened her eyes and returned the gaze. "Hi," she said.

"Good morning," Sydney replied, returning the smile.

"Is everything—I mean, are you okay with..."

"Yes," Sydney said without hesitation, tipping her head up to meet Alex's lips in a brief and tender kiss. "I'm wonderful. When can we do it again?" Sydney's laugh was muffled as Alex pulled her into a strong embrace and a passionate kiss.

When the kiss ended Sydney reached up and brushed a lock of hair from Alex's forehead, an intimate gesture quickly becoming habitual for her.

"I wish I could stay here all day with you, just like this," Sydney whispered.

"So do I." Alex bent down and kissed Sydney's forehead then looked over at the clock beside the bed. Sydney's gaze followed hers to the clock, then her head dropped to Alex's chest and she sighed in exasperation.

"Damn." Sydney gave Alex a final quick kiss then rolled out of bed. She moved to a nearby chair where she retrieved a short silk robe. "I'm going to jump in the shower," Sydney said. She turned back toward the bed as she pulled the robe on. Alex had turned on her side with her head propped up in the palm of her hand. She was silently watching Sydney's every move. Sydney paused as she took in the almost hypnotized look on Alex's face.

"Sergeant Chambers?" Sydney smiled as she stood before the bed with the robe hanging open down her front. Alex's eyes roved up her body, pausing occasionally. Sydney felt herself becoming turned on simply by Alex's sultry gaze and obvious desire. Alex's eyes finally met hers and they looked at one another without speaking for a moment.

"God, you're beautiful," Alex said, her voice almost hoarse. Sydney smiled and moved the few steps to the bedside. Alex reached out a hand and moved it inside Sydney's open robe, running it along the warm flesh to rest on Sydney's bare hip as Sydney leaned over and their lips pressed together.

"And you're virtually irresistible," Sydney said when she ended the kiss. "And I'm going to end up back in this bed if I don't focus and turn around now and head for that bathroom." Alex's hand drifted toward her derrière and she reached around to still Alex's trespass in places Sydney knew would cause "virtually" irresistible to become just plain irresistible.

Alex simply smiled up at her. "Go take your shower and get ready for work," she said. "I'll head down and try and figure out how to make some coffee."

Sydney gave Alex one more quick peck on the lips then turned and went into the bathroom.

AFTER SEVERAL MINUTES of simply enjoying the sensations running through her mind and body, Alex got out of bed and dressed, then went downstairs and retrieved her backpack from where she had dropped it in the entryway the night before. She smiled as she recalled the passion that had erupted between them.

Alex proceeded to the downstairs bathroom where she brushed her teeth and washed her face then ran a comb through her hair. She couldn't recall the last time she'd actually been comfortable and engaged enough to spend an entire night with a woman and wake up with her the next morning. Not since Regina. Even then, the level of comfort, of certainty, had not equaled what she felt now in Sydney's presence.

Alex was still smiling as she made her way into the kitchen to figure out the coffee machine. By the time Sydney came downstairs the rich caffeine mixture was successfully brewing and Alex was leaning on the counter checking messages and email on her cell phone.

Alex pocketed her phone as Sydney approached. She visually admired the now professionally attired, yet undeniably sexy woman in whose arms she had spent the prior night. Sydney moved directly to her and leaned up to kiss her once again.

"Mmm, minty fresh," Sydney said as she pulled away. "I was going to offer you some toiletries if you need them."

"Not necessary. I brought some." Alex nodded toward her backpack sitting on the counter nearby. Sydney looked over at the indicated bag, then back at Alex with a raised eyebrow.

"That sure of yourself, huh, Sergeant? You knew you'd end up spending the night with me?" she said with a slight smile.

"No! That's not what—I'd never—" Alex stopped and took a deep breath, feeling slightly panicked. She tried to start over. "It's just because I get stuck at work sometimes." Alex took Sydney's hands in each of hers. "I swear to you I would never presume—"

"Relax, Alex," Sydney said. Then added, "It's not as if I didn't make my intentions pretty clear at my office yesterday." The mischievous smile and Sydney's reassuring squeeze of her hands did relax Alex a little.

"Well, just the same," Alex said, returning the squeeze. "I want you to be thoroughly comfortable with this, with us, wherever we may go with this. I won't ever pressure you and I want you to tell me if anything makes you uncomfortable, okay?"

Sydney nodded and they embraced. "Thank you," she mumbled into Alex's chest. She gave Alex a final squeeze then they released each other.

Several minutes later they exited the house through the garage, both carrying travel mugs of coffee and Alex carrying Sydney's soft satchel briefcase. Sydney pressed the button for the garage door, then opened her vehicle's passenger door. Alex placed the briefcase on the passenger seat then closed the door, immediately moving the arm not holding her coffee to wrap around Sydney.

"When's your next day off?" Sydney asked.

"I'm working through Friday night," Alex said. "I almost forgot to ask. Are you free this weekend?"

"I don't think I have any plans," Sydney said as she leaned comfortably against Alex.

"My friend Sal and his girlfriend, Tiffany, would really like to meet you. You've met Sal, Sergeant Donatelli? They've invited the two of us to their place on Saturday. I think they plan to barbeque if the weather isn't too cool. Does that sound like anything you'd be interested in?"

"It sounds nice."

Alex looked away nervously then back to Sydney. "Spend the rest of the weekend with me?" she asked. "After the barbeque, I mean."

"Absolutely," Sydney said. "It can't come soon enough." Alex smiled and leaned down for another gentle but lengthy kiss.

"Drive safe," Alex said when they broke apart. She grasped Sydney's hand and brought it to her lips. "Call me when you get to your office?" Sydney nodded, then they kissed once more before Alex winked at her and turned to make her way out of the garage to her truck parked in the driveway.

THIRTY MINUTES LATER Sydney parked in the subterranean garage below the courthouse and made her way up to her office. She hung up her suit jacket and sat down. She picked up her phone and dialed Alex's cell number from memory.

"I've arrived safely," she said when the familiar voice answered. "Are you on your way to the gym?" she asked, having already learned of her daily workout habit. She more than appreciated the results of that habit.

"Yep. I'll call you later today," came the reply. "I miss you already."

"So do I. The weekend can't come soon enough."

Sydney leaned her head back and closed her eyes after hanging up the phone. She let her mind once again recap the events of the previous night. She was tired. She and Alex hadn't gotten a lot of sleep, but she felt strangely energized at the same time.

"You, my friend, are absolutely glowing."

Sydney opened her eyes to see Tyler leaning on the door frame looking at her. He entered and sat down across from her, leaning forward on her desk and lowering his voice to a conspiratorial whisper.

"You have the distinct look of someone who is supremely sexually satisfied," he said with a knowing grin. "You got laid." Sydney could only grin in response. "I knew it." Tyler said. "It's about damn time."

Chapter Eleven

THE REST OF the week progressed slowly for Alex. Her mind frequently turned to Sydney and the strength of her attraction for the woman. An emotional attraction, not just a physical one. Why were these emotions so different than anything she'd felt before? Her relationship with Regina had been comfortable and she'd cared about her, but the intensity of that relationship was nothing compared to what she felt now. Her other encounters with women in recent years hardly deserved the title relationship, they were better described as conquests with no need or want for future or continued contact. But Alex couldn't escape the fact her feelings toward Sydney were entirely different. Beyond an undeniable desire and physical attraction, Alex felt an emotional attachment and attraction to Sydney—a need to protect her, to nurture the relationship.

ON FRIDAY ALEX and Sal ventured into Rampart Division for a late lunch at Tommy's Burgers, a hangout and mainstay in downtown L.A. As was their habit, they chose to eat near their cars, rather than amongst the small number of crowded tables situated around the corner burger stand. The conversation naturally turned to the upcoming Saturday get together and the emerging relationship.

"Syd's looking forward to meeting you guys tomorrow," Alex said as they leaned on the hood of Alex's black and white.

"Uh-huh."

Alex had a feeling Sal's noncommittal response was not entirely due to his mouth being full of French fries. Alex finally bit the bullet. "Syd and I, we slept together." She looked at Sal with a question in her eyes, uncertain what his reaction would be. "I really care about her, Sal. I'd really like your support."

"Look," Sal finally said, wiping grease and chili remnants from his fingers. "You know I want what's best for you. I just can't help thinking you've been down this road before. A straight chick looking for a fling toyed with you once. And you got screwed, my friend. I don't want that happening to you again."

Sal had been there many years prior, when Alex was in her twenties and become enamored with Tamara Walker, a slightly older supervising detective introduced through mutual friends. Their flirtation had turned into a steamy relationship and eventually discussions turned to long-term plans. Alex, in her first really serious committed relationship, thought she had found the woman she would spend the rest of her life with. They made plans to move in together and travel, but everything was always put off for one reason or another at Tamara's insistence.

Alex soon became concerned about a certain male officer with whom Tamara seemed to spend a lot of time. To make matters worse, the officer was a peer of Alex's, assigned to the same division. When she finally confronted her girlfriend about it, Tamara told Alex he was a long time family friend, the son of her father's business partner. She described their relationship as a close friendship. She said that though he wanted more, Tamara wouldn't allow it to progress to that level. She added a fear that if he were to discover she was a lesbian then he would expose this to her family as well as use it against her and jeopardize her career. Tamara was heavily in the closet, something Alex hadn't been for several years, though she considered it a personal decision and respected Tamara's wish to have her sexuality concealed.

This went on for months with Alex acquiescing to the requests for patience, believing Tamara's claims that at some point—soon—they would be together permanently. Tamara continued to express a fear of emotional distress. Alex even offered to leave if Tamara felt that was the best and safest thing for her. Tamara insisted she didn't want her to go, saying eventually they would be together, begging her to continue their relationship in secret.

Alex accepted her role as essentially—the other woman—sneaking around to clandestine meetings, believing she was Tamara's first love, that the relationship with the other officer was platonic.

Finally, after almost a year, Alex got to the point deep down inside where she knew she was being played. She still hesitated to admit it or act on it. It came to a head one weekend when Tamara told Alex she had to spend the weekend with the other officer as part of a family get together. Alex was working the Sunday afternoon when he came to the station to pick up his paycheck. Alex, who was in the station preparing an arrest report, finally decided to confront him. She asked him to step outside, telling him she had a question for him. Once outside she asked him the precise nature of his relationship with Tamara.

"Are you together? Like boyfriend and girlfriend together?" she asked.

"Yep," he said, appearing as if he wasn't surprised by the question.

Alex took a deep breath. "I was led to believe that Tamara and I had a relationship."

"Well," he replied. "She said you'd created something like that in your head. She told me you've been aggressively pursuing a lesbian relationship with her, a relationship she obviously has no interest in. She's tried to be nice and communicate that to you. But you're making her uncomfortable with the way you're forcing yourself on her. She says you just won't let it go. So I'm telling you to back off."

Alex mailed Tamara's apartment key back to her that afternoon and never spoke to her again. Since then, she'd been unable to commit to any relationship, finding company and sexual satisfaction when the opportunity arose, but never submitting at any real emotional level. Regina was the first to push that limit and it was the first long term relationship Alex had since Tamara.

"Don't get me wrong," Sal broke back into Alex's thought process. "I'm not saying Sydney's intentions are the same, or that she's as messed up as that manipulative, two timing whore. What if she doesn't even know where she's at in life? Straight, bi, gay, whatever. What if she doesn't even realize she's using you to sort her own feelings out?"

"That was ten years ago, Sal. I like to think I've grown up a little since then — that I know better." Alex took a deep breath. "Did you ever tell Tiffany about Tamara?" she asked.

Sal shook his head. "Nope. I'd never reveal it without your permission. Not even to Tiff. Besides," Sal added with a smile. "Tiff loves you to death, and you know how she is with her protective, maternal instinct thing. She'd probably hunt down — she who shall not be named — and flatten her tires, or something, if she knew how the bitch had messed with your head." Then he grew serious once more. "Tiff knows something happened that made you afraid of commitment. She's also noticed this seems different for you as well. You're more intense about this. It's clearly not casual dating.

"No offense my friend," Sal went on. "If Sydney were anyone else you would have screwed her and moved on by now, just like every other woman before and after Regina. For some reason you're approaching this differently. As your friend, I can't help but notice certain similarities with Sydney. You can't even be sure she's gay." He took a deep breath. "I'm just saying take it slow, don't get too wrapped up until you're sure of where you both stand. I see you falling fast here. I don't want to see you get your heart broken again.

"Anyway," Sal said, "Anything interesting happen lately with that asshole Ramos?"

Lieutenant Ramos had been a thorn in Alex's side since they were young police officers together at Hollywood Division. Ramos was a member of L.A.P.D.'s infamous "God Squad," a group of officers from various ranks who were bonded through their evangelical beliefs and were led by a high-ranking command officer known as "Bible Bill." The group was known to protect and promote one another within the department, putting their evangelical similarities before professional competency.

Ramos had not hesitated to reveal his chauvinistic beliefs to Alex from their first meeting, constantly ridiculing her and making quiet remarks regarding women not belonging in law enforcement. When Ramos found out Alex was a lesbian the harassment became openly hostile. It didn't help that the general consensus amongst their peers was that Alex was a better street cop than Ramos.

The conflict reached its head when Alex beat out Ramos for a highly coveted position within a gang unit. Ramos had intentionally revealed to the unit's supervisors and senior officers Alex's sexual orientation and made numerous disparaging remarks about her in an effort to destroy her selection chances. The plan backfired. The unit had not been impressed by Ramos's personal attacks against a fellow officer. Alex was selected for the gang unit, and Ramos had been counseled about his attitude and conduct. He was also reminded about the department's zero-tolerance policy for discrimination.

As usual, the "God Squad" closed ranks to protect one of their own. Ramos was transferred to a new command shortly thereafter and his career was not hindered. He'd gone on to have all the right positions to promote, while Alex progressed slowly, proving herself a peer leader, a strong tactician and a well-respected street cop in each of her assignments.

Years later, when Alex transferred to Central Division in her second year as a sergeant, she found Ramos, now a lieutenant, assigned there as the Commanding Officer of Central Detectives. While she didn't work for Ramos, her position with a specialized unit created an environment in which she had to interact closely with detectives on occasion. Ramos maintained his strong dislike of Alex, something the rest of Alex's unit, and many detectives, picked up on.

Ramos was known fairly universally as a "climber" who cared more about his own professional aspirations than he did about any mission, the personnel under his command or even the community. That fact, coupled with Alex's competence and professionalism, won over most officers very quickly. Ramos's repeated verbal attacks and back stabbing comments had little negative effect except to frustrate Alex at times.

"Ramos is Ramos. Fuck him," Alex said. "He's harmless."

"I don't know," Sal replied. "I have a feeling that man's got no boundaries. He's dangerous. He's dangerous to his own people and to anyone he set his sights on, and you are definitely in his sights."

Alex shrugged. "I can manage him. It's not as if he really has any direct impact on me."

ALEX IMPATIENTLY PACED before the window as she waited for Sydney to arrive. The plan was for her to come to Alex's so they could head to Sal and Tiffany's together, then for Sydney to spend the night at Alex's afterwards.

Alex mentally chastised herself for standing at the window like a nervous schoolgirl watching for Sydney's car. Moments later the distinctive Mercedes roadster turned the corner at the end of the street. Alex headed out the front door and down the walkway to the curb, reaching it just as Sydney pulled up.

"I see you found the place," she said as Sydney climbed out of the two-seater. "Any problems?"

"Not at all. I like your neighborhood." Sydney popped open the trunk.

Alex smiled as she noted the overnight bag. She reached in and retrieved it. "I'll just put this in the house and we can head out," she said as she closed the trunk.

"Uh-huh," Sydney said.

Alex smiled to herself when she noticed Sydney following her back up the walkway to the front door. Alex took a few steps into the front room and put the case down, then turned back to the door. Sydney closed the door behind her. Neither said a word as they stepped into each other's arms and kissed.

"How is it possible I can miss you this much when we were together just a couple nights ago?" Alex said when their lips finally separated.

Sydney smiled. "I know, I feel the same way." She forced herself to pull away. "But we have to be on our way. I'm not being late to my first meeting with your best friend." She put her keys in Alex's hand. "You drive."

"Your car?"

"Yes."

"Uh, okay." Alex briefly wondered about the value of the vehicle she was about to drive. Perhaps ninety percent of her annual salary? The thought was forgotten as they pulled away from the curb and she was quickly intoxicated with the power and agility of the German machine.

They drove the few miles to Sal and Tiffany's town home, pulling up to park at the curb in front. Alex followed Sydney to the trunk and watched her remove first a bottle of wine—Chardonnay, she presumed without seeing the label—then a six-pack of Sam Adam's Light.

"I wasn't sure exactly what I should bring," Sydney said, handing the six-pack to Alex. "So I brought a variety." Sydney then reached back into the trunk and retrieved a bouquet of seasonal flowers.

"You really didn't have to bring anything," Alex said as she took the beer. "Sal and Tiff are really down to earth and informal."

"They're your friends," Sydney replied as Alex reached past her to close the trunk. "And it's important that I make a good impression." This was added with a sincere smile as Sydney proceeded up the sidewalk toward the front door.

Alex wondered why that statement struck her as important, but it was. Again she was forced to admit that the way her friends felt about her dates had not been important to her in a long time. Not because her friends' opinions weren't valuable to her, but because she knew the dates were most frequently short term flings with no chance of lasting longer than a few weeks.

"Hello, ladies." Tiffany's zealous greeting from the front porch broke Alex's thought process. "You must be Sydney." Tiff displayed her normal bubbly personality, hugging Sydney in welcome, not waiting for Alex's introduction.

"Syd, this is Tiffany," Alex said with a smile.

"Hi, Tiffany. It's great to finally meet you," Sydney said as she presented the bottle of wine and flowers.

"And this is Sal."

"Hi, Sal. You definitely look familiar. Aren't you one of the ones who tries to keep this one out of trouble at work?" Sydney shook his hand while nodding toward Alex.

"Yes, ma'am," Sal said with a smile. "I try and usually fail." Sal appeared equally welcoming, but Alex could tell by the look in his eyes that her best friend still held reservations.

The four of them had an enjoyable afternoon, with Sal and Alex manning the grill as Tiffany prepared a variety of salad, side dishes and dessert. The afternoon was cool but bright and they ate on the patio in the backyard. As the sun set on the horizon Alex and Sal stood in the backyard sipping beers and playing with Sal's dog, Maestro, an excitable Labrador mix.

"I know how you feel about this, about Sydney," Alex said quietly. "I appreciate how good you're being toward her despite all that."

"Hey, it's like I told you before," he said. "I'm not saying she's out to burn you or take advantage of you. From the looks I see her giving you I think she's genuinely, uh, interested in you." Sal smiled before continuing. "I'm just not sure even she knows exactly what her intentions are, where she intends to go with this, or how far. Remember, from everything we know this is all new to her. She may get to a point where she freaks out and takes the easy road back to the socially acceptable life of heterosexuality. She's what, thirty-something? That's a long time to go before a self-discovery like this." All Alex could do was nod, the same thoughts had flashed through her mind on more than one occasion. "I want you to be happy, but just be careful. That's all I'm gonna say," Sal added.

SYDNEY THOROUGHLY ENJOYED the afternoon. She found Sal and Tiffany fun and accepting and extremely pleasant company. She and Tiffany quickly bonded and they now sat in comfortable padded deck chairs, sipping coffee.

"It's been a long time since she's had someone she actually wanted to introduce to us," Tiffany said.

Sydney broke her gaze from Alex and turned to look at Tiffany with a question in her eyes.

"Don't get me wrong," Tiff continued. "It's not as if our Alex has been without social company. She's not a nun." This added with an affectionate smile. "But you're different for her, special. You should know that."

"I know Alex seems like she's unbreakable," Tiffany said. "But I assure you she's not. They don't talk about it," she nodded toward the two standing in the yard playing with the dog. "But something happened years ago before I came along. Alex got hurt somehow in a relationship and she's never really recovered. They think I don't know, but every once in a while I pick up things that are said, or unsaid. I'm sure Sal is sworn to secrecy, and Lord knows Alex would never knowingly reveal a vulnerability or weakness." She took a deep breath.

"Alex is like a sister to Sal—" she was interrupted by yelling and growling from the yard and they both looked to see Alex lying on the ground wrestling with Maestro like an eight-year-old as Sal stood over them egging them on. "And I can't help but love the silly oaf." She turned to look Sydney in the eye. "You seem to be good for Alex. I haven't seen her happy like this, excited about a relationship with anyone, in a long time. This could be a huge step forward for her, or a gigantic step back." Silence hung between them for a few minutes. "I don't ever want to see her hurt the way I think she was hurt back then."

Sydney was silent for a few moments. She didn't take Tiffany's words as a threat in any way, but accepted them as a statement of a loving friend who was looking out for Alex's best interest. If anything, it warmed her to know that Alex was the kind of person who could foster such strong loyalty and concern from those closest to her. Sydney was also strangely drawn to Tiffany, sensing she could speak openly with this woman she had just met, that this was the beginning of what could be a wonderful friendship.

"I know you must have reservations about me. I'm sure Alex has revealed my background, or lack thereof." Both women smiled at Sydney's careful terminology. "But I've never felt this way about anyone, man or woman. It's so powerful, so all consuming and it all happened so fast. I care about Alex, deeply. None of us may know where this is going to go, but I assure you, the last thing in the world I would ever knowingly do is hurt her."

"I GUESS YOU need the grand tour, huh?" Alex asked as she unlocked her front door and held it open for Sydney.

"Sure, I'd love to take the tour."

"It's going to be a short one." Alex closed and locked the door behind them. "You can probably fit my entire house into one or two rooms at your place."

They entered into a small but tidy two bedroom, two-bathroom bungalow.

"Well, this is obviously the kitchen," she said a couple minutes later as she handed Sydney a mug of coffee. "I gutted it and rebuilt it a couple years ago. Then did the same thing to each of the bathrooms last year."

"Very impressive," Sydney said. She ran her hand across the granite counter top, noting the color variations blended nicely with the dark walnut cabinets. The walls were the color of a creamy hot cocoa and gave everything a warm homey feel.

Alex led her back out to the living room and Sydney took the time to take in the comfortable setting. It was outfitted with a plush couch and recliner positioned to enjoy either the stone fireplace or the large, wall mounted flat screen television. A short entertainment shelving system was situated under the television and Sydney noted several framed photographs displayed there. One was Alex and Sal in uniform, obviously taken years prior.

"That was taken the day we graduated from the Academy," Alex said.

"You look so young. Both of you." Sydney's eye traveled to the next photo, which captured Alex and Tiffany smiling together at the camera. They were dressed in shorts and t-shirts and looked very relaxed. Sydney could see a body of water in the background. "Where was this taken?" she asked, pointing to the second photo.

"Sal took that while we were camping at Lake Havasu this past summer."

Sydney followed Alex down a short hallway.

"Guest bedroom," Alex said, pointing to a neatly maintained room off the hallway. Sydney noted the desk and a small love seat sized sofa. "I use it more as an office, but the sofa folds out to a bed whenever it's needed. That's the guest bathroom." She pointed directly across the hallway at a spotless full bathroom. They continued on to the end of the hallway, passing a laundry closet containing a stackable washer and dryer.

"And my bedroom," Alex said. She pushed the door open revealing a decent sized master bedroom. A queen sized bed was centered along one wall along with two bedside tables and lamps. A dresser was along the opposite side, centered between two windows. On the wall between the windows was a flat screen television, not quite as large as the one in the living room. Sydney walked through the room and looked into the attached bathroom.

"Wow. You rebuilt this as well?" Sydney asked as she took in the large walk in shower and twin vanity.

"Yep, that was my final summer project last year. I practiced on the spare bathroom first."

"It's beautiful. I love the travertine," Sydney said, indicating tile utilized on the floor and within the shower.

She then followed Alex out through the French doors onto the rear patio. Alex showed her the fire pit she had installed recently in the small patio and backyard.

"Well, Sergeant, if this cop thing doesn't work out for you, it looks like you could always pick up construction or building of some kind."

Alex shrugged. "I like staying busy. And I like working with my hands."

They soon wandered back to the kitchen and continued talking casually as they leaned on the central island counter finishing their coffee. After gazing into Sydney's eyes for several seconds, Alex removed the coffee mug from her hands and placed it on the counter beside her own. She leaned in close to Sydney, their bodies touching.

"Have we sufficiently satisfied the rules of decorum and civility?" Alex asked. "Because right now I can't really think of much more than getting you into my bed."

Sydney nodded.

Alex took her by the hand and silently led her from the kitchen down the hallway to her bedroom.

SYDNEY AWOKE WITH the pleasant sensation of Alex's body pressed to her back and Alex nuzzling her neck just behind her ear. She smiled and pressed back into Alex's body as they spooned together.

"I like waking up with my arms around you," Alex said, pulling her closer.

"Mmm, and I like waking up with your arms around me." Sydney rolled over in her embrace until they were facing one another, kissing Alex lightly. "What are the plans for today?"

Alex closed her eyes briefly as Sydney swept the hair away from her forehead. "Anything you want."

"Well," Sydney said, smiling. "I think I'm beginning to know you well enough to figure what you would like."

"Oh, really?"

"You usually get in a workout in the mornings, don't you?" Sydney asked.

Alex nodded. "But that's no big deal," she said. "I'd prefer to spend the time with—"

Sydney's fingers stopped her words. "I'd say you got a bit of workout in last night."

Alex blushed. "True," she said after a moment. "And it was a very enjoyable workout. Not quite my norm, but very enjoyable."

"Then let's go to the gym and get you your normal workout," Sydney said.

"You want to go with me?" Alex said, a little surprised but judging by the smile quite enamored with the idea.

"If you don't mind."

"Sure," Alex said with enthusiasm. "I can probably get you a guest pass."

"Not necessary," Sydney said. She rolled out of bed and started dressing. "I saw the membership card in your truck. I belong to the same gym. There's one in Hollywood just down the hill from my house."

"Hmm, isn't that handy."

An hour later they were both well into their respective workouts at the gym a couple miles from Alex's house. Alex concentrated mainly on the heavier dumbbells and barbells and worked almost exclusively within the free weight area that few women ventured into. Sydney's routine, on the other hand, consisted mainly of the machines out on the main floor.

As Sydney finished a set of leg curls on one of the machines she overheard a conversation between three young women loitering nearby.

"Hey, Vicky," one voice said. "Isn't that the cop you've got the hots for in the weight room?"

"Where?" came the voice in reply.

"Right there, sitting on the bench near the dumbbell rack. The one in the blue shirt, right?"

"Oh, yeah. That's her all right."

Sydney glanced up between the machines and recognized the woman as the same law clerk who had been flirting with Alex at the courthouse. She looked toward the weight room and confirmed that Alex was indeed sitting on one of the work out benches near the dumbbell rack. As Sydney watched, Alex got up and retrieved two thirty-five pound dumbbells and began a set of standing bicep curls.

"God, she's hot." Vicky's statement invaded Sydney's mind, which had coincidentally been thinking very similar thoughts at that moment.

"So when are you going to get her to go out with you?" asked one of Vicky's friends.

"Better still, when are you going to get her into your bed?" asked the third woman with a giggle. "Come on, you keep talking about it."

"I've been workin' it," Vicky said. "I haven't seen her in a while. But now that we've run into each other..."

Sydney saw the two friends smile as they watched Vicky wander toward the free weight room. Sydney's eyes also followed her progress and a fire began to burn in her. She was practically on autopilot as she picked up her towel to follow the woman.

ALEX FINISHED HER last repetition and moved forward to re-rack the dumbbells when she felt a presence beside her. She looked over to see Vicky standing next to her, smiling.

"Lookin' good, Alex, as usual," Vicky said. She moved closer.

"Uh. Hi, Vicky," Alex said. She stepped back as she immediately felt a little uncomfortable with the invasion of her personal space. Vicky again stepped closer, putting her hand on Alex's arm, her breast brushing against Alex's bicep.

"I was wondering—" Vicky started to say, only to be interrupted.

"Hey, hon," Sydney said, approaching from the other side and putting her hand intimately on Alex's back. "About ready to go?"

Alex smiled in relief. "Yeah." She turned back to Vicky. "Nice to see you," she said. "Have a good workout."

Vicky gave a weak smile to Alex, then looked at Sydney who gave a smile that in no way reached her eyes.

Sydney pulled Alex down for a fiery kiss that lasted several seconds.

When they broke apart Sydney remained leaning into Alex.

"Wow," Alex said quietly. "Uh, Syd, you do know we're not at the West Hollywood gym, right?"

"Uh-huh," Sydney replied, fire still burning in her eyes. "Tell me something, sport. Is she still looking."

Alex was momentarily confused, then caught on. She surreptitiously glanced around, her eyes pausing momentarily on Vicky, then coming back down to Sydney. Alex's eyes were now dancing with amusement.

"Uh-huh, both she and her friends."

"Good. She better get the clue and back off. What a bitch."

Alex almost laughed out loud at Sydney's exclamation.

"Uh, Syd? Would you like me to stand still so you can pee on me, thereby marking your territory?"

"Don't tempt me." Sydney said with an amused smile. "Come on, you." She grabbed a fistful of the front of Alex's t-shirt as she pulled her to the door.

"YOU WANT TO jump in the shower first?" Alex asked as she pulled into her driveway several minutes later.

"No, that's okay. You jump in," Sydney said, though Alex thought she caught a mischievous look in her eyes as she climbed out of the truck. She couldn't help but notice the smoldering look that remained in Sydney's eyes as she headed toward the bathroom. She bent down over Sydney who was seated on the end of the bed, taking off her shoes.

"Don't worry, babe." Alex gently kissed Sydney's cheek. "She's got nothing on you." Alex leaned over, kissing the other cheek, then straightened up and headed into the bathroom.

She was rinsing the shampoo out of her hair when the shower door slid open and a naked Sydney stepped in. Sydney pushed Alex against the wall of the shower, leaning into her and trapping her in a passionate kiss. When she pulled away Alex was speechless as Sydney simply leaned back and put her head under the nozzle, then lathered her hair with shampoo. She looked at Alex.

"Make this fast," she said. "I've got plans for you, sport."

Alex had never before experienced being turned on by a mere look, but she was now. Sydney never said a word, and never touched Alex as they finished their shower together. But the looks she directed at Alex's body spoke wonders. And Sydney wasted no time when they were done.

Alex was standing beside the bed and hadn't even finished drying off when Sydney came out of the bathroom and pulled Alex's towel from her grasp. She reached up, grabbing fistfuls of hair at the back of Alex's head, bringing her down for a forceful kiss. Sydney's tongue demanded entry, which Alex immediately surrendered. When Alex reached up with her hands to caress Sydney's towel wrapped torso, Sydney broke the kiss and grabbed Alex's hands in each of her own, pushing them away from her body.

"Nu-uh," Sydney said. "On your back, Sergeant."

ALEX BECAME AWARE of her surroundings some time later as she felt a slight pinch and stinging sensation to the top of one shoulder, near her collarbone. She opened her eyes just as Sydney's head pulled up to look into her eyes. "Syd?"

"Yeah?"

"Uh. Wow." Alex tried to order her thoughts, still somewhat overwhelmed by what she had just experienced. "Um, are you sure you've never been with women before? 'Cuz that was...um...wow." She took another deep breath. "Was that because of, you know, what's her name?"

Sydney put her head down on Alex's chest and ran her fingers lazily across Alex's shoulder and up and down her arm, causing goose bumps to rise.

"Well, I didn't want there to be any doubt in your mind about my intentions, or how I felt about you, or how I feel about other people even looking at you the wrong way."

"I see." Alex closed her eyes and put both arms around Sydney, drawing her closer. Sydney ran a finger around Alex's breast and up to her shoulder, hitting a particular sore spot. Alex glanced down at herself, seeing a large hicky now emblazoned below her left collarbone.

"So you did mark me as your territory." Alex's head fell back on the pillow. Sydney smiled and shrugged and Alex could only hug her tighter as she laughed.

"Well, better be careful. Because if your response is always gonna be something like that, then I just might start paying people to do stuff that'll make you jealous."

They spent the entire middle of the day in bed, intermittently dozing and making love, though in the late afternoon they did find their way to the phone to order a pizza to be delivered.

"So, what are the chances of me convincing you to have dinner with me again this week?" Alex reached for another piece of pizza from the box lying on the bed between them.

"Your chances of convincing me are outstanding," Sydney replied. "But I kind of have the week from hell."

"What's hell about your week?"

"There's a strategic planning retreat this Monday, Tuesday and Wednesday for all the unit supervisors. It's the D.A. offices from L.A., Orange and Ventura Counties, plus the federal prosecutors. We're supposed to discuss strategies on vertical prosecutions for major crimes, mainly gangs and organized crime," Sydney said with a tired sigh. "But Stan called yesterday morning to tell me he came down with the flu, and then his wife and kids got sick. So I've been asked to stand in for our unit. Everybody is driving out tomorrow and the first session is Tuesday. I have some pre-trial motions tomorrow I can't miss, but I'm supposed to be on the road right after that."

"Hmm. A retreat on the county's dime. That sounds nice."

"Please," Sydney said. "It's in Oxnard."

"Oh, okay." Alex smiled. "Not exactly Palm Springs or San Diego, is it?"

"Nope, and I'll probably be driving out there in the afternoon commuter traffic and I think it's supposed to rain. I'm not looking forward to it."

"So you'll be gone until Thursday?" Alex asked. Sydney nodded, leaning back against the pillow, clearly not happy about the circumstances. "Well then," Alex said, reaching for the now empty pizza box and dropping it over the side of the bed onto the floor. "We need to make the most of the time we have left together." She grabbed Sydney by the hips, pulling her downward in the bed, off the pillow to lay flat. Then leaned over her, pressing their lips together in a crushing kiss. She immediately felt Sydney's arms wrap around her shoulders, pulling them together.

By the time the sun went down that evening, the two were cuddled together in exhausted sleep.

Chapter Twelve

WHEN SYDNEY ARRIVED at work the next morning she ran into Tyler in the break room as she went in to fill her coffee cup.

Tyler turned and leaned on the counter. "So," he said, stirring his coffee. "How was the barbeque?" The two had spent Friday evening together and Sydney had told Tyler of the invite to meet Alex's friends.

"Barbeque was nice," Sydney said. She put the mug to her lips and walked out of the break room toward her office with Tyler following close behind.

"Uh-huh," Tyler said as they entered her office and he took a seat without invitation. "And what about the rest of the weekend?"

"What about the rest of the weekend?" Sydney said, shuffling files on her desk.

"I knew it." Tyler leaned forward in his chair. "You spent the weekend together, didn't you?" Sydney gave up on the files, picked up her coffee cup and leaned back in her chair. She looked at him and couldn't keep the smile from her face.

"Yes, we spent the weekend together."

"And?"

"And, it was," she paused. "Amazing."

SYDNEY FINALLY CHASED Tyler out of her office, but only after being forced to share the full details of the previous two nights. She got to her first pre-trial hearing before lunch, then managed to finish her second one by three. She went home to pack, then immediately got on the freeway in hopes of beating the afternoon commuter traffic heading out of L.A. to the Simi Valley and Thousand Oaks areas. Unfortunately, a big rig overturned in the rain on the northbound 101 Freeway and abolished any hopes of spending less than several hours on the freeway. Sydney called Alex once she was on the road in hopes of passing the time away. The cell phone rang and then went to voicemail, so she left a message.

Hours later, after surrendering to the traffic congestion somewhere east of Thousand Oaks and stopping for a quick salad for dinner, she finally pulled into the parking lot of the conference hotel. At eight p.m. she checked into her room and picked up the phone to call Alex.

"I was hoping that was you," Alex said when she answered. "I'm sorry I missed you earlier. So how is the exotic retreat to Oxnard? All you expected it to be?"

"Oh, sure. The view from my room looks over a beautiful parking lot and across the street to a strip mall that includes an adult video store and a restaurant that advertises both Chinese and soul food on the same menu."

They talked for several more minutes about nothing in particular, both just enjoying the comfortable companionship and hearing the other's voice, then reluctantly said their goodbyes.

THE CONFERENCE CONCLUDED on Wednesday afternoon and Sydney returned to her room with a new urgency. The group of rooms was actually booked through that night and none of them were expected in their offices until mid-day on Thursday, allowing them several hours to commute back from the Oxnard area.

Sydney's mind, however, drifted through the afternoon sessions of the conference thinking more and more about Alex and the need to see her. She didn't want to wait for the weekend. She begged out of a dinner invite from several other attorneys, figuring if she got on the road she could make it home by eight or nine o'clock. Maybe she and Alex could get together depending on when Alex got off work.

She took a last look around the room to ensure she wasn't missing anything, then zipped up her case as her phone rang.

"Speak of the devil," Sydney thought to herself when she noticed who the caller was.

"Hey, I was just thinking about you." Sydney gathered her things as she spoke, now even more determined to get back to Los Angeles as soon as she could.

"And I was thinking about you," Alex said. "I miss you. I wish I didn't have to wait until Saturday to see you."

"I was thinking the exact same thing," Sydney said. "I'm leaving now. I can hopefully make it back in about three hours." Sydney exited her room and made her way down the hall to the elevator.

"You're leaving now?"

"Yes. I'm about to check out now. I'm getting in the elevator so if I fade out just hold on."

"You really shouldn't leave yet. When you get to L.A...." Alex's voice was lost when the call dropped in the elevator.

"Damn," Sydney muttered. She punched the button on her phone to re-engage the call as soon as the elevator doors opened and she stepped into the lobby. Alex picked up instantly.

"What do you mean I shouldn't leave?" Sydney asked as she stood in the hotel lobby. "You cut out, what's going to happen when I get to L.A.?"

"I'm not going to be there." Alex's voice, rather than coming to her through the phone, was spoken from lips only inches from her ear. Sydney turned to find her standing there, a grin on her face. Sydney immediately fell into her arms, saying nothing. Several people exiting another elevator were forced to step around them, some looking at the two grown women in curiosity.

"I think we should go to your room," Alex said. "Come on." She picked up her duffle bag and took Sydney's rolling case from her hand. They entered the elevator and the doors fortunately closed before anyone else had a chance to enter. Sydney pushed the button for the eighth floor then was immediately in Alex's arms once again, this time their lips met in a deep kiss. They broke only when the elevator dinged, indicating they were arriving.

They made it to the room and inside before they kissed again, followed by a gradual dance toward the bed. Various items of clothing were shed along the way and they fell into bed as the setting sun came through the window.

Several hours later they lay in one another's arms. They had made love as if they hadn't seen each other in months, rather than days. Then they ordered room service and enjoyed an intimate dinner together.

"One of the other sergeants mentioned this morning he needed to get out early to drive to Santa Barbara for a family thing. I just kind of hopped a ride with him at the last minute," Alex said as they lay in bed together after dinner. "I hope you don't mind me showing up like this."

"Mind? Of course I don't mind," Sydney said. "You answered my prayers by showing up here."

Alex rolled over and pushed herself up, coming to rest on top of Sydney. She intertwined her fingers with Sydney's and raised her arms over her head, pressing them into the pillow.

She leaned down and their lips met. Then Alex moved down to nuzzle Sydney's neck, gradually working toward her collarbone.

"So is that all you prayed for? Just me showing up?" Alex asked, her voice husky with passion. She dipped her head to one of Sydney's breasts, taking an erect nipple into her mouth.

She lifted her head momentarily waiting for Sydney to respond, but her hand kept massaging Sydney's nipple.

Sydney gasped, trying to concentrate. "My prayers definitely involved you doing a little more than that."

Alex smiled and returned her lips to Sydney's chest, eventually working her way even lower.

"THIS IS KILLING you, isn't it?" Sydney squeezed Alex's hand with her own as they rested together on the center console of the small Mercedes two-seater. She'd noted Alex fidgeting that Thursday morning from the moment they left the hotel.

"I don't know what you're talking about."

"Come on. Tiffany told me all about your control issues. It's killing you not being the driver right now, isn't it?"

"Hmm."

"Let's see, you have control issues which include the need to always be the driver and sitting in restaurants with your back to the wall or facing the door, even when you're off duty. How am I doing?" Sydney said with a playful smile.

"I don't think that's really a control issue, it's more of a precaution. I'm a very cautious person."

"And you have an unhealthy affinity for pizza and those carbonated energy drinks."

"Well, I wouldn't categorize it as entirely unhealthy, really," Alex said. "And I'm going to have to be angry at Tiffany for a while since she decided to reveal my issues to you so early in our relationship. I'm still trying to woo you, after all."

"Oh, hon, you successfully wooed me a long time ago."

"Really?"

Sydney smiled as she nodded in reply.

"Cool," Alex said with a self satisfied smile.

About forty-five minutes later Sydney pulled off the freeway as they entered Thousand Oaks, the halfway point back to downtown Los Angeles.

"I'm going to get some gas," she said as she pulled into a gas station.

Alex already had the gas pumping when Sydney came back out of the gas station mini-mart. She turned to Sydney after returning the nozzle to the pump and was met with a can of one of her favorite zero calorie energy drinks, as well as the car keys.

"Here ya go, sport," Sydney said with a smile. "These should help you relax."

The smile was still on Alex's lips as she entered the freeway headed for L.A.

"THANK YOU FOR coming out to spend the night with me," Sydney said as they stood together just inside the front door of Alex's house. They'd made good time from Oxnard and had returned as far as Burbank where they ate a late brunch together. Sydney was dropping off Alex before she headed in to work the rest of the day at her office.

"When will I see you next?" she asked.

Alex stood with her arms around Sydney. "I've got a really early morning warrant service tomorrow. I guess it was very hush-hush and so my squad just got told about the assignment yesterday. I'm gonna hit the sack now, I think. I've got to be at the station a little after midnight tonight. But I can meet you for dinner tomorrow night."

"Is that the Temple Street gang warrant?" Sydney asked. Alex nodded, surprised Sydney knew about it.

"I just got asked on Monday to work the D.A.'s command post for that." Alex was familiar with the D.A. assignments to multi-location, multi-suspect, or other high profile search warrants such as this one.

City Attorneys, District Attorneys, even federal prosecutors would be assigned to command posts and staging areas to provide advice on appropriate booking charges and to coordinate prosecutions amongst the various agencies.

The two women discussed it further and agreed they would definitely get together the next evening.

"You're sure that's not too long a day for you?" Sydney asked.

"Not at all. It's worth it to see you."

Sydney reluctantly started for the door. She did, after all, have to be at work at least for the afternoon. Alex turned to Sydney before opening the door and they found themselves looking at each other in the entryway. Sydney pulled Alex to her as she tilted her head back. Alex complied without resistance, leaning down to meet Sydney's expectant lips. Her hands found their way around Sydney without conscious thought.

The kiss broke and they stepped back, both smiling. Sydney opened the door and Alex followed her to her car at the curb, opening the driver's door for her.

"So we'll see each other tomorrow evening?" Sydney asked as she got behind the wheel. Alex nodded, still smiling. She stood in the road, unmoving, until Sydney's taillights turned out of sight.

Chapter Thirteen

THE AFTERNOON WAS busy for Sydney as she attempted to catch up on the work left untouched the last several days. On her way home she received a call from Alex.

"Hi," Alex said. "How was your afternoon?"

"Not bad. Aren't you supposed to be sleeping?"

"Well, yeah. I napped, then I woke up hungry. So I ord...I, uh, got something to eat and then I'll nap again before heading in later tonight."

"Uh-huh. And what did you have to eat?" Sydney asked, having caught the hesitation in Alex's voice. There was a slightly mumbled response. "What was that?" she prompted.

"I ordered pizza," Alex said with a sigh. Sydney laughed.

"Well, I know you have to get some rest since you're up early tomorrow morning. And I know we'll see each other tomorrow evening, but I'm glad you called," Sydney said, then added quietly. "I wanted to hear your voice. Please be careful tomorrow."

"No worries. I'm pretty sure we're getting one of the boring locations. Probably someone's girlfriend or grandma's house," Alex said. They wished each other a pleasant night and promised to see each other the next evening.

Sydney had been given the case file summary for the warrant service and spent the rest of the evening reviewing it. The intent was to serve search and arrest warrants on over forty locations, searching for over sixty individuals associated with the Temple Street gang in Rampart Division, just west of Downtown Los Angeles. The charges ranged from weapons and narcotics sales to robbery, witness intimidation and accessories to the attempted murder of a police officer.

The investigation had begun seven months prior when three Temple Street gang members carrying illegal automatic weapons had been the subjects of a simple traffic stop by uniformed officers. Knowing they had the weapons in the car and they would likely be found, the gangsters decided to just shoot it out and conducted a surprise ambush on the officers. In the gun battle that followed, one of the gangsters was killed and one officer was seriously wounded. The two remaining gangsters tried to flee the scene on foot. One of them was caught within the perimeter the responding officers had set up. But the second, who it was later determined was the primary shooter in the ambush, did manage to escape and had evaded capture for months. It was believed he possibly fled to Mexico.

They launched a multi-agency task force to not only identify and capture the outstanding suspect, and anyone who assisted him, but also in hopes of dismantling the Temple Street gang and its ability to function as an organized criminal enterprise. This warrant service was the result of over a year of investigative work, surveillance and undercover buys.

Sydney was told she didn't need to be at the command post and staging area until six a.m. since her role involved primarily giving advice on the warrant results and appropriate booking charges. That role would not begin until arrestees started being brought into the command post, likely not until seven or eight. But she decided she wanted to be there for the actual warrant services scheduled to begin at five a.m. She knew from prior experience the teams of officers would be briefed early then respond to secondary staging areas they selected closer to their assigned target locations. It was imperative that when the warrant services began, the time each team made their entry had to be simultaneous at all forty-plus locations. Otherwise there would be phone calls made from friends in the neighborhood to other gang members at un-served locations and suspects could potentially flee or discard contraband prior to the officers' arrival.

Sydney pulled into the Los Angeles Convention Center's West Conference Hall parking garage at four-thirty the next morning and drove amongst barely organized chaos. Hundreds of police officers were gathered there. Many were already pulling away in caravans consisting of multiple vehicles. Others were gathered around their supervisors receiving briefings or were leaning on trunks of cars analyzing maps and photographs.

She parked out of the way then followed the signs into the adjacent building complex and soon found the convention hall that was outfitted as the command post for the operation. She checked in, noting the additional assistant district attorney assigned to work with her for the morning had not yet arrived. She then wandered to other tables and made the appropriate introductions and notifications to some of the other investigative and prosecutorial personnel present.

Sydney made her way to the end of the hall near some tables and a large map and white board display. She knew this would be the nerve center of the operation, where the command staff would be and where the primary information would be collected. She took a closer look at the map and saw it indicated all the locations to be served, the suspects being sought and the teams assigned. She knew from talking to Alex that her team was assigned location twenty-seven. She found location twenty-seven and confirmed the assigned team was "Central VC Squad two." Central Division's V.C.T.F. was Alex's Violent Crime Task Force, and Squad two was the group of twelve officers assigned to her, or "my guys" as she always referred to them.

Sydney went on to note the details of location twenty-seven. It belonged to the girlfriend of a Temple Street gang member. He and his brother, the second suspect believed to frequent the location, utilized the house to stockpile and sell weapons and drugs. The outstanding suspect who was involved in the shoot-out with officers was also reputed to have stayed in the house prior to fleeing to Mexico.

Not exactly the boring location Alex tried to say it would be, Sydney thought to herself. Then she told herself this was a taste of what it's going to be like as a cop's girlfriend. The thought process literally stopped her in her tracks. They'd had a few dates. What was she doing thinking that way?

This is crazy, she silently chastised herself. We haven't even talked about a commitment or anything. Girlfriend? Where did that come from? She had to admit she felt differently about this relationship than she ever had about any other. Was that just because Alex was a woman? Or was it because this relationship was going somewhere emotionally that no other relationship had gone? Was she possibly falling in love with her?

Sydney's mind came back to the present when she overheard an officer announce to the command post personnel that all teams had reported they were at their forward staging areas and the orders for the entries to begin could be given at the incident commander's discretion.

Sydney backed away and took a position near the communications unit. This was a table staffed by seasoned dispatchers who were assigned to manage radio communications in each of the four sectors. Sydney knew that at this stage of the operation all the important information would flow through these radio positions and would be dutifully documented and displayed by these dispatchers working behind the scenes. Sydney had noted from the organizational chart that locations fifteen through thirty were considered Sector Two, so she positioned herself near the radio table designated to handle Sector Two communications.

Moments later an officer with collar insignia indicating he was a captain turned to the communications tables.

"We're a go," he said. "Green lights all teams and all sectors."

The dispatcher for Sector Two immediately broadcast the green light one at a time to each team, ensuring they acknowledged the operation was now active. When the dispatcher got to team twenty-seven Sydney was sure it was Alex's voice she heard provide the verbal acknowledgment. She smiled. Alex sounded so crisp, professional, and all business. She was reminded again how she had first been so impressed with Alex's calm and professional demeanor on the stand at the murder trial, how nothing had rattled her despite the best efforts and word games the high priced defense attorneys had engaged in.

For a minute or two after the green light was given there was silence on the radios, then teams gradually starting reporting their arrivals at their assigned target locations. The dispatchers again tracked the times for each team's report.

"Now we get to see how successful we are," the dispatcher

assigned to Sector Two said to Sydney. She had obviously noted Sydney's apparent interest in the radio traffic on her frequency.

Sydney acknowledged with a smile and a nod. She too knew the next radio broadcasts from each team would indicate their control and neutralization of the target location and whether they had any sought after suspects in custody. Later reports would include the results of searches, to include weapons, narcotics and money or any other evidence that was recovered.

Sure enough, within minutes reports started coming in regarding secure target locations and several included details and names of specific suspects in custody. Then suddenly all hell broke loose on the Sector Two frequency.

"Shots fired! Shots fired eight-ten North Coronado! Location twenty-seven!" said a male voice that sounded as if he was running. "Officer needs help, eight-ten North Coronado!"

"All units, officer needs help, shots fired. Eight-one-zero North Coronado in Rampart Division. Search warrant location twenty-seven."

Sydney couldn't understand how the dispatcher could remain so calm as she put the information out over the radio. There were several quick broadcasts from units responding, then silence on the air. Somewhere behind Sydney another officer switched to the Rampart Division patrol frequency and additional units were heard broadcasting their response to the help call in their own division.

Then suddenly Sydney heard Alex over the radio.

"Suspect is to the rear of eight-ten North Coronado. Male Hispanic, white shirt, blue pa—" Alex's statement was interrupted by the sound of automatic weapon fire. The radio was left open for a second or two as the gunshots were heard repeatedly, then there was what sounded like static and the radio went silent.

Sydney stood still in horror, having difficulty breathing, feeling dizzy and terrified. An older dispatcher wearing the insignia of a supervisor on her uniform sweater was standing nearby and saw the look on Sydney's face. She was immediately beside her, guiding her to a chair.

"Here you go, honey. Sit down here. Do you know someone on that team?" the dispatcher asked. Sydney could only nod in reply.

"Air Three is overhead." The radio crackled as the police helicopter broadcast they were over the incident, then added, "Start rolling a rescue ambulance. We've got one down in the backyard."

Sydney closed her eyes. Who? She was screaming inside. Who do they need the ambulance for? Why isn't anyone saying anything?

Then she heard another broadcast.

"You can show a code four at eight-ten North Coronado, suspects are in custody. We need an RA unit for a male, approximately twenty years of age, suffering from a gunshot wound to the shoulder."

Sydney gasped in relief when she heard Alex's voice come over the air. She sounded unhurt, calm and commanding. Sydney covered her face with her hands, and concentrated on pulling herself together. The senior dispatcher seated beside her rubbed her back.

"There now. Everything's good. Sounds like the only one hurt is the bad guy."

Sydney nodded and quietly thanked her for her kindness. She looked up to see numerous members of the command post staff talking on cell phones while simultaneously giving orders to subordinates. Sydney pulled her cell phone from her pocket but realized she couldn't call Alex. Alex was probably on her phone right now with one of the command staff here. She would be way too busy to stop and talk to Sydney. Sydney decided all she could do was her job, hoping that the dispatcher was right and that it was only the bad guy who was injured.

Sydney took her position at the District Attorney table amongst the investigative entities who would be processing the arrestees and evidence. Another attorney soon joined her from her office and together they began working through the cases as officers filtered in with arrestees, weapons, money, narcotics and other evidence of criminal activity and gang affiliation. Most of the weapons cases were referred to federal prosecutors, as well as one or two high-level narcotics cases. But the vast majority of the arrests fell to the District Attorney's Office, and Sydney and her partner had to conduct a preliminary case review and provide guidance on the most appropriate booking charges.

Over an hour later there was a slight lull in the activity and Sydney leaned her elbows on the table and put her face in her hands. She was drained and finding it hard to concentrate on the task at hand. If she could talk to Alex, be absolutely sure she was okay, if she just had some reassurance.

A moment later Sydney was startled by a tap on her shoulder. She lifted her head and turned to find Sal standing next to her. Sydney wasn't sure if she should be relieved or concerned by his presence.

"Hi," he said. "We have a mutual friend in common who was hoping to speak to you. Do you have few minutes?"

Sydney knew that friend could only be one person. She turned immediately to Steve, the assistant district attorney working beside her. "Can you hold the fort for a few minutes, Steve?"

"Not a problem," he said. "Take your time."

Sydney got up and followed Sal as he walked out of the command post and convention hall into the adjacent parking garage. There he headed away from the loitering police officers to a distant dimly lit corner where a lone black and white police car was parked behind a convention center maintenance van, both positioned next to the wall.

As they neared the two isolated vehicles Sal stopped at the back of the van and indicated that Sydney should continue around to the other side, between the van and the wall. Sydney peeked around the corner and saw Alex standing there, nonchalantly leaning on the wall, out of view of the rest of the garage occupants.

Sydney stood still, overwhelmed by her own emotions and the relief she felt. She once again felt as if she had difficulty breathing and her knees were shaky. She was aware of Sal saying something to Alex.

"Five minutes, Alex. That's all I can give you. I'm gonna go make a head call."

Alex nodded acknowledgment then noticed Sydney's distress. She was beside her instantly.

"What's wrong?" she asked as she reached out to support Sydney, concern in her eyes.

"I was here," Sydney said. "I heard the radio...your voice...the shots...the call for an ambulance..."

ALEX DIDN'T KNOW what to say. It had never occurred to her that Sydney would have heard anything. Her current status involved essentially playing hooky, escaping momentarily from where she was supposed to be to come surprise Sydney and say hi. That and she figured she would have to explain why she might be a little late for their dinner date that evening. She was somewhat overwhelmed by Sydney's reaction. Sydney had been scared for her, concerned about her wellbeing. Alex hated that she had caused this wonderful woman such distress. She pulled Sydney into a tight embrace.

"I'm fine. There's nothing to worry about. Everything is fine," she said soothingly.

Sydney took a deep, ragged breath, then looked up into Alex's face. "I'm sorry—" she started to say. But Alex stopped her, placing a finger gently across her lips.

"No," Alex said. "I'm sorry for scaring you. For upsetting you. I don't want to be the cause of that." They stood embracing one another silently for several minutes until Alex finally broke the silence.

"I'm not supposed to be here, you know." Alex chuckled as she spoke. "After a critical incident like a shooting all the involved and witness officers have to be separated and escorted by a department supervisor until they're officially interviewed. Luckily Sal was here with his squad and they'd already secured their location. He got himself to the scene and assigned as my babysitter. As far as everyone is concerned we're en route to Rampart Station. We went a little out of the way to make a bathroom call here. At least that's our excuse. I actually just wanted to see you."

Sydney looked up into Alex's face once again and asked quietly, "Did you shoot him?"

Alex shook her head. "Nah," she said, not adding that she was more than a little pissed at herself for not reacting faster. "One guy was in the house and went to guns there as soon as we came through the door. Then he ran, so a couple of us chased him out the back door and across the yard. I never even saw the other guy come out of the shed in the backyard and start shooting the AK. One of the perimeter officers assigned to the rear alley took him down while I was diving for cover and trying to figure out where the bullets were coming from." Alex smiled. Sydney didn't seem to see the humor in it.

Sydney put her head on Alex's shoulder then squeezed her arms around Alex tighter.

"I think I might be a little late for dinner tonight," Alex said quietly. "These things can take a long time."

"That's okay," Sydney said. "Come by when you're done."

"You sure?"

"Absolutely. I don't care what time it is." Sydney stepped back as Alex released her, running her hands down Sydney's arms to hold each of her hands within her own. "I'll wait for you," Sydney said with a reassuring smile, squeezing Alex's hands in return.

Sydney looked over to see Sal approaching. "You guys need to get on your way before you're missed by someone far more important than me," she whispered. "Go. Maybe the sooner you go and get this done the sooner you can see me tonight." She leaned up to give Alex a light kiss then turned to walk around the van and back toward the convention hall. As Sydney passed Sal coming the other way, she reached out and squeezed the man's arm.

"Thank you," she said quietly, then disappeared into the command post.

THE FIRE WAS burning in the fireplace in the den as Sydney sat on the couch, staring at nothing. She had returned from work in the early evening and tried to relax after the emotional day. She knew she was exhausted but had been unable to sleep as the sound of Alex's voice during the shooting kept playing over and over again in her head. She looked frequently at the clock on the mantel, counting the minutes until Alex would arrive.

Sydney finally gave up trying to relax and went down to the kitchen. She began wiping counters and cleaning the stovetop, for the second time that evening, as the thoughts kept speeding through her mind. The truth was that up until this point Sydney had been downplaying her feelings for Alex. True, she was confused about some things, but she could no longer deny how she cared for this woman and the depth of her feelings. She wanted, needed, Alex in her life and they would have to figure out how it would all work.

Just as this mantra was playing in her head she heard a light knock on the door. Sydney shot down the hall and was at the entry way in seconds. Her abrupt opening of the door caused Alex to take a step back in surprise. Alex dropped her bag and Sydney was instantly in her arms, burying her face in Alex's chest. Several moments later Sydney raised her head to look into Alex's face.

"Hey," Alex said. "You okay?"

"Shouldn't I be asking you that?"

"I'm fine, really. I promise."

"God, this cop thing is going to take some getting used to." Sydney felt Alex's arms tighten around her and a hand rub gentle circles on her back.

"Have you slept at all today?" Alex said. "Its eleven o'clock and you were up way early this morning."

"I couldn't sleep before I saw you."

Alex leaned down for a brief kiss. "You've seen me now, so let's get you to bed." She leaned down and picked up her bag then took Sydney by the hand and led her to the stairs. "And I really need a quick shower."

Alex pulled Sydney into her arms once more as they entered the master bedroom. "You get ready for bed. I'll be out of the shower in a few minutes." Sydney nodded and pulled Alex down for one more kiss before Alex turned to go into the bathroom.

Sydney heard the shower water running as she climbed into bed a few minutes later with every intention of waiting for Alex. She tried to stay awake, but the exhausting tension of the day, and the relief that came with seeing and holding Alex was overwhelming and she drifted to sleep within moments of her head hitting the pillow.

ALEX AWOKE TO faint sunlight beginning to peek through the back window of the master suite. Sydney's head was pillowed against her shoulder. Alex smiled and tenderly kissed the top of her head then relaxed back onto the pillow to simply enjoy the closeness. Minutes later she felt the head on her shoulder move and looked down into brown eyes gazing back at her.

"Hey, beautiful," Alex said and smiled down at the still sleepy face.

"Good morning," Sydney replied, somewhat sheepishly.

"What's wrong?"

"I'm sorry I fell asleep on you last night. That wasn't my intention."

"There's no need to apologize, silly." Alex brought Sydney's hand up to her lips and gently kissed her knuckles. "You were exhausted. I was just thankful to be able to see you, to hold you."

"You're sure?" Sydney leaned up on her elbow beside Alex, leaving the fingers of her other hand entwined with Alex's.

"Of course," Alex said, rubbing her back reassuringly. "It's not just about, you know, sex. I enjoy being close to you. Thank you for that."

"No," Sydney whispered. "Thank you." Sydney leaned down and kissed Alex. She worked her kisses down Alex's jaw to her neck. She pushed herself up and rolled her body fully on top of Alex, propping herself up and looking down at her with a slight smile on her face.

Alex was a little surprised to see the lust in Sydney's eyes as she gazed down at her. Before she could say a word Sydney's lips covered hers once again. She felt Sydney's tongue demanding entry and her lips parted. "Syd?" Alex struggled to say, her brain barely retaining that last responsible thought as her head was thrown back against the pillow, exposing her neck more fully to her partner. "Your work? Time?"

"Don't worry," Sydney said between nips of Alex's neck and earlobe. "Plenty of time. It's Saturday, silly." Her lips met Alex's once again as her hand found the bottom of Alex's shirt and made its way underneath as both women surrendered to the passion.

AN HOUR LATER Sydney rolled over to find bright sun streaming through the windows and turned in bed to find Alex lying beside her, sleeping once again. She reached out and ran her finger along Alex's forehead, moving an errant lock of hair. She saw the slight scar that still remained at the edge of Alex's eyebrow and smiled to herself as she rose, deciding to let Alex sleep while she took her shower.

When Sydney got out of the shower a short time later, she pulled a short silk robe over her naked form and walked out into the bedroom. She glanced again at the form still lying in the bed. Just then Alex opened her eyes.

"Good morning, beautiful," Alex said.

"Good morning...again." Sydney stepped forward, closing the distance between them and sat on the edge of the bed.

"I'm sorry I fell asleep again," Alex said. "Have you been up long?"

"Only long enough to jump in the shower. I didn't have the heart to wake you."

Alex looked over at the clock beside the bed. She was startled at the hour and almost sat up in bed. "Oh wait, Saturday, right?"

Sydney nodded. "You want to jump in the shower while I think about making us some breakfast?"

Alex nodded. "I'll be down soon." Alex leaned over and gave her a lingering kiss, then got up and made her way into the bathroom. Sydney watched her go, struck again by her physical attraction to the strong broad back and tight butt as it walked away from her. Then she proceeded down the spiral staircase toward the kitchen below.

ALEX STOOD FACING the wall under the shower head, leaning into the stream of hot water as it cascaded against the top of her head and shoulders and down her back. As she reached for the soap on the shelf beside her she heard the shower door click open behind her and turned to look over her shoulder. Sydney stood in the open glass doorway. Alex was speechless as she watched the robe slip from

Sydney's shoulders revealing her fully naked form beneath.

Sydney stepped into the shower and Alex's breath caught at the nearness of their bodies. Without saying a word Sydney reached around and took the soap from Alex and began lathering her back.

"I thought you were going to make breakfast," Alex said when she was able to speak. "And I thought you already took a shower."

"I believe I said I was going to think about making breakfast. So I thought about it and decided to do something else instead. And as for the shower, two is always better than one." Sydney put the soap back on the shelf and began massaging Alex's back with both hands, soon moving them to the sides of her ribcage and around to the front of her body. Her hands moved gradually upwards.

When Sydney's soapy hands brushed her breast, Alex could barely contain herself. She turned quickly to face Sydney, no longer able to keep from touching her. Alex pulled Sydney into her and their chests met, skin on skin, damp and warm. Their mouths quickly found one another and the kiss was aggressive, demanding. Alex pulled Sydney toward her, pushing her thigh between Sydney's legs. Sydney gasped and began to move in a rhythm against her. Alex was confidant the warmth and wetness there was not entirely because of the shower.

Sydney forced her tongue into Alex's mouth, probing and demanding contact. Then she broke away and threw her head back, moaning and increasing her tempo.

This friction, coupled with Sydney's moans of ecstasy, drove Alex to climax along with her lover. Sydney shuddered and her body went limp. She collapsed against Alex, who with her own sexual release found it a challenge to keep them both upright. They stood for several minutes in each other's arms under the falling water, slowly recovering.

Sydney eventually pulled back and looked into Alex's eyes. Alex leaned down and kissed her, gently, passionately, a tender contradiction to the feelings of aggressive sexual desperation they had shared just moments earlier.

"I guess I should go make breakfast now," Sydney said after the kiss ended. Alex could only grin as she watched Sydney exit and dry off, wrapping a towel around herself and retrieving her robe, looking back at Alex with a smile as she left the bathroom.

Chapter Fourteen

ALEX SPENT MOST of the next week in a bit of a haze. Her squad was back to working primarily afternoons and into the nights. She found it difficult at times to keep her mind off of Sydney. They spoke several times a day on the phone and would frequently text one another. Her emotions were almost juvenile, but Sydney seemed to be responding with the same youthful enthusiasm.

They had promised to get together again Friday evening and Alex found it difficult to wait. She'd hoped to meet with Sydney sooner, but Sydney had to attend an event on behalf of her office that Thursday evening.

As it so happened, Alex was soon roped into a similarly unpleasant work commitment. Not feeling confident at the networking skills that higher management tended to engage in, she generally hated the occasional social and political events that her position and assignment required of her. Alex's lieutenant had received this particular invitation but due to a family emergency was now unable to attend. So, at the last minute Alex was asked to fill in as the representative for their task force. She went prepared to be bored by the highly political environment, but knew it was important for good community relations and interaction.

Tonight's event was a recognition dinner for outstanding volunteerism in the community and couldn't be avoided. It was sponsored by various charitable organizations throughout the downtown area and one of them had purchased a table and presented invitations to several senior members of Alex's division as well as the commanding officer. Other tables included various additional officials from city and county agencies and elected officials and prominent members of the business community.

The crowd was growing outside the ballroom at the Bonaventure Hotel as they waited to enter the function. Alex was hot and somewhat uncomfortable in her Class A uniform which included a long sleeved wool uniform and tie, freshly polished leather gear and boots, and her various department and military ribbons. She wondered how long she would have to stay past the dinner hour before she could escape without being judged impolite.

Would anyone even notice if I snuck out?

She was standing off to the side, against the wall at the edge of the crowd in the atrium area outside the ballroom. A small part of her was wondering if Sydney's event would prove more entertaining for her than this one likely would for her. Then she looked across the concourse and her heart stopped for just a moment as she saw the specific focus of her thoughts and desires standing near the middle of the room. By chance her prayers were answered—this was the same event Sydney had been required to attend.

Alex gazed at the woman she'd been thinking about to distraction over the past several days. Sydney looked gorgeous in a black cocktail dress. Her brown hair hung loose across her shoulders and even with the conservative neckline and three-quarter length sleeves the woman screamed sexy in a very classy way. She was by far one of the most attractive, if not the most attractive, women in the room.

Sydney was locked in conversation with someone Alex believed she recognized as a field deputy to one of the city council members. Alex slid behind a large decorative planter containing trees and statuary taller than she. From there she watched Sydney, trying to determine if she looked truly engaged or if she was as bored as Alex was. Her answer came when the council deputy looked down briefly to pull a business card from an interior jacket pocket. Sydney very distinctly looked around her as if searching for an avenue of escape or an excuse to depart. Alex smiled as she moved farther behind the planter and pulled out her cell phone.

SYDNEY PASTED A polite smile back on her face when the council deputy drew the business card from his pocket and handed it to her. The man had engaged in not so subtle flirting with her when she first arrived for the evening and had somehow tracked her down again. She was finding it more and more difficult to put up with his arrogance and was desperately hoping for an interruption.

"Here's my card," he said. "Just give me a call or an email and we'll hook up and discuss our council office plan for gang intervention. The District Attorney's office will have to be engaged and I'm in the position to ensure you're on the leading edge of it. This is going to be big politically. It will be a benefit to the career of anyone involved. I can take you to dinner sometime soon and we'll discuss it."

At that moment Sydney was thankful to hear her cell phone chime indicating an incoming message. "I'm sorry," she said before she even looked at the display. "I'm expecting an update on a warrant service I'm going to have to take this. It was very nice talking to you." Sydney turned and walked away before he had a chance to respond. She looked at the cell phone view screen and smiled.

```
I'm watching you
```

Moments later her phone chimed again.

```
You look fantastic.
```

Sydney moved to the edge of the large hallway outside the ballroom, scanning the crowd in search of Alex, a frustrated smile on her face.

ALEX WAS HIDDEN from view in a darkened area of the concourse, still largely concealed behind the decorative bushes. Sydney was walking almost directly toward her, and finally stopped less than ten feet away, still scanning the crowd.

```
Where are you?
```

Sydney's text reply appeared. Alex read the response then pocketed the phone. She watched Sydney unknowingly drift nearer, now actually leaning on the corner of the large rectangular planter that Alex stood behind.

Alex leaned toward Sydney's ear. "I'm right here," she whispered, placing her hands gently on Sydney's hips from behind.

Sydney almost jumped at the close contact, then turned with a smile. Alex smiled back and watched Sydney's gaze travel over her dress uniform.

"I didn't know you were going to be here," Sydney said.

"Neither did I," Alex replied. "Last minute stand in for my lieutenant." Alex hands were still on Sydney's hips, and she glanced over Sydney's shoulders to scan the area. No one seemed to be looking in their direction so she gently pulled Sydney toward her.

"Now I'm thinking maybe this thing won't be quite so boring after all," Alex said.

Sydney brought a hand up to rest against Alex's chest and allowed herself to be pulled closer. Sydney ran her fingers along the several rows of military ribbons mounted below Alex's badge and there was no doubt in Alex's mind this would be a much better evening than she had originally thought.

"I was just thinking that very same thing," Sydney said quietly, with more than a little seduction in her voice.

Alex looked over her shoulder once again and noticed they were virtually alone in the hallway, everyone else having entered the main ballroom. Her eyes came back to Sydney's lips and her breath caught. She fought the urge to drag Sydney towards the closest dark corner and finally dragged her eyes back to meet Sydney's. She found Sydney smiling at her as if she knew exactly what she'd been thinking. "We'd better stop or we'll never make it in to dinner," Alex said. She took a small step back. "What table are you at?"

"Table nine," Sydney said. "You?"

"Fourteen."

"Hmm. I'll be watching you." With that Sydney turned and walked toward the doorway, looking back briefly to give Alex a blatantly seductive smile. Alex caught her breath and paused, leaning on the planter for a few moments before she regained her composure sufficiently to proceed into the room with some semblance of professionalism.

    Alex entered the ballroom shortly after Sydney and walked through the room, pausing at several tables where various citizens, officials and fellow officers caught her attention. She shook hands and exchanged pleasantries with several people. Alex's gaze passed over the tables and she quickly located Sydney. Their eyes met and each of them smiled. Alex located table fourteen and was able to choose a seat positioned to face table nine. Her seat placed Sydney clearly within her view. The director of a local Business Improvement District, the organization who had sponsored the table, greeted Alex. After being introduced to the rest of the table, a waiter placed the salad in front of her and the dinner presentation began.

    A FEW TABLES away, Sydney was having a hard time keeping her mind on the various polite conversations that took place around her. Her gaze kept drifting to a specific occupant at table fourteen. When the dinner service finished Sydney became aware of her cell phone vibrating within the clutch purse on her lap. She carefully removed the device and looked at the view screen, while she held the phone out of view below the edge of the table.

```
You're distracting me.
```

The text from Alex said. Then another text seconds later.

```
You really do look incredible.
```

Sydney tried to appear casual when she looked at Alex seated several tables away. Alex gave her a barely concealed smile and a wink. Moments later Sydney felt her phone vibrate once again.

```
That's not my favorite outfit on you, but its
close.
```

Sydney smiled and sent a response.

```
And what would be your favorite outfit?

     Absolutely    nothing...as    in    you,    wearing
absolutely nothing.
```

Then another few seconds later came another text.

> Wearing nothing and lying beneath me.

Sydney almost gasped audibly and a tingle went through her body. She took a deep breath before looking up. Alex leaned back casually in her chair and sipped at her coffee. But when her eyes met Sydney's there was no denying the mutual desire that passed between them. Sydney finally forced herself to look away. She tried to look casual and controlled when she reached out to add sugar and stir her own coffee, but she couldn't seem to keep her hand from shaking.

When she looked up again she saw Alex get to her feet and leave her table, exiting the ballroom. Simultaneously, her cell phone vibrated once again.

> Follow me

Without hesitation Sydney excused herself from the table. She exited the ballroom into the concourse area and paused to look around. Seeing no one she preceded down the concourse, thinking perhaps Alex had headed for the ladies' room. When she passed an alcove leading to the now closed hotel management offices, strong arms reached out and pulled her into the dimly lit nook. Sydney was swept into a comfortable embrace and Alex's lips found hers for a quick but passionate kiss. Sydney's arms automatically encircled Alex's neck.

"God, I've been waiting all week to be able to do that again," Alex whispered when their lips parted.

"It's driving me crazy being in the same room but not next to you," Sydney said.

Alex nodded. "I know," she said. "How quickly can we get out of here?"

Sydney laughed. "We have to stay for the awards. That's the whole point of the evening."

"At least tell me you'll come home with me," Alex whispered.

"Yes, I'll come home with you." Sydney leaned in and kissed Alex briefly. "Now come on, we have to get back inside before we're missed." Sydney pulled away, giving Alex's hand one more squeeze before she released it and walked back down the concourse toward the ballroom.

ALEX WAITED SEVERAL moments, allowing Sydney to return to her seat before following her into the ballroom, taking her seat just as the awards presentations began. As the evening proceeded Alex wondered if anyone else at the table had figured out how unengaged she was. She and Sydney continued to exchange increasingly flirtatious glances and subtle smiles.

As the last presentation ended and the master of ceremonies thanked everyone for coming, Alex was on her feet and giving her regards to her table mates. She gradually made her way to the ballroom doors, talking sporadically with various people as the rest of the occupants filtered out into the concourse. She was briefly sidetracked again by her deputy chief and had to engage in polite conversation as he introduced her to several other significant downtown business owners.

When she was able to extricate herself, Alex drifted toward the wall then turned to view the atrium lobby, searching for Sydney. She located her in the midst of the crowd making her way in Alex's direction but pausing occasionally to speak with a few people. Her eyes broke away from Sydney and came in contact with Lieutenant John Ramos as he gazed back at her. The Lieutenant's gaze left hers and panned over to Sydney, then back to Alex, now with a look of barely concealed contempt.

SYDNEY FINISHED SPEAKING to the last person and walked toward Alex at the side of the room. As she watched, the look on Alex's face completely changed and Alex's entire body stiffened. Sydney followed her gaze and it come to rest on an individual she recognized as the police lieutenant who Alex had argued with on the day the flowers had been delivered to her office.

"Hey," Sydney said, reaching out to touch Alex's elbow as soon as she was in reach. She pulled Alex away and into a deserted pay phone alcove. "Are you all right?" Alex took a deep breath and smiled at Sydney then briefly ran her fingers over Sydney's.

"I'm fine, now that you're here."

Sydney let her concern go for now, passionate fire reignited by Alex's touch. The rigid and angry posture left Alex and was replaced by a look of unmistakable desire.

Alex pulled Sydney to her, taking her in a passionate kiss. "How about we get out of here?" she said in a husky voice when their lips parted. "I want to see you in my favorite outfit."

Sydney shuddered at the thought of having Alex's naked body on hers once again. She leaned up and their lips met once more, tongues battling for supremacy as they each communicated their deep need to be with the other.

"God, yes. Leave. Now." Sydney said between gasps as Alex's lips worked their way down her jaw and neckline.

"Where are you parked?" Alex asked between caresses.

"I used the valet. You?"

"I've got a black and white. I'm parked on the street—" They were interrupted by Alex's cell ringing. Her head dropped to Sydney's shoulder in exasperation before she pulled the phone from her pocket, glancing at the screen.

"Yeah, Sal."

Sydney listened as Alex's eyes widened and grew serious. Her own concern grew as she listened to Alex's half of the conversation and felt Alex's body tense in her arms.

"How bad are they?" Alex asked. She paused, then, "Which hospital?"

Alex's eyes met Sydney's and Sydney saw the apology written in them. She squeezed Alex's hand reassuringly as the conversation continued.

"Okay, I'm en route. I should only be about fifteen minutes." Alex looked at Sydney as she put the phone back in her pocket. "I'm sorry, Syd. That was Sal. He was covering my guys tonight while I'm here. I gotta go."

"I understand. It sounded serious. Come on." Sydney saw the internal struggle in Alex's eyes and pulled her out of the alcove, leading her through the lobby toward the front doors. "Someone got hurt?" she asked.

"I guess a couple of my officers ended up in a pretty good fight with a parolee. They fought him down to the floor and were handcuffing him when his girlfriend, who had called the police when he beat her, came at them from behind with a knife. They both got cut pretty good. They'll be okay, but..."

By that time they had reached the valet line. Sydney, aware they were now once again in the public view, simply squeezed Alex's hand.

"Go. Take care of your officers," she said, trying to communicate her support and understanding through her eyes and the chaste touch. "Until tomorrow?" she asked quietly. Alex squeezed her hand in return and gave her a sexy knowing smile.

"Absolutely. Drive home safe," she said, then turned and jogged to the police car at the curb in front.

Sydney watched her all the way to the car, her mind still fantasizing about the evening that was no longer going to be. Well, she'd made it through the week so far, she'd somehow manage to make it one more night without her sergeant's touch.

SYDNEY WAS RETURNING from picking up a cup of coffee and a snack the next afternoon when she saw a familiar form approaching the court building drinking from a large can of carbonated energy drink.

"Good afternoon, Ms. Rutledge," Alex said as she met Sydney at the door, opening it and giving her a smile that made Sydney almost melt on the spot. From the gleam in Alex's eyes as Sydney passed her through the doorway, the effect did not go unnoticed.

"So, what are you doing here?" Sydney asked, trying to sound casual and ignore her own increase in heart rate. How did Alex do this to her every time they were near one another?

"I got a call from," Alex paused to pull a paper from her pocket and look at it as they came to a stop in front of the elevators. "Assistant

District Attorney Niles." She leaned past to push the elevator call button lightly brushing the front of Sydney's breast with her forearm as she did so. "He wants a meeting with some of us about an attempted murder case that's going to jury next week. I came over a little early. Just because you never know what issue might pop up." Alex looked up and into Sydney's eyes. "Or who you may run into."

Sydney had to look away as her knees started to shake. "I'm sure Dan Niles will appreciate the personal attention and dedication," she said with a smile then turned toward the opening elevator doors.

"There are others here I would much prefer to give my personal attention and dedication to," Alex said in a sultry whisper from behind Sydney just before they joined the other people crowding their way into the elevator. Sydney pressed the button for the eighteenth floor with slightly shaky fingers. Alex casually sipped from her drink and leaned against the wall in the back corner of the elevator car, extending one arm outward to the side along the waist level hand rail.

With the other passengers taking up most of the remaining space, Sydney was forced to stand close beside Alex, leaning on the handrail upon which Alex's arm rested. The doors closed and the car began moving up, jerking slightly as it started, driving Sydney to momentarily lean more heavily on the rail and wall. Alex's arm rested against her back behind her as she leaned on the wall to keep her balance. She glanced at Alex, noting the look of feigned innocence on her face as Alex looked upward and watched the lighted numbers above the door go from one to two.

The elevator stopped on the third floor and half of the passengers exited. As the doors closed Sydney sensed a soft touch through her suit jacket and blouse. Alex's hand caressed her lower back, unseen by the other occupants. Sydney took a deep breath at the contact and closed her eyes momentarily. The sexual frustration she'd been dealing with since the previous evening, the urges she had fought throughout the entire night and morning, returned in a rush.

The car stopped again on the fourth floor as several more exited and additional people entered, chatting noisily. Sydney shifted to make room for the additional people, moving slightly closer to Alex. As she leaned back, and the elevator began to move again, Alex's hand resumed its soft contact, this time her fingers inched lower, moving in a circular pattern. The car stopped two more times, disgorging all but one of the other passengers as it moved on to the less popular eighteenth floor. When the doors opened to the floor containing the offices of the various assistant district attorneys the last occupant exited. By that time Alex's hand had continued its stealthy downward movement and came to rest squarely on the left cheek of Sydney's derrière. Alex gave a final gentle squeeze just as Sydney forced herself to move away from the wall and out of the elevator. She turned and looked over her shoulder at Alex, her eyes afire with frustrated passion.

"Not nice, Sergeant," she said in a tense whisper. "So not nice."

Alex followed Sydney out of the elevator and through the waiting area, raising her hand in acknowledgment to the clerk sitting behind the window. The clerk smiled back and buzzed the security lock allowing them through the door leading from the lobby back to the various cubicles and offices.

"So, Ms. Rutledge, would you be so kind as to point me in the direction of Mr. Niles's office?" Alex asked with a slight smile on her lips.

Sydney came to a stop when she reached the intersection in the hallway, a turn to the right leading to the doorway to her office. She pointed in the opposite direction.

"That way," she said. "Second door from the corner I believe." She stood there, looking at Alex, the coffee she had originally left the building for all but forgotten in her hand. Her eyes still burning with frustrated passion.

"All righty then," Alex said, the slight smile remaining. "Shall I stop by your office on the way out?"

Sydney took a deep breath to control her response. She looked around and saw no one in the immediate vicinity. She took a sharp step toward Alex and grasped Alex's uniform shirt in a fist, pulling her forward, their bodies almost touching and their lips within inches of one another.

"After last night, and then...that," Sydney said in a low voice. "You owe me a hell of a lot more than just a drive by office visit, Sergeant." She let her hand slide down the uniform front, sending tingles through Alex despite the insulation of the bullet resistant vest. Sydney took some satisfaction in the effect she read through Alex's eyes. Then she turned and headed toward her office.

Sydney entered her office and carefully put the coffee down with a slightly trembling hand. She fell backwards into her comfortable leather executive chair and let out a sigh, heavy with sexual frustration.

"This is craziness," she muttered quietly to herself. "How does she do that to me?"

Sydney spent several minutes shuffling papers around on her desk, finding it difficult to concentrate. She finally gave up, simply turning the high backed chair toward the window behind her and leaning her head back, gazing at the afternoon sky and trying to relax her mind to the point of being able to do some kind of work.

She lost track of time and wasn't sure how long she engaged in this pointless exercise before she heard a knock on the frame of her open door. She turned to find Dan Niles standing in the doorway. Sydney knew him as a bright up and coming lawyer in the office and she had a part in mentoring him from the time he'd arrived.

"Hey, Syd," he said with a shy smile. "I'm heading for a quick pre-trial meeting with the officers on that drive by shooting I'm handling next week. I was just wondering, if you're free for the next thirty minutes or so, would you mind sitting in with me? I'd appreciate your oversight, just to make sure I don't miss anything."

Sydney knew this was Dan's first complex case, with multiple suspects each facing multiple charges and gang enhancements. His willingness to have a second set of eyes on his case, to not let ego interfere with his judgment, was simply more evidence of his talent and dedication.

"Absolutely." Sydney stood and gathered a legal pad and a pen, a satisfied smile on her face. She knew a certain individual was waiting in the conference room for this specific meeting. That unsuspecting and cocky sergeant was about to be the target of well-deserved payback. Sydney was carrying her cup of coffee and glanced at the conference room occupants as she came through the door. Her eyes came to rest last on Alex and she quickly moved her cup to cover her lips and hide the resulting smile. She quickly looked away, fearing she might be unable to maintain her professional demeanor if she allowed her gaze to linger too long.

"Afternoon everyone," D.A. Niles said as he sat down. "Thanks for coming in. I know its Friday and I'll get everyone out of here as quickly as possible. I appreciate you all coming in on such short notice." He took a seat after putting the stack of files on the large conference table. "Jury selection went more smoothly than I expected and finished this morning so we'll begin testimony Monday."

Sydney took the seat directly opposite Alex, at the end of the table. The remainder of the meeting participants extended around the rest of the table in a horseshoe shape. This, coupled with Sydney's position pulled slightly away from the table, put D.A. Niles in a position blocking the rest of the officers view of her. Except Alex, who had a clear and unobstructed view.

Sydney crossed her legs, placing the legal portfolio on her lap and then casually placed her cell phone on top, concealed from the other occupants of the room.

"I've asked Ms. Rutledge to sit in as another set of ears and eyes, just to make sure we don't overlook anything," Niles said as he looked towards Sydney.

At that Sydney nodded in greeting to each of the officers, her eyes meeting Alex's last and pausing slightly longer. She let her tongue peak briefly from between her lips and slightly moistened her lips. Alex's gaze immediately dropped to her mouth. Sydney was satisfied her devious plot was already in motion and working. She sent her first text then watched as Alex glanced down to read it. When Alex looked back up, Sydney raised an eyebrow and then very slowly uncrossed her legs, shifting in her seat and re-crossing them the other way. Her hand dropped to the hemline of her skirt as if she was going to pull the skirt to her knees. Instead her fingers ran upwards toward her hip, bringing the edge of the skirt higher, revealing more of her thigh. The move effectively invisible to everyone except Alex. Sydney knew how Alex loved to run her hands up her thighs and under her skirt when they engaged in foreplay. She smiled when Alex sat up straight and swallowed nervously.

AS ALEX TRIED to concentrate on what was being discussed, her cell phone vibrated in her pocket. With additional officers within her squad still operating in the field, there was always the possibility of a time sensitive issue or emergency popping up. She removed the phone from her pocket and placed it on her thigh beneath the level of the table, then as discreetly as possible glanced down to read the message.

```
Am I distracting you yet, lover?
```

Alex read the message then slowly brought her eyes back up, trying without success to keep them off of Sydney. Moments later the phone vibrated against her thigh once again.

```
I'm thinking about how much I want to touch you.
```

Alex immediately imagined the feel of Sydney's hands on her flesh. The thought was so strong she couldn't stop herself from sitting straight up and taking a deep controlling breath. She was startled when she realized the room was silent and A.D.A. Niles was looking at her.

"I'm sorry, what was that?" Alex said, realizing she must have missed the question.

"You directed the search for the weapon after the termination of the vehicle chase and the foot pursuit of the shooter?"

It vibrated at her thigh once again.

```
And how much I want you to touch me
```

Alex coughed before replying. "Yes, that's correct. We knew he had the handgun when he ran from the car into the alley, and that he no longer had it when he was taken into custody running out the other end of the alley. So we held the alley and conducted a thorough search. I found it tossed behind a dumpster and had it held for fingerprints."

"Okay, good," Niles said. He glanced down at his notes. "I spoke to the fingerprint analyst today. He's ready to testify on the print match, and the firearms analyst will testify to the ballistics match to the rounds collected at the scene, and removed from the victims. Now, about the driver of the suspect's vehicle..."

His voice faded into the background again as the phone on her leg vibrated once again. She tried to fight the urge to look. That effort was successful for about two seconds before her eyes drifted once again to the illuminated screen below the edge of the table.

> Do you want to touch me?

After reading the text Alex barely kept the groan from being audible. Her uniform pants were getting tighter and more constrictive, especially around her crotch. She sat up straight and actually grasped her inseam near her knee, pulling the pants downward as she tried to minimize the contact to the increasingly sensitive area. The next text was almost more than Alex could handle.

> I want you inside of me.

Alex leaned her head forward and stared at the table surface in front of her, concentrating on keeping her breathing slow and even. Fortunately, the meeting wound down several minutes later when Niles thanked the officers for coming and stood, signaling the close of the meeting.

Sal turned to Alex and asked as he stood up, "Wanna grab a cup?" Alex still felt a little dazed when she looked up at him. She noticed a slight smile on his lips and wondered if he had noticed what had been going on.

"Sergeant Chambers," Sydney said from across the table as she stood. Both Sal and Alex looked over at her. Alex saw her run one hand down her thigh, as if straightening an invisible wrinkle in the material of her skirt. Alex's eyes followed the motion of her hand.

"I have a couple of questions about another case you're involved in," Sydney said. "Do you have a few minutes to chat in my office?"

Alex nodded. "Uh-huh," she said. Then cleared her throat and spoke with more clarity. "Yeah, sure." She turned to Sal as Sydney headed out of the room. "Give me a few minutes, Sal."

"Sure," he replied. "Take your time. I'll meet you at Central City Café. I'm working through tonight and I haven't eaten yet."

SYDNEY WAS LOOKING out her office window when she heard the click of the door latch closing quietly behind her. She turned in her chair to see Alex leaning on the now closed door, looking at her with what appeared to be barely controlled lust.

"Do you have any idea how much you drive me crazy?" Alex asked quietly.

"Really?" Sydney said, trying to control her own urges. "I'm not the one who started this."

"That's what I mean." Alex's head fell back against the door, her eyes remained locked on Sydney's. "Sometimes I just can't keep my hands off you. You do that to me." Alex took a step away from the door and moved toward Sydney. "God, you make me want to—"

"Stop." Sydney stood and held her hand up to emphasize the point. "You know you deserved every bit of that." She smiled as she continued. "Don't come near me, Alex Chambers. You stay on that side of this desk or so help me..."

Now Alex smiled in a roguish way.

"Or so help you what?" she asked, raising an eyebrow and taking a small step toward the desk. Sydney shook her head and took a half a step back. She felt the back of her knees make contact with her desk chair and knew she couldn't back any further.

She crossed her arms in front of her chest, her eyes breaking from Alex as she looked at the ceiling. She took a deep breath and worked hard to maintain physical and mental control of both herself and the situation.

"We've got to come up with some ground rules," she said. She closed her eyes and continued to breathe deeply for several moments.

"Okay."

The whispered voice came from directly in front of her and Sydney opened her eyes to find that Alex had silently closed the space between them. Alex now stood with their lips inches apart, separated by Sydney's crossed arms.

"How about we discuss it in more detail tonight?" Alex rested her hands on Sydney's hips and Sydney grasped Alex's wrists, holding the hands in contact with her body and allowing Alex to move closer. "You know, just so we can establish the ground rules." As she spoke, Alex leaned in slightly, gently grazing Sydney's lips.

With this contact Sydney abandoned any vestiges of control. She grasped Alex by the nape of the neck, drawing her head down in a passionate kiss. Alex's arms wrapped around her, their bodies crushing together, tongues battling for dominance.

When the kiss ended they stood, foreheads resting against one another, catching their breaths. Sydney ran her fingers down Alex's collar, and gently fondled the top buttons on the uniform shirt. Alex's fingers caressed her back and she could tell Alex was thinking of taking the contact further. If that happened Sydney was unsure of her ability to maintain any limits on conduct. And she couldn't remember if she'd heard Alex lock the door behind her.

Sydney laid her hand flat on Alex's chest and firmly pushed her away.

"Go," Sydney said. The look on Alex's face was priceless. Sydney quickly turned and sat down, pulling her seat toward her desk and picking up an important appearing legal document. She pretended to inspect it but in fact could barely see straight and was unable to make out the words on the paper.

"We'll finish this discussion this evening," she said, finally looking back up at Alex who stood unmoving with a slightly dazed look on her face. Sydney had a mental surge of triumph when she saw proof Alex was suffering at least as much as she was. "Turn-a-bout's fair play, Sergeant Chambers. Don't ever forget that."

Alex took a deep breath, clearly working to get her own passions under control. It obviously took a moment and some serious effort, but the roguish smile returned and the passion in Alex's eyes diminished slightly. She leaned forward, putting both hands on the desk and bringing her head down to meet Sydney's. Once again their lips shared the same air. Sydney sat completely frozen, willing herself to maintain total control of her body and breathing as she met Alex's look from only inches away.

"Like I was saying," Alex said quietly. "You drive me completely, utterly..." Alex leaned in and kissed Sydney very tenderly, sucking Sydney's bottom lip momentarily as she pulled away. "Crazy." Alex straightened and moved to the door, opening it.

"Oh, Sergeant?" Sydney said, just loud enough to be heard only as far as the door. Alex turned. "You better drink enough of those energy drinks of yours." She looked up into Alex's face. "You know, so you're sure to be properly energized for that discussion tonight."

Alex paused, and Sydney was once again convinced she'd had the desired effect. Then Alex smiled and gave her a wink before disappearing into the hallway. Sydney finally let her body go, wilting into the seat and moaning. She looked at the clock on her desk and knew there was probably no way she would get any real work done over the next hour before she left for home. She silently willed the time to move more quickly.

Chapter Fifteen

THEY SPENT FRIDAY night together and it more than lived up to the tension and expectations they had established with their teasing verbal foreplay. Alex had been forced to work each night over the rest of the weekend and when Sydney returned to her demanding work schedule on Monday they had once again been forced into mostly telephonic communication.

It had proved thus far to be a relatively quiet Wednesday for Alex as she looked forward to her evening with Sydney after their several day stretch without each other's company. That was suddenly shattered just before noon by the dispatcher's broadcast of a violent robbery in progress.

"Any available Central unit, two-eleven in progress, five-four-six South Hill Street at the jewelry store. Four male black suspects wearing ski masks and hooded sweatshirts. One suspect is holding the employees at gunpoint. Suspects are inside the store smashing jewelry display cases."

A rash of such takeover style robberies had plagued downtown in recent months. The suspects were believed to be gang members from South Los Angeles. Alex knew from prior incidents the suspects would likely run to a waiting getaway car and head west to the 110 freeway to get back to South L.A. Knowing that other units would respond directly to the robbery location, Alex drove west on Seventh Street, intending to cover what she believed would be a likely avenue of escape for the suspects.

As she drove westbound on Seventh Street and approached the intersection with Hill Street, the first unit arrived at the jewelry store and broadcast over the air that the suspects were last seen southbound on Hill Street in a gray four door Honda.

Simultaneous to the officer's radio broadcast, Alex pulled to the intersection of Seventh and Hill Street just in time to see a gray Honda run the red light and turn onto Seventh Street directly in front of her. As the car made the turn she noted four occupants and caught sight of one of the rear passengers wearing what appeared to be a black sweatshirt with the hood pulled up.

She pulled behind the vehicle and reached for the radio microphone.

"One-zebra-one-thirty, I'm requesting back-up and an airship, following two-eleven suspects, westbound Seventh Street from Hill. It's a gray Honda four door with four male black occupants."

She listened as the dispatcher repeated her broadcast and request for back-up, alerting units in the area and any available police helicopter. Alex heard several units in the downtown area broadcast their response as she continued to follow the vehicle, choosing at that time not to activate her lights or siren until additional units were closer. She strongly believed the suspects would not easily surrender.

The two rear passengers turned to look out the rear window at the black and white police vehicle, then the driver accelerated, swerving dangerously across the double yellow centerline into oncoming traffic in an effort to escape.

Now left with no choice but to warn the public of the oncoming dangerous driver, Alex activated her light bar and siren.

"One-zebra-one-thirty, show me now in pursuit of two-eleven suspects, now northbound Grand Avenue from Seventh Street."

Alex accelerated after the suspects, now heading into the high rise business district at the heart of the busy downtown financial district. She heard additional Central units broadcasting they were en route to assist with the pursuit as the suspects hit sixty miles an hour through the streets crowded with lunchtime pedestrians. She momentarily thought the suspects might turn left and head for one of the freeway on-ramps, but was surprised when they made a sudden right turn on Second Street, back toward the Civic Center and away from the freeway.

The driver tried to take a right turn going way too fast, skidding across the intersection sideways and sliding the driver's side of the car into a thick telephone pole on the opposite corner. Alex skidded to a halt, positioning her vehicle facing the passenger side of the wrecked vehicle, quickly exiting and crouching behind her armor paneled driver's door with her weapon drawn. She fought the rising adrenaline to ensure her broadcast was clear and un-rushed.

"One-zebra-one-thirty, suspects have crashed, southeast corner of Second and Main."

Alex heard the sirens of approaching officers as she attempted to ascertain the status of the four occupants of the vehicle. She saw the right rear passenger, who was in the seat closest to her, moving and bending down in his seat. He looked out at her then suddenly threw the door open and ran from the vehicle southbound down the street as the first back-up units screeched to a halt in the intersection.

Seeing multiple officers focusing on the crashed vehicle with the remaining three occupants, Alex holstered her weapon and took off in foot pursuit of the fleeing suspect. He made it across the street and less than half a block down the sidewalk before Alex caught him. Just as she got close enough to reach out and grasp his upper body, a vehicle suddenly pulled out of the mouth of an alleyway immediately in front of them. Neither she nor the suspect were able to stop or adjust their trajectory. Alex saw the suspect reach toward his waistband as both of them skidded across the hood of the vehicle and crashed to the pavement on the other side.

She rolled to her feet, turned toward the suspect and heard the distinctive sound of metal hitting pavement at the same time she recognized a blue steel semi-automatic handgun skidding along the sidewalk within a few feet of the suspect. She drew her handgun and took aim at the suspect as he reached for the fallen weapon.

"Don't fucking think about it!" Alex said with authority. "Hands up! Move away from the weapon!"

The suspect froze momentarily, as if measuring her intent, gauging her willingness to pull the trigger. Alex's finger was already on the trigger and she was more than ready to apply the necessary pressure if his hand moved much closer. Although she was zeroed in on the suspect, in her periphery, she noticed the numerous unprotected pedestrians in the immediate vicinity. She knew she couldn't permit an exchange of uncontrolled bullets on the busy downtown street.

The suspect apparently sensed her willingness to shoot and slowly straightened up, moving away from the handgun at her direction. As the first officers ran up to assist Alex, the suspect dropped to his knees with his hands behind his head and was taken into custody.

Several minutes later Alex was organizing the scene. Two suspects had been transported to the hospital by ambulance as a result of the collision and officers had to accompany each of them to maintain custody. Witnesses were transported from the jewelry store to identify the remaining suspects and the vehicle and to claim the collection of jewelry and money, which was found in the car.

Alex was in the midst of briefing the newly arrived robbery detectives from Central Station when her cell phone vibrated. She excused herself from the detectives for a moment and stepped aside. She pulled the phone from her pocket and smiled.

"Good afternoon, Ms. Rutledge," Alex said. "How are you doing?"

"Just fine," came the reply. "Are you busy?"

"Uh, not really anymore. Just cleaning up some loose ends at a scene."

"Uh-huh, just cleaning them up?" said the slightly amused voice on the other end of the phone. "Or did you perhaps have a hand in creating the need for the clean-up?"

"Why, Ms. Rutledge, what could possibly give you the idea that I —" At that precise moment, Alex's eyes drifted across the street where she noticed a familiar person standing in the entryway to a café on the corner. Sydney was looking directly her and had a cellular telephone to her ear.

"Ms. Rutledge, how long have you been spying on me?" Alex asked, though she couldn't keep the smile off her face as her eyes met Sydney's across the four lanes of roadway.

"Long enough," Sydney said. "We were just finishing lunch inside when you made your rather spectacular arrival."

Alex couldn't help but snicker at Sydney's terminology. "So you saw that, huh?"

"Uh-huh." Alex watched from the opposite side of the street as Sydney shook her head in mock frustration. "Are you okay?" Sydney asked.

"Sure. I'm not the one who crashed into the telephone pole," Alex said lightly.

"You know you're bleeding," Sydney replied. When Alex looked up at her she saw Sydney gesture toward her own elbow, then nod at Alex. Alex looked down at her arm and noted a rather large and bloody abrasion to her elbow and forearm. The adrenaline had obviously kept the discomfort from registering yet, though it looked like it would sting a little bit later.

"Oh. Uh, I guess I hadn't noticed. That's just from a stumble, when I, uh, kinda tripped. It's just a little road rash."

"Uh-huh. You mean when you were chasing the one with the gun and pretty much got hit by the car?" Sydney asked.

"Hmm. You saw that too, huh?"

"Yes, Sergeant Chambers. I had a front row seat for the entire terrifying episode."

Alex heard Sydney take a deep breath.

"I'm going to have to work with you on this whole concept of full disclosure, aren't I, Alex?" she said quietly.

Alex could think of nothing to say in response and so she shrugged and attempted to look suitably chastised. Sydney smiled back at her from across the four lanes of traffic, then shook her head again in feigned frustration.

Alex looked over at the waiting detectives. "Your mere presence is extremely distracting, Ms. Rutledge. Perhaps you could vacate the area so I might actually get some work done without inappropriate thoughts invading my mind."

"Come over later?" Sydney asked. "We can discuss those inappropriate thoughts?"

"You bet. As soon as I'm off. Bye." Alex looked up again and they exchanged a smile as Sydney turned to walk the few blocks back to the courthouse and Alex returned to the detectives.

RAIN WAS FALLING heavily outside when Sydney faded off to asleep on the couch in her den waiting for Alex to arrive. Alex had called earlier to say she would be a little delayed due to some minor complications with the robbery case. Sydney assured her that she should come over whenever she got off.

The first time the doorbell rang Sydney resisted waking from the exceptionally erotic dream she'd been having about a certain police sergeant. The second time it rang she awakened fully. She noticed the time on the mantel clock read eight fifteen as she ran for the entryway and threw the front door open. Standing before her was the subject of her recent fantasy.

Alex stood there, soaked to the skin, rain streaming down her face.

"You really need to check the window or peep hole or something before you go throwing the door open like that," she said. "You never know who could be standing here."

"Get in here, silly." Sydney reached out and pulled Alex inside. Alex closed the door behind her, then turned back to Sydney. She dropped the duffle bag she was carrying, initially startled when Sydney suddenly wrapped her arms around her.

"Hey," she said, playfully trying to pry Sydney from her. "You're gonna get soaked."

"I don't care," Sydney said, pushing past Alex's resistance and pulling her into her embrace. "God, I've missed you."

Their lips met as Sydney's arms moved inside Alex's wet jacket, pushing it from her shoulders and allowing it to slide down her arms and drop to the floor. Alex wrapped her arms around Sydney's slim waist, pulling Sydney fully into her embrace. Sydney ran her fingers through Alex's wet hair, pulling her head down, pressing their lips together more aggressively. Alex pulled Sydney's blouse from her waist and worked her hands underneath the silk material. Sydney groaned with desire when Alex's hand met the bare skin of her back.

The spell was broken when Alex broke from the kiss and they both stood looking at each other, lips lingering inches from each other.

"Not that this was anything but unbelievably enjoyable," Alex said with a smile, "but I'm getting you soaked. I've spent the afternoon rolling around on a downtown street and then doing parole compliance searches on less than clean houses in South Central L.A. I should shower before I..." She looked down at the front of Sydney's blouse, now soaking wet, clearly exposing a lacy bra beneath. Sydney watched as Alex's eyes lingered on her visibly hardened and excited nipples. Alex paused, temporarily unable to speak.

"Maybe you're right," Sydney said. "How about you clean yourself off and I'll get changed into something more comfortable and we'll relocate to somewhere more appropriate?"

Alex's eyes returned to Sydney's face and she nodded. She picked up her bag and followed Sydney up the stairs to the master suite. Sydney led her into the bathroom.

"Take a hot shower before you catch your death of a cold, Sergeant Chambers. Take your time. I'll be here when you get done." She leaned up and gently kissed Alex, then backed from the room, partially closing the door behind her.

Several minutes later Sydney returned, glancing through the partially open bathroom door. The glass shower door was steamed up and the view was obscured, but Sydney could make out the outline of Alex's naked body. Even through the steam she could see the streamlined muscular build. Her breath caught as she relived the feel of having those strong arms around her, the lips on hers. She brought herself back to the moment and averted her eyes from the open doorway, instead raising her voice to be heard above the running water.

"When you're ready to join me, I've got the fire going and I brought a beer up for you."

By the time Alex exited the bathroom, Sydney had lowered the lights and had the fire burning at a low level. She was dressed in a lacy sleep camisole and matching briefs. Both accentuated her sleek build and firm breasts and the way the silky material hung across her body she hoped would leave little to Alex's imagination.

Sydney straightened up after lighting the candle and noticed Alex standing in the middle of the room looking at her. The tight athletic cut t-shirt accentuated Alex's strong arms and muscular shoulders, slimming to her trim waist. The nylon sweatpants were barely snug against Alex's legs and Sydney believed they showed off what she had always thought was an exceptionally good looking butt. Sydney noticed how a curl of Alex's short damp hair still fell forward across her forehead in that classic roguish fashion she was now so fond of.

Sydney smiled at Alex and motioned her to come closer. She picked up a cold beer and a wine glass from the table and handed Alex the bottle as they met in front of the fire.

"Feeling better, Sergeant Chambers?" she asked. "A little more dry at least?" Sydney took a sip of her wine. She licked her lips and leaned up, kissing Alex. Alex responded with her lips, but made no move with her hands.

Sydney pulled away and said, quietly and seductively, "Make love to me, Alex. Now."

Saying nothing in response, Alex took Sydney's wine glass from her hand and placed both the glass and her bottle down on the coffee table. She straightened up and gently pulled Sydney to her until their bodies met.

Sydney leaned her head back, exposing her neck and Alex's lips gently caressed the exposed skin. Sydney gasped and wrapped her arms around Alex's neck, her fingers stroking still damp hair.

Alex slipped her hands under the silky camisole and Sydney took a ragged breath. Their bodies pressed closer, hips and groins pressing against one another. Alex trailed kisses up Sydney's neck, across her jaw and found her lips again. They were hungry with desire. Lips parted and tongues reached for one another.

Alex's fingers stroked Sydney's lean, taught stomach then up the front of her camisole. Sydney groaned as the fingers brushed her breast, then quickly found her erect nipple, gently squeezing. Sydney's breath caught and her lips broke away from the kiss as she gasped quietly.

"Oh God, Alex."

Alex quickly stripped the camisole up over Sydney's head as she raised her arms, willingly allowing it to go. Sydney then pulled at

Alex's t-shirt and Alex quickly acquiesced, pulling the t-shirt off.

"I need to feel your skin against mine," Sydney said and pulled Alex's mouth to hers again.

As they kissed, Alex lifted Sydney off her feet and carried her to the bed, lowering her to the sheets.

THE NEXT MORNING found them enjoying breakfast together. Sydney looked up to see Alex smiling fondly at her.

"What are you smiling about?" Sydney asked.

"I'm just liking the idea that we get to spend the whole day together."

Sydney returned the smile then reached across the table to squeeze Alex's hand, and again considered how grateful she was for Alex's presence. Alex's strength and confidence were reassuring, and Sydney found her emotional attachment was quickly matching her physical and sexual attraction to the woman sitting next to her.

They sat comfortably enjoying coffee together, looking out at the still damp morning. Sydney thought about how comfortable she found this very normal behavior, simply enjoying breakfast together. She wondered what it would be like to have this available to her every morning. That thought surprised her as she realized how early in the relationship it really was. She wondered if she was allowing her emotions to overrun her rational mind and move too quickly.

Alex broke the silence and interrupted her internal debate with a query. "I noticed the path through the trees out there." She pointed with her fork to a footpath leading from the backyard through the tree line. "Where does that go?"

Sydney gave a smile. "It goes through the trees and into the canyon and around a little stream fed pond. It's really quite nice, very peaceful. We could take a walk this afternoon if the weather stays clear."

They passed the rest of the morning in comfortable companionship, spending most of the time in the den curled up together on the couch, reading the newspaper, occasionally watching TV and napping in each other's arms. Late in the afternoon Sydney went out briefly on the back deck. She noted the sky was clear and the afternoon was cool but crisp and bright.

"Come on," she said to Alex with enthusiasm as she came back into the house. "Go get some shoes on and a jacket and let's take a walk."

Alex put her shoes on, tucked her Glock into the rear of her waistband and ensured her sweatshirt was pulled down to conceal it. She then joined Sydney on the back deck. Alex noticed Sydney had a canvas tote bag over her shoulder.

"What's that?" she asked, indicating the bag.

"It's a surprise," Sydney said with a smile. "You'll see."

"Well, let me carry it." Sydney pulled away with a question in her eyes and an accusatory look. "Don't worry, I won't look inside," Alex said, laughing.

Apparently satisfied with the guarantee, Sydney handed her the bag and together they walked across the yard to the entry of the pathway through the trees. Twenty minutes later they stepped from the path into a small clearing in the hillside containing a moderate pond, approximately fifty feet across.

"Wow." Alex stopped at the edge of the trees and looked around the glen. "I wasn't expecting this. It's impressive. Who knows about it?"

Sydney shrugged. "Maybe no-one. I've never met anyone else out here. I come out here a lot in the summer to sit and read or nap. Come on." Sydney took Alex by the hand and pulled her to the edge of the pond to a plush grassy area brightly illuminated by the afternoon sun. She relieved Alex of the bag and placed it on the ground, removing a blanket followed by several additional items. Alex smiled as a romantic picnic for two took form before her, including champagne, cheese, crackers and fruit.

Time passed as they fed themselves and each other and spoke about anything and everything that came to mind. After finishing the champagne and food, they reclined together on the blanket. Sydney lay on her back on the blanket looking up through the treetops, Alex beside her. Alex was lying on her side, leaning propped up on her elbow with her head in her hand.

Sydney glanced over to find Alex gazing at her. "What are you thinking?" she asked.

Alex smiled as she looked down at Sydney's lips then back up into her eyes. "I'm thinking I can't keep myself from doing this."

Alex leaned down for a kiss, and as their lips met she shifted, bringing her body in full contact with Sydney's. Alex continued to shift coming to rest on top of, and slightly between, Sydney's legs, her crotch resting against Sydney's hip. As the kiss became stronger, Sydney put her arms around Alex, one hand on the back of her head entwined in her hair. Alex caressed her breast and Sydney moaned with pleasure. In response, Alex tugged at the base of Sydney's shirt.

Sydney grabbed Alex's wrist and pulled away from the kiss, laughing.

"Sergeant Chambers, you're about to start something we have absolutely no business finishing here," she said breathlessly. Alex's head dropped in submission, her forehead resting on Sydney's chest. She slowly removed her hand from where it had been working up Sydney's shirt as Sydney giggled again. "Maybe we should take this back to the house?"

"Definitely," Alex said. "And as quickly as possible."

They repacked the bag and folded up the blanket, then headed out of the clearing and back up the path. After they'd been walking for a few minutes Alex's cell phone rang. Alex paused and looked at the screen. "It's Chuck Severs from R.H.D.," she said as she answered. Alex came to a sudden stop as she listened and Sydney knew immediately that something was terribly wrong.

ALEX STOPPED IMMEDIATLEY when she heard the seriousness in Chuck's voice.

"Alex, there's been another copycat murder," Chuck said without preamble. "Happened probably thirty-six to forty-eight hours ago. Victim was just found this afternoon. I'm still at the scene."

Alex looked up to see that Sydney had also paused when the phone rang, and was now looking back at her, a question in her eyes. "Where?" Alex already knew the news would not be good. The only reason Chuck would be at the scene was if this murder occurred in the city of Los Angeles.

"The victim was found in North Hollywood Division. As far as we can tell, the last place she was seen alive was at work."

"Where did she work?" Alex asked.

"Alex, all the latest victims have been attorneys. This one was with the public defender's office. She worked at the Central Courts Building." Alex looked at Sydney again, concern in her eyes.

"There's something else you need to know," Chuck said quietly. "And this is very close hold. Just today the medical examiner conducted a comparison of the autopsy reports and photographs from the first three copycat murders and the original twelve by Sinclair. The ligature marks on the neck are the same. It's the same murder weapon."

"Holy shit!" Alex understood the gravity of the situation. This definitely wasn't just a copycat killer. This was, without a doubt, someone connected to Sinclair. Someone continuing the work he began. Someone who now appeared to have their sights set on Sydney and had been working their way closer.

Alex put her phone in her pocket and reached for Sydney's hand and they began walking together up the path with Alex setting a hurried pace.

"Come on," she said. "We need to get back to the house."

"What's happened?" Sydney asked.

"There's been another murder. I'll fill you in on the details when we get to the house."

Sydney turned and looked at Alex with eyes filled with shock and fear. No longer looking at the ground in front of her, she tripped over a large tree root and lost her balance, falling to her hands and knees.

Alex leaned down and helped Sydney to her feet. "Are you okay?"

Sydney brushed off her hands and then the knees of her jeans. "Yeah, I wasn't watching where I was—" Sydney's eyes focused on something behind Alex. A look of terror in her eyes.

Alex pushed Sydney back and began to turn, reaching for the

handgun tucked in the small of her back. She never made it. A fraction of a second later something slammed into the left side of her head. Then her world went dark.

Chapter Sixteen

SYDNEY WATCHED IN horror, powerless to do anything as the huge figure came out of the trees behind Alex, a snarl on his face, swinging a solid tree branch the size of a baseball bat. She tried to scream a warning but was without a voice as the scene unfolded in what appeared to be slow motion.

The huge man moved faster than his size should've allowed as he closed the distance before Alex could react. The branch connected with the side of Alex's head and Sydney could do nothing as Alex fell to the ground, her face covered in blood.

"Alex!" Sydney tried to move to her, but the attacker stepped between them, grasping at Sydney. When she struggled in an effort to move past him to the fallen woman, he backhanded her across the side of the head. Sydney was thrown several feet across the clearing where her back struck a tree and she fell to the ground.

Sydney collapsed, dizzy and struggling for breath, her ears ringing and the side of her head throbbing. She saw through teary eyes as the man leaned over Alex's still form, searching her clothing and removing Alex's cell phone, tossing it aside into the brush. He pulled Alex's sweatshirt up and rolled her over, then removed the handgun from her rear waistband. The man straightened up and turned back to Sydney, advancing on her with a leering smile.

Sydney tried to crawl backwards away from the approaching form as she looked frantically for an avenue of escape. She ran into something solid blocking her way and she found her back against another tree. She saw the man's smile grow, apparently amused by her efforts. As he loomed over her, her fear increased as she became very aware of his size. He was at least six-two and stocky with a shaved head. She looked at his face and into his eyes and Sydney felt she was seeing into a soul that was completely without compassion or conscience. She knew immediately that any plea on her part would only prove fruitless. She looked again toward Alex, hoping to see movement, some sign of life, but she remained motionless. Her terror grew.

Sydney rolled to her knees and attempted to climb to her feet to run but the man grabbed at the front of her sweatshirt, fisting the material and holding her effortlessly. With Alex's handgun still grasped in one hand, he pushed her to the ground on her back, lowering himself to his knees and straddling her hips. Sydney struggled against him, trying to pry her shirt from his grasp and he laughed out loud. The weight of his lower body trapped her upper legs and hips to the ground with no effort. He released his hold on her shirt and reached down toward her waist with his now free hand.

Sydney struggled more violently when she determined his intent. In desperation she flailed her fists at his arms and face, then finally scratched at his face and neck as she screamed for him to stop. The smile on his face dimmed momentarily, then before Sydney could raise her arms in defense he brought his fist forward against the side of her face. The blow sent her head backwards, striking the ground beneath her. She was once again stunned by the impact. His hands returned to her waist area.

"He said I could have you first," the giant man kept repeating as he began to unsnap and unzip her jeans.

ALEX'S FIRST CONSCIOUS knowledge was an incredible pain in her head. After a moment she heard the sound of a struggle and recognized Sydney's voice crying out in pain and resistance. Mustering her energy she rolled to her side and saw Sydney lying on the ground several yards away. A large man was crouched over her with a gun in one hand. He grabbed at the front of Sydney's pants and then punched Sydney as she struggled against him. Anger filled her with the adrenaline she needed. She fought the dizziness as she climbed to her knees, grasping a nearby tree and struggling to her feet. Then she launched herself at the form stooped over Sydney.

Alex hit the man in a football style tackle, shoulders down, ramming his upper body from the side, knocking him clear of Sydney and throwing both of them to the ground a considerable distance away. The handgun flew from his hands, landing in the dirt roughly halfway between the two of them.

"Run, Syd! Just run!"

The man jumped to his feet far too quickly and Alex struggled up once again, fighting the ongoing dizziness, determined to stand between the attacker and Sydney. She glanced at Sydney and saw her hesitate. "Go!" Alex yelled again. Their eyes met, then Sydney turned and fled, running up the path in the direction of her house.

Alex saw the attacker's eyes follow Sydney and knew she had to keep his mind on her. She moved laterally toward the handgun and his eyes moved back to follow her. He moved quickly, closing in on the weapon ahead of her. His fingers were just brushing the handgun's frame when she finally met him, again bowling bodily into him. He fell to the ground on his back and Alex managed to position herself above him and quickly brought a knee into his ribcage, resulting in a satisfying grunt of pain. He was quick to recover while Alex's energy was draining. The feelings of exhaustion, dizziness and nausea were almost overwhelming. She knew in her current physical state she would be unable to continue very long in a one-on-one, close quarters combat scenario. She simply hoped to fight long enough to give Sydney time to get herself to safety and call for help.

Alex and the man struggled for several moments, and Alex delivered several elbow strikes, driving his head back. Alex looked with satisfaction as the blood streamed down his face. Then he lashed out with a fist. The strike seemed to pass effortlessly through her defenses, striking her on the left side of the head where he had already done the initial damage with the wooden staff.

She reeled backwards and was unable to stay on her feet. She fell to the ground in agony, seeing stars, feeling nauseous, and fighting unconsciousness. She battled through it, knowing what was at stake, and forced herself to rise to her feet. She focused on him and then once again charged back at the man, who was now also on his feet. As she stormed forward she realized what she had missed while she was struggling in near blackness. The man had retrieved the handgun from the ground nearby and was now bringing it to bear on her.

For a fraction of a second she stared down the dark muzzle, then heard the sharp crack of the weapon firing. Alex felt a shocking pain to the left side of her torso. The momentum of her charge still carried her into the man, knocking him back and over a nearby fallen tree limb. She had a vague sense of the handgun falling to the ground nearby as she fell on top of him. Instinctively, her hand closed over a nearby rock. Alex was thrown off the attacker, his strength clearly overpowering her. But she stretched out, aiming for his face, and hitting him with the rock as she fell. She connected with a glancing blow to the side of his head, then she was once again on her back on the ground, dizzy and nearly out of breath. She looked to her right and saw her handgun lying nearby. She struggled to roll toward it, reaching out and taking a grip then bringing it up to aim. The attacker was no longer there. Alex heard crashing in the underbrush and observed him running deeper into the woods. She tried to bring the handgun up to take aim at his retreating back, but her eyesight wavered with dizziness and she was unable to maintain a sight picture on the fleeing figure. Within seconds he had disappeared out of sight.

Alex glanced down and pulled her left hand away from her side where she had been unconsciously grasping at her own torso. Her hand came away covered in blood and she realized she'd been shot. With that realization the pain set in, almost doubling her over. Again she fought through the pain, determined to follow Sydney to the house. She was scared to death the attacker might circle around in the woods and approach the residence before help arrived. Sydney was alone at the house. Alex had to get to her. Struggling to move, she slowly began the walk up the path, moving from tree to tree as she leaned on them for support.

SYDNEY RACED BACK up the path as fast as her legs would take her. She'd struggled momentarily with the internal battle. Part of her felt her place was to stay and help Alex. But with Alex's second command to run she had. She was now set on making it to the house to get help for Alex. As she ran her mind registered the growing darkness as the sun continued to set. The terrain became more treacherous and she found it harder to see. She tripped and fell several times, but refused to slow. She was approaching her back yard when she heard the shot. She paused momentarily, terrified of what it might mean, and then continued up the path. It seemed far too long before she broke out of the trees and across the backyard. She quickly unlocked and entered the house, snatched the phone from the wall and dialed nine-one-one.

"Nine-one-one emergency. What are you reporting?" came the voice of the dispatcher.

"We need help. Shots fired. Officer needs help!" Sydney repeated the words she had heard over the radio just days prior, figuring it would bring assistance faster. "We were attacked by a man in the woods behind eighty-two ten Summit Ridge Road. There's an off duty police officer fighting with him and I've now heard gunshots!"

"You're at eight-two-one-zero Summit Ridge Road?"

Sydney confirmed her address then listened as the dispatcher repeated the information, presumably over the radio frequency that would dispatch officers to the scene. She then began asking Sydney a series of questions regarding the suspect, his appearance, who the officer was and what she looked like. Sydney provided all the information she could, emphasizing that Alex was already injured and that an ambulance was also needed. The dispatcher assured her officers and an ambulance were already en route, but Sydney knew it would be several minutes before anyone would arrive at the secluded canyon location.

Sydney watched through the window, hoping to see some evidence of Alex, while she gave the dispatcher the requested information. She saw movement at the edge of the trees and watched a figure emerge, stooped over and moving slowly. In the darkness Sydney was unable to tell who it was so she watched, unmoving and unspeaking as the dispatcher continued to ask if she was there and if she was all right. Sydney saw the figure stumble and fall at the edge of the deck, just within the envelope of the rear patio lights. Sydney recognized Alex as she struggled to rise. Her face was covered in blood.

Sydney dropped the phone, threw open the French doors and bolted across the deck to Alex's side. She grasped Alex around the waist and helped her toward the open doors, looking back and around her as they moved, afraid the attacker would emerge from the trees at any moment. Once inside she turned to lock the doors as Alex picked up the discarded phone on the counter. Alex gave hurried information on the suspect and his direction of travel through the woods.

Sydney was shocked at Alex's appearance. Blood covered her face and had spread down the front of her sweatshirt. She was leaning heavily on the counter and her breathing was labored. Her speech slowed and it looked to Sydney as if simply holding the phone was becoming a challenge. Sydney moved quickly to the kitchen and grabbed clean hand towels from a drawer. She returned just as Alex began slipping down the side of the counter in obvious exhaustion. Sydney tried to steady her, slowing her fall. The phone slipped from Alex's hands to the floor, now forgotten by both women.

Alex came to rest sitting on the tile, slouched against the base of the counter with the handgun still clutched in her right hand. It was obvious she was fighting unconsciousness. Sydney used one of the towels and gently wiped the head wound, noting the large gash along Alex's forehead and temple. As she did Alex's drowsy eyes studied Sydney's face, coming to rest on the split and bloodied lip. Alex's eyes grew wider for a moment and she released the weapon, bringing her right hand up and gently caressing Sydney's face.

"You're hurt," she whispered. Sydney brought her own hand up to meet Alex's and her eyes watered.

"Don't worry about me, I'm fine," she said as she fought to maintain her composure. She continued her inspection of Alex's injuries, silently pleading for the ambulance to arrive more quickly. The head wound had bled heavily and Sydney initially thought this was the cause of all the blood on Alex's sweatshirt. But then she saw Alex grasping at her left side, just above the waist of her jeans. Sydney drew a sharp breath as she noticed the fresh pattern of blood soaking the sweatshirt material and spreading outward from beneath Alex's bloody hand.

She mentally prepared herself for what she might see, then reached down and gently tried to remove Alex's hand. She felt Alex weakly resist and she looked into her eyes.

"Let me help," Sydney said. "I need to look."

Alex gave an almost invisible nod, then her eyes closed and she let her hand fall away to the side. Sydney moved the sweatshirt up, and then pulled away the t-shirt beneath, revealing what Sydney knew had to be a bullet wound. She gently placed one of the folded towels against the wound and applied pressure. Alex gasped in pain and her hand came back up to cover Sydney's. Fresh tears came to Sydney's eyes as she looked Alex in the face.

"I'm sorry," she said and touched Alex's cheek softly. "I have to stop the bleeding." She saw a weak smile come to Alex's lips as her eyes opened and she looked at Sydney. Alex's hand came up and took Sydney's hand in hers.

"You're doing great," Alex whispered. "We're gonna be fine." Alex gently squeezed Sydney's hand, then her eyes closed once again.

At that moment Sydney heard approaching sirens. She gently disengaged her hands from Alex's and ran for the door. Sydney exited onto the front porch and waited impatiently as the first police officers were arriving at the base of the driveway many with their weapons drawn. A sergeant, identified by the stripes on his uniform sleeve, approached her quickly.

"Where's the officer?" he said with no introduction.

"She's in the kitchen at the back. She's been shot," Sydney answered as she led him into the house and made her way back to Alex

"And the suspect?" he asked as they walked rapidly, followed by several other officers.

"I last saw him in the woods out the back. I heard Alex tell the dispatcher he ran westbound from the path." At that moment they entered the kitchen. Alex hadn't moved.

The sergeant paused for a fraction of second. "Shit," he said then knelt beside Alex and took her hand. "Alex!" he said, prodding her to respond. "Come on, kid. Wake up and talk to me."

Sydney saw Alex's eyes flutter and she looked up at the sergeant, a look of recognition passing momentarily across her face.

"The R.A.'s almost here, Alex. Hold on for me." The sergeant put Alex's hand down gently, stood up and was immediately in charge again as more officers arrived. He turned to Sydney as she went to her knees next to Alex, again applying pressure to the towel at Alex's side.

"Where exactly in the woods were you?"

"Down that path about a third of a mile," Sydney said as she partially turned and pointed to the footpath at the edge of the trees. "You'll find a bag with a blanket that I dropped." The sergeant nodded.

"Sandoval, you're here with Sergeant Chambers. You stay with them all the way to the hospital and get anything either of them may need," he said, clearly indicating that taking care of Sydney was included in that responsibility.

"Jacobs, get down the driveway and guide the paramedics in here as soon as the R.A. pulls up. Sanchez, Eldridge, Thomas and Deamer, you guys are perimeter security, we have no idea where the bad guy is right now, so you protect this house. The rest of you, you're with me." Without saying anything further he turned and exited via the French doors, followed by four officers.

Moments later Officer Sandoval returned, leading four paramedics behind him. They immediately surrounded Alex and began providing medical care. Sydney was forced to stand and back away to make room for them. She stood silently watching, crossing her arms in front of her and holding tight in an effort to keep control of herself physically and emotionally. She grew more concerned as she noticed Alex was clearly unconscious. When the paramedics carefully rolled Alex over she gasped as she heard one of them say, "I've got a second bullet wound here. Looks like we've got entry and exit."

They soon had Alex on a gurney and began wheeling her out of the house. Sydney and Officer Sandoval followed close behind. As they loaded Alex's unmoving form in the back of a waiting ambulance,

Sydney asked, "Can I ride with her? Please?" She looked first to Officer Sandoval, then to the paramedics. One of them looked to the officer who gave a slight nod.

"Yes, ma'am," the paramedic said. "Come this way." He led her to a side door of the ambulance and helped her up to a cushioned bench seat near the head of the stretcher. The second paramedic was already inside the ambulance beside Alex, hanging a clear bag of solution which fed a line to an intravenous needle now in Alex's arm.

"I'll follow right behind you." Sydney heard Officer Sandoval say. "I'll meet you at the hospital."

Sydney heard the siren activate as the ambulance pulled away to begin the drive to the hospital. Her attention was focused on Alex, who lay unmoving on the stretcher, eyes still closed. She watched as the paramedic placed an oxygen mask over Alex's nose and mouth and placed the small oxygen tank between Alex's knees on the stretcher. The paramedic asked her if she had been present when Alex was injured.

"I was there when she got hit in the head, but not when...when she was shot."

"How did the head wound happen?"

Sydney struggled to tell him, the terrifying image rolling once again through her mind. "He...the man...he swung a tree branch at her head...like a baseball bat."

"Was she able to defend herself at all? Deflect the blow in any way?" The paramedic leaned over and lifted Alex's eyelids, shining a small penlight at one pupil then the other.

"No...she didn't even see it coming."

The paramedic nodded and entered the details onto the electronic data pad.

Sydney stroked Alex's cheek, willing her to open her eyes. Soon afterwards the ambulance slowed and came to a stop. The paramedic tending to Alex was immediately out the doors when they opened, reaching back and pulling the stretcher from the ambulance. Sydney followed close behind and as soon as her feet hit the pavement she reached out and took Alex's hand. Committed to staying close to Alex as long as she could, Sydney remained beside the stretcher as it entered the emergency room doors. She looked up to see the E.R. crew moving to meet the gurney and her eyes fell on a familiar figure. There was no mistaking Tiffany's shocked expression, then as Sydney watched a professional mask fell over her face.

The paramedics were yelling vital signs and information on the nature of the injuries as the stretcher was wheeled into a nearby emergency bay. Sydney shifted slightly out of the way as they moved Alex from the stretcher onto the bed. Tiffany assisted in hanging the I.V. bag, starting oxygen and connecting additional monitoring devices. The E.R. doctors began collecting additional vital signs and carefully removed the bandages covering the gunshot wound. Meanwhile, another nurse began cutting away Alex's clothes.

Still standing off to the side, largely forgotten by the medical staff, Sydney watched as Tiffany leaned over and quietly whispered to Alex.

"You're doing great, Alex. You're going to be fine." One of the doctors yelled out the order to draw blood for typing and Tiffany quickly responded.

"She's O-Positive and she has no allergies." Both doctors looked at Tiffany.

"Tiffany, do you know this officer?" one doctor asked. Tiffany nodded. "Tiffany, we've got enough E.R. staff. The swing shift already came on. You need to let us handle this." Sydney thought that Tiffany was going to argue, then the nurse looked over at Sydney standing silently nearby. She nodded at the doctor and stepped back. As the work around Alex continued, Tiffany moved away and joined Sydney.

"Come on," she said. "She's in the best of hands. We need to let them work."

Sydney allowed Tiffany to guide her out of the E.R. bay then down the hallway and into a small private family waiting room. As soon as the door closed Sydney began to shake. By the time Tiffany sat down beside her she could no longer keep the sobs contained. She collapsed against Tiffany's shoulder. Tiffany leaned over and took a box of tissues from a nearby coffee table, offering them to Sydney.

When Sydney's sobs died down Tiffany rubbed her back. "I've got to call Sal. Then I'm going to get some stuff and we'll get you cleaned up." Tiffany kept one arm around Sydney as she pulled her cell phone from her pocket. In the silence of the empty room Sydney could hear the voice come through Sydney's phone.

"Hey, babe," Sal's voice answered on the second ring. "Are you on your way home?"

"Sal, you need to come to the hospital. They brought Alex in. She's been shot."

"What? What happened?"

"I don't have the whole story yet. She was with Syd and it looks like there was some kind of attack. I was only in the E.R. for a few minutes. It looks serious but I don't think it's fatal." Sydney felt Tiffany's arm tighten around her, sending a sense of reassurance.

"Drive carefully. There's no point in rushing. It'll be a while before we know anything."

THE NEXT FEW hours passed as an exhausting, confusing whirlwind for Sydney. Tiffany helped her clean up, treating her split lip and giving her an ice pack for her swollen cheek. Sal arrived and shortly thereafter various detectives and command staff members made their way to the hospital. Detectives from Hollywood Division interviewed Sydney briefly, then Chuck Severs arrived and took over. Sydney immediately recognized him as the detective from R.H.D. who had responded after the bouquet of white roses was delivered to her office.

"I know this isn't the best time for you," Detective Severs said after he sat down next to Sydney. "But it's important we get as much information as we can as quickly as possible." Sydney nodded and the detective continued. "I've spoken to my partner. He's at your house walking the scene, so I have a bit of an understanding of where you were. Can you tell me what happened?" Sydney took a deep breath to steady herself and then began her story.

"We were on our way back to the house, coming up the path through the trees. It was right after you called Alex." She looked up and saw the detective nod. "I don't know where he came from. I had tripped and Alex helped me up when he just suddenly appeared. He had a large branch." Sydney couldn't keep the tears from her eyes as she once again relived the attack. "I just froze...I didn't even warn her." Sydney sobbed as the guilt washed over her. "Maybe if I had said something she could have defended herself."

"Hey, none of this is your fault. He was lying in wait and timed his attack for when he could do the most damage." Detective Severs reached for a nearby box of tissues, handing one to Sydney. "I seriously doubt if anything you could have done in that split second would have made a difference."

Sydney wiped her eyes then gathered herself to continue.

"Alex seemed to realize something was wrong at the last moment. She started to turn, but he was already swinging at...at her head." She looked up to see understanding in the detective's eyes.

"What happened next?"

The detective carefully talked Sydney through the entire incident, gathering as much information as he could.

Sydney was exhausted when she finally finished working her way up through the arrival of the first officers after her nine-one-one call. Chuck closed his notebook after asking a few clarifying questions.

Sydney was told canine units supported by SWAT officers had swept the wooded area behind her house. The attacker had not been found and the trail followed by the dogs indicated he had possibly made his escape through the trees to a car parked further down the street. Alex's phone had been located. The phone, along with Alex's weapon and a rock found at the scene with blood on it, were all being forensically studied for fingerprint and DNA evidence that would hopefully lead to identifying the suspect.

"Listen. We think it's likely you were the focus of this attack, that it was committed by the same person who sent you the flowers." Sydney nodded in acceptance. This possibility had run through her mind over the last hour as she sat waiting for news of Alex. "And we're pretty sure it's related to the copycat murders."

Sydney's breath caught and she fought to remain calm. "What does that mean? What exactly happens now?"

"Well, you'll be assigned an R-one-hundred detail. They'll be with you twenty-four hours a day." Sydney nodded, recognizing the reference to the security teams provided by the L.A.P.D.'s elite Metropolitan Division in high risk situations. "Two officers have already arrived. They're just outside this room in the hallway. Another detail will be attached to Alex in case she was a target. They'll stay with each of you until he's caught."

Sydney nodded, barely aware of the detective leaving and Sal taking his place by her side. She looked up when Sal placed her purse and keys in her lap.

"How're you doing?" he asked, giving her hand a gentle squeeze before letting go. Sydney gave a weak shrug in response.

"Have you heard anything about Alex?" she asked.

"Nothing yet. Tiffany's out there and will let us know as soon as she hears anything." He pointed to her purse and keys. "The sergeant who arrived at your house first brought those by. He made sure everything was cleaned and locked up." Sydney pictured the tall supervisor who had taken command of the scene.

"He knows Alex, doesn't he?"

Sal nodded. "Yeah, he was her first partner when she first got off probation almost fifteen years ago."

At that moment Tiffany entered and Sydney leapt to her feet. "Any news?"

"Nothing yet. She was stable when they took her in to surgery. They want to make sure they have identified all the damage." She approached Sydney and put her arms around her. "We should know something soon. They know to send the doctor in here as soon as he's done."

It was over an hour later when the doctor finally entered the room.

"Mr. Donatelli. I understand you're listed as Sergeant Chambers's next of kin?"

"Yes, sir."

"I'll run you through what we've determined. Let me know if anything doesn't make sense, or I'm sure Tiffany can also help with any questions that may come up." He glanced at Tiffany who nodded in response. "The bullet entered and then exited through the lower left area of her torso. It glanced off her rib, cracking it before it exited her back. We determined it passed through without striking any organs. Although there was significant blood loss, the wound was not life threatening. The head injury did cause us some concern and I ordered full x-rays and C.T. scans in order to eliminate skull fractures or brain swelling."

"How did the scans look?" Tiffany asked.

"Overall, I think she's out of danger. She's got a serious concussion and, of course, some stitches. The blood loss will leave her extremely lethargic. Between that and the drugs we've put her on, she's going to sleep for a while. But she's resting comfortably. She's going to have a hell of a headache for a while and will be a guest here for several days."

"Oh, she's gonna love that," Sal said with a relieved smile and a squeeze to the shoulders of the women on either side of him.

"Can we see her?" Sydney asked.

"Sure," the doctor said. "She likely won't wake for a while, quite possibly not until sometime tomorrow morning. And even then it'll be sporadic due to the painkillers. But there's no reason you can't sit with her if you'd like. We're moving her to a private room. We'll let you know as soon as we have her situated."

Chapter Seventeen

SYDNEY OPENED HER eyes and stretched in the cushioned seat beside the bed. She turned to see Sal and Tiffany asleep, leaning on one another on two seats placed together nearby. The fully lighted, windowless white hospital room provided no clue as to what time it actually was and Sydney glanced at her watch—just minutes after five a.m.

The night before had been terribly draining and a whirlwind of activity. Tiffany had finally gotten the three of them into Alex's private room and extra chairs were brought in. They were all permitted to stay, despite the normally restrictive visiting hours in the unit. Sydney wasn't sure if that was due to Alex being a police officer or Tiffany being on the E.R. staff, but she was thankful for those allowances. On the few breaks Sydney had taken to get a drink of coffee or water or to use the restroom, she noticed the two uniformed officers stationed outside Alex's room. These were obviously the security detail she'd been told about. While their presence was somewhat disconcerting, on a different level Sydney knew they were necessary.

She looked up at Alex in the bed nearby. She had yet to awaken, though both Tiffany and the medical staff gave assurances she was out of danger. Sydney couldn't help but think about the emotional rollercoaster of the last couple of weeks. They'd been filled with fear and terror. There had also been the comfort provided by Alex's presence and their new relationship. Was the intensity of her bond simply a result of this tumultuous series of events? Was this just another relationship for Alex, or did she feel the same way? How would she feel when she woke up to find Sydney there? Sydney had no answers to these questions, she only knew she wanted to be there, needed to be there. Not just because she felt responsible for Alex being injured while protecting her, but also because she was so incredibly attached to her.

"How are you doing?" Sydney turned to Tiffany when she heard the question quietly asked. Tiffany was awake and looking at her as Sal remained asleep leaning against her shoulder.

Sydney gave a weak smile. "I'm okay. I was going to get a cup of coffee. Can I get you something?"

At that moment Sal woke up, opening his eyes and yawning. He saw Sydney looking at him and immediately looked from Alex's still form to Tiffany beside him and then back to Sydney. Concern burned in his eyes.

"What? Any change?" he asked, looking between the two women.

"No change. She's been sleeping comfortably," Tiffany said as she put a calming hand on Sal's knee.

"I was just going to go for some coffee. Would you like some?"

Sydney asked as she rose. Sal shook his head as he yawned and stretched again. Sydney then looked at Tiffany with a question in her eyes. When Tiffany also shook her head Sydney started for the door. Her hand was on the doorknob when a quiet moan was heard from the bed.

Tiffany reacted the quickest and was immediately at the bedside. Her practiced eye reviewed each of the nearby monitors, then leaned over the bed to look at Alex. Sal was close behind her, joining her on the left side of the bed. Sydney approached the opposite side of the bed more slowly as Alex's eyes fluttered then opened, soon focusing in on Tiffany who was leaning over closest her.

"Hey, you," Tiffany said quietly. "You're in the hospital. You're going to be fine."

Alex appeared to nod slightly. Her eyes moved to Sal and a small smile appeared on her lips. Then her eyes closed momentarily, only to open suddenly.

"Sydney? What happened to Syd?" she quietly demanded, speaking with effort. Tiffany put her hand on Alex's shoulder and seemed about to speak when Sydney stepped in.

"I'm right here. I'm fine." Sydney reached out and took Alex's hand in hers. Alex moved her head and eyes to look at her and visibly relaxed. Sydney felt Alex lightly grip her fingers in return. Her eyelids fluttered and it was obvious this little bit of activity had exhausted her. Moments later her steady breathing revealed she was once again sleeping soundly.

Sydney's eyes filled with tears she couldn't keep from flowing. They were soon streaming down her face as she stood beside the bed, still holding Alex's hand. Sal guided her into a chair that had somehow appeared behind her. Sydney sat and leaned forward, resting her head on the edge of the bed, still not releasing Alex's hand.

Tiffany placed a hand on her shoulder and gave it a supporting squeeze. "Sydney, you're exhausted. You need to go home and get some rest." She moved to Sal and put her arms around him. "Both of you do."

"I don't want to leave Alex alone," Sal said. "She shouldn't wake up alone."

Sydney nodded in agreement.

"She's not going to wake up again for quite a while," Tiffany reassured them both. "I'll stay here until you come back. I don't want to see you back here for at least six or eight hours. They'll probably move her out of ICU this afternoon and start reducing the meds a little. She may wake again this evening."

"Come on." Tiffany moved back to Sydney's side and helped her to her feet. Sydney begrudgingly nodded and stood. She leaned over and placed a kiss on Alex's forehead, then allowed Tiffany to guide her out of the room.

SYDNEY ARRIVED HOME a couple of hours later. The two officers who were to provide security for her drove her home and, at her insistence, took up posts in the ground floor rather than sitting outside in the cold. She told them to make themselves at home and showed them the kitchen basics, then quickly retreated to her bedroom.

As she entered from the top of the spiral staircase, she looked at the unmade bed and her mind immediately recalled the previous night spent with Alex. Was it just over twenty-four hours before that she and Alex had spent a wonderful night together? It felt like it had happened a lifetime ago. How could that incredibly joyful period of romance and tenderness have transitioned so dreadfully to the moments of terror that followed?

Sydney shed her clothes and fell into bed and, overcome by exhaustion, she cried herself to sleep.

Hours later Sydney was awakened by the sound of the front doorbell ringing. At first she was disoriented and momentarily terrified when she heard the front door open and male voices. Then she remembered the security detail that was currently assigned to her. Sydney hurriedly threw on sweats and a sweatshirt and went down the main stairs to the entryway. There she found one of the officers from the security detail in conversation with Detectives Chuck Severs and Robert Kim. The conversation went silent as they all turned to watch her descend the stairs.

Sydney paused near the bottom of the stairs, suddenly fearful there may be a very tragic reason for their arrival.

"Is anything wrong?" she asked. "Is Alex—"

"Alex is fine," Chuck answered quickly. "I checked a couple of hours ago and there's no change. She's still resting comfortably. They just moved her out of ICU to a private room on one of the floors."

The sense of relief almost dropped Sydney to her knees. She paused and leaned on the banister, then looked up at a clock in the entryway and saw it was just after three p.m. "I should get back to the hospital." She began to turn to return to her room and get properly dressed.

Chuck spoke up. "I wanted to run some information past you and have you look at some pictures. Then we'll make sure we get you right to the hospital."

"Have you found him?" Sydney asked, eyes wide.

"We may have identified a possible suspect. Can we sit down somewhere and talk for a few minutes?" Chuck said.

She nodded and led the way to the kitchen.

"Why don't I make some coffee for everyone? Officer Davis, would you and your partner like some coffee?"

"Coffee is always welcome, ma'am," one of the Metropolitan Division officers who had today's security detail said.

"Have a seat, detectives," Sydney said, indicating the informal dining area next to the kitchen as she reached for coffee and filters. "Coffee?"

"Thank you, Ms. Rutledge," Chuck said as his partner nodded.

Sydney busied herself making coffee, trying not to look at the tile area inside the French doors. It was there that Alex had lain bleeding just twenty-four hours prior. The officers had done a spotless job of cleaning the area after Alex was transported, but the picture was clear in her mind and she still found it unsettling.

When the coffee was done she handed out mugs to each of the four officers, providing cream and sugar as requested, then poured herself one and sat down at the table. She took a slow sip of coffee, preparing herself for whatever was to come.

"I believe you said something about some pictures, detective?"

"Yes, ma'am," Chuck said.

He had what appeared to be a file folder in front of him. Sydney immediately recognized what was about to happen. The file folder was a photographic six-pack, a folder containing a display of six similar appearing individuals, usually photos from Department of Motor Vehicle files, or possibly old booking photographs. One of the individuals in the line-up was a possible suspect in the crime being investigated. Sydney had viewed photo six-packs numerous times in her career as they were frequently utilized for witness or victim identification of suspects. She had questioned detectives and witnesses on the stand on prior occasions to admit photographic six-packs into evidence in her trials. But she had never imagined she herself would be a victim viewing the photo line-up.

"I'm going to show you a group of photographs, one of whom may or may not be the man who attacked you yesterday," Chuck said without emotion. "Please know the backgrounds in each photo may be different, hair styles may have changed, that sort of thing. If you see the man who attacked you and Sergeant Chambers, please point him out. Do you understand?"

"Yes," she replied simply.

With that response, he turned over the folder, revealing a series of six small photographs. Sydney forced herself to look at each photograph carefully and fully despite knowing she would recognize the attacker at a moment's glance. His image was burned into her memory. When she got to the head shot in position number four she paused and her breath caught. Her finger came up immediately and pointed to the photo.

"That's him. I'm positive," she said, looking at Detective Severs. "That's the man who attacked us." The detective showed no reaction, but Sydney knew he couldn't, and shouldn't. He was likely making an effort to do everything absolutely by the book due to the important and personal nature of the investigation. The last thing they needed was for a defense attorney to be able to question the impartiality of a suspect identification.

The detective handed Sydney a pen and a photocopy of the line-up and had her circle the photograph she identified, then write and sign a brief statement. These handwritten notes on the photocopy would serve to document her independent identification to be presented later in court. As he collected the paperwork and folder he told Sydney that a rush DNA analysis had been conducted on various items collected in the clearing where the attack had occurred. One of the tests had matched to the suspect she'd just identified.

"Now we know who we're looking for. We'll get his photograph out to every cop in the county and we'll try and figure out what connection he has to Sinclair, if any," Chuck said, then finished off his coffee. "And I'll make sure the officers assigned to you and Alex have good photographs of this guy. He won't be getting near you again."

"Thank you, detective," Sydney said as she rose from the table. "Now if you'll excuse me, I'm going to get changed and get back to the hospital."

LESS THAN AN hour later Sydney was showered and en route back to the hospital with her two escort officers. A cell phone call by one of the officers while en route provided them with Alex's new hospital room number and she entered the room shortly thereafter. She found Tiffany sitting in a chair near Alex's bed. Tiffany smiled at Sydney as she entered the room.

"Hey. Do you feel better?" Tiffany asked.

Sydney returned the smile and nodded, then looked at Alex's sleeping form. "Is there anything I should know?"

"They started pulling back the sedative a bit, so she's likely to wake up anytime this evening," Tiffany replied. "I'll talk to the staff before I leave and make sure they know you're here."

"Have you been here the whole time?"

"I crashed in our staff bunk room and had a friend stand by with her for a while," Tiffany said. "But now that you're here I'll head home. I'm sure Sal will be back this afternoon at some point. There's a newspaper and magazines there on the bedside table if you're interested." Tiffany gave Sydney a hug then handed her a piece of paper. "Here's both Sal's and my cell numbers. You keep those and call if you need anything."

"Thank you."

Tiffany left the room and Sydney settled herself into the seat next to Alex's bed. She moved the chair closer, leaning over to rest her elbows on the thin mattress and taking Alex's hand in hers. It was clear that Alex was resting comfortably and that helped to calm Sydney's mind. Unlike the restless sleep she'd found earlier at home, Sydney soon put her head down on the bed beside Alex and gradually fell asleep.

Sydney awakened when Alex's hand moved, twitching and then tightening around her fingers. She lifted her head and saw Alex's eyes flutter and then open. Their eyes met and a tired smile slowly appeared on her face.

"Hi," Alex whispered.

Sydney grasped Alex's hand and stood, leaning over her. "How are you? Are you hurting? Do you want me to get the doctor?"

"Shh. I'm fine," Alex said, squeezing Sydney's hand. Sydney lowered herself back to the chair and Alex released her hand and reached up, moving slowly and coming to rest gently against Sydney's cheek.

"You're hurt." Alex was looking at Sydney's swollen and bruised cheek and split lip.

"I'm fine. Don't worry about me," Sydney said, finding it difficult to fight back the tears. Alex was lying in a hospital bed, recovering from a bullet wound and a concussion, yet her first reaction was concern for Sydney's injury. "How do you feel, really?" Sydney asked.

"A little, uh, high, I think," Alex said, still sporting the sleepy smile.

Sydney couldn't help but smile back at her. "I'm told they've weaned down the medicine, but I'm sure you're still flying pretty good."

"Uh-huh," Alex said. She then closed her eyes and took a deep breath, as if trying to pull her thoughts together. When her eyes opened they were slightly more focused and her look was serious.

"What happened? I don't remember much after..." Alex paused and Sydney could see her mind trying to put things together. "Did you make it to the house? Did he come back? I remember trying to get back to the house. But it's all fuzzy after that."

"You made it to the house," Sydney said, unsure of how much information she should be giving Alex in her current state.

"Did they catch him?"

Sydney paused, which was all the answer Alex needed. Her eyes closed in frustration. "Geez, how did I let him get the drop on me? Why didn't I just shoot him? I should've ended this."

"No. You did everything you could." Sydney squeezed Alex's hand.

"But he almost—"

"But he didn't," Sydney interrupted. "Because you stopped him. You saved my life, Alex," she added quietly. "And they know who he is." Sydney nodded as Alex looked at her. "They got DNA from the woods where it all happened. I just identified him in a photo six-pack today."

"Who is he?" Alex asked.

"Who's who?" The voice came from the doorway and Sydney turned to see Sal entering through the open door. He came to the bedside opposite Sydney and looked down at Alex.

"Hey, chica." Sal leaned down as if examining Alex's eyes. "You're way high."

"Yeah, no shit," Alex said. "I gotta get 'em to cut down on that stuff. I hate having my mind all fuzzy."

Sal pulled up the other chair and sat down. "So, who we talking about? What he?"

"They got DNA at the scene. I was asked to look at photographs today and I.D.'d him," Sydney said.

Sal nodded. "Yeah. The wanted bulletin is already out there. It's posted at the nurse's station outside as well. Every cop in the county is lookin' for this guy. Don't worry, we'll get him."

Sydney could see Alex's eyes growing droopy and she leaned toward her, gently touching fingers to her cheek.

"Don't worry about it, Alex. It's all under control. You just concentrate on getting healthy. You need to rest." Alex barely nodded, her eyes already closing. She was asleep again almost immediately.

OVER THE NEXT two days Alex continued to show improvement. At her insistence the pain medications were reduced and she became more aware of the discomfort to her side and an ongoing headache. When asked about the pain by medical staff she insisted it was bearable, refusing increases in the pain medication, determined to work through the discomfort. She was at the point where, with assistance, she was able to make her way slowly to the attached bathroom to use the facilities, and engage in light activities such as brushing her teeth. She was not yet permitted to shower. Sal and Tiffany found amusement in the fact Sydney had insisted on taking over Alex's daily sponge baths.

Additional friends and co-workers were gradually permitted to visit, including Alex's lieutenant and the officers from her unit. Sal and Sydney spent shifts each day at the hospital. Sal would spend most mornings prior to going to work the rest of his shift. Their lieutenant assigned him to the hospital on duty for the first half of his shift each day, knowing he was family for the injured sergeant and following the prevalent mantra that "cops take care of cops". Sydney would come in late in the morning and stay through the evening.

Like the police department, Sydney's boss had taken the attitude that the attack was a result of her duties as a D.A. and had administratively assigned her to home pending the apprehension of her attacker. He relieved her temporarily of her caseload. Tiffany, who returned to her regular daytime duties in the E.R., also stopped in as frequently as possible.

It was mid-day of Alex's third day in the hospital. She was flicking aimlessly through television channels when Lieutenant John Ramos walked into the room. He stood at the foot of the hospital bed as Alex looked him up and down.

"And you would be here why, exactly?" she asked, not even attempting to disguise her disdain.

"I'm here because I'm currently the acting Patrol C.O. and it's my responsibility to check on the progress of injured officers," he said.

"Great, you've checked on me. Now you can log it and leave."

Instead, Ramos walked farther into the room, coming to a halt off to the right side of Alex's bed. "Your lieutenant's trying to make this an injured-on-duty caper. He submitted the paperwork this morning and it's come to me for approval. I'm not seeing this as I.O.D."

Alex rolled her eyes. "Really?" she said, her voice dripping with sarcasm. "No, I guess I can see where you wouldn't consider being attacked by a serial murderer something that could be construed as in the line of duty."

"There's no evidence this is some serial murderer," he said, then lowered his voice. "And remember, I know what you two are."

"You two were probably out there flaunting what you are. That kind of deviant behavior instigates violent reactions. You should've expected that kind of a response from someone."

"You son of a..." Before she consciously knew what she was doing Alex started to rise in an effort to physically confront Ramos. She was sitting up and swinging her legs over the side of the bed when a sharp pain in her side stopped her short and she staggered.

"Alex, no!" Tiffany lunged forward, physically pushing Ramos back away from the bed as she stopped Alex, gently pushing her back. Alex gasped in pain as Tiffany helped her lie back down.

"Out!" Tiffany yelled as she turned on Ramos. She had entered the room in time to hear the last of Ramos's statements. "Out of my hospital, now!" At that moment Detective Chuck Severs appeared at the door, then entered rapidly.

"I think you'd better leave now, sir," Chuck said harshly. Ramos eyed him, then started to walk away, turning back toward Alex.

"I'm sure we'll have a chance to discuss this further at a later time, Chambers," Ramos said as he headed out the door.

Tiffany turned back to Alex, who was sweating and breathing hard from the exertion and discomfort.

"You can't be moving around, especially not like that."

"What going on?" Sydney asked as she came through the door and moved to the bed. She took Alex's hand as she studied her face and noted the sheen of pain-induced perspiration.

"God, he's a prick," Alex said as she grimaced.

Tiffany circled to the left side of Alex's bed and raised the edge of Alex's shirt to check her bandage. "I'm giving you some extra meds for the pain," she said.

Alex shook her head. "No, I'll manage. I don't want to be nodding off." Alex indicated to Chuck, who was waiting quietly inside the door.

Sydney looked at Tiffany and raised an eyebrow as they exchanged a glance. Alex seemed to read the look.

"I'm fine, you two," Alex said, squeezing Sydney's hand. "Seriously. I need a clear head for this."

"Fine," Tiffany said. "But I'm coming back after this interview and we're getting you doped up. I'm betting that's going to hurt for a while. You're lucky you didn't open it back up. How's your head?"

"I'm okay," Alex said, still grimacing. "I'll manage." She tried hard to ignore the throbbing of her head causing the slightly nauseous feeling.

"What happened?" Sydney asked again after Tiffany left.

"It was just Ramos, again," Alex said, squeezing her hand again. "He was here and he... irritated me."

"I thought that was him I saw leaving when I got off the elevator," Sydney said. "Are you sure you're okay?" Sydney reached out and wiped the perspiration from Alex's forehead, gently brushing aside the few strands of hair.

"I'm fine, really," Alex said. "But I think since you're the only other witness, it would be bad form for you to be here right now." Alex nodded toward Chuck, who had been standing silently off to the side for several minutes, simply watching the interaction.

"I'll go grab a cup of coffee and wait outside until you two are done."

After Sydney left Chuck proceeded with the interview to get Alex's statements and recollections from the attack.

Chuck pulled out the familiar photographic line up folder. "I know you know how this works," he said. "But be patient and let me go through the formal process just to make it all perfectly legal, okay?" Alex nodded and Chuck's voice turned formal and professional. "I'm going to show you a series of photographs. Pay no attention to the background or clothing. Hair styles or facial hair may be different. I need you to look at these photographs and tell me if you recognize any of them." He then turned over the folder, displaying the six photographs. Alex was able to identify the suspect without hesitation from the photo line-up.

"Him. He's the guy." She pointed to the mug shot in the fourth position. "He's the one who attacked us and shot me." Minutes later she had written and signed a brief statement regarding her photo identification of the suspect. She put the pen down and handed the statement form to Chuck. "Now tell me what you know about him."

"His name is Raymond Garvis," Chuck said as he carefully gathered the paperwork. "He's thirty-seven with a history of theft, drunk driving, violent assault and sexual battery. Sinclair employed him for several years prior to his arrest for the White Rose Murders. According to both neighbors, and Sinclair's financial managers, Garvis had essentially been Sinclair's Man Friday. You know, handling odd jobs, running errands or any other task that Sinclair put him to."

"And?" Alex felt there had to be more. Chuck shrugged.

"We don't know much else. It looks like Garvis must have been at least partially involved with Sinclair's murder spree. Maybe helping in some limited fashion. But we never had any forensic evidence to tie him to a scene. We're working on the premise Sinclair left Garvis with instructions to continue the spree, though it's possible he acted independently, basing his copycat murders on what he learned from Sinclair." Chuck paced as he spoke.

"The only part that's a little off is everyone claims Garvis isn't the sharpest tool in the shed. According to Sinclair's neighbors he was too dumb to do much more than odd jobs, mowing the lawn, washing the car, easy errands, that sort of thing. Even Garvis's sister, his only living family, says he has never been able to maintain a job. He dropped out of high school..." Chuck shook his head as he read the file. "Any way you look at it, he must've really paid attention to Sinclair, because every indication is there's no way he could've masterminded this whole thing on his own.

"Anyway," Chuck finished as he gathered his things to leave. "We've got every cop looking for him and bulletins going out to the press. Don't worry, we'll pick him up. Probably real soon."

"ALL DONE?" SYDNEY asked, rising to her feet from the hallway chair as Chuck stepped out of the room. He let the door close behind him as he nodded.

"All done," he said. "You should get some pain medication in her. Looks like she's hurting pretty good now."

"What happened before I came in? With that lieutenant? And what's his problem with Alex?" Sydney asked.

"From what I know, he's had an issue with Alex for a lot of years. He's, well, somewhat intolerant. Some of it's a religious thing with him. He made some insinuations that she brought the attack on the two of you, because she's..." Chuck paused and looked away, unsure how to continue.

"Because we're together?"

"Yeah. So when he said it Alex pretty much tried to climb out of the bed to go after him. But don't worry," he continued after a pause. "While his opinion might not be completely isolated it certainly isn't wide-spread. Alex is extremely well respected. Nobody is going to let him influence the investigation."

Sydney re-entered Alex's room as the detective departed, observing Alex lying in bed with her eyes closed, obviously grimacing in pain. Sydney moved closer and took Alex's hand, watching Alex's eyes open at the touch.

"Hey, how're you doing?"

"I'm okay."

"You're a liar," Sydney said gently as she pulled out her cellular phone and typed a quick message on her cell phone. "I'm getting Tiffany in here to make sure you get some pain medication."

"Oh, my God," Alex grumbled. "You traitor. You're not supposed to take her side."

"You won't heal if you don't relax. Your body needs rest. That's what the doctor keeps telling you." Moments later Tiffany came through the door.

"I spoke to the doctor and explained you may have overextended yourself a little bit. I figured you might prefer I administer this rather than a duty nurse you may or may not know."

"Come on, Tiff," Alex said, trying to plead her case. "This isn't necessary. You just need to get me released and out of here."

"Uh-huh." She uncapped the syringe and turned toward Alex's I.V. bag. "Keep up that attitude and I'll make you roll over and give it to you in the butt cheek. I know for a fact you haven't been sleeping as well as you should be, Alex. You need to accept the pain meds, not just the antibiotics."

"You'd love to give it to me in the butt cheek. Everyone knows you medical professionals have a thing for seeing people naked and in pain."

"Yeah, and I've got Sal at home to satisfy that tendency in me, so lucky for you I don't need you to provide that satisfaction," Tiffany replied. "Speaking of which, I have a date this evening with Mr. Soon to be Naked and In Pain, so you two have a pleasant evening." She lowered her voice as she moved behind Sydney.

"Give her about ten minutes and she's gonna be out," she said quietly.

THE NEXT DAY around lunchtime Alex was sitting propped up with pillows in the bed thinking about her interview and the information Chuck had provided. She was frustrated by the feeling there was something at the edge of her mind she should remember, something important, but she just couldn't grasp it. The thought process was interrupted as Sal broke through the door, quickly entering then looking up and down the hallway before closing the door behind him. He turned with a large pizza box in his hands and a smile on his face.

"Figured you've gotta be tired of hospital food by now," Sal said. "And Tiff told me about your visitor yesterday." Sal put the pizza box down on the end of the bed then continued. "I'm assuming it was Ramos, so I figured this might be a welcome addition." He reached into the backpack he had slung over one shoulder and removed a cold six-pack of Sam Adam's Light.

A short time later Tiffany and Sydney came through the door. Tiffany came to an abrupt halt just inside as she observed the open box of pizza sitting on the bedside table. Tiffany noted the slice of pizza in Sal's one hand and his other hand quickly moving out of view behind his body. Alex was similarly holding a piece of pizza and was sliding her other hand beneath the bed sheet, obviously concealing something. Tiffany folded her arms and looked back and forth between them with a stern expression.

Alex looked at Sal. "You're toast," she said, trying to hide the smile. Tiffany rolled her eyes as she approached the bed, then she saw the beer carton below Sal's chair, partially concealed by a jacket.

"Tell me that is not what I think it is." she said, coming to an abrupt stop.

"Oh yeah, you're definitely toast," Alex reiterated, still apparently finding the situation quite amusing.

Tiffany leaned down and picked up the carton, noticing one empty bottle in the carton and another one missing.

Tiffany turned to Alex with a questioning look on her face. "Tell me you're not drinking alcohol?"

Alex removed the hand concealed beneath the bed sheet, revealing a plastic cup containing about an inch of frothy amber liquid.

"Are you supposed to be drinking that?" Sydney said as she approached the bed.

"Hmm, now who's toast?" Sal said, smiling as he took another bite of pizza then a sip from the bottle he had hidden behind his back.

"You brought it here and gave it to her!" Tiffany took the beer from Alex's hand. "She's on medication!"

"Yeah, I'm on medication," Alex said, putting on her most innocent look. "I can't be held responsible for my actions. I don't quite know what I'm doing most of the time."

"You're incorrigible is what you are," Tiffany said. "And if you don't know what you're doing most of the time then clearly you're not ready to be released." Tiffany couldn't help but smile at the look on Alex's face at that comment. They all knew Alex had been impatiently awaiting word of her release and practically bribing the medical staff to sign off on it. Sydney started giggling quietly as she also noted the desperate look on Alex's face.

"That's got nothing to do with it," Alex said quickly. "I'm fine to leave. Get me the hell outta here."

"Well," Tiffany said, as she returned from dumping out the remainder of Alex's beer in the connected bathroom sink. "The doctor said possibly tomorrow afternoon you can be released if," she put a finger up to stop Alex's next comment, "and only if, you have somewhere to go where you'll have some assistance and can continue with bed rest and very little activity for a while."

All three had a good idea exactly what Alex's reaction to that would be. She was not one to ask for assistance or be coddled.

"Please," Alex said as she let her head fall back in exasperation. "I don't need a friggin' babysitter. I can do just fine."

"You can't even make it to the bathroom to pee without help, you jackass," Sal said with a smirk. He brought his beer bottle up to his lips to take a sip only to have it snatched away by Tiffany.

"Hey! I'm not the one on medication."

"No alcohol in my hospital," Tiffany said sternly, once again walking to the adjacent bathroom.

"Damn," Sal said under his breath, then refocused on the issue at hand. "Well, the obvious answer is you can stay with us in our downstairs guest room. Tiff and I have somewhat varying schedules, so at least one of us will be around most of the time."

"And I'll fill in the rest of the time." This came from Sydney, who was now seated on the edge of the bed and had taken Alex's hand in hers. "You shouldn't be alone, Alex. Let us take care of you for a while."

"I hate to impose on any of you," Alex said, giving Sydney's hand a squeeze. "You're sure this is the only way I can get out of here?" she asked Tiffany as she returned from the bathroom.

"Yep. It's with us, staying here, or I suppose a decent board and care facility is another possibility."

Alex rolled her eyes and let her head fall back onto the pillow. "Fine. Please just get me out of here."

At that moment the door burst open and Chuck Severs came through.

"We got him," he said. "We just found Garvis's body. He committed suicide." Everyone turned toward him.

"How?" Sal asked the question on everyone's mind.

"Anonymous nine-one-one call came in to Long Beach P.D. It came from a pay phone. The caller said he'd seen someone looking like Garvis going into a dive hotel. You know, the kind that rents by the hour as well as the day or week. When the officers got there they found the door unlocked and Garvis inside. He shot himself in the head."

Alex squeezed Sydney's hand and gave her a smile.

"I just came from the scene," Chuck continued. "Garvis had been renting the place for the past couple of weeks. When we searched it we found a box with newspaper articles about the last four murders and photographs of all four victims. He'd been stalking them just like the prior White Rose Murders." Chuck reached into his jacket pocket and pulled out his cell phone.

"There's something else you should see before it goes public," he said with some obvious discomfort. "There were some other photos. They're being held for prints and everything, but I snapped some quick shots with my phone." Chuck punched a couple buttons and handed the phone to Sydney first.

Alex looked at Sydney's face, heard her sharp intake of breath and saw her pale visibly. She immediately reached out and put her hand on Sydney's leg as Sydney swiped her finger across the screen of the phone, working her way through a series of photos. After a few moments she wordlessly handed the phone to Alex.

What Alex saw shocked her as well, but it took root as anger and frustration. How could she have let this guy get so close to Sydney without noticing him? She worked through a series of photographs obviously taken over the last several weeks. There were several of Sydney in and around the courthouse, taken close up. The others were obviously taken from a distance, probably utilizing a telephoto lens of some kind. There was one of Sydney walking with Tyler through the subterranean garage at the courthouse building, another of her in the window of her Oxnard conference hotel, talking on a cell phone. Then came the photographs of Alex and Sydney. One of Sydney standing on her front porch as Alex parked in the driveway, another of them embracing at the open front door of Sydney's residence, then another of them embracing in front of the window to what Alex immediately recognized as Sydney's master bedroom.

"He was in your backyard. That's the only way he could've taken that." Alex flicked through the last several photographs again then handed the phone to Sal as Tiffany leaned over his shoulder and they too looked through the photos.

"How could I have missed this guy?" Alex reached for Sydney's hand once again and gave it a squeeze. "I'm so sorry, Syd. I should never have let that happen."

"Don't be silly. You had no idea to even suspect this, and he made sure he wasn't seen." Sydney gave a brave smile and squeezed her hand back. "And it's over now. He's dead."

"Yep," Tiffany said as she handed Chuck back his phone. "So everything's back to normal now. And we can get you out of the hospital tomorrow and everyone can start moving on."

Chuck nodded. "Yeah, that's pretty much it. I'll keep you informed if anything comes up, but it's not as if there's going to be a trial or anything." Chuck said his good-byes and departed. Moments later the four Metropolitan Division officers came in and wished Alex the best in her recovery and thanked Sydney for her hospitality during their assignment to her. As was expected their detail had been canceled with the discovery of Garvis.

Shortly afterwards, the evening nurse came in with Alex's medication. "Good evening ladies. Time for the evening meds."

Tiffany leaned over to Alex and asked her, too quietly for the charge nurse to hear, "How much beer did you drink, Alex? Seriously?"

Alex knew she was wondering about complications with the medication. "He only poured that little bit in the cup, that's all I was going to drink. And I'd only had a tiny sip or two of that."

Tiffany nodded, apparently satisfied, then turned to Sal as she picked up the remaining beer and dropped it in his lap. "Let's go, you. We can leave these two some time alone together before the meds kick in and Alex is dead to the world."

Sal turned to Alex as he stood. "So we'll pick you up tomorrow afternoon. Tiffany will be here on shift, so she'll let me know when it looks like they'll release you. Then one of us will call you, Syd."

"Your keys are at my place. Why don't I head over to your place in the morning on my way in to the office and pick up some stuff for you? I'll bring a bag by here tomorrow afternoon before you leave."

They all agreed on the plan and Sydney and Alex found themselves alone in the room soon afterwards. Alex once again squeezed Sydney's hand and looked into her eyes.

"So, how do you feel about all this? About the pictures?" she asked. "And Garvis? Are you okay?"

"I'm just glad it's over," Sydney said with a deep sigh. "And in a twisted way at least something good came out of all this."

"What's that?"

"You," Sydney said quietly. "Us."

"Come here," Alex said and pulled Sydney toward her on the bed. Sydney leaned forward and kissed Alex lightly on the lips. When she began to sit up, Alex pulled her back for another kiss.

"We can't. You're hurt. We have to be careful."

"Shh. I'm not that hurt," Alex said, not releasing Sydney. "Come here."

As they kissed Alex moved her hand down to Sydney's hip, pausing there for a moment. Then she moved up Sydney's side and cupped her breast. Sydney groaned as Alex squeezed lightly, then gently massaged the hardening nipple with her thumb. As their tongues met and probed Alex moved her hand down again to Sydney's waistband and pulled the bottom of the shirt from her pants, moving her hand underneath.

Sydney suddenly broke the kiss and grabbed Alex's wrist, halting its upward progress.

"You have to stop," she gasped, lips hovering only an inch away from Alex's as she looked into her eyes.

"Why? I want to touch you. To feel you."

"And I want you to touch me. You have no idea how badly I want that. You're hurt and you need to rest and save your energy. Not to mention we're in a hospital room and anyone could walk in at any moment."

"God, but its driving me crazy. I want to touch you so bad."

"So do I. But this is for the best. We just can't. We need to wait until you're healed a little more." Sydney brushed her fingers across Alex's forehead, pushing an errant lock of hair aside. "I have an idea," she added after a pause. "Let's go away together."

"Like away where?"

"The mountains. I'd like to go spend some time in the snow, Sydney said. "We can be lazy together, get a lot of room service, and spend the evenings in front of a fireplace. It'll be nice. You can't go back to work for a while anyway. How does that sound to you?"

"It sounds great. When do we leave?"

"Well, we can check with the doctor and see when you can make the drive."

Alex pulled Sydney to her again, re-engaging the kiss, which once again quickly became passionate and demanding. Alex's hand, which hadn't moved from just beneath the base of Sydney's shirt, began moving upward along the skin of her rib cage and brushed the underside of her lacy bra. Alex felt Sydney's body move into hers, their chests touching as Sydney leaned farther forward, her kiss becoming more forceful. Alex's hand moved over the lace and again her thumb began massaging the erect nipple through the thin material.

Sydney suddenly pushed away, sliding off the edge of the bed to stand beside it. Alex's hand fell from inside her shirt to the bed as Syd stepped out of arm's reach. Sydney was breathing hard and had a glint in her eye and a slight smile on her lips.

"God, Tiffany's right. You really are incorrigible." she said with a quiet laugh. "I need to leave before I let you start something we shouldn't."

"I've got a better idea," Alex said, also smiling. "Let's just give in to it and do something we shouldn't. Please?" Alex reached out to Sydney but found the motion took more effort than it should and lacked her normal coordination. The pain medication Alex was given to help her sleep was clearly starting to take effect, her body becoming incapable of following where her libido clearly wanted to lead.

Sydney shook her head, but took Alex's hand in hers. "No, Sergeant Chambers. It's for your own good." She moved forward, grasping both of Alex's hands so they could no longer stray and seated herself again on the edge of the bed.

"I'll call you tomorrow morning and you can walk me through packing what you need at your place. Then I'll see you tomorrow. I'll be here in time for your release." She leaned forward and kissed Alex lightly on the lips and then on the forehead. "You get some rest," Alex heard her say just as she drifted off to sleep.

Chapter Eighteen

THE NEXT AFTERNOON Sal waited with Alex as her doctor reviewed her latest test results prior to releasing her. Alex was still moving slowly. The wound to her side was healing but remained quite painful. As a result she tended to walk hunched over, favoring the left side. She also suffered frequent throbbing headaches that increased in intensity when she moved too quickly or became fatigued. Sal helped her to the bathroom to use the facilities and change into regular clothes.

"How ya doin'?" Sal called through the closed bathroom door. "Have you fallen and you can't get up?"

"Ah geez, just shut up already." The door opened a moment later and Alex shuffled out wearing lose sweats and a t-shirt. "I can't manage to put on a bra and putting on socks and shoes is completely impossible. God, this is pathetic."

Sal laughed and took Alex by the arm. "You're not leaving yet anyway, we'll put your shoes on later. Come on, shuffle your ass back onto the bed."

Alex sat down on the edge of the bed and her attention was drawn to the door by a quiet voice.

"Hey, Alex."

Both Sal and Alex went silent as they turned and saw Regina standing in the open doorway.

"I wanted to come by and see how you are," Regina said as she walked into the room and looked briefly at Sal. "Hey, Sal, how're you doing?"

"Good," he said. "How about you?"

"I'm okay." Regina's eyes returned to Alex as she came to a stop near the bed.

Sal cleared his throat and looked at Alex. "You good?" he asked, raising an eyebrow. Alex nodded in reply and Sal continued. "I'm gonna go find Tiff and we'll see what the plan is to get you out of here." Alex nodded again.

There was a moment or two of awkward silence after Sal walked out, then Regina finally spoke again. "I wasn't sure when I should come to see you," she said. "Or if I should come at all. Whether you'd even want me to."

Alex started to shrug then winced in pain as it tugged the wound on her side. "I don't mind you visiting," she said. "How are you doing?"

"I've been worried about you. I was terrified when I heard what happened. When I heard it was you."

"Regina, I—"

"I just came to see with my own eyes that you were okay."

"I'm fine. I'm leaving the hospital sometime today. The sooner the better."

"Yeah, I'd imagine this hospital stay has been pretty frustrating for you. You don't play helpless very well."

"So tell me," she continued after a pause. "Does this have anything to do with that information you asked me to get?" Alex nodded. "And this district attorney I read was with you when this happened, I assume she's the friend you're helping?" Alex could only nod again as she looked Regina in the eyes. "Well, I don't have anything yet, but I can keep looking."

"Thank you," Alex said. "I know this guy is dead now, but I still have unanswered questions. Something isn't fitting." There was a pause between them before Regina spoke quietly again.

"Is it serious between you two?"

Alex answered as honestly as she could. "I think it may be getting serious. I'm not exactly sure how she feels about it. We haven't had a lot of opportunity to talk about it recently." Now it was Regina's turn to nod silently.

"Regina, I'm sorry I hu—"

"Don't." Regina shook her head. "You don't need to be sorry about anything." She stepped forward, positioning herself between Alex knees as they hung over the side of the bed. Alex was uncomfortable with the intimate position Regina had taken, and unsure where to look. She flinched when Regina reached out and put her hands on Alex's shoulders.

"I just want you to be happy," Regina whispered. She moved her hands to caress each of Alex's cheeks, drawing Alex's face up to look her in the eye. "Do you remember there was a time when we were happy together?"

When Regina leaned down and kissed Alex on the lips it came as a surprise and Alex was somewhat slow to react. Alex could sense the longing, almost desperation, in Regina's kiss. She quickly reached up and grasped Regina's wrists, pulling the hands away from her face and pulling back from the kiss.

Alex started to speak, "Regina, this isn't what I—" but then she heard the quiet sobbing gasp from the doorway.

"Oh, God!"

Alex turned to see Sydney standing in the open doorway, one hand to her mouth and her eyes large and growing moist. Then Sydney dropped the duffle bag containing Alex's belongings and fled down the hospital corridor and out of sight.

"Syd!" Alex launched herself from the bed without thinking, taking two hurried steps before almost collapsing from pain and dizziness. She felt arms wrap around her and she was helped back to the bed.

"Come on, you can't chase after her right now," Sal said as he and

Tiffany tenderly pushed Alex back onto the bed. Alex lay there with her head back and eyes closed, attempting to catch her breath and stop the nauseous feeling. Tiffany immediately lifted the edge of Alex's shirt to inspect her wound.

"I'm sorry, Alex," Regina said quietly from several feet away. "I should go." Regina was out the door before anyone could react.

A couple of minutes later Alex had caught her breath and was able to open her eyes. "Where'd she go? Where did Syd go?"

Tiffany shook her head. "She ran down the hall toward the elevators. What happened? When we were walking up the hallway we saw her standing at the door, then she suddenly turned and ran."

"She saw Regina kiss me." Sal's eyebrows rose and Tiffany's eyes got big. "It wasn't like that! She just surprised me. I don't know what she was trying to do. I didn't kiss her back. I stopped her and pulled away and I was trying to tell her. Shit! Syd saw the kiss and must've thought..." she paused with her eyes closed as she imagined exactly what Sydney saw and what her likely conclusion had to be.

"Fuck! I've got to find her." Alex pushed up in an effort to get out of bed, but Tiffany immediately put her hand out to stop her.

"You're not going anywhere right now. You don't even know where to start looking," Tiffany said. "Try calling her."

Alex picked up her cell phone and called Sydney's number. The phone rang and then went to voicemail.

"Syd, it's Alex. Please call me. It wasn't what you think. Please let me explain." Not knowing what else she could say, Alex hung up.

TYLER MOVED ASIDE as Sydney stormed through the doorway. Sydney threw her purse on a chair in his small living room and began pacing.

"That lying, manipulative...God! How could I be so stupid?" Sydney was interrupted by the ringing of her cell phone. She pulled it from her purse and glanced at the caller I.D. She threw the phone back into her purse without answering it and continued into the family room.

"Wanna tell me what's going on, or are you just going to wear out a trail on my carpet with your pacing and cursing? I assume this is about Alex?" He poured two glasses of wine and handed one to Sydney.

Sydney stopped, looked at Tyler, and then looked at the glass of wine in her hand as if suddenly recognizing it for what it was. She took a large sip of the wine, swallowed, then sighed deeply. She sat down on the couch near Tyler, taking another large sip, more of a gulp. Then she slumped back in the couch in a completely defeated posture.

"Yes, it's Alex. She's supposed to get out of the hospital today. So I went there to help get her settled at Sal and Tiffany's. I had thought about taking her home with me, you know. But I figured with Tiffany being a nurse and everything, that was the best place for her." Sydney took another large swallow of wine. When she started to speak again it was almost in a whisper. "There was another woman in the room with her when I got there. They were kissing." A tear slid down her cheek and she brushed it away, anger taking over again. She tipped the wine glass, draining the last of its contents, then leaned forward and reached for the wine bottle. She refilled her glass, drinking again.

"God, Ty. How could I be so stupid?" Sydney asked for probably the third or fourth time. "How could she make me think this was somehow special?"

"How do you know it isn't?" he asked.

"Please! She was lip-locked with that woman! Trust me, that was not a friendly, sisterly kiss. That woman was sending a clear signal that she wanted all of Alex."

"And what signal was Alex sending?"

"I don't know." She said quietly as tears came to her eyes again. "I'm not going to cry over this. I'm not going to allow Alex Chambers to have that much control over me!" She drained her wine and reached forward to refill the glass once again. As she was pouring her phone could be heard ringing from within her purse.

"I'm not answering that. She already tried to call me once. I don't want to hear any chicken shit excuse." Sydney was beginning to slur her words as she worked her way quickly through her third relatively large glass of wine. Moments later Tyler's cell phone began to ring.

ALEX WAS RELIEVED when the call was actually answered.

"Hello?" Tyler's calm and quiet voice came over the line.

"Tyler, it's Alex. Do you know where Syd is?" There was a pause and for a moment Alex was afraid Tyler wasn't going to answer her.

"Yes," he said slowly, giving no more detail.

"Is she okay?"

"That's a relative question." Tyler's voice was noncommittal.

"Can I talk to her? Please?"

"I don't think that would be a good idea right now."

"You've got to believe me, Tyler. She's got to believe me. It wasn't what she thinks she saw. It didn't mean anything."

"Well, I can tell you it most certainly meant something to Syd."

"Shit," Alex muttered as her worst fears were acknowledged. "It was my ex. She came to the hospital to see how I was. She started to kiss me and as soon as I realized I pushed her away. But I guess Syd was standing at the door when it happened." Alex knew she was rambling but couldn't seem to fight the desperation she was feeling.

"I'm not the one you need to explain this to," was all Tyler said.

"You've got to get her to listen to me. Please?" Once again there was a long pause before he replied.

"That is not going to happen tonight, I can assure you. I've got to go."

"Shit! He hung up on me." Alex looked up at Sal and Tiffany standing patiently nearby. She took a deep breath, trying to calm her racing nerves.

"She's with Tyler," she said. "So at least I know she's okay. He's not going to let me talk to her right now, though."

"Well, maybe that's for the best. Let her calm down a bit and think through what she thinks she saw. She'll realize she didn't see you reciprocating that kiss," Tiffany said. "Let's get you out of here and we'll try and come up with a strategy to get her to listen to you. You can try calling her tomorrow."

Tiffany had already ensured Alex was processed for release and all the paperwork had been signed, so they simply gathered her few belongings and headed out of the hospital with Tiffany pushing Alex in a wheelchair, per hospital regulations.

A short time later the three of them arrived back at Sal and Tiffany's house and the two of them helped Alex into the spare bedroom. Alex didn't say much but kept her cell phone in her hand and repeatedly looked at it, silently willing it to ring. She fought the urge to continue making calls to Sydney, knowing they would likely go unanswered.

When Tiffany prepared pasta for dinner, usually one of Alex's favorites, Alex ate little. She had very little appetite and spent the time simply pushing the food around her plate. Despite her mind racing with the anxiety and frustration, Alex was physically exhausted. She put up little resistance when Tiffany suggested she head for bed.

TYLER SAT DOWN beside Sydney on the couch and she lifted her head and took a deep breath.

"So who was that?" she asked.

"Alex." Tyler said simply.

"How does she have your number?"

"I gave it to her after the flowers, just in case you or she needed anything."

Sydney turned away, thinking of that day. Of the concern Alex had shown and how she had comforted her, stood guard for her, expecting nothing in return. How was that possible if their relationship was just a conquest? Sydney was confused by her own feelings as she tried to work through the chain of events. Soon her emotion, her anger, egged on by too much wine, again overpowered her logic.

"I hope you told her to fuck off and hung up on her." Sydney's anger was not backed by a lot of energy and her body fell back against the couch once again. She looked up to see a slightly shocked look on Tyler's face. She rarely used language that caustic. He looked down at the empty wine bottle, then at his still half full glass, and Sydney realized she'd finished the last of the wine while he was on the telephone. Tyler put his arm around Sydney's shoulders, drawing her against him, her head resting on his shoulder. Sydney couldn't stop the tears and quiet sobs.

"I told her tonight probably wasn't a good time for you guys to talk. But maybe you should think about talking to her tomorrow," Tyler said quietly as he rubbed her arm and shoulder in an effort to comfort her. "Maybe there's more to the story than what you saw."

"Oh, I'm sure there's more to the story than just the kiss I saw."

Tyler and Sydney remained on the couch in that embrace, saying little. Sydney was eventually overcome by emotional exhaustion, assisted by the excessive amount of wine.

Sydney woke early the next morning with a moderate headache and cotton mouth. She found herself lying on the couch covered by a blanket, her shoes sitting beside her on the floor. She realized she had either fallen asleep or passed out on her best friend. She quietly got up, putting on her shoes and folding the blanket. She wrote Tyler a quick note thanking him for listening and promising to see him at work. Then she silently let herself out of the house and headed home.

ALEX SLEPT WELL into the next morning, though it was a restless and disturbed sleep despite the medication Tiffany had insisted she take. Her eyes came to rest on the phone on the bedside table and she fought the urge to try another call to Sydney.

She sat up, then gradually stood, testing her own strength and abilities. When she found she could stand and walk without assistance, she made her way to the bathroom across the hall. She decided that she would shower first, then call Sydney. It was almost twenty minutes later that she shut off the water and carefully climbed from the shower. Moments later she heard a knock on the door.

"Hey, Alex, you good?" Sal called.

"I haven't had a real shower in almost a week. I needed that. Don't worry, I'm fine. Just moving a little slower than normal, that's all."

"When you're ready come on out and we'll figure out some breakfast for you."

Alex dressed then went back across the hall to the guest bedroom. She sat down on the bed and reached for the cell phone. Fear caused her to hesitate, but she eventually pressed the speed dial and put the phone to her ear.

When Alex arrived in the kitchen several minutes later, virtually shuffling into the room, Sal pointed to a seat at the table and put a plate of scrambled eggs and toast in front of her, followed shortly thereafter by a glass of juice.

"If you don't eat all of that Tiff will have my ass," he said as Alex sat down.

"She leave for work already?" Alex put her cell phone

down on the table next to her.

"Yep."

"Did she tell you she slipped me a mickey last night?" Alex caught Sal's slight smile.

"She might've mentioned something along those lines," he said. "We both knew there was a possibility you'd try and drive your dumb ass somewhere you don't need to be right now."

Alex noticed Sal pause as if debating his next words. "Did she call?" he finally asked, nodding towards the cell phone. Alex shook her head in reply.

"Did you call her this morning?"

Alex looked at Sal and then back at her plate. "I left another message," she said, then quickly shoveled her mouth full of eggs and toast so she wouldn't have to say anything more for a moment.

Sal sat down across from Alex at the table.

"What are you gonna do?"

"Keep calling. Try and get her to talk to me, to understand." Alex took a deep breath. "I talked to Tyler. He said she went to work. She shouldn't be alone right now. Something's not right with this Garvis thing. It's just not making sense." Alex shook her head and picked up the phone to try again.

SEVERAL HOURS LATER, when Sydney had not returned any of the previous messages left on her cell phone, Alex called her office number. She was surprised when Cathy, the receptionist, answered the phone.

"Hi, Cathy. It's Sergeant Chambers from the L.A.P.D. I thought I was calling Ms. Rutledge's direct office line."

"Oh, hi, Sergeant. Yes, you've got the right number. Sydney forwarded her line to my desk for the day and asked not to be disturbed. I think she's just trying to get back in the groove of things after everything that's happened. I'll tell her you called the next time she opens her door."

"Okay, uh, thanks." Alex hung up and sighed in exasperation. She was relieved to at least confirm Sydney was safe at work, but surely Sydney couldn't ignore her calls forever? Surely she would open up and let Alex explain at some point? Alex returned to flicking the channels on the TV remote until Sal announced he was going for a run.

"You sure you're okay here for a while? Need anything before I head out?" he asked as he tied his running shoes.

"I'm good. Get out of here already." As soon as he left Alex muted the television and called Sydney's cell phone for the first time since calling her office number that morning. After ringing several times it went to voicemail.

"Syd, please call me. We need to talk. Please let me explain. It wasn't what you think. God I miss you. Please call me." Alex hung up when she was unsure what else to say. She looked at her cell phone for several minutes then selected another number from her contacts list.

"Hello?" Alex heard Tyler say.

"Hey, Tyler, it's Alex again. How is she?"

"All things considered, she's better than she was last night."

"She won't pick up my calls. And she's had her office line forwarded to the receptionist. Is that just to avoid me?"

"Probably. She may not be happy that I'm talking to you either." After a while he finally brought up the question Alex knew he'd been wanting to ask. "Who was the other woman?"

"She's not another woman. I swear, there is no other woman, Tyler." Alex knew her best shot was to convince Sydney's best friend of her sincerity.

"She was my ex, from a long time ago. She came to see me at the hospital. That's the first time I've seen her in over a year. I don't know why, but for some reason she moved in and kissed me. I didn't kiss her back and I broke it off as soon as I registered what was happening. But that's all I think Syd saw. I tried to go after her to explain, but I couldn't. I yelled to her to stop, but she just kept going." Alex took a deep breath, then continued more slowly.

"God, Tyler, I feel terrible. The last thing in the world I want to do is hurt her. And Tyler, she shouldn't be alone right now. Something's not making sense about this whole copycat thing and Garvis." Alex paused. "Be there for her, Tyler. If she won't let me near her please promise me you won't leave her alone? Not until I'm sure everything is good."

"Okay, I'll try."

She heard Tyler take a deep breath.

"It's almost the end of the work day," he said. "I'll talk to her. Maybe I can get her to give you a call, or at least answer yours."

"Thanks, Tyler." Alex hung up, hoping Tyler could help her make some progress with Sydney.

SYDNEY HAD JUST finished listening to Alex's most recent voicemail when there was a soft knock on her door. She looked up to see Tyler peeking his head into her office. She waved him in and leaned back in her chair as he closed the door and took a seat across from her without saying anything.

Sydney's first reaction to Alex's messages was that Alex sounded concerned and sincere and Sydney admitted to herself that a part of her, a big part, missed Alex greatly. But then the anger took over again. Anger at Alex, but also at herself for allowing herself to be so swept off her feet. Angry with herself for being jealous of a woman she didn't even know and a relationship she didn't understand.

When she leaned forward and looked at Tyler he handed her two telephone messages.

"Cathy gave me those when she saw me heading this way."

The first was work related, a junior attorney calling with a question about a prior case. Then Sydney turned to the second one. It was from Alex, a message to call her. Sydney tossed both messages onto her desk and once again leaned back in her chair, rubbing her tired eyes.

"She called me too," he said. When Sydney raised her eyebrows in question he went on. "She wanted to know if you were okay. She tried to explain to me what happened. What you saw. She tried to put it in context."

Sydney looked at him skeptically.

"Hey, for what it's worth, she sounded sincere. Are you going to dodge her forever?"

"I don't know." The angry look left Sydney's face. "I need to figure out how I feel. What I feel. To use your words, I need to put my life and Alex's in context."

"She also made me promise not to leave you alone," Tyler said. Sydney just looked at him. "She said something about Garvis doesn't make sense."

Sydney began to gather her files. "Well, I don't need a babysitter, but I was going to invite you to dinner anyway."

Chapter Nineteen

ALEX SPENT THE afternoon and into the evening hoping Tyler had a chance to talk Sydney into calling her. Anxiety and frustration had driven her almost to the point of exhaustion. She waited patiently until after dinner before finally calling Tyler once again.

"Tyler, how is she?" Alex asked without preamble.

"Listen, she's really shaken up about this. I don't think it's so much anger at you as it is doubt about herself and where she fits. Part of her thinks you led her on and she's angry she fell for it."

"Nothing could be further from the truth, Tyler. I swear it," Alex said in a pained voice.

"Well, it's up to you to convince her of that," Tyler said. "I had dinner with her and now she's sending me home. She insists she doesn't need a monitor."

"You can't leave, Tyler!"

"Well, she's insisting on kicking me out."

"Shit!" Alex rose from the couch and began walking toward the hallway and the guest bedroom beyond. "Don't leave until I get there," she said as she went to gather her belongings.

When Alex exited the bedroom with her bag she found Tiffany and Sal waiting for her near the front door. They had clearly heard part of the conversation and knew what she intended to do.

"How do you intend to get there?" Tiffany asked. "It's not safe to drive while you're on that medication." She crossed her arms in defiance.

"Not a problem," Alex replied. "I haven't taken the pain meds today."

"I knew it," Tiffany grumbled under her breath. She shook her head in exasperation. "Do you have them with you at least?"

"Yeah, they're in here somewhere." Alex indicated to the bag she carried as she continued toward the door.

Sal walked beside her to her truck with Tiffany trailing behind. "Call if you need anything."

"Thanks, buddy." Alex slowly climbed into the cab of her truck. Ignoring the pain the movement caused. She started the engine and rolled down the window. "You're handling this better than she is." Alex nodded toward Tiffany, still standing behind Sal looking angry.

"I know you, Alex. The way I see it we were kinda lucky keeping you reined in this long."

"She's pissed at me, isn't she?"

Sal turned and looked back at Tiffany. "She loves you, Alex. She's just worried." He reached out his hand and Tiffany finally gave in and joined him beside the truck.

"You damn well better be careful, Alex," she said as Sal put his arm around her. "Don't you dare ruin all my hard work."

"I will, Tiff. I promise."

"Good luck," Sal added. They both waived as Alex backed from the driveway.

EXACTLY THIRTY MINUTES after leaving Sal and Tiffany's, Alex's phone rang. She had just turned her truck around in Sydney's expansive driveway and backed up to face down the sloping drive. With her back to the structure she felt at least she would see anyone approaching from the street. She looked at the caller I.D. on her phone then answered as she shut off the engine.

"Yeah, Tiff?"

"Are you there?"

"Yes," Alex said. "I just pulled up."

"What are you going to do next?"

Alex sighed in response, letting her head fall back against the seat. "I don't know. I hadn't really thought that far ahead."

"Uh-huh."

Alex could almost picture Tiffany rolling her eyes as she spoke.

"You need to be in bed, Alex. You need to take your pain medication and get some rest. It's the only way your body will heal. You keep going like this and you're just going to end up back in the hospital."

"I will, Tiff. I just..." Alex paused because she didn't really know what to say next. She didn't know how to express her remorse over what happened between her and Sydney. She had no idea how to explain the feeling that Garvis's death was not the end of that horror. Alex just knew she had an overwhelming need to protect Sydney, whether the woman wanted that protection or not.

"Just get yourself some real rest as soon as possible, Alex."

"I will, I promise, Tiff. As soon as I can. Don't worry." Alex signed off and slipped the phone in her pocket. "Now what?" she quietly asked herself as a surge of exhaustion washed over her. The simple thirty minute drive from Sal and Tiffany's place to Sydney's house had taken a lot out of her. "What exactly are you gonna do now?"

SYDNEY LEANED BACK on the counter, her arms crossed over her chest. Tyler had been delaying his departure, finding every excuse to stick around. He'd insisted on helping clean up after the meal and was now wiping down the kitchen counter for the second time.

"Really, Ty," she said. "I'm fine. I can take care of myself you know."

Tyler looked up with a sheepish smile and shrugged. "Yeah, well—"

Sydney's cell phone rang and she glanced at the screen, part of her somewhat disappointed that it wasn't Alex, though she wasn't sure if she would have answered it then. Alex's insistent calls and pleas, and apparent non-stop concern, were slowly but surely breaking down Sydney's stubborn barrier.

Sydney noted the call was coming from Tiffany and a spark of concern shot through her as she answered.

"Hello?"

"Hi, Sydney. It's Tiffany."

"Is everything okay?" Sydney asked, resisting the urge to inquire directly about Alex.

"Well..."

Concern shot through Sydney at the woman's hesitation and the last barrier dropped.

"What's wrong? Tiffany, is Alex okay?"

"Alex isn't exactly cooperating with proper medical advice."

"What do you mean?" Sydney asked. "Was she released from the hospital?"

"Unfortunately, yes. She was released yesterday."

"What's going on, Tiffany? Where's Alex right now?"

"How about you go to a window and look out at your driveway. Tell me what you see," Tiffany said.

"What the..." Sydney made her way to the front window in the living room, Tyler following behind her, gathering his jacket and keys as he went. Sydney looked out toward her driveway and saw Alex's truck backed in. The silhouette of a solitary figure could be seen seated in the cab.

"She's here," Sydney said quietly into the phone. "Why is she here?"

"Because she's worried sick about you, quite literally actually. The two of you in the cumulative sense, but also you in the singular. She seems to believe you may still be in danger." Sydney watched out the window as she listened.

"Listen, she's been a mess since yesterday. She's refusing to take the pain medication and hasn't been resting. The last place she needs to be right now is sitting in a damn car trying to stay alert," Tiffany said. "I know what happened yesterday, and I think you may have misinterpreted a thing or two. Maybe you can reserve judgment for the night just to get Alex out of her truck? I promise we can talk tomorrow and maybe I can shed a little more light on this."

Sydney replied after only a brief pause, the decision having been made in her mind long before the end of Tiffany's plea.

"Okay," she said. "I'll get her inside and get her to bed."

"Syd, get her to take the pain medication and the antibiotics, they should be in her bag," Tiffany added. "And she just needs to stop and rest."

"I'll take care of it. We'll talk tomorrow? You'll tell me whatever it is that's going on with her and this woman?"

"Yes," Tiffany said. "How about I come over tomorrow morning before I go to work, maybe around seven-thirty? I'll check on our patient and you and I can talk."

"I'd like that," Sydney said quietly. "I'll see you then." Sydney turned as she hung up the phone and finally noticed Tyler standing at the door, jacket on, ready to depart.

"You knew about this, didn't you?" she said.

"Alex insisted I not leave until she got here. She didn't want you left alone. She had just texted me that she'd arrived as your phone rang."

"Humph," Sydney mumbled. "So what exactly was she planning on doing? Freezing to death on my driveway?" Sydney shook her head as she opened the door and moved out onto the front patio. She paused at the top of the steps leading to the driveway. Tyler gave her a quick hug.

"I'm outta here," he said. "Call me if you need anything." Sydney nodded. "And for what it's worth, Syd, I think she's sincere. I'm not sure what happened at the hospital yesterday, but I get the feeling it isn't entirely what you saw, or think you saw." He shrugged. "That's just my gut feeling."

Sydney watched Tyler walk past the front of Alex's truck to his car parked beside it. He gave a wave to Sydney on the porch then backed out of the driveway. Sydney took a deep breath and then made her way down the stairs toward the truck.

The windows were somewhat foggy and she couldn't see clearly into the cab, but as she came within a few feet the door was pushed open and she could make out Alex's figure sitting in the darkness.

"I know you're mad, Syd," Alex said. "And I know I'm the last person you want to see right now. But I just can't get rid of the feeling this isn't over. I think we've missed something." She paused, then looked into Sydney's eyes.

"I want so badly to try and explain what you saw. What you think you saw. I hope one day soon you let me. But I understand if you're angry and have no interest in me being in your life. That's the last thing in the world I want, but I'll respect your wishes. But I would never forgive myself if something happened to you, even if you do hate me. So I'm gonna stay here just in case. I won't bother you. I'll make some calls tomorrow and figure something else out for your protection."

Alex reached out to pull the truck door closed, her face partially illuminated by the front porch light.

Sydney saw the wince and heard the slight gasp as Alex stretched to reach for the open door. Alex's face was drawn and pale, with dark circles beneath her eyes. She was obviously exhausted and appeared to be in considerable pain, though Sydney could see she was making a valiant effort to conceal that.

"Alex, wait," Sydney said and reached out to stop the door from closing. "This is ridiculous, Alex. Just come inside."

"Are you sure?"

Sydney nodded without hesitation. "You're going to freeze out here, and Tiffany made me promise to keep you alive at least until tomorrow morning. Come on."

Alex slowly climbed from the raised truck cab, confirming for Sydney just how much discomfort she was experiencing. Remembering Tiffany's admonition about the medication, Sydney was prompted to ask about it.

"Where's your bag with your medication?"

THE SENSE OF RELIEF was almost overwhelming for Alex as she climbed from the cab of her truck. Sydney was at least speaking to her. There were no guarantees, but they were starting to communicate. When Sydney asked about her medication she reached for her bag, the movement sending agonizing pain radiating through her body. She gasped in pain. Sheer will power kept her from falling to her knees on the pavement. Instead she fell toward the truck, leaning into the open doorway and folding her upper body across the driver's seat in an effort to at least stay on her feet. The pain was closely followed by an overwhelming sensation of dizziness and nausea.

Sydney moved quickly to her side. "Alex!"

"I'm good," Alex said, trying to sound sure as she attempted to breathe and clear her head. "I should know better than to move like that." She made another effort to reach for the bag, which seemed so close yet so far away.

"Let me get it," Sydney said. "Just move over here a bit." Alex felt a supporting hand on her arm and she looked up into Sydney's face and found eyes full of concern. She reached for Sydney's hand, grasping it gently.

"Syd, please, can we talk? Please let me explain what happened." Sydney squeezed back reassuringly.

"Don't worry, we'll talk," she said quietly, then reached to grab the bag and closed the truck door. "Come on."

Alex didn't resist when Sydney took her arm and looped it over her shoulder, then grasped Alex gently around the midsection. She concentrated on putting one foot in front of the other as they made their way into the house.

"Can you make it up the stairs to the bedroom?" Alex only nodded in response and they slowly took the steps. By the time they reached the top, Alex was coated in sweat from the effort and accompanying pain.

Alex wasn't sure where they were going or what she could expect. Was she even welcome in Sydney's bedroom any longer? She paused briefly at the top of the stairs, unsure which way they would turn. Was she to be relegated to a guest bedroom? She gave an inner sigh of relief and joy when Sydney didn't hesitate to turn her gently to the right toward the master bedroom. They entered and Sydney led her to the bed, helping her to sit down. She dropped the duffle bag then kneeled in front of Alex and began unlacing her shoes.

"How do you feel? Are you okay?" Sydney asked as she looked up into Alex's face.

"I'm good," Alex said. "Much better now than I was yesterday at this time," she added with a slight smile.

"Don't downplay it. I can tell you're hurting." Sydney reached up and brushed a lock of hair off Alex's forehead. The familiar and tender motion always sent Alex's heart skipping.

"It's nothing. I was stupid and twisted when I shouldn't have. I should know better."

Sydney gave her a skeptical look. "And that's all?" she asked as she removed Alex's second shoe and placed a hand on her knee. "Alex, you can barely see straight, much less walk straight."

"It's just a little bit of a headache as well," Alex replied. "The doctor warned me I may have them for a little while. Maybe a little too much activity too soon." She gave Sydney's hand a gentle squeeze and they had several moments of companionable silence, just looking at one another.

"Bed," Sydney finally said. "We need to get you into bed. Let's get those pants off."

Even through the discomfort and dizziness, Alex couldn't help the smile that crossed her lips when she heard those words. She slowly stood up and put her hands on Sydney's shoulders as Sydney unbuttoned her jeans. Alex leaned down and kissed Sydney, until Sydney pulled away.

"Stop it," Sydney said. "That's certainly not what we're here for. We still have a lot to talk about, you and I."

Alex sat down on the edge of the bed again once the jeans were moved down over her hips.

Sydney pulled Alex's pants over each foot and off, then reached for her shirt, pulling it gently over Alex's head. Her eyes paused momentarily on the bandages that remained prominent around Alex's torso.

Alex remained silent as Sydney removed a loose t-shirt from her duffle bag and helped her put it on. Alex's gaze no longer met Sydney's as she accepted Sydney's assistance and silently followed her directions. Warring sensations of doubt and hope flooded her mind, further complicated by an overwhelming sense of pain induced exhaustion.

Alex couldn't get a read on Sydney and was unsure exactly what she was feeling. Hurt? Disappointment? Alex just knew she needed very badly to make Sydney understand what had happened with the kiss with Regina.

"Stand up for a second," Sydney said, then helped Alex to her feet. She pulled the bed covers down then moved back to Alex's side. "Come on, get into bed."

Alex complied without comment or resistance, wincing as she lay down and stretched out. Sydney pulled the covers over Alex then disappeared into the bathroom, returning a moment later with a glass of water. She sat down on the edge of the bed and put the water down on the bedside table, then reached for the pill vials she had removed from Alex's bag earlier.

"I spoke to Tiffany this evening," she said as she shook out the pills from the two vials of prescription medication. "If you're not careful you're going to end up back in the hospital. Come on, take these."

"I don't need two of the pain pills," Alex said. "Two of them knock me on my ass. I don't need that." Sydney simply looked at her as she resealed the pill bottle.

"Uh-huh," was all she said. The two prescription strength pain pills remained in her hand. She held the pills out to Alex and then handed her the glass of water. Alex looked into Sydney's eyes and saw the determination there. She surrendered after only a moment's hesitation, accepting both pills.

When Alex finished and handed the glass back she finally found the courage to ask once again, "Can we talk, please? About what happened at the hospital. What you saw."

"Okay," Sydney said quietly as she placed the glass on the bedside table. She sat and waited quietly for what Alex would say next.

Finally confronted with the opportunity she'd been hoping for over the past twenty-four hours, Alex suddenly found she was nervous and unsure of herself. She realized how much she feared losing Sydney and could only hope that her explanation rang true.

"The woman you saw with me," she began. "Regina. She's my ex. We were together for over a year and it ended a little over a year ago." Alex looked at Sydney and couldn't gauge her reaction. She simply sat on the edge of the bed listening. She was close enough for Alex to reach out and take her hand, but Alex didn't, fearing Sydney would pull away. "I broke it off when she insisted we take our relationship to the next level. She wanted to move in together, I wasn't ready for it. She set the ultimatum and I wouldn't budge. So that was it." Sydney continued listening silently, so Alex drove on.

"Sometimes I think maybe she expected me to come back to her, to change my mind. But I never did. I guess in a way I loved her, but I know I made the right decision. Living with her wasn't what I wanted. It wasn't what I was ready for. Somewhere deep inside me I knew we weren't meant to spend the rest of our lives together. But in her mind I guess it was what she really wanted and so it hurt her when I wouldn't give her that commitment." Alex paused again, realizing she was rambling. Part of her was hoping Sydney would respond, react somehow, ask a question, and say something. But Sydney just sat there, waiting for Alex to continue.

"I called her a little while ago, right after you got the flower delivery." This finally got a reaction from Sydney. Alex saw her stiffen noticeably and her eyes got a little wider. "It was the first time I'd spoken to her in almost a year. She's a social worker and has contacts within the Department of Children and Family Services. I thought she could maybe get me some information on Sinclair's background. After the flowers got delivered I just couldn't let go of my belief we were missing something about him. She was the only one I could think of who might be able to help with his history.

"Evidently she heard what had happened and showed up at the hospital. I swear to you I didn't call her, didn't ask her to come. I haven't spoken to her except for that one phone conversation about Sinclair. She just showed up. I think..." Alex leaned her head back against the pillow and took a deep breath again. "Shit, I don't know what to think. A part of me thinks she was looking to get back together, to see if I was open to..." Alex let the thought hang as she paused once again, now looking down at her own hands resting in her lap as her mind tried to understand what had happened. "I don't understand why she would have thought there was any way. I mean, when I called her before I pretty much told her about us." Alex glanced up at Sydney and then quickly looked back down at her hands.

"I don't know how she ended up kissing me. She just suddenly was there and I stopped her and started to push her away. I was going to explain to her how there was no chance, but then I saw you in the doorway. Then you ran and I tried to chase after you but...God, Syd, I'm so sorry I hurt you. I know it sounds unbelievable but I swear I didn't kiss her. I didn't do anything to invite it, not purposely at least. Maybe I shouldn't have called her before, but I couldn't think of anyone else who could help with the foster system information. Maybe I gave her the wrong idea somehow. I just don't know how. All I know is I'm scared to death I messed this up. Messed us up. Messed up what we have here, or what we could have."

Alex found it increasingly difficult to focus as the pain pills started to kick in. She tried to get everything out, feeling compelled to make Sydney understand before the drowsiness overcame her. Her head fell back against the pillows once again, but she found the strength to look up once more when she felt Sydney take her hand. "I swear to you there's no one in my life right now except you, Syd."

"No one else?" Sydney asked quietly.

"No one but you."

"And you didn't kiss her back?"

"Not at all, I swear." Alex was whispering now, concentrating on trying to stay awake and hoping her honesty was reassurance enough to convince Sydney.

"And you think we could have something here? Between us?" Sydney asked as she once again reached out and brushed the errant lock of hair from Alex's forehead.

"God, yes. You're almost all I can think about," Alex said, her eyes half closed. She heard Sydney take a deep, relaxing breath.

"Go to sleep," Sydney said. She adjusted the pillows behind Alex so she could lie down. "We'll talk more tomorrow."

Alex was comforted by Sydney's continued presence, seated beside her on the bed. When Sydney started to stand up, Alex's reached for her hand.

"Please don't leave."

Sydney said nothing for several seconds, then kicked off her shoes and carefully lay down next to Alex.

"Does this mean you forgive me?" Alex asked as she felt Sydney's head rest gently on her shoulder.

"I don't know," Sydney said. She rested her hand on Alex's stomach. "You may need to grovel a little bit more."

"I'm not above a little groveling." Alex turned her head and kissed Sydney's forehead, silently grateful the empty feeling that had been hanging over her for the last twenty-four hours was finally gone. "This whole day, ever since yesterday, I've hated it. I hated being without you. I hated knowing I'd been the cause of your hurt." Alex moved her left hand to her stomach, finding Sydney's hand there and interlacing their fingers. "I started to feel a little crazy thinking you might be gone from my life, out of reach."

Alex's entire body tensed as she thought about it again. Sydney reached up to her chin, gently turning Alex's face to meet hers. The kiss Sydney initiated was tender and Alex felt it full of regret and forgiveness. When Sydney pulled away she placed her finger to Alex's lips to keep her from speaking.

"Shh. We can talk more in the morning. You need to get some sleep," Sydney whispered. Alex released a very contented sigh and she finally allowed her body to relax as her eyes closed.

SYDNEY AWOKE THE next morning and carefully got out of bed, hoping not to wake Alex. The night before, after she was sure Alex was sleeping soundly, she had gotten up briefly and changed into her own pajamas. Then she'd gone downstairs and made herself some hot cocoa, sitting in the den and thinking about all that had happened. She couldn't deny the relief she felt having Alex nearby again. They may need to talk a little more, but Sydney was convinced they were well on their way to getting over this recent incident and moving on with their relationship. She returned to bed shortly afterwards and snuggled against Alex's larger body. To Sydney's knowledge Alex had never stirred, but when she woke Alex's arm was firmly wrapped around her pulling them together as they slumbered.

Sydney put on some comfortable sweats and made her way to the kitchen, leaving Alex to sleep as long as possible. She had just finished making coffee when there was a soft knock on the door.

"Good morning," Tiffany said when Sydney opened the door.

"Hi. Come on into the kitchen," Sydney said. "Can I get you some coffee?"

"I'd love some." Tiffany put down her purse and seated herself in the kitchen nook area. "You have a beautiful home," she said after glancing at her surroundings. "What smells so good?" she asked.

Sydney smiled a little bit as she placed two mugs on the counter, poured coffee, then slid one mug toward Tiffany. She placed the sugar bowl and a carton of creamer on the counter before replying.

"I just put some coffee cake in the oven. It'll be ready in fifteen minutes or so if you'd like some," she said.

"So," Tiffany said after taking a sip of coffee. "What happened last night? Obviously you got her to come in and get some rest? I'm assuming she's still here since her truck is."

"Yes, she's still upstairs in bed."

"Any problems with that?"

"Well, to be honest, she scared me a little," Sydney said. "She looked terrible and I could tell when she moved that she was in pain. She tried to turn at one point to get her bag out of the truck and she just about collapsed. I got her to take the medication, though, and she slept the whole night through. I tried to be very quiet this morning when I got up so she would keep sleeping."

"I'll take a look at her this morning before I leave," Tiffany said, then took another sip of coffee. "But how are you feeling about everything else that happened? I mean at the hospital?"

Sydney sighed as she stirred her coffee. "After what happened at the hospital...I don't know. I guess I felt like I needed to try and figure everything out. Maybe I blew things out of proportion. I keep questioning what I saw now, or what I think I saw. I'm honestly not sure." Sydney looked away and shook her head. "But I've never experienced anything like what I feel for Alex. It's so all consuming, like I can't get her out of mind. And when I saw that other woman with her—"

"You mean Regina?"

"Yes, Regina. I saw that and just lost it. In reality I guess I didn't really have a right to react that way. We've only been seeing each other a little while. And it's not as if we've even discussed being exclusive. It's not as if I had a right to expect it. But seeing her like that still drove me crazy."

"Well, if it's any consolation, that whole Regina thing drove Alex more than a little crazy too. The only thing that kept her from going after you at the hospital was that she was physically incapable of it. She still tried though, and Sal and I had to scrape her off the floor when she collapsed." Tiffany tried to look innocent when she added, "Probably the only thing that kept her from trying again that night is the fact I pretty much drugged her into oblivion."

"You what?" Sydney asked, half shocked but half giggling.

Tiffany nodded as she took another sip of coffee, pausing before she went on. "Listen, I'll admit I wasn't there to see what happened between Alex and Regina. I didn't see what you saw. But I can tell you this for sure, you were the only thing on Alex's mind from the point she saw you turn and run. Regina didn't even exist anymore at that point." Tiffany looked seriously at Sydney. "And there's another thing you need to know. Whatever Alex tells you about her and Regina, it'll be the truth. She's not going to string you along or play you. She doesn't lie her way into relationships, or into someone's bed."

Sydney let out a sigh as she visualized again what she had seen that day at the hospital. She was no longer sure exactly what happened, what she had seen. She'd been so upset and overwhelmed by the scene she wasn't too clear any longer on the details. But she had sensed the sincerity in Alex's words the night before.

"She told me that woman, Regina, is her ex and that she showed up unannounced. That Regina initiated the kiss before Alex knew what was happening."

"Well, from a medical standpoint, keep in mind Alex wasn't all together at the time. It's completely reasonable her powers of observation and her reflexes would have been slow on the pick-up." Tiffany said. "And the other thing you should know is Alex is the one who broke that relationship off. And I can assure you she hasn't been pining about Regina for the past year. However..." Sydney looked up at Tiffany when she paused in her statement.

"Listen," Tiffany said after taking a deep breath. "This is just my intuition speaking, but it seems like Regina hasn't completely wanted to let it go. We run into each other from time to time, Regina and I, both socially and professionally. She always asks about Alex and I've sometimes gotten the feeling she was waiting, hoping Alex would eventually come back to her. I guess what I'm saying is it's well within the scope of possibility, if not probability, that Regina would make a play under those circumstances." Tiffany took a deep breath and shook her head.

"But like I said," she continued. "The bottom line is Alex wouldn't lie about her intentions. Her relationship with Regina ended because she was honest about where it was, or wasn't, going. Whatever Alex has told you about how she feels about the two of you, you can count on it being the absolute truth."

Several moments of comfortable silence followed as Sydney thought over what had been said.

"Hey, you two."

Sydney turned to see Alex coming down the spiral staircase into the room. She moved slowly, almost stiffly, one step at a time, and kept her left arm hovering near her wounded side. But she did look better, more rested than she had the previous night. Her eyes had regained some of their spark. Sydney turned her chair to face Alex as she came to a stop standing between Sydney's legs.

Alex drew Sydney into a somewhat tentative embrace, and Sydney noticed the hesitancy. In an effort at reassurance, she returned the hug, carefully encircling Alex's midsection. When she pulled back and looked up into Alex's face she saw a timid smile on her lips, and what looked like relief in Alex's eyes.

"You're looking a little better," Sydney said. She reached up and ran a finger across Alex's forehead, brushing away that constantly rebellious lock of hair. She could literally feel the tension leave Alex's body at the closer contact.

"I'm much better, now that I'm here with you again," Alex said, tightening her arms around Sydney. Sydney returned the hug and then motioned to the other seat.

"Sit down, you," she said. "I'll get you some coffee." She got up and moved into the kitchen.

"So, Tiff," Alex said as she sat down. "What are you doin' here? Checking up on me?"

"Yes. I thought I'd stop in and check on how you were doing."

"I'm good, Tiff. Everything's fine. Seriously, I don't need a babysitter." Sydney turned to watch the interaction between the two and saw Tiffany roll her eyes as Alex responded.

"First of all you could have, shit, you probably should have, ended up back in the hospital last night," Tiffany said. "You pushed it too hard, failed to take your meds and refused to rest. Second, do you forget who I'm living with? I know how you macho cops operate. I know damn well that you need a babysitter more than the average patient, not less. I'm just not quite sure how to best manage that yet."

"She's going to stay here with me," Sydney said. "I'll make sure she stays put and gets rest."

"Are you sure you're up for it?" Tiffany said with a smile. "She can be a handful."

"Uh, hello," Alex broke in, looking from Tiffany to Sydney who was cutting slices of the coffee cake she'd recently removed from the oven. "She's sitting right here and I'm pretty sure she should have a say in this."

"Oh, I think I'm up for it," Sydney responded as if Alex had never spoken. "She can stay with me. It's the weekend now so I've got a couple days to make sure she knows the rules before I go back to work. Anything special I need to know?"

"Not really," Tiffany said. "Change the bandages daily. I'll give you extras. You know the directions for the meds are on the bottles. She shouldn't take any baths or soak the wound directly for long periods of time, not for a few more days at least. The ribs are going to take a couple weeks to heal. The head is the question mark. Headaches, dizziness...that'll stick around a while because of the concussion. Bottom line, you," she pointed at Alex, "need to rest."

Sydney nodded in agreement as she moved toward the table carrying slices of coffee cake, putting a plate down in front of Tiffany and then one in front of Alex. Alex put her arm around Sydney's hips as she stood next to her.

"Are you really sure you're okay with this? With me staying here with you?" she asked. "I don't want to impose."

"Don't be silly," Sydney said. "You're not imposing. And I'd like to continue what we started, from where we left off. Well," she added with a slight smile as she moved away to retrieve the coffee and refill everyone's cups, "maybe not exactly where we left off. You're a little under the weather now, after all."

Alex turned slightly red and Sydney was happy with herself as she sat down with her own breakfast.

TIFFANY DEPARTED A short time later and Sydney directed Alex to the couch in the den with orders not to move. Sydney proceeded to rush about playing nursemaid. She ensured Alex's medication, a glass of water and the television remote were within easy reach, and brought in an extra blanket and pillows for her. Sydney then announced she was going to check on options for lunch later, and that after lunch Alex would need to take her medication.

Alex reached out and grasped her hand as she passed by.

"Hey," she said. "How about you stop and sit down and relax with me a while."

"But is there anything else you want? Anything you need?" Sydney asked.

"Yes." Alex pulled Sydney to the couch beside her. "I want, and need, you to be here with me, right now." As Sydney sat down Alex put her arm around her shoulders and pulled her close. "Just relax."

Sydney allowed Alex to pull her into her embrace beside her, tucking into Alex's right side and lowering her head to Alex's shoulder.

"I guess I'm still a little freaked out about the last couple days. Everything, emotionally, has happened so fast. It was kind of overwhelming."

Alex stiffened slightly as Sydney spoke. Inside Alex felt a part of her fearing the answer, but she asked the question anyway.

"Do you want to slow things down?" Alex asked.

"No." Sydney said without hesitation. "That's just it, I don't want to slow down. I want to grab on to you and not let go. It's like I'm thinking of you during every waking hour, but I like it. I like knowing you're there, that you're with me. But then part of me is afraid that I'm making a presumption, that maybe you feel differently about it, that it's not—"

"Stop," Alex said. "You can stop being afraid of that. I feel the same way." Alex paused and struggled for words. She had never been one to talk a lot about her feelings or emotions, but she felt this was an important point in their relationship and sensed the need to be open and honest with Sydney.

"I know this happened fast and a lot of weird stuff has gone down. A lot of stress has been put on us during these first few weeks. But we're still here, together, right now. What I do know is I want to put everything I can into us. You've captivated me, Sydney Rutledge. I want you in my life. That's the most important thing to me right now, making sure you know that. I think the pull, the attraction, of this relationship is new to both of us. But we're here right now, together. We'll figure the rest of it out as we go."

Alex had been gazing forward out the window as she spoke. She now looked down at Sydney nestled into her right side and found the woman gazing up at her. She noticed Sydney's eyes were moist with emotion and Alex pulled the woman more protectively into her embrace.

"Are you okay?"

"Yes," Sydney whispered. "Now I'm wonderful."

Alex bent down and their lips met, gently at first, then with growing passion. Alex's right arm was wrapped around Sydney, pulling her closer to her side. She reached up and caressed Sydney's cheek. As the kiss became more urgent Alex felt Sydney's hand come to rest on her thigh. Her libido immediately responded and without thinking about it Alex began to guide Sydney backwards onto the sofa beneath her. As Alex twisted her torso she was suddenly overcome with a flash of pain ripping out from the wound in her left side. In that moment she had completely forgotten about her own physical limitations. The sudden pain staggered her and she gasped, almost collapsing. She pulled away from Sydney to her seated position on the sofa.

"Oh, God. Alex?" Sydney gasped. She saw the pain in Alex's eyes and the sheen of perspiration that had broken out on her face. She took Alex's hand in hers, then reached up to Alex's cheek. "I'm sorry," she said. "Please tell me you're okay."

Alex looked at Sydney and smiled weakly. "You have nothing to be sorry about, silly," she said, bringing Sydney's hand to her lips and kissing it. "I'm fine."

"You're not fine. You're hurting." Sydney leaned over and picked up the vial of pain pills, shaking one into her palm. "Here, take this," she said, holding out the pill and the nearby glass of water.

Alex initially hesitated to accept the pill and water. "I hate those things," she said. "They knock me on my ass."

"You need to rest and this will make you more comfortable," Sydney said. She forced the pill into Alex's hand then held out the water for her. "You heard what Tiffany said, your body heals faster at rest. And you need to be more careful. Geez, we need to be more careful." Sydney added the last part with a shake of her head and slight smile.

Alex handed the glass back to Sydney after swallowing the pill. "I just forgot about it. I got carried away in the moment." Her crooked smile now matched Sydney's. "You kinda have that effect on me."

Alex reached out as Sydney started to stand, grasping each of her hands, guiding Sydney to stand between her legs in front of her. Sydney bent at the waist, allowing Alex to pull her downward. She disengaged her hands from Alex's and moved them to brace against the back of the sofa on either side of Alex's head and hovered there, leaning over Alex, their faces only inches away from one another.

"You, Sergeant Chambers, are incorrigible." Sydney leaned down, intending only to give Alex a quick parting kiss. But when their lips met the passionate current flowed through her and she was again caught up in the moment. She soon felt Alex's hands on her hips, sliding gradually upwards. Sydney forced herself to pull away from the kiss.

"Stop it," Sydney said in mock frustration, but with a smile on her face. "I'm going to walk away, for both our sakes. I'll go make some lunch." Sydney reached for the nearby remote, pushed the button to turn on the television then handed the remote to Alex. "You're going to sit here and relax." Sydney reached up and ran fingers across Alex's forehead brushing aside that rebellious lock of hair she was so fond of. Then she straightened up and walked from the room. Alex leaned back and smiled as she listened to Sydney's steps retreat through the archway into the kitchen.

An hour later they had finished eating the lunch Sydney had put together. As Sydney cleared the dishes away and cleaned up in the kitchen, Alex flicked aimlessly through television channels with the remote. She was obstinately fighting her body's urge to succumb to the drowsing effects of the medication. Sydney sat down at the end of the sofa, lifted her stocking feet onto the edge of the coffee table in front of her.

"Come here," Sydney said. "Lie down." She patted the sofa next to her. Alex gingerly turned on to her back and lay down, putting her head in Sydney's lap. Sydney removed the remote from Alex's grasp, meeting no resistance. She brushed hair back from Alex's forehead, then leaned down and gave her a kiss.

"Would you just stop fighting it and go to sleep. You need your rest," she said. Alex's eyes closed and she smiled as she realized how truly content she felt. Moments later her breathing tempo changed as she allowed sleep to overcome her.

SYDNEY RETURNED TO work the following Monday, leaving Alex at home to continue her recuperation. As she sat in her office reviewing witness statement for an upcoming case, she was suddenly aware of a presence in her doorway. She looked up to see Lieutenant John Ramos standing there. He entered without an invitation and stood before her desk. Sydney lowered the case file she'd been reading and leaned back in her chair. She didn't stand, nor did she offer the man a seat.

"Something I can do for you, Lieutenant?" she asked brusquely.

"Yes, as a matter a fact," he said. "You can explain to me exactly how someone such as yourself, who by all appearances is a nice young woman, gets mixed up with a deviant like Chambers."

"I don't see where that's any of your professional concern, or personal business."

"Chambers is a bad cop. She's careless, a hothead and she does a half ass job. You'd be better off distancing yourself from her. Word about the two of you spreads and it could have negative ramifications for you, personally and professionally."

Sydney stood as she asked, "Is that a threat, Lieutenant?"

"That's reality," he replied. "I know for a fact there are high ranking members of your office who see things for what they are. They would be disappointed to learn the things I've learned about you."

"Get out." Sydney said in a low voice. "Get out of my office."

Tyler's voice came from the doorway. "Mary Claire is ready for you in her office, Lieutenant."

Ramos gave Sydney one last look then turned and walked out of her office. Tyler watched Ramos retreat down the hallway to the deputy in charge of the Major Crimes Unit, then entered Sydney's office, closing the door behind him. Sydney was slowly lowering herself into her chair.

"I take it that was the infamous lieutenant you told me about?" Tyler said. "The homophobe who has it out for Alex?"

Sydney nodded. "Geez, Alex is right, he really is an asshole."

"Are you okay?" Tyler asked.

"Yeah, I'm fine." Sydney picked up the file to resume her work. "Oh, Ty," she caught him as he began to exit her office. "Let's keep this between us. If Alex hears about this she's liable to hunt him down and kill him. She doesn't need the aggravation right now."

Chapter Twenty

THE REST OF the week progressed relatively quietly. Alex was waiting each evening when Sydney returned home from work and they would spend the evenings cuddling on the sofa in front of the television or fireplace, then retire to the master bedroom together. She knew Sydney worked hard not to allow either of their libidos to override her caution due to Alex's injuries. Alex thought she was being too cautious, and their lack of intimacy became a source of frustrating humor between them on almost a nightly basis.

One afternoon Alex found a photo album on a shelf of the entertainment center and pulled it out. They spent some time together that evening turning through the pages of photos together. Sydney pointed out her now deceased parents and their Midwestern home, as well as photos of her and her sister growing up. They soon came across a couple of family photos that included a young man. In many he had his arm around Sydney. Alex simply pointed to him in one of the photos and looked at Sydney. She raised her eyebrows in a questioning expression.

Sydney nodded slowly. "Richard Morrison," she said. "We were engaged for a while, up until a couple years ago."

Alex's heart skipped momentarily and she silently told herself to relax. The relationship had ended a long time ago.

"Engaged?" she said. "Really? So you were almost a Mrs. Richard Morrison?"

"Yeah. Well, no, not really." Sydney hesitated. "It was never going to work. He seemed like a good guy, and for a while I thought it could work. But he was a little controlling and not entirely supportive of my hopes and aspirations." Alex had the distinct feeling Sydney was minimizing some of the facts, but didn't interrupt as Sydney continued.

"I finally figured out it just wasn't right and I couldn't go through with it," Sydney said. "I guess now I know why, huh?" Sydney smiled and looked into Alex's eyes, then leaned over and kissed her. Alex let her trepidation fade away and returned Sydney's kiss, then they moved on with the photographs.

When they finished looking through the photo album Alex asked a difficult question as Sydney got up to put the album back on the shelf of the entertainment center.

"What's your sister going to think about you and...women?"

Sydney once again paused before answering. She straightened the various albums on the shelf as she seemed deep in thought.

"I'm really not sure," she finally said. "I hope she's okay with it. She's the only family I have. I guess we'll find out eventually, won't we?"

Alex nodded in response, then her mind returned to something she'd been contemplating over the past couple of days. She reached down inside herself and tried to develop the courage to say what she wanted to.

"What?" Sydney asked, coming to a standstill in front of Alex, apparently sensing there was something hanging between them.

Alex reached out with her hand, indicating that Sydney should come closer and take a seat. She gently pulled Sydney to sit on the couch beside her.

"I want to tell you something. And I don't want you to feel like you have to even respond. It's just something I want you to know. Especially if you're even thinking about talking to your sister, about us, or maybe just about you. You deserve to know how I feel." Sydney nodded and Alex plunged ahead.

"Syd, I have no interest in dating anyone else. I haven't had any interest since you and I...well, since our first date. I don't want you to feel pressured at all, but I have no intention of seeing or being with anyone." She looked up into the eyes of the woman sitting beside her and felt Sydney's hand come to rest against her cheek. She drove on with her thoughts.

"I think our relationship is moving to the next level, at least for me. I mean, I don't spend repeated nights at just any woman's house. That's something that people who are in a relationship do."

"In a relationship?"

"Yeah," Alex said. "You know. Like a step beyond just dating."

"So you think we've gone a step beyond dating?"

"Well, yeah. Don't you?"

Sydney smiled. "Alex, I feel the same way. I want to be with you, and you exclusively."

Alex smiled when she heard this statement, then figured she's make it formal.

"Well, in that case," she took Sydney's hand in hers. "Sydney Rutledge, will you be my girlfriend?"

Sydney smiled and leaned in and kissed Alex. "Yes, Sergeant Chambers, you better believe I'd like to be your girlfriend." She kissed Alex again, then added. "And if Regina or that little law clerk even look at you wrong, from this point on, they answer to me."

THURSDAY EVENING CAME and Sydney and Alex retired once again to the sofa in the den. Alex sat at the end of the sofa, leaning back and partially reclining against several pillows arranged against the corner and armrest. She sat with one leg extended along the length of the sofa and the other leg hanging over the edge.

"Come here," she said when Sydney moved toward the other end of the couch. Alex patted the cushion, indicating to Sydney that she should have a seat on the sofa between her legs. Sydney sat down and Alex drew her backwards to recline against her chest. Sydney initially hesitated.

"What about your side?" she said as she sat but resisted leaning back against Alex.

"Don't worry about that," Alex said. "I'm good." She put her arms around Sydney and pulled her into her. "And getting better," she added with a smile.

They sat together just watching the fire for a while, Sydney leaning back with her neck and throat exposed as she reclined with her eyes closed. Alex gently brushed Sydney's hair from her neck and then kissed the tender area. She continued kissing Sydney's neck and worked the kisses down to the base of her neck, gradually moving the loose fitting blouse aside.

Sydney smiled and leaned her head back farther, allowing Alex greater access. Alex gently turned Sydney's head, granting her access to her lips. Sydney reached up and cupped her cheek as they met in a passionate kiss. Lips parted and tongues met. Alex allowed her hand to drift to Sydney's chest, coming to rest lightly on her breast.

She massaged Sydney's breast through her blouse, feeling her nipple immediately respond. She moved her hand lower and slowly pulled the bottom of the blouse from Sydney's waistband. She began to release one button at a time, opening the garment from the bottom up.

Alex was pleasantly surprised when Sydney brushed her slow moving hands aside and began rapidly unbuttoning her blouse from the top down as the kissing continued, now more intense, more demanding. When their hands met in the middle, freeing the last button, Sydney covered Alex's hand with her own and moved it beneath the material. She pressed Alex's hand against her breast and Alex heard as well as felt Sydney's quiet moan of pleasure.

Alex's body responded and her hand seemed to move downward on its own and she deftly dealt with a second article of clothing that stood in her way.

Alex moved her kisses down Sydney's chin to her neck and felt Sydney's quickened heart rate as her lips caressed the skin covering her pulse point. Her heart sang as she was once again able to bring such pleasure to her lover's body.

Moments later Sydney collapsed against her as the final ripples of orgasm faded away. Alex wrapped her arm around Sydney and pulled her close, her head rested against Alex's chest and shoulder. Sydney lay there with her eyes closed as her breathing gradually returned to normal.

Alex was spent, yet exhilarated. She leaned her cheek against the top of Sydney's head as she recovered, her heart rate gradually slowing. Alex knew she'd been close to orgasm herself simply from the sight and feel of her lover. She soon felt Sydney's fingers stroking her arm and

Sydney's lips caressing her neck.

"Are you proud of yourself, Sergeant Chambers?" Sydney asked quietly. "Because you should be," she added with a smile. Alex smiled back at her.

"You inspire me," Alex said. "Sometimes I just can't keep my hands off you." She leaned down, intending to deliver only a fleeting tender kiss.

Sydney met the kiss with greater passion and their lips lingered. She turned within Alex's arms, as she maneuvered to face Alex.

It was now Alex's turn to moan. Sydney pulled away from the kiss with a sultry smile on her face and looked deep into Alex's eyes.

"I want to touch you," she said, then leaned down and kissed Alex once again. "I'll be careful." Sydney moved her lips farther down Alex's neck. "But I want to touch you everywhere." She stopped and looked at Alex again and Alex found herself unable to speak. She could only nod in response. "Good." Sydney rose to her knees on the cushion, kneeling between Alex's legs. Without hesitation she grasped the bottom of Alex's t-shirt.

"Let's take this off."

Alex sat forward and allowed Sydney to pull the shirt over her head. She wore no bra and Sydney smiled as she dropped Alex's shirt to the floor.

"Now lay back and relax," Sydney said and guided Alex back to partially recline against the pillows at the end of the sofa.

Sydney's still unbuttoned blouse allowed the exposed skin of their stomachs to come in contact. Alex couldn't keep her hands from responding and she tried to reach under the blouse with both hands. Sydney pushed up to a kneeling position, just out of Alex's reach. She slowly let the blouse drop from her shoulders and join the t-shirt on the floor beside the sofa. She reached back to unclasp her bra and that too dropped away. Alex reached up for Sydney's now fully exposed breasts but Sydney stopped her.

"No way," Sydney said with tender forcefulness. She took each of Alex's hands and pushed them down to the pillow on either side of Alex's head.

"It's my turn now. I'm going to make sure you realize you belong to me." She kissed Alex again. "Make sure you have no doubt in your mind."

Sydney again brought her lower body into contact with Alex, this time allowing her hip to grind a certain very sensitive area.

This brought an audible gasp to Alex's lips and her shoulders and arms tensed, her fists clenched against the pillow. Alex pushed her hips up to meet her, to force greater contact, but then gasped in pain.

Sydney stopped immediately and pushed up, looking into Alex's face.

"Alex? Are you okay? Should I—"

"Don't stop! For Christ's sake, don't stop!" Frustrated arousal was written all over Alex's face. "I just have to let you...please...don't stop."

Sydney nodded then lowered herself to kiss Alex's lips once again. "Tell me if anything hurts." She kissed Alex's neck. "Don't move. Just let me do all the work."

Alex's breathing quickened and she moaned in pleasure as Sydney's lips ventured over her body. She was vaguely aware of Sydney removing her remaining clothes, then nothing existed for her except the amazing sensations being created by her lover.

Later, she felt Sydney move and Alex opened her eyes to watch her pull a light blanket from the back of the sofa and draped it over the two of them. They lay together after their lovemaking, with Sydney resting partially atop Alex, her cheek lying against Alex's chest.

Alex rested against the pillows with her eyes closed, comfortable in the silence and the close contact she had with Sydney. She felt Sydney's hand rest gently against her cheek.

"Hey, are you all right?"

Alex grinned and opened her eyes.

"All right? I can assure you, I'm much better than all right." Alex raised her head to kiss Sydney. "You're amazing," she said, stroking Sydney's bare back beneath the blanket.

"We should head for bed," Sydney said. "I think you've had enough activity for the day."

Alex examined Sydney's clothing, hanging off her in disarray providing clear evidence of their recent lovemaking, and couldn't disguise her small smile of satisfaction. This was not lost on Sydney, who pulled Alex to her feet.

"Come on, stud. Off to bed with you." She gathered their discarded apparel and led the way up the spiral stairs to the bedroom above.

Moments later Alex was dressed in her boxers and an oversized t-shirt, her standard sleeping attire, and was lying in bed awaiting Sydney. When Sydney came out of the bathroom and approached the bed, Alex couldn't help but admire her lover's body, which was by then covered by an old worn t-shirt of Alex's. When Sydney joined her Alex pulled their bodies together.

"You look delicious in a t-shirt," she said as she began to nuzzle Sydney's neck. "But you look more delicious without it."

Sydney laughed and pushed Alex away.

"Sergeant Chambers," she said. "You're incorrigible. Remember I have to work tomorrow. Besides," she continued, "you need to conserve your energy. You're still healing."

Sydney rolled over, putting her back to Alex as Alex muttered in mock frustration, "I don't know, I thought I did pretty damn well for an invalid."

Sydney giggled and reached behind her and took Alex's hand, pulling her over to enfold Sydney in a spooning position. She kissed the palm of Alex's hand then held it around her, tucked to her stomach.

"Yes, Sergeant. You did pretty damn well."

They were both fast asleep in each other's arms within minutes.

THEY AWOKE THE next morning and lay in one another's arms for several minutes. Alex finally spoke the words she'd been thinking for a couple days.

"You know," she said. "As wonderful as all this has been, I think I'm healthy enough to be on my own again." She glanced down at Sydney to measure her reaction. "I don't need to be a burden on you anymore."

Sydney's head came up sharply.

"You haven't been a burden," she said. "I understand if you feel well enough to go home, but you haven't been a burden. It's been nice having you here."

"Nice?" Alex asked, a mischievous smile on her face. Her hand drifted lower to gently squeeze Sydney's derrière.

Sydney matched the smile. "Yes, nice." She leaned up and kissed Alex. "Enjoyable. Stimulating. You know, nice."

"Well, I'd like to show my appreciation for your hospitality," Alex said, her hand moving to massage Sydney's back once again. "Let me take you away for the weekend?"

"Sounds enticing. What did you have in mind?"

"Well, I know we've talked about the mountains. Maybe Big Bear or Arrowhead? Running Springs?" Alex said. "Somewhere with snow, fireplaces, candlelit dinners?" She could tell from Sydney's expression she liked the idea.

"We can head up as soon as you can get out of work today," she continued. "Maybe you can pack a few things before you head downtown. I'll drive home and pack some stuff and wait for you there and we'll head out from my place in the afternoon. Does that sound the slightest bit enticing?"

"Absolutely enticing," Sydney said. "But are you sure you're okay to drive?" she asked.

"Uh, you do remember last night? We...I mean..." Alex laughed quietly. "Yeah, I think I can make a twenty-minute drive home on my own. We'll figure the rest of it out from there."

Sydney buried her face in Alex's neck and giggled as well. "Yeah, okay," she said, kissing Alex's jaw. "I guess you've proven you've got enough energy for a quick twenty minute drive." She worked her way to Alex's lips, pressing a lingering kiss there, then pulling away and looking once again into Alex's eyes. "I have something to ask you, too." Alex raised her eyebrows in query.

"If I were to clear a drawer or two for you, and maybe some room in the closet, and make some room in the bathroom, would you use it?"

Alex was shocked for a moment as she thought about what such an action meant. "You mean keep some stuff here? Are you sure that's what you want? I mean, are you comfortable with that?" she asked.

Sydney leaned in and kissed her once again, then nodded. "Yes," she said. "I'm absolutely sure."

Alex hesitated for a moment, knowing this was the first step to a really serious commitment. She had fled from Regina over the "move in" conversation and that had been after almost a year of a dedicated relationship. So why was she not running now? Why did this feel different?

"Yes," Alex finally said. "I'd like that."

Sydney displayed a mischievous smile. "Good, since I already put your clean clothes and toiletries away yesterday afternoon."

"Really? Just a little presumptive, aren't you?" Alex replied with a smile as Sydney climbed out of bed. "Am I really that easy?"

"A girl can hope, can't she?" Sydney said. "Why don't you go back to sleep for a while and I'll see you at your house this afternoon." She leaned down and kissed Alex then retired into the bathroom.

About thirty minutes later Alex was nodding off when Sydney gave her a tender kiss goodbye. She awoke again on her own a couple hours later and finally got out of bed. She smiled when she went into the bathroom to shower and discovered her small collection of toiletries carefully placed amongst Sydney's and her few items of clothing carefully folded in a drawer. It was a virtually empty duffle bag she carried with her downstairs to the kitchen.

There she found a second, equally pleasant, surprise waiting for her. Sitting on the counter with her keys was a single key, obviously to Sydney's front door, and a garage remote. A note in Sydney's handwriting read:

```
Alex—this way you can come and go as you please.
Your truck is in the garage. Can't wait to see you
this afternoon. Drive home safely. XOXO Syd.
```

Alex smiled as she hooked the new key onto her keychain, tucked the note in her pocket, picked up the remote and headed out the door. She managed to convince the doctor's office to fit her in for a last minute appointment then headed home to research and make reservations for the weekend getaway, and pack. Her heart skipped a beat when the knock came at the door in the early afternoon.

Chapter Twenty-one

SYDNEY RUSHED THROUGH the day in hopes of escaping as early as possible. She had two preliminary hearings that were fortunately heard before lunch, then met with detectives handling another upcoming high profile case being prepared for jury trial. She worked through lunch on some related issues and was heading northbound up the 110 Freeway by two p.m., arriving at Alex's house shortly afterwards.

Sydney stepped forward into Alex's arms the minute the door opened.

"Hi, there," Alex said after the welcoming kiss was shared. "You were able to get off early. That's great."

"Yep, I'm looking forward to the weekend," Sydney said. "I was hoping to beat some of the afternoon traffic. Ready to go?"

"You bet." Alex gave Sydney one more quick kiss then retrieved her bag and they headed out to the driveway. "How comfortable do you feel about driving my truck if it's necessary?"

"Okay, I guess. Why?"

"Well, the weather report says Arrowhead might get some more snow over this weekend, so I figured my truck is a little more practical than your cute little sports car. But I want to be sure you're comfortable with it in case you should happen to drive it."

"In case I should happen to drive it?" Sydney asked. "You say that as if you think it's not likely, like you'll be doing all the driving. Sure you're up to that?"

"Uh-huh," Alex said. She set her bag down in the rear of the quad cab and proceeded to the trunk of Sydney's car parked next to her truck in the driveway. "Pop the trunk and I'll grab your bag."

Sydney activated the button on the key fob and the trunk popped open to reveal a suitcase that, while somewhat small, was still twice the size of Alex's duffle.

"You do know this is just a weekend trip, right?" Alex was smiling as she gingerly removed the case from the trunk. Sydney saw Alex wince and had to fight the urge to step forward and help. She knew Alex was frustrated with her ongoing physical limitations and so she was trying not to overreact and add to the discomfort.

"Yes, silly," Sydney said. "I'm know it's just for the weekend. I just didn't want to leave anything important behind."

"Clearly." Alex smirked as they entered the truck. Alex set the GPS from a slip of paper in her pocket and backed out of the driveway. "All right," she said. "We're off." She looked at Sydney and reached across the center armrest to take Sydney's hand in hers. "Thank you for coming away with me."

Sydney squeezed her hand in response. "Thank you for taking me away. So, what can you tell me about where we're going?"

"Actually," Alex said. "I'd kind of like to keep it as a surprise. I'm just hoping it lives up to my expectations."

They traveled a few minutes in comfortable silence, then Sydney spoke once again.

"So, how was your first day of unsupervised freedom?"

Alex chucked. "Not bad. I do have some good news. I got a last minute appointment with the doctor this morning on the way home from your place. He agreed to put me back to work on Monday. It's just light duty and half days, but that's something at least."

Sydney's heart sped up slightly. She had known this was coming and that Alex would likely push to return to work as quickly as possible. She knew from the beginning she was getting involved with someone in a potentially dangerous profession and that she would have to deal with that. That potential had already been presented to her in very vivid detail in recent weeks. To her credit, Sydney showed little, if any, of the trepidation she was feeling. She simply squeezed Alex's hand.

"Are you sure you're ready for that?"

Alex gave her hand a reassuring squeeze in return. "Absolutely," she said. "It's just a release to light duty. I'll be riding a desk and pushing paper for a while, and working shortened hours. It'll be boring as hell but at least I'll be doing something."

"Just promise me you'll be careful. Don't push too hard?" Sydney said.

"Of course." Alex raised Sydney's hand to her lips and gave it a kiss.

Sydney gave her a critical, slightly disbelieving look.

"Uh-huh. I'm gonna hold you to that, Sergeant Chambers."

They moved on to a discussion of other casual topics for the next hour as they continued east on the 10 Freeway then turned off at Highway 38 to begin the drive up the mountain toward Arrowhead.

Sydney noted Alex began to grow quiet and her movements stiff. In the dimming late afternoon light she noticed Alex wince the few times she adjusted in her seat. It was clear her first active day was starting to take its toll and had possibly been a little too much. Sydney pointed to a strip mall with a Starbucks in it.

"Let's stop here for a second," she said. "I'd love a coffee."

Alex obeyed and they parked and exited. Alex's breath caught as she climbed down from the raised truck and her movements were slow and stiff. Sydney pretended not to notice as they moved inside and awaited their order.

Several minutes later as they made their way back to the truck, coffee in hand, Sydney reached over and took the keys from Alex.

"I'll drive the rest of the way." Alex opened her mouth to protest and Sydney put a finger to her lips. "No. I can see you're uncomfortable. This is the first time you've been up and active for most of a day. You've probably pushed too hard and done too much. I'm not letting you drive us over the edge of the mountain just for the sake of trying to prove you're infallible."

They re-entered the truck and Alex clipped her seatbelt.

"Just for the record," she said with mock indignation. "I am infallible. And I most certainly would not have driven us over the edge of the mountain."

"Yes, sport," Sydney said, not even attempting to hide her patronizing tone as she reached out and patted Alex's leg. "Why don't you put the seat back and try and relax."

Several minutes later, as they began the winding turns that would begin the steeper climb upward, Sydney looked over to find her clearly exhausted companion fast asleep in the seat next to her.

ALMOST FORTY-FIVE minutes later Sydney followed the directions provided by the GPS unit and passed through a very small community called Fawnskin. Soon afterwards she pulled off the mountain highway onto a somewhat secluded smaller road called North Shore Lane. She would occasionally see the glint of moonlight off water through the trees as she made her way farther from the highway. After a couple of miles she turned into a partially full parking lot and saw before her a moderate sized ski chalet style resort surrounded by trees and snow. She smiled at the beautiful setting. It was going to be a wonderful weekend. She parked then leaned over to Alex and gently stroked her cheek.

"Hey, you. We're here."

Alex opened her eyes and looked at Sydney, then looked out the window and smiled, apparently satisfied with what she saw.

"Hmm, it looks like the web site so far. Well, shall we go check in?"

They proceeded into the lobby and noted the large sitting area, still carrying the ski chalet look. A large bar took up one corner, and a casual sitting area was gathered around a large central fireplace and windows looking out onto a shoreline meadow and Arrowhead Lake beyond. Sydney admired the view as Alex checked in then joined her and led her to the elevators and up to the third floor.

They entered a large mini-suite room with a king bed to one side and a sitting area surrounding a large fireplace to the other. Sydney moved to the covered window and drew back the curtains. The view from their window was unobstructed, giving the impression they were looking out the picture window of a single cabin on the shoreline as opposed to an exclusive fifty-room resort. The lake glistened in the light of the full moon, which could be seen over the trees on the opposite shoreline across the lake.

Alex walked up behind Sydney as she stood looking out the window and reached her arms around her.

"Happy to be here?" she whispered in Sydney's ear. Sydney leaned back into Alex's embrace.

"God, yes. It's beautiful." She turned in Alex's arms to face her then leaned up to kiss her. "Thank you."

Alex smiled. "I'm glad you like it. But I've got something else to surprise you with. Why don't you go have a nice relaxing bubble bath in what should be our Jacuzzi tub." She nodded toward the yet uninspected bathroom. "And I'll see you when you're done."

"What about dinner? Should I dress for the restaurant downstairs? It looked kind of nice," Sydney asked as she removed toiletries from her suitcase.

"Nah. Why don't you just put on something comfortable and we'll figure it out. Maybe I'll just pick something up and we can save the restaurant for tomorrow night."

A little more than twenty minutes later Sydney exited the bathroom wearing a silk negligée and short silk robe. She first saw the bed covers drawn back expectantly. As she looked farther into the suite she saw Alex seated in front of the large picture window at a small candlelit table set for two. The lights in the suite were dimmed, allowing the candles to cast a romantic glow. Alex stood and walked to Sydney, taking her once again into her arms.

"Maybe you'll just pick something up, huh, Sergeant Chambers?" Sydney asked quietly with a smile as she looked at the table setting.

"Well, yeah, something like that. Do you like it?" Alex asked, leading her by the hand to the table and holding the chair for her as she sat. Sydney could only nod as she took in the candles and dinner. Alex removed a bottle of Champagne from a nearby ice bucket and filled two glasses. She sat down and lifted the champagne flute. Sydney followed suit and Alex gently tapped the glasses together.

"To us," she said. Once again Sydney could only nod.

When dinner was finished they moved to the sitting area in front of the crackling fireplace. There they cuddled and polished off the champagne while feeding one another dessert from a platter of chocolate covered strawberries.

After several minutes of cuddling and watching the fire, Sydney took Alex's empty champagne glass and placed it on the low table in front of the couch. Then she turned and climbed onto Alex's lap, straddling her hips with her knees on the couch on either side of her. Sydney rested her hands on Alex's shoulders as she gazed into her eyes.

"Thank you," Sydney said. She leaned down and tenderly kissed Alex. "This is all wonderful." She kissed her once again, then pulled away slightly. "You've definitely made me feel special," she said with their lips just touching, then she re-engaged the kiss, gradually increasing its intensity.

Alex undid the sash of Sydney's robe, then moved her hands up each of Sydney's hips within the garment. Sydney removed her hands from Alex's shoulders momentarily, shrugging the robe off and allowing it to fall to the ground. Sydney pulled at Alex's shirt, drawing it up and over Alex's head in one smooth move, then plunged her tongue into Alex's mouth once again.

Alex slipped her hands under the front of Sydney's negligee to her breasts where she gently massaged and squeezed. "Bed?" she asked.

"God, yes," Sydney replied in a gasp, rising from Alex's lap, taking her by the hand and pulling her toward the bed across the suite.

Chapter Twenty-two

SYDNEY AWOKE TO the comfortable sensation of Alex's arm draped protectively across her stomach. She gently traced the wrist and fingers as she looked over at her lover. A smile slowly developed on Alex's face and she opened still drowsy eyes.

"Hi," Alex said, somewhat seductively, as she tightened her arm around Sydney. Sydney didn't resist as Alex pulled her into her embrace. The kiss that began gently soon grew more aggressive, and just as Sydney extended a leg over Alex's hip and began to pull Alex on top of her they were disturbed by a knock on the door.

"Damn. Didn't we put out the 'Do Not Disturb' sign last night?" Sydney said in humorous exasperation.

Alex smiled down at her from her position on top of Sydney.

"Uh, this is probably my fault," she said. Sydney raised her eyebrows in question and Alex continued. "I arranged for room service at eight a.m. You know, breakfast in bed." She gave Sydney a quick kiss then started to rise. "I'll get it," she said.

"Wait a minute. You can't just throw the door open to room service. I'm naked!"

Alex removed a hotel robe from the nearby closet and turned back to Sydney smiling. "And you're gorgeous when you're naked," she said as she leaned down and kissed Sydney.

A second knock came at the door, slightly louder and more insistent, accompanied by a male voice. "Room service."

"Just a second!" Alex called, then returned her attention to Sydney, momentarily resuming the kiss. "Don't worry," she said. "I'll protect your virtue." She straightened up and walked to the door, ensuring the robe was secure around her own otherwise naked body.

Alex opened the door to the room service delivery, leaving it standing only partially open so it obstructed the view of the bedroom portion of the mini-suite.

"I'll take it from here," she said, pulling the rolling cart into the room then turning back for the bill. She signed the bill, handed it back to the uniformed gentleman, and then closed the door.

Alex pushed the cart closer to the bed then began uncovering several plates. Sydney started to get out of bed to help but Alex stopped her.

"Nope," she said, pushing Sydney back into the pillows. "Allow me." She placed a tray containing an assortment of pastries and juice across Sydney's lap. "Besides," she added as she poured coffee for each of them. "This is likely as close as you'll ever get to me cooking for you." Alex sat down on the bed, lounging against the pillows beside

Sydney as they enjoyed a leisurely breakfast together. Neither was in a hurry to get out of bed, even long after the breakfast was done.

IT WAS EARLY afternoon when the two finally dressed warmly and walked down to the lobby of the hotel. Alex had convinced Sydney they should at least take a walk along the shoreline, if for no other reason than to allow the maid service access to the room at some point. Alex carried a folded wool blanket under her arm and both were dressed warmly. They picked up a map of the immediate area from the concierge desk, then headed out of the hotel and down to the shoreline. A path ran along the edge of the lake, between the trees and the water, ending about a hundred yards down the shore from the hotel at a small hotel dock. They turned and took the cleanly shoveled path in the opposite direction, headed away from the marina. Within minutes they had rounded a slight bend in the path and were completely out of sight of the hotel.

Looking back and noting their apparent solitude, Alex took Sydney's hand in her own, interlacing their fingers. Sydney responded by giving her hand a gentle squeeze and moving closer to Alex as they walked on for several minutes in companionable silence. They soon came across a rocky outcropping that jutted out into the water. Alex laid the folded blanket on the top of the rock and they sat down with Sydney leaning back into Alex's embrace. There they sat and watched the sun get lower on the horizon, sending shimmers of shifting light across the lake.

"I could get used to this," Sydney said after a while.

"What's that?" Alex asked. "Being served breakfast in bed? Staying in bed after breakfast? Making love for most of the day? Spending the weekend in a romantic secluded resort on the side of a mountain lake? Snuggling together in the cold watching the sun set?"

"All of that is very nice, wonderful in fact," Sydney said, snuggling against Alex as they sat together. "But I was actually referring to you."

"What about me? You could get used to me?"

"Yes. I could get used to waking up next to you. When you go back home and then go back to work next week I'm going to miss you. I enjoyed coming home to you each evening last week, and waking up with you next to me each morning."

"Well, I have a key now. So I can stop by whenever I please. I can surprise you anytime."

"Promise you won't be a stranger?" Sydney asked.

"I can definitely promise that," Alex said and hugged Sydney to her. Moments later she felt Sydney shiver.

"I think I heard it may snow later," Alex said. "And it's going to be a cold night." She drew Sydney closer, wrapping both arms around her then leaning down and nuzzling Sydney's neck. "We'll have to figure something out to stay warm."

Sydney giggled. "Subtle, Sergeant Chambers, very subtle." She pressed her body further into Alex's embrace for a moment then leaned forward to climb off the rocks, pulling Alex with her. "Come on, let's head back before it gets too cold and dark."

"What about dinner?" Alex asked. "What would you like to do tonight?"

When they returned to the hotel lobby they decided to have dinner in a little Italian restaurant they'd been told about in the small town of Fawnskin a few miles down the lake front highway from the hotel. They checked with the hotel desk and discovered the restaurant was casual dress and a local favorite. The desk clerk told them the restaurant did not take reservations and on a Saturday evening was likely to get busy. They decided to set out immediately in hopes of beating the rush.

The restaurant turned out to be all that it promised. They found parking close by, and while the restaurant looked popular it was not yet packed. They were immediately seated in a private booth near the back. They found the food very good and the service was outstanding. When they made their way out almost two hours later they found a light dusting of snow had gathered on the road and parked cars. The snow continued to fall and seemed to be growing heavier.

"WE'D BETTER GO right back to the hotel," Alex said to Sydney as they made their way back to the truck. Sydney climbed into the cab as Alex held the passenger door for her. "I'd like to get back to the hotel before chains become necessary. I don't want to get stuck trying to put them on in the dark," Alex added.

As they pulled onto the lakeside highway Sydney reached out almost unconsciously as Alex's hand met hers near the center console. This had become a very natural act for the two of them. Sydney found it very comfortable and reassuring, with no words needing to be spoken.

The ringing of Alex's cell phone broke the silence several minutes later. Sydney let go of her hand as Alex retrieved the phone from her jacket pocket and took her eyes off the highway just long enough to look down at the caller I.D.

"It's Regina," she said. The glance she gave Sydney was somewhat nervous.

"Well, you better answer it," Sydney said, squeezing her arm reassuringly. "She may have that information you were asking for."

Alex nodded then pushed the button to receive the call, putting Regina on speakerphone.

"Yeah, Reg," she said. Having had no reason to use their cell phones in the last twenty-four hours, neither woman had realized how bad the reception was along the less developed northern shore of the lake. It became evident as they barely heard every third word spoken by Regina.

"...lex...formation you..."

"Reg, the reception is terrible here. Let me get to a landline and call you back in a little while," Alex said as she leaned forward toward the wheel.

Sydney looked out the window and saw the snow beginning to fall more steadily, now impacting visibility on the roadway. She was relieved they only had a short distance to go to get back to the hotel. Regina's voice cracked through the speaker again.

"...need to...important..." Sydney was frustrated with the incomplete and garbled statements and saw Alex reach toward the phone to hang up when one partially complete statement came through and chilled her to the bone. "...nclaire has a twin..." The phone connection died immediately after that.

It all clicked into place for Sydney at that moment. The comment she heard Garvis make repeatedly during the attack came back to her.

"He told me I could have her first."

That statement had been stuck at the edge of her mind for days now, not making sense. But now it did. Sinclair had a twin. Garvis had been a pawn. Sinclair's twin was the "he" in that statement, and he was still out there. The threat was still there.

"Oh my God!" Sydney said. "I wasn't imagining things at the elevator — it was Sinclair's twin. The flowers, the pictures. It's been him all along."

Alex stuffed her phone back into her jacket pocket and reached once again for Sydney's hand, giving it a reassuring squeeze.

"We'll get back to the hotel and I'll get all the details then we'll make some phone calls. This could mean nothing."

"I know," Sydney said. "Or it could explain—"

"What the hell is this asshole doing?" Alex exclaimed as a large dark SUV pulled up beside them as if attempting to pass on the thin mountain roadway. The truck suddenly swerved to the right into their lane, forcing Alex to swerve toward the shoulder in an effort to avoid a collision.

ALEX HEARD SYDNEY scream as she attempted to maintain control of her truck when the wheels hit the loose dirt on the shoulder. She almost made it, but the driver of the dark SUV swerved to the right again, this time actually colliding with her front door and quarter-panel, forcing her completely off the pavement. The wheels on the right side of the truck caught in the soft gravel at the far right of the shoulder where the edge began to drop off steeply.

Alex fought to keep the truck on the solid portion of the shoulder and roadway, but knew it was a losing battle as the truck began to drag to the right and tilt dangerously. In the end she had no choice but to turn into the drop, hoping to at least keep the vehicle upright and avoid as many large trees as possible as it barreled down the ravine. But luck was not with her in that effort as the left front tire finally hit a large boulder, sending the front left portion of the vehicle airborne and flipping it onto the passenger side. Alex felt the truck make almost a complete roll as the vehicle continued forward and down. What she could see of the earth spun through the windshield as first the passenger side hit the ground, then they turned completely upside down, sliding on the roof for what seemed like seconds. They came to a bone-jarring stop when the bottom of the car collided with a large tree, halting the truck as it now lay on its driver's side.

Neither of them moved for several minutes. Alex closed her eyes against the dizziness and felt the now all too familiar sensation of warm blood trickling down the left side of her head. She knew she'd reopened her head wound. She eventually heard a voice calling to her. Alex opened her eyes and looked to her right, which was now up, and saw Sydney suspended above her, restrained by her seatbelt. Sydney's concerned eyes looked back at her.

"Sydney?" Alex said, somewhat frantically as she reached for her own seatbelt release. "Are you okay?"

"Yes," came the shaken reply. "I think so." Alex saw Sydney struggling with her seatbelt.

"Not yet! Let me get up and help." Alex released her seatbelt and carefully stood, her feet actually on the now shattered driver's door window and her upper body well into the suspended passenger seat area. She ignored her own pain and put her arms around Sydney to take her weight, and as Sydney released her seatbelt Alex was able to ensure she was lowered carefully to a standing position with her. They both stood there in each other's arms for a moment.

"You're sure you're okay?" Alex said, pulling back and inspecting Sydney for any evidence of injury. "Does anything hurt?"

"Nothing serious. I just got the breath knocked out of me, I think. What about you? I thought you were fading out on me for a minute there." Then Sydney caught the dark blood streaming down Alex's face. "Your head! You've re-opened your stitches."

"It's okay. I just banged my head on the window or the door frame when we rolled. Let's get out of here and make our way to the road for help. I wonder if the idiot who ran us off the road stuck around." Alex began kicking out the already cracked windshield, which eventually fell away in a full sheet of safety glass and the two of them stepped out into the night. The snow was now falling more heavily.

Alex looked up the hill and was surprised at how far off the road they had traveled. She looked the other way, down the hill, noticing they had traversed the steepest portion of the hill and come to rest as the ground began to even out and the trees became more populated. She knew somewhere beyond those trees was the lake, but they were too dense to allow the water to be seen.

Alex's gaze returned to the hill once again. It was going to be a difficult climb back to the roadway in the snow. The hill was quite steep and the snow was growing deeper by the minute. But they had no choice. No one would to see them from the road at night, and by morning the car could be covered in a blanket of snow. She knew they weren't dressed for being stuck outside on a night like this. They had to make it to the road and hope to flag down a passing car.

Alex reached for her pocket, finding her cell phone missing. Then she reached for her rear waistband. The holster that was usually tucked into her pants there was missing as well. She figured both must have been jarred loose during the violent rolling of the vehicle.

Alex gave Sydney's hand a quick squeeze. "Give me a quick second," she said, then stepped back through the open windshield into the cab of the truck and began feeling around, almost blindly, for her weapon, her phone and anything else that may be important or useful.

Alex was bent over, feeling around under the driver's seat and beneath the dashboard below the steering wheel. That lucky position likely saved her life. She suddenly heard the sound of gunshots, then heard Sydney scream. The first round fired pierced the thin metal of the roof about two feet above her head, right about where her chest would have been had she been standing. The second round passed through about ten inches lower and slightly to the left.

"Run for the trees, Syd!"

A third round came through the roof, still lower and this time slightly to the right. It became clear to Alex the shooter intended to stitch a continuous pattern of bullet holes until he eventually got lucky. A moment of relief came over her as she also realized he seemed to be concentrating on her, so Sydney had hopefully escaped and was out of sight and behind cover. All of this passed through Alex's mind in a few seconds, closely followed by her determination that she had no choice but to make a break for it. She launched herself out through the open windshield before the next round was fired.

Alex saw Sydney running into the trees and moved to follow. She was two steps out of the truck when the sole of her insulated hiking boot hit the unseen sheet of glass that used to be her windshield. Her foot slipped along the wet and snowy glass and she fell. That slip saved her life, as the fourth round sailed past where her head had been a fraction of a second before. She hit the ground and rolled to her right, past the front of the truck and behind it. To follow Sydney now would mean Alex would have to expose herself to her assailant. Instead, she backed into the trees, keeping the bulk of the vehicle between her and where she believed the shooter was. She maintained that cover, keeping low and pausing momentarily behind large tree trunks to listen for movement. She would attempt to circle toward the lake in the direction Sydney had taken, hoping to find her before whoever was out there did.

SYDNEY HEARD ALEX'S shouted order and complied without further thought. Not sure where the shots had been fired from, she dashed down the remaining slope for the cover of the nearby tree line, assuming Alex was close behind her. She heard another round fired and again strike the truck. Somewhere in her conscious mind she realized the gunfire was not focused on her, but on Alex. As soon as she reached the heavier trees she stopped and listened for Alex, thinking she must have been behind her when she ran. She heard and saw nothing and suddenly realized she hadn't heard anything after the fourth shot. Was Alex lying back there in the snow, possibly wounded?

Sydney wasn't going to go on without her. No matter how terrifying this was she had to go back for Alex. She began to slowly make her way back in the direction she believed the truck lay, slowing as the trees grew thinner, pausing occasionally to listen. She was sure she had to be close when she crouched behind a particularly large pine tree trunk. She closed her eyes and took a deep breath, trying to raise the courage to move on, knowing she was becoming more exposed. At the last minute she heard the soft crunch of snow beneath boots behind her and to her right. She began to turn when the open-handed blow caught her in the side of the head, sending her reeling to the ground.

He was on her before she recovered, shoving the gun against her chin as he roughly lifted her off the ground. It was then she recognized him and the terror almost caused her to collapse again. It was Sinclair. Sinclair's twin actually, her mind registered from somewhere. At that moment Sydney had no doubt she was about to be subjected to all the horrors she had been witness to during Sinclair's trial. The rape, the torture, the death. She couldn't keep the tears from falling as he pushed her up the incline and slightly to the right, back in the direction the gunfire had originated.

As they progressed he talked.

"I've been watching you since my brother's trial. You were very impressive, Ms. Rutledge. Very professional." Even with the almost overwhelming sensation of terror, Sydney's mind was putting it all together. They were clearly identical twins, so the DNA would be the same, only the fingerprints would be different, and those are more easily hidden or protected by a smart offender.

"Of course, that doesn't change the fact that you had no business being in that courtroom. If you were smart you would have stayed in your place, in your proper world. You're a woman, you should be a mother, not trying to do a man's job in a man's world." He began to rant quietly and Sydney started to gain a deeper understanding of the sociopathic thought process that had led to the murderous crime spree.

"But you took it even one step further than that, didn't you?" he continued. Sydney sensed he was possibly working himself into a dangerous frenzy. This belief was confirmed when he suddenly slammed her into the trunk of a tree, turning her around and taking her by the throat again, the gun pushed painfully into her ribs and his body pressing against hers. Sydney could feel his erection against her abdomen.

"You and that other woman," he continued. "That sergeant. She's worse than you are, thinking she has any business in that line of work. And you two violate the natural order of things. You flaunt your violations for the world to see. You both deserve the ultimate punishment." He shoved his hips into her crotch, physically making his intentions clear and smiling at the tears that ran down her face. "I'll take care of her first though. I'll make you watch while I kill her. Maybe I'll play with her a bit first while you watch. But when that's over you and I are going to spend a long time together."

His next order surprised her. "Now scream."

She looked at him, unsure how to react. Suddenly a fist crashed into the side of her head, knocking her to the ground once again. He was immediately standing over her, shoving the handgun into his waistband and reaching for the front of her jacket, pulling her off the ground and raising his hand to hit her again. "I said scream, bitch!" he ordered again then slapped her.

"No! Stop!" Sydney let out a strangled cry.

"Again!" This time he shook her and again raised his hand, this time in a fist.

"Stop it! What do you want?" Sydney raised an arm in an effort to defend herself, now half sobbing she closed her eyes.

The blow never came. She opened her eyes to see him looking back the way they had come. He appeared to be listening carefully. She soon heard the sound of someone crashing through the trees, moving toward them in the forest. She saw the sinister smile develop on his face and he pulled her roughly to her feet.

"Good. Now we keep moving." He once again removed the handgun from his waist and grasped her by the back neck of her jacket, propelling her forward. Sydney suddenly realized what was happening. She was being used as bait. Bait for Alex. He intended to follow through on his threat to torture and kill Alex in front of her, then rape and kill her afterwards. And she was powerless to stop him. Ten minutes later Sydney was still being pushed forward at gunpoint as snow continued to fall. The Sinclair twin prodded her to continue her progress, occasionally adjusting their direction of travel. As she tripped over a branch and fell hard to the ground she looked back at him as she rose and noted he was looking at a handheld GPS device. He put the device back in his jacket pocket then pulled her roughly to her feet.

"Scream again. Scream for help," he ordered.

Now knowing what he planned, Sydney was determined not to help him lead Alex into a trap. She shook her head in refusal.

"Don't try and play games with me." The open palm connected with her left cheek. Sydney would have fallen to the ground had he not been holding her by the front of her jacket. The world spun momentarily as he pushed her back up against another tree. "I said scream," he said with menace.

"I won't help you," Sydney said quietly.

Sydney saw him reach into his back pocket, then gasped and flinched when the switchblade knife clicked open just inches from her eye. She took a deep breath and once again shook her head in refusal. She couldn't help but notice the dangerous glint of anger that flashed through his eyes.

Sydney closed her eyes, unsure of what would happen next but determined not to help summon Alex. She flinched and tried to pull her head away as the cold steel touched her cheek below her left eye. He dragged it, relatively gently, down her cheek and jaw to her neck. She felt the sharp edge held across her neck as his other hand roughly unzipped her parka then ripped her shirt open, tearing the top several buttons off. The sudden cold and the instant up-tick in fear caused her to gasp.

Sydney had an immediate understanding of what might be about to happen. She had seen the photos and vivid written descriptions of the torture and knew exactly what Sinclair's victims had been subjected to. She kept her eyes clenched shut and sobbed quietly, but still she didn't scream.

The point of the knife trailed down her neck. The pressure increased at her collar bone and she bit her own lip to keep from crying out as the sharp edge cut into her skin, getting deeper as it inched down across her sternum toward her breasts. She knew the warm wet sensation was her own blood as it trailed down her now exposed chest. She held on as long as she could, but the pain and fear was soon overwhelming and a terrorized cry eventually escaped from her lips, growing louder and then ending in a wracking sob as the knife was withdrawn and Sydney fell to the ground crying.

The Sinclair twin returned the switchblade to his pocket and leaned down, again grasping Sydney by the arm, pulling her to her feet and resuming their forward progress. Within a few minutes they entered a clearing containing a large cabin with a gray Ford Taurus parked nearby. Sydney noticed the cabin was on a slight rise above the water, with what appeared to be a boat ramp traveling along the side of the cabin and down to the shoreline. She briefly glanced at what appeared to be the top of a set of stairs on the lakeside of the cabin leading down the shore and a small wooden dock.

"Get inside," he ordered as he dragged Sydney across the clearing and up the front porch of the cabin. Once inside Sydney observed a surprisingly well-equipped modern living area. She was pushed into the middle of the large main room. Suddenly feeling very exposed in the relative light of the interior, she pulled her jacket closed about her, covering her torn shirt.

"So now," he said with a sadistic smile. "We wait. And you stay out of trouble." He drew his arm across his body and brought his fist forward in an upwards-backhand swing, striking Sydney before she could react or prepare for the blow. She was lifted off her feet and thrown backwards, crashing through a wooden coffee table, which splintered beneath her. Then blackness overcame her.

Chapter Twenty-three

ALEX MOVED THROUGH the woods, working her way around to the left in the direction she believed Sydney had gone. She paused at one point, thinking she'd heard a woman's muffled cry.

"Stop it! What do you want?" This time Alex distinctly recognized Sydney's voice. It came from ahead of her and slightly off to the left. She corrected her direction and took off at a headlong run through the trees, unconcerned with the noise she was making.

Several minutes later she heard another terrified and pain filled scream and immediately adjusted her course. It appeared they were moving back toward the lakeshore. A few minutes later she saw a lakeside cabin through the trees. She paused behind a tree trunk near the edge of the clearing, studying the scene. She noted the Ford Taurus parked nearby. Nothing she saw helped her determine if Sydney was being held here or if the assailant had taken her past this cabin and onwards into the woods.

Alex studied the dim light that could be seen through the partially covered windows. She knew she had no choice but to approach the cabin and try and get a look inside. After taking a last look around she dashed across the open space, running low to the ground through the gently falling snow flakes. She came to a stop flush with the exterior wall of the cabin, near the corner of the front porch. She inched her head slowly toward the window, scanning the dimly lit room. She saw no movement, no apparent occupants, and was about to draw her head back when she leaned far enough to see the floor in the far corner of what appeared to be a family room area.

Her heart was in her throat as she saw Sydney lying on the floor, bloody and obviously beaten, her wrists bound and extended over her head, secured to the sofa frame. Alex forced herself to carefully observe the entire room and the darkened doorways that appeared to lead into the bedrooms. There was no movement, no evidence of another occupant.

Alex scanned the clearing and surrounding tree line, still seeing no movement. She knew he had to be here somewhere. There was no way he would just leave Sydney behind. She knew there was a good chance she was being baited—set up. She also knew she had no choice. Sydney was obviously hurt. She may need immediate medical attention. She had to take the chance and make her move now.

Alex silently climbed onto the porch and approached the front door. She reached out and tested the doorknob, finding that it turned easily in her hand, not locked. Alex's suspicions grew. Instinct told her it was a set up, but she didn't have any other choice. She pushed the door open and entered swiftly, moving immediately across the room to the opposite wall. She confirmed there were no occupants in the attached kitchen area. The older model phone lay broken on the floor, the cord, having been removed, eliminated any chance of a call for help. Alex moved next to the two darkened doorways. They also appeared empty. She made her way to Sydney and knelt beside her.

Sydney was lying on her side in a semi-fetal position. Her wrists were bound with the phone cord with her arms extended past her head and secured to the frame of the sofa. Alex's breath caught again as she saw Sydney's battered face. Bruises were already rising at her cheek and temple and her lip was swollen and split. Alex brushed her hand gently across Sydney's cheek.

"Syd? Hon, I need you to wake up."

Sydney groaned in response and tried to move. Alex attempted to untie the line, but her cold and stiff fingers could not seem to manipulate the tight knots. She rose and moved back to the nearby kitchenette. She noticed a set of Ford car keys, likely to the Taurus sedan parked out front. She slipped the keys into her pants pocket then retrieved a steak knife in a butcher block on the counter and returned to Sydney's side. She carefully cut the line allowing her to remove the binding from Sydney's wrists.

Sydney groaned as Alex slowly rolled her onto her back, revealing the torn shirt and bloody gash extending across her sternum. Alex's mind was immediately drawn to the memory of the pictures she had seen of Sinclair's former victims. The thought brought tears to her eyes as she imagined the horror Sydney must have endured. At that moment Sydney's eyes opened.

"No," Sydney said weakly. "Alex, it's a set up. He's here."

"We're getting out of here, Syd. Just come with me."

As gently as possible she lifted the groggy woman to a seated position then helped her to stand. Sydney leaned into her as they moved slowly to the still open doorway where Alex paused and scanned the area around the cabin. Seeing nothing she moved with Sydney onto the porch and turned toward the vehicle as Sydney's steps grew slightly stronger. It was then Alex saw the fresh footprints in the newly fallen snow. They went from the side of the Taurus back in the direction of the corner of the house at the other end of the porch, behind Alex.

Alex mentally kicked herself as she realized her failure. In her haste to get to Sydney's side she hadn't cleared the vehicle. The voice that spoke from behind her a fraction of a second later did not surprise her.

"So, the indomitable, Sergeant Chambers. We finally meet face-to-face."

Alex turned slowly and saw the Sinclair twin smiling sadistically from across the porch. "You made better time than I thought you would," he said. "You almost caught me unprepared. Allow me to introduce myself. I'm Lucas Brooks. You managed to best my brother,

Matthew Brooks, though you know him as Matthew Sinclair. You won't find me quite as easy to vanquish as he was, I'm afraid."

Alex watched the gun carefully for a moment, then her eyes moved up to study his face. Even having been prepared for a Sinclair twin, the match was shocking. Sydney also raised her head from Alex's shoulder and her eyes settled on the man. Her hand came up to grasp at Alex's jacket as if fearing he would pull her away. Alex instinctively pulled Sydney closer to her in an obviously protective motion, taking a step back as the man holding the gun came toward them across the porch. Alex looked at the still open doorway between them, then immediately discounted the idea of escaping into the cabin before he could intercede. Her inspection did not go unnoticed.

"Like the place, Sergeant?" Brooks asked, indicating the cabin. "The owner was kind enough to tell me about this private, secluded, romantic cabin when I sat next to him at a breakfast counter in town yesterday. Apparently he rents the place when he's not using it and was willing to show it to me on the off chance I might be interested in the future. He didn't realize my needs were more immediate. But he certainly won't need it anymore. It's terrible how many misfortunes can befall you when you're alone in the middle of nowhere in the dead of winter."

The sinister smile left no doubt in Alex's mind what had befallen the owner of the cabin.

"And his SUV came in handy as well. It allowed me to keep my own car here and use his to assist with that little accident you had.

"The bottom line is this," he continued. "No one is going to miss him. No one is going to miss either of you for a while. And even when they do, they won't find your car or either of you out here for some time. We have this place, and everything around it, all to ourselves for a while. Just the three of us."

Alex slowly stepped in front of Sydney, standing between her and Brooks. She watched carefully as he moved closer, the gun held level and pointed directly at her midsection. Brooks seemed to notice this protective movement and Alex noted he seemed to be working himself almost into a psychotic frenzy as his anger clearly grew.

"Look at you, cavorting together as if you were a man and a woman. You two are disgusting deviants! Both of you! You'll pay for violating nature, for defying the natural order of things! I'll personally make you pay, the way the others have. They also thought they could fit into a man's role. Thought they could do a man's job better than men. You'll be punished just as they were. You first." Brooks looked at Alex. "I'll kill you before I teach Ms. Rutledge a more lengthy lesson."

As he ranted the wind kicked up and was gusting against them, blowing flurries of fresh snow up onto the porch. It soon became difficult to hear and the visibility lessened. The car parked nearby was no longer visible.

"Inside," Brooks said, almost having to yell. "Both of you." He emphasized this by waving the gun, indicating the still open cabin door a few feet away.

Alex used the gusting wind as an excuse to try and draw him closer. "What?" She shrugged her shoulders and held her hands up in simulated surrender. "I can't hear you," she hollered. It had the desired effect. He moved closer and raised his voice.

"Get inside!" He gestured again toward the open door. He now stood only about six feet away.

Alex nodded in understanding, then pulled Sydney to her right side and began moving toward the door that stood between them and Brooks. She continued to keep her body between Brooks and Sydney. As she held Sydney around the waist she slipped the car keys into her pocket, her actions concealed by their bodies. She leaned closer to Sydney's ear, unsure if she could hear what was said but trying anyway. "As soon as you can," she whispered below the level of the wind. "Run for the sedan and get out of here." She looked into Sydney's eyes and saw the understanding.

They neared the open doorway and Alex noted she had cut the distance between herself and Brooks, who stood on the porch just a few feet to the other side of the door. Alex inched closer as she allowed Sydney to precede her through the doorway. She looked to her left and saw her opportunity as Brooks looked away momentarily, glancing at the blowing snow and the Ford Taurus parked beyond. Alex didn't hesitate, shoving Sydney through the doorway out of the line of fire and rushing the few feet between them before Brooks turned back to face her.

The weapon fired just as she got her hand on his wrist and shoved the gun outward and away from her body. Her other hand came up and clenched his throat as she drove him backwards, moving with him and maintaining her hold on his gun wrist as the back of his thighs hit the porch banister. Alex continued pushing, driving him over the top of the banister and carrying her with him. She concentrated on maintaining control of the gun hand as they went over the side, dropping six feet to the ground below and landing with a bone jarring crash.

Brooks, who landed on his back and shoulders with Alex partially on top of him, seemed momentarily stunned. Alex took advantage of this moment to devote her efforts to relieving him of the gun, throwing her upper body across his right arm and shoulder, pinning it to the ground then grasping the weapon hand with both of hers. Unfortunately he recovered with amazing speed and used his free hand in a fist to pummel at her head and the side of her face from his position behind her. Still she concentrated on the weapon, finally working her way to the magazine release and seeing it partially dislodge from the base of the weapon's grips. She frantically pulled at the magazine, removing it and throwing it as far as she could, hoping it disappeared in the snow.

Alex knew she was now left with the one round in the chamber, then the weapon would be empty. Brooks continued to batter her from behind. He was now concentrating rabbit punches to her kidney area, the blows landing on the still healing gunshot wounds and cracked ribs. Alex fought through the rising pain, cleared her hands away from the slide of the semi-automatic handgun, then forced the trigger of the weapon backwards. It fired, discharging what Alex knew would be the final round. The slide on the semi-automatic handgun locked back, proving it was indeed empty. She released his gun hand and rolled away from Brooks, trying to create distance.

Alex realized too late the beating she had taken during the struggle for the weapon had taken its toll. She was slow in rolling to her feet. Brooks, however, was much faster. As Alex turned to face him and tried to raise her hands in defense he plowed into her, driving the two of them to the top of the stairway leading to the boat deck. Alex crashed to the ground with Brooks on top of her and looked up to see him raising his right hand back with a glint of metal clenched in his fist. She realized he still had the empty handgun as it began coming down toward her head.

Alex shifted her weight and drove her hips up, forcing Brooks off balance from his position straddling her. As his body tipped she rolled, reaching for the front of his clothes with her hands and throwing him sideways over the top of the stairs. In her exhaustion, the throw was not made cleanly and Brooks grasped at her arm and clothing as he fell, pulling her over the edge with him. They rolled together down the dozen hard steps, losing grasp of one another as they reached the bottom.

Alex rose to her knees and looked up just in time to see the glint of metal again coming at her head. She tried to dodge, leaning away from the incoming object and falling off balance again to her side. She rolled to her hands and knees and tried to rise to her feet but was suddenly taken with a booted kick to the ribs. She tried to roll out of the way but a second kick caught her in the side of the head and her vision began to tunnel.

SYDNEY, THOUGH STILL woozy from the earlier abuse, knew Alex had placed a set of keys into her pocket. She heard the directions Alex gave her before pushing her through the doorway. She heard them crash over the banister to the ground below then the shot go off shortly afterwards. They had moved out of sight down the side of the cabin by the time Sydney exited, but she heard the grunts and cursing of the altercation as they battled toward the lakeshore.

Sydney removed the keys from her pocket and looked through the driving snow to where the now barely visible sedan was parked. She made up her mind in seconds. She had left Alex alone once before in the woods behind her house, she would not do it again, no matter what the cost. She tucked the keys back into her pocket and moved rapidly off the deck.

She made her way through the falling snow at the back of the cabin and slowly down the stairs, following the sounds of the ongoing struggle. As she neared the bottom of the steps the shoreline appeared before her through the wind driven falling flakes of white. Two figures could be seen, locked in combat on the ground near the beginning of the dock. Then one stood, towering over the other, and she immediately recognized the figure as Brooks. He swung at Alex, who Sydney saw fall off balance, then he began viciously kicking her.

Sydney looked frantically about her for a weapon, seeing only a pile of discarded wood apparently left over from the deck construction. She picked up a short piece of two by four and moved toward the two. Her approach was unnoticed by Brooks as he continued his vicious attack on Alex who was doing her best to defend herself from the repeated kicks, covering her face and head with her arms, which left her ribcage exposed.

The roar of the wind through the surrounding trees covered any sound Sydney made as she hurriedly approached. Bringing the board up over her head and swinging downward with all her might, Sydney aimed for the back of Brooks's head. At the last moment, leaving no opportunity for Sydney to adjust her aim, he suddenly leaned down to grab Alex and pull her to her feet. Sydney's blow took him in the upper back instead of the head. The blow staggered Brooks, who dropped Alex's almost limp body as he fell forward to his hands and knees.

Sydney, distracted by Alex's inert form, was not expecting his quick recovery. Brooks rose to his feet and rushed at her, angry and in obvious pain, but still moving with surprising speed. She brought the wood beam back for another baseball swing but he had already moved within arm's reach and Sydney's blow did not have much power or speed behind it. Brooks blocked it at her wrist with one large hand and ripped the wood from her grasp with the other. He backhanded her across the head, sending her to the ground at the edge of the deck. When Sydney looked up Brooks was once again advancing. Looking behind her she saw the large dark platform of the dock extending over the water. She had no other avenue of escape and so she backed slowly away from him, across the wooden platform extending over the cold water.

Sydney suddenly remembered the keys in her pocket. She reached for them, positioning the ring in the palm of her hand with three of the keys protruding between her fingers as she made a fist. It was a technique taught in the most basic of self-defense courses and it was pretty much all she had left. She cocked the arm slightly back, somewhat concealing her fist behind her body as Brooks came closer.

He was soon within arm's reach of her and Sydney lashed out with all her energy, swinging her fist at his face, specifically at his eyes. Her fist connected in a slashing motion, driving the keys across his vulnerable face and left eye. Brooks was caught unprepared and staggered backwards, his hand covering his face as he partially turned away from Sydney. Seeing a possible opening, Sydney tried to run past Brooks's doubled over form. But once again, his speed was alarming. He reached out, grabbing Sydney around the waist as she tried to get between him and the edge of the dock. Holding her around the body with one arm he grabbed at her wrist with the other, ripped the keys from her hand and threw them over the edge of the decking into the water below.

Sydney looked into Brooks's now bloody face and saw the rage. The next open-handed blow caught her in the side of the head and face, sending her back down the length of the dock and leaving her lying dizzy on her stomach on the wood. Brooks's strong hands grabbed at the back of her jacket and lifted her to her knees, pulling her back against his legs. Then something wrapped around her neck. She knew immediately what was happening as the leather belt tightened. Her hands came up and grabbed uselessly at the belt. When that didn't work she tried to reach back and claw at the hands near the back of her neck. Nothing worked and the belt began pulling tighter, cutting off her air. She heard Brooks's laughing above her as her breathing became more labored. Her vision soon began to tunnel and the laughter faded out as she lost consciousness.

ALEX HAD TRIED in vain to deflect the repeated kicks to her body and head. She swore she felt multiple ribs crack beneath one particularly vicious blow, and the warmth of the blood as the partially healed wounds to her side were reopened. There was a pause to the blows then strong hands grabbed at the front of her jacket and started to lift her upper body off the ground. Just as suddenly the grip was released, dropping her back to the ground on her back and allowing her a respite from the beating. She rolled to her side and opened her eyes in time to see Brooks tear a board out of Sydney's hands and lash out at her, sending her staggering down the dock.

Alex fought to get to her knees as she watched Sydney continue her valiant battle with the attacker almost twice her size. Alex saw Brooks stagger backward with Sydney's strike at his face, and was climbing to her feet when Sydney made her running attempt to escape past him, only to be struck down once again.

By the time Alex managed to stagger unsteadily to her feet and step onto the dock, Brooks had already removed his belt and pulled Sydney to her knees before him. She watched in horror as the belt went around Sydney's neck and Sydney battled to breathe. Everything seemed to move in slow motion as she made her way down the raised platform, anger and desperation driving her faster and calling on energy reserves she didn't know she had. She picked up the discarded two by four as she moved, bringing it over her shoulder as she came within range of Brooks, the movement being masked under the sound of the wind.

Brooks was turned sideways to Alex, partially hunched over at the waist as he leaned down, pulling the belt tighter around Sydney's neck. This left Alex a less than ideal target. She took the best aim she could, driving the wood beam down toward the base of his neck. In that last second before she connected, she saw Sydney's hands dropping away from the belt at her neck as she lost consciousness.

As the blow struck, Brooks fell forward on top of Sydney's inert form. Alex, weakened and off balance, staggered as well, going to her knees but maintaining a grip on the wood. She was again amazed at Brooks's recovery as he shook his head and then rose to his feet. He looked down at Sydney, who was lying motionless on her side near the edge of the dock, then up at Alex who was climbing to her feet several yards away. He smiled at Alex, then reared back with one foot, bring it forward in a vicious kick to Sydney's exposed midsection, sending her over the end of the dock.

Alex staggered to her feet as she watched this happen, hopelessly screaming as she watched Sydney go over the edge, splashing into the close to freezing water below. She slammed into Brooks a fraction of a second too late and they both went down, Alex straddling him about his midsection. She brought the edge of the board to his throat and applied pressure. Brooks concentrated his punches at her midsection, his fist connecting with the bleeding wound to her left side. He continued to fight as she weakened, then he suddenly threw her sideways, using the same tactic she had earlier, twisting and shifting beneath her and sending her off balance.

This time, however, Brooks wasn't as quick to recover, rolling slowly to his hands and knees and grasping at his throat. Alex was on him again in a second, her body weight driving him down onto his stomach as she now straddled his back at the waist. Alex knew she had to get to Sydney. She knew she had been at least unconscious when she went over the edge into the lake. Alex prayed Sydney was holding on and she could get to her in time. She had no time to waste and acted on desperation.

Alex brought her hands to Brooks's head, one reaching down and grasping his chin as the other placed pressure on the back of his head. She then placed a knee across the top of his shoulders and applied her bodyweight.

Bringing forth every ounce of strength she could muster, she yanked his chin savagely upwards and to the right as she simultaneously pushed downwards and to the left with the hand at the back of his head. Alex heard the sickening crack of vertebrae breaking even over the winds. His struggle ceased immediately and his body went limp.

Alex hurriedly pushed off Brooks and moved to the end of the dock where Sydney had gone over the edge. She leaned over the end of the wooden platform, searching the surface, desperately screaming for Sydney, terrified she had sunk beneath the surface of the cold water. Finally, she saw Sydney's arms wrapped around the upright leg of the dock, eyes closed and barely conscious, oblivious to the voice yelling down to her. Just as Alex reached for her, Sydney's grasp of the wooden pylon slipped and she sank below the surface.

EVERYTHING HAD GONE black for Sydney as she finally succumbed to the belt's stranglehold and the lack of oxygen. Then suddenly the restriction around her neck was released and she fell forward. Her head and face struck the wooden planks, driven downward by a tremendous weight falling on top of her. In the back of her mind somewhere she knew she owed her release to Alex. She rolled onto her side, gasping as her lungs filled with oxygen again. Except for her desperate breathing, her body refused to respond and she couldn't seem to see through the blackness. A sudden blow to her ribs knocked what little wind from her had been recovered, then she was falling.

Sydney struck the surface of the cold lake and plunged under. She struggled back up and gasped for air as her head broke the surface, the cold immediately sapping what little strength she had left. It took all she could muster to grasp at the nearby post and put her arms around it. At first she was able to hear the sounds of a struggle through the wood above her. Then her teeth even stopped chattering as she sank once again toward unconsciousness. She tried desperately to hold on but her arms slipped from the wooden pylon and she sank once again beneath the surface.

ALEX PLUNGED INTO the frigid water a moment after Sydney disappeared from sight. She dove, desperately searching and finally seeing a flash of color through the water. Her hands closed around cloth then she wrapped her arms around Sydney's limp body and pushed off the sandy bottom. Alex pulled Sydney back to the surface, careful to keep her head above water as she dragged Sydney the fifty feet back to the shoreline.

By the time Alex was able to feel the bottom of the lake beneath her feet her own teeth were chattering uncontrollably. She knew she had a short period of time to get them both back to the cabin and out of the wet clothes. She pulled Sydney out of the water and up onto the shore, noting her blue lips. She ensured Sydney was breathing, then somehow found the strength to lift the limp body into her arms and begin the journey back to the cabin through the snow and wind.

It seemed like forever before she was climbing back up the porch, struggling through the still open door into the now chilled interior of the cabin. Alex had recalled seeing a thermostat and paused momentarily to turn up the heat. Somehow she made it into the bedroom, some still operational part of her mind telling her that they had to get out of the wet clothes and under covers.

She undressed Sydney, then stripped off her own clothing. As gently as she could she partially lifted, partially dragged Sydney onto the bed and beneath the covers, climbing in next to her and wrapping her body around her. She was relieved when she felt Sydney move, shivering and moaning. When she next looked down at Sydney she found haunted and exhausted eyes looking back at her.

"Is he—"

"He's gone. You don't have to worry about him. Right now we're just going to get warm and then we're going to rest."

As Sydney's eyes closed again Alex noticed her bruised and bloodied face. She briefly lifted the bed covers and inspected her once again, noting the redness to her ribs that was beginning to darken into purple. Alex remembered the vicious kick that had sent Sydney into the water. She knew there was a good chance Sydney had some broken ribs. She could only hope there was no greater internal damage.

Alex knew their only choice at this point was to stay in the cabin and wait out the storm and regain their strength. The phone was inoperable and there was no cell phone reception. They had no keys and therefore no transportation. And they had no real idea of exactly where they were, even if they could navigate in the storm. They would need to make do here for a while. Fortunately the cabin was well built, modern and appeared well equipped.

Alex fought her own urges to give in to exhaustion as she lay huddled around Sydney. Her wound was re-opened and bleeding and needed to be addressed. She pushed herself from the bed and tried to stand, staggering and almost falling to her knees as the pain and exhaustion nearly overwhelmed her. She looked down and saw the blood seeping from the wound. She would have to do something about that.

She moved to a linen cabinet outside the bathroom and found what she needed. She folded a pillowcase into a compress then used another to wrap around her torso and hold it in place. Not ideal, she figured, but good enough to work in the short term. Then she made her way back to the bedroom and climbed back into bed with Sydney, who was still shivering slightly. Alex pulled Sydney close, knowing their shared body heat was likely the safest and most efficient way to warm them. Sydney tucked into her body in welcome and it was only moments before each of them fell into an exhausted sleep.

Chapter Twenty-four

SAL AWOKE TO the ringing of Tiffany's cell phone. Tiffany rolled over and grabbed the phone from the bed stand, speaking quietly. He looked at the nearby clock. It was almost midnight. The timing of the call alone caused concern and Sal was instantly awake.

"Yeah, Regina. What's up?" Tiffany said, turning away from Sal. He stopped her and reached up to tilt the phone away from her ear then leaned in so he could listen as well.

"Tiff, I'm sorry to bother you," came the reply. "I was trying to get hold of Alex with some information that might be important. I got through to her briefly this evening but the cell reception was bad and she said she was going to get to a regular phone and call me back. With everything that's been going on, and with what I found out, well, I'm just a little concerned that she never called back."

"She's up in the mountains for the weekend with...someone," Tiffany said. "What information are you talking about?"

"Alex asked me to do some research on Matthew Sinclair. Everyone knew he was adopted, but Alex was wondering what his real background was. She thought maybe everyone was missing something and possibly there was something in his past. I had to call in a couple favors because we had to go back into the archived paper files, before things were computerized. But it turned out Matthew Sinclair's real name was Matthew Brooks. Matthew Brooks had a brother at the time he entered foster care, a twin brother."

"Sinclair had a twin brother?" Tiffany was immediately wide-awake as the implications of Regina's statement hit her. She turned to meet Sal's eyes, then pulled the phone away from her ear and put it on the speaker setting.

"Tiffany, the Brooks twins, they had a history," Regina's voice came from the device. "They did weird, mean stuff to animals and then later to other kids. Things we now realize are indicators of mental illness—sociopathic tendencies. They were separated in the system because they seemed to feed off each other. Matthew was eventually adopted. Lucas, the other twin, never was. When he got to his teenage years he grew more violent. There were allegations of sexual attacks against young women. He finally disappeared off the map when he turned eighteen. The records from their time together seemed to express an opinion that Lucas was the ringleader and Matthew the follower. I had some friends look at the actual events and they think the evidence more appropriately supports that in fact Matthew was the ringleader and directed Lucas to commit most of the atrocities at his direction."

"Did you tell Alex any of this?" Sal asked, already rolling out of bed and reaching for his clothes.

"No, that's just it. We had a bad cell connection. I tried to tell her there was a twin but she said she'd get to a landline and call me back. I've been waiting all night and she never called back. I've tried her cell phone a couple of times but it just goes to voicemail."

"Alex would've called you back if she said she was going to," Sal said as he pulled on a shirt and sat down to start lacing up shoes. "Something might be wrong. I think I know where she's at up in Arrowhead. I'll start by calling there. Thanks, Regina. Once I start making notifications on this you'll probably be getting some phone calls."

Tiffany disconnected the phone and started getting dressed herself as Sal turned on his laptop then began a search of resorts and hotels in the Arrowhead Lake area. Alex had called him Friday before she and Sydney headed out of town and had given him a rundown of their plans. Sal finally hit on a resort that sounded familiar from the previous day's conversation with Alex. He dialed the number, reaching the night shift front desk clerk. Sal explained that he was a sergeant with the Los Angeles Police Department and that he was attempting to make emergency contact with another sergeant who was staying at the resort. The manager confirmed an Alex Chambers was staying at the hotel and connected Sal with the room. The phone rang unanswered and went to the message service.

"Alex, it's Sal. It's important I get hold of you as soon as possible. You need to call me as soon as you get this, no matter what time it is."

Sal hung up and called the hotel clerk back again. He explained he had left a message but he needed to ensure the message was received and requested the clerk to arrange for a visit to the room. Sensing the clerk's hesitation, he finally advised him the occupant may have been the victim of a crime and he needed to determine if they were present in the room. He soon found himself speaking to the night shift manager and after explaining the circumstances he agreed to check the room and call Sal back. He followed through as promised, and minutes later Sal was informed the room was empty and it did not appear it had been occupied since the maid had made it up at mid-day. Sal advised the manager he and other law enforcement officers would likely be en route and to please call him back should he notice the occupants had returned.

"What do we do now?" Tiffany asked as Sal hung up the phone.

"Unless Alex shows up or calls, I'm heading up to Arrowhead. I'll start making some other phone calls on the way."

Tiffany began gathering her own warm clothing. "I'm going with you."

"No, hon, this isn't—"

"I'm going with you. I can keep you company on the drive. I can make phone calls. If we get there and it turns into a big police investigation, I can run for coffee or do whatever needs to be done." Tiffany took Sal's hand and leaned down to give him a kiss. "I care about Alex, too. We'll go up together and figure it out. And you may need me." They both knew what she meant. Tiffany's medical background might come in handy.

Sal nodded and stood up, then hugged her. "Thank you," were the only words he could find.

An hour later they were well east of L.A. making their way into the foothills of the San Bernardino Mountains. Sal had notified Detective Chuck Severs, telling him what he knew and suspected and giving him Regina's number, then advising the detective he was heading for Arrowhead. Chuck called Sal back as they reached the foothills and began heading up the mountain.

"After I talked to Regina I made a few notifications then contacted the San Bernardino County Sheriffs. They're going to meet up with you. I gave them the description of Alex's truck and the license number. They've already confirmed it's not in the parking lot of the hotel and they're searching for it. They had a storm blow in this last evening that made getting around difficult for a while but it's starting to lighten up. Do you have chains?"

"Yeah, I'm good," Sal said.

"Okay, look for the sheriff's car at the chain inspection point on the mountain highway. They'll be waiting for you and will guide you up to the hotel. I'm going to make some phone calls to initiate some checks on Alex's phone signal and some other things, then I'll be en route. I'm hearing the cell signals are sporadic at best up there, so I'll get hold of you through the Sheriff's Office if I don't see you there first."

"Sounds good. I'll see you up there." Sal ended the call then immediately called the hotel, asking the clerk, who was now familiar with him, if Alex had returned to her room. The clerk said he was quite sure she hadn't, but put Sal on hold momentarily to call Alex's room. He returned a minute later to advise him there was no answer in the room. Sal ended the call and put the phone down, reaching for Tiffany's hand beside him as his concern continued to grow.

SEVERAL HOURS LATER the sun was just beginning to rise over the eastern horizon. A San Bernardino County Sheriff's Deputy had guided Sal and Tiffany into the hotel after meeting them at the snow chain checkpoint partway up the mountain. The young deputy had extended every courtesy, filling in the L.A.P.D. sergeant on the actions his department had taken so far. Unfortunately, that hadn't been much. Not for a lack of willingness, but simply because they had little information to work with and the region had been hit with a short but fierce snowstorm. But all the S.B.S.D. units on duty had been provided with not only Alex's photo—compliments of L.A.P.D. records—but also the description of her vehicle, as well as Matthew Sinclair's photo. This last effort was based on the presumption Sinclair's twin brother likely looked like him and just in case Lucas Brooks was in fact in the area.

At six-thirty a.m. Chuck Severs and his partner, Robert Kim, arrived at the hotel. The hotel had graciously offered one of their meeting rooms off the main lobby for use by the law enforcement personnel. That room now contained the two L.A.P.D. detectives, Sal and Tiffany, the original deputy who had led them through the snow, and now a sergeant from the sheriff's department. Chuck got right down to business after making a phone call utilizing the hotel landline provided.

"Okay, here's what we've got. I've managed to get some quick responses from Alex's credit card company and her cell phone provider." He leaned over a map of the region that had been provided by the deputy. "It looks like there was a charge on her credit card last night at about seven p.m." He referred to his notes. "It was at a restaurant in Fawnskin."

The deputy pointed to the small town on the map. "That's right here," he said. "It's about eight miles straight down the highway. What time was that at?" he asked.

"The charge was processed at seven-thirty-two p.m.," Chuck said after referring to his notes.

"That was a little before the storm really blew in," the deputy said. "If they left shortly after that charge, they should have made it back here without any serious issues. There's not a lot between here and there except some small private roads leading into other properties along the lake, cabins and things. I can't see any reason why they would've stopped anywhere between here and there."

Chuck nodded as the rest looked at the map, then turned to his notes again.

"Alex's cell provider recorded an incoming call to her phone at a seven-thirty-eight. That has to be the call from Regina Carlisle. According to the cell phone company, it connected through a tower on the west side of the lake. They said their reception is spotty up here, but they're sure the town of Fawnskin would be on the very edge of their service area and her phone would not have connected had she been too much farther from the tower than that."

Chuck straightened up and took a breath. "I've had them trying to ping her phone since I first called them early this morning. When I spoke to them just now they said they had a momentary connection that failed almost immediately. It went through the same tower."

Sal looked down at the map. "So the phone is somewhere between here and Fawnskin? Chuck nodded. Sal turned and looked at the deputy. "That call went through just before the storm started?" The deputy nodded.

"Geez, so what are we saying here? They drove off the

edge of the road?" Tiffany asked.

Sal looked up at Chuck, knowing they were thinking the same thing.

"Or they were forced off the road," he said quietly. "Alex wouldn't have driven if the weather was too bad. And she wouldn't have driven faster than the conditions allowed."

"Okay," the sergeant interjected. "So we concentrate our efforts between here and Fawnskin. We pay attention to any evidence of cars going off the road."

He was immediately on the radio, making notifications. After further discussion it was agreed that Sal and Tiffany would ride with the deputy and begin their search from the hotel. Chuck and Robert would ride with the sergeant and respond directly to Fawnskin, then begin working their way back eastbound along the highway.

ALEX WOKE UP to sunlight coming between the blinds on the bedroom window. She was at first confused in the unfamiliar surroundings, then her memory returned. She sat up slowly, feeling the discomfort the movement brought, and the exhaustion that still invaded her body. She turned to Sydney, still asleep beside her, then reached over to run her fingers down a bruised cheek.

"Hey, how're you doing?" she asked when Sydney's eyes began to flutter. Sydney tried to sit up then gasped, grabbing her ribcage and falling back.

"Don't move," Alex said. "Just rest and stay warm. I'm gonna get us some clothes and then we'll work on a way out of here."

Alex swung her legs off the bed as she moved to stand up. As the bed covers fell away the improvised compression bandage she had created the night before was revealed, now stained with blood. Sydney gasped again when she saw the bloody bandage and Alex's bruised torso. She reached for Alex's hand.

"Don't worry," Alex said, squeezing Sydney's hand gently. "I'm fine."

She made her way slowly into the bathroom, finding their clothes on the floor where she'd left them. They were still wet and rumpled. Considering the chilly conditions outside, Alex figured it would not be prudent to put those clothes back on. She went back into the bedroom and began rooting through the chest of drawers and a nearby suitcase. Sydney watched from her position in bed.

"It feels kind of wrong," Sydney finally said. "Just searching through someone's cabin like this."

Alex returned to the bed, now carrying two pairs of sweatpants and a couple sweatshirts.

"I know, hon. But our clothes are still wet." She sat to put on the sweats. "And it's not as if the owner is going to need these anymore."

Sydney nodded silently in response.

"Here, why don't you put this on. It'll be large, but it's clean and warm." Alex helped Sydney sit up and put on the loose sweatpants and sweatshirt, then tried to get her to climb back in bed. "We've got no keys, so no car. I'm going to head up the road away from the lake. I figure it's got to hit the main highway a little ways up. I'll flag down a car and get someone to call for help."

Sydney shook her head. "I'm coming with you."

"Sydney, you're hurt. You're cold. You were almost..." Alex stopped momentarily as she visualized the horror of the previous night. Sydney had been choked into unconsciousness. She'd almost drowned. "It looks like there's two feet of snow out there. There's no point in both of us going."

Sydney stood slowly and leaned into Alex. The two of them embraced, neither wanting to let go for several moments.

"Be careful, please?" Sydney finally said, leaning back and looking into Alex's eyes.

"I'll be careful," Alex said, then leaned down and kissed her. "And I'll be back soon."

They moved together out of the bedroom toward the front living room, Alex helping Sydney, who still seemed unsteady on her feet. She intended to leave Sydney on the sofa there, beneath a blanket. They were both startled by the sound of footsteps on the front porch, immediately outside the door. Before Alex had time to react or remember whether she had locked the door, the doorknob turned and the door swung open.

OVER AN HOUR into the search Sal and Tiffany, along with their escorting deputy, had covered almost three miles. The radio crackled with a notification from the sergeant advising them to come immediately to a point two miles east of the Fawnskin town limits. Sal's heart was in his throat as they drove west on the highway. Tiffany reached forward from the back seat and squeezed his shoulder as they pulled up to the scene. Chuck met them as they climbed from the sheriff's cruiser.

"We found her truck," he said, pointing down a steep ravine. Sal and Tiffany looked down and saw the truck lying on its side lodged against a tree, partially covered under a blanket of snow.

"Oh, shit!" Sal said. "Are they there?"

"It doesn't look like it. Rob is down there now with the sergeant taking a better look around."

Sal reached for Tiffany's hand. They had no choice but to wait and watch as the two figures worked their way around the overturned truck and the surrounding area. They then began to trudge back up the ravine through the snow. It was not an easy trek, taking the two of them a good ten minutes. When they reached the edge of the road they were breathing hard as Detective Kim told them of their observations.

"There's no one in the truck. Looks like they kicked out the windshield to exit. It's got a solid layer of snow on it and there's no footsteps in the snow, so they crashed at the beginning of the storm." He looked uncomfortably at Sal and Tiffany, clearly needing to add something. "There are four rounds through the roof. Someone was shooting at the truck after it came to rest. And there's blood inside, on the driver's side."

Almost an hour later they were still there. Due to the evidence of shots being fired this was no longer a simple missing persons case. The San Bernardino County Sheriff's Department had called in additional resources. Deputies were searching the woods surrounding the overturned truck, though there was little hope of any obvious evidence due to the snowfall.

Sal, Tiffany and the two R.H.D. detectives were standing by the various vehicles gathered at the road's edge waiting for any news that might come in. A deputy soon drove up and the four of them listened as he reported to the sheriff's sergeant who had taken command of the scene.

"We've got an SUV parked off the road in the underbrush just about a couple hundred yards up the road. Almost looks like it pulled off the side and intentionally parked out of sight. It's got collision damage to the right side. Paint transfer looks like it may match." The deputy nodded his head at Alex's truck at the bottom of the ravine. "It's locked up and other than the damage to the outside, nothing looks suspicious. Here's the license." He handed the sergeant a slip of paper.

The sergeant nodded, then turned to the detectives. "Well, let's see who it's registered to." He climbed into his car to work on the mobile computer as they all gathered around. Moments later they had an address for the registered owner in Marina del Rey, California.

"That doesn't help much, does it?" Tiffany asked Sal.

"Well, M.D.R. is L.A. County Sheriff's territory. How about we have them do a drive by on the owner's address and see if anyone can tell us where the owner is up here?" Sal said to the sergeant.

He nodded. "Already done. Our dispatch is making the request to the L.A. Sheriff's Office now."

Another thirty minutes later their reply came in via the sergeant's computer terminal. The adult daughter of the registered owner had fortunately been dog-sitting for her father and was able to provide the location of the cabin he owned, with rural directions to a private road off a mile marker a short distance down the mountain highway. Having been briefed by the R.H.D. detectives on the history of Sinclair/Brooks, and unsure of what they would find, the sergeant had gathered four additional deputies to accompany them to the cabin. They set off in a caravan of several vehicles.

Sal turned in his seat and told Tiffany, "Stay in the car until we know what's going on, okay?" She nodded and they proceeded down the dirt road toward the cabin.

The vehicles pulled directly into the clearing and the cabin was suddenly in front of them, a single sedan was parked in front and the lake visible beyond.

The various sheriff's personnel exited their vehicles and deployed on the house at the direction of the sergeant as he and a second deputy approached the front door. Sal, Chuck and Robert stepped out and gathered behind the vehicle parked in front of the cabin, wanting to be available but knowing it was the locals' operation. They watched as the two sheriff's deputies took each side of the cabin's door, then the sergeant reached up and turned the knob. The door swung open without resistance and the two uniformed officers brought their drawn weapons up.

TRAPPED IN THE exposed center of the room, Alex tried to turn and shield Sydney as the door fully opened. She first saw the two handguns pointed at her, then noted the weapons were brandished by uniformed officers. She slowly raised her free hand to show she had no weapon, her other arm was wrapped around Sydney.

"Don't shoot," she said clearly. Then added, "I'm a cop."

"Sergeant Chambers?" The inquiry came from the uniformed deputy wearing sergeant's stripes. He entered, lowering his weapon slightly, eyes sweeping the rest of the room. Alex nodded, relief flooding through her. The sergeant waved for the second deputy to follow and they quickly cleared the rest of the rooms in the small cabin.

"Sit down," the sergeant said, pointing at the sofa. "You look like you're about to fall over. We'll get you some help." He turned to his deputy, "Let them know they can come in. And make sure to get the nurse." The deputy nodded and headed for the door. Moments later Alex heard him yell from the porch.

"Get the nurse and you can all come on in."

Rapid footsteps were heard traversing the porch. Alex looked up at Sal as he entered, smiling weakly at him as he sat down in a chair next to her.

"Geez, Chambers, you really are a shit-stirrer, aren't you?" Sal shook his head, looking back and forth between them, unable to hide his look of relief.

Less than an hour later they were en route to Mountains Community Hospital on the east shore of Lake Arrowhead, compliments of the San Bernardino County Sheriff's Department. Both were admitted for their multitude of injuries and the residual effects of moderate hypothermia.

Chapter Twenty-five

THE NEXT MORNING Alex was perched on the edge of Sydney's bed, refusing to move despite Sydney's efforts to convince her otherwise.

"You shouldn't be up, Alex. You should still be in bed." Sydney gave Alex's hand a squeeze as she gently argued.

"I'm fine. I just need to be near you," Alex replied. A noise at the doorway drew their attention as Sal and Tiffany entered their shared hospital room.

"Glad to see you two looking a little more healthy and alive," Tiffany said as she gave each of them a hug, dropping a duffle bag beside the bed.

"Yeah, and I want to thank you for the romantic evening Tiffany and I spent in your nice mountain suite," Sal said with a smile. He looked around at the sparse hospital room furnishings, his eyes settling on the remains of the breakfast they had been provided. "I'd venture to say our night was certainly far better than yours was."

"Yes," Tiffany added. "And better than the night you'll spend this evening, I'm afraid."

"Ah, you're kidding me." Alex said. "Tell me we're not stuck here for another night!"

"Afraid so," Tiffany said. "It's for the best, Alex. You guys both went through a trial."

"Yeah, but—"

"You've got another mild concussion on top of your previous one, re-injured your cracked ribs and re-opened your bullet wound." Tiffany countered.

"Yeah, but—"

"Sydney almost drowned, she's got her own cracked rib and her case of hypothermia was not minor, Alex."

"Just stay and keep me company, Alex. Please?" This came from Sydney, as she blatantly manipulated Alex in an effort to get her to voluntarily stay at the hospital.

Alex took a deep breath. "Okay," she said quietly, ceasing her arguments. She looked down at their entwined fingers as Sydney gave her hand another squeeze. Sydney looked up to exchange a knowing look with the other couple and stifled a giggle when Sal silently mouthed, "She's whipped," to the two women.

Later that afternoon the San Bernardino Sheriff's investigators, accompanied by Chuck and Robert, visited Alex and Sydney at the hospital. Alex had her cell phone and weapon returned to her by the Sheriff's investigators, who told her the items had finally been located inside her truck. The vehicle, she was told, had been dragged back to the roadway, but was unfortunately a total loss.

They all made themselves comfortable in order to fill the women in on what had been discovered over the past twenty-four hours.

Working with the crime scene information, along with statements provided by Alex, Sydney and Regina, and from follow up by Chuck and his partner in reviewing the old manual children services and adoption records, a full picture of what happened had been put together.

"Matthew and Lucas Brooks were indeed twins," Chuck began. "From what we can gather they were raised by a single mother. Dad left and completely disappeared when the boys were still very young. Mom had her own issues and evidently abused the boys both physically and psychologically. She locked them in a small closet for days at a time and beat them sometimes with a belt when they caused her problems. Evidently she blamed them for holding her back from what she believed would otherwise be her own great professional success. A teacher discovered this abuse when the boys were ten years old and a court removed them from mom's custody. She didn't really fight the process or make any effort to keep them when they were taken.

"Regina was able to locate the county foster and adoption records, which is when she tried to make that phone call to you." Chuck paused to look around the room before continuing and Sal jumped in.

"She called me after her call to you dropped and she wasn't able to get back to you. Then, when I couldn't get hold of you, that's when I reached out to Chuck and we all headed up here." Both Alex and Sydney nodded.

"How did you figure out where to start looking for us?" Sydney asked.

"We traced the cell tower closest to you when that last call went through. We asked around and figured out where you had been to dinner and were pretty sure you never made it back. So we started looking for your car along the route from the restaurant," Roger said. "We found your car, then soon after found the car Brooks used to run you off the road. We were able to contact the owner's family and that led us to the cabin where we found you."

"What happened to the owner of the car? How did Sinclair, or Brooks, get a hold of it?" Sydney asked.

"We found his body today," one of the Sheriff's investigators said. "He was buried in the snow in the woods beside his cabin. He'd been shot. We think it's likely ballistics will show it was the same weapon Brooks shot at you with."

Alex leaned back against the raised bed and pillows beside Sydney and put her arm around her. Sydney leaned into Alex, comforted by their contact as she contemplated how close to death they had both come.

Chuck then took up the narrative once again.

"The foster records Regina found show what we now know were activities that indicated serious psychological issues. They were abusive to small animals and cruel to other children. Various foster families took them in only to return the twins when the problems surfaced. Notes indicated they were too difficult to control, dangerous and violent. Social workers finally determined the only way to handle the two would be to separate them. They believed their misbehavior fed off one another and so separated they would be more manageable. This seemed to work out for Matthew, who was taken in by a financially well off couple who had been unable to have their own children. They gave him their family name and he grew up in a life of privilege, becoming Matthew Sinclair."

"Lucas Brooks, on the other hand, carried on with his socially unacceptable behaviors and acting out," Roger said. "He developed into an angry teenager and juvenile delinquent. There were even some allegations of sexual abuse made against him by other young women he encountered, but none of those charges ever stuck because all of the victims seemed too afraid to follow through with any formal investigations. Lucas was never adopted and spent his time in the system until he turned eighteen."

"It looks like sometime after Lucas turned eighteen he was able to track down Matthew." Chuck took over the story. "Now that we know where to look and the name to look for, we're finding some banking records that show Matthew Sinclair was providing large amounts of money to Lucas Brooks, and has been doing so for years."

Alex nodded. "So they reconnect and the two psychopaths start feeding off each other all over again. And let me guess, the White Rose Murders were all about them being pissed off at mommy? That's why they chose professional women for their victims?"

Chuck nodded in the affirmative.

"What about the man who attacked us in the woods?" Alex asked.

"Ah, yes. Garvis. No one knows exactly how Sinclair, or perhaps Brooks, recruited Garvis," Chuck said. "But we're pretty sure Garvis knew about the murders, probably even actively helped out on the recent copycat killings, maybe the original White Rose ones. Plus he has his own history of sexual attacks. It clearly wouldn't have taken much to recruit him to make an attack on you two. We're pretty sure Brooks murdered him and the stuff left there was planted to throw us off and make you lower your guard."

"The belt Brooks had," Sydney said, her hand unconsciously going to her own throat as she remembered her own experience. "It was the missing murder weapon from the original case, wasn't it?"

"We think so," Chuck said. "We haven't done a forensic match. But I've looked at the stitching and I'm pretty sure it's going to be a match. And that's pretty much the whole story." Chuck stood and was joined by the rest of the visitors. The two detectives and their sheriff's department counterparts wished the two women a speedy recovery and departed, leaving Sal and Tiffany.

"Well, you two are supposed to be released tomorrow morning. We'll be by then to pick you up," Tiffany said. "I packed some clothes and necessities and brought them in for you," she added, pointing to the duffle she had dropped beside the bed. "So you two get some rest and we'll see you tomorrow."

Alex and Sydney soon found themselves alone once again.

"You okay?" Alex said, looking at Sydney beside her and they remained snuggled on the same small bed.

"Yeah, it's just, I don't know, a little overwhelming," Sydney said.

"But it's over now," Alex said. "I have no doubt about it now."

"Yeah, it's over. Now we can just concentrate on more important stuff." Sydney leaned down, tucking her head into Alex's shoulder and below her chin. "Like us."

ALEX AND SYDNEY were dressed and ready to leave when Sal and Tiffany entered the hospital room the next morning.

Sydney was reclining on the hospital bed, Alex once again seated beside her, hand in hand.

"Well, your ride has arrived. You guys ready to go?" Sal asked.

"Yes, definitely," Sydney said.

"You're all checked out of the hotel. We packed up all your stuff. The deputies even brought the clothes from the cabin," Sal said. "So we're ready to hit the road. Any idea where we're heading?"

"What do you mean?" Alex asked. "Home. We're heading home. I think we've had enough adventure for a few days."

"Uh huh," Tiffany said. "Which home? Both homes?" She turned to Alex. "You got a plan to get around for the next few days, considering you don't have a car?"

"Shit. I hadn't even thought of that." Alex turned to Sydney. "And your car is at my place."

Sydney squeezed her hand. "Well, it looks like maybe you're stuck with me for another day or two, Sergeant Chambers," she said with a smile. "We're both moving a little slow. So we'll just have to take care of each other for a while."

Alex's smile matched hers. "Are you sure you can put up with me?"

"I'll manage somehow," Sydney said as she stood to walk out hand-in-hand with Alex. "Thanks, Sal. We'd appreciate it if you'd take us to Alex's place and we'll figure it out from there."

Just over twenty-four hours later the two women were safely snuggling together beneath blankets in front of the fireplace in Alex's bungalow as the February rain fell gently outside. After being dropped off by Sal and Tiffany they had retired to bed and slept most of the afternoon away, awakened only by hunger. Then they had reclined amongst throw pillows in front of the crackling fire.

"So, what are the chances I can beg a ride tomorrow to go new car shopping?" Alex asked as she ran a hand through Sydney's hair and lightly touched the still bruised cheek.

"I'm sure I can work that into the schedule," Sydney replied. "I should probably think about going back to work on Tuesday though."

"Yeah. Me too. Hopefully everything can get back to normal now. Really back to normal, with no more surprises."

"What's normal?" Sydney asked, turning within Alex's embrace to face her. "With us I mean. With everything that's happened, our relationship has kind of been formed around crazy drama and crisis. How do you feel about that?"

"How do I feel? I feel that I want you in my life. We're just going to have to figure the rest out. We go back to work. We go on with our lives. We work out the rest of it as we go." Alex leaned in and kissed Sydney lightly. "I think we'll figure it out together."

Sydney's only response was a deeply passionate kiss as she wrapped her arms around Alex. Tomorrow could bring whatever challenges it may. They would meet them together.

Other Quest Titles You Might Enjoy:

Murder and the Hurdy Gurdy Girl
by Kate McLachlan

It's 1897, and Susan Bantry is on the run from the law. She ends up in Needles Eye, Idaho, where she works in a hurdy gurdy as a dancing girl.

Jo Erin, Susan's childhood friend, is the cross-dressing Pinkerton agent sent to track Susan down. Before she can complete the job, a mining war breaks out and interferes with Jo Erin's plans. Complicating matters even further are the feelings that resurface between Susan and Jo Erin, as events from their past come back to haunt them.

ISBN 978-1-61929-126-3
eISBN 978-1-61929-127-0

Hearts, Dead and Alive
by Kate McLachlan

When fifth grade teacher Kimberly Wayland finds a human heart in the middle school dumpster, she has some explaining to do. Like why she was in the dumpster in the first place, and why she didn't tell the police about her gruesome find. But after giving the police a fake alibi, explaining is the last thing Kim wants to do. Instead, with the help of her friends—hot "best friend" Becca, co-worker "lesbian wanna-be" Annie, and lawyer "stickler-for-rules" Lucy—Kim sets out to solve the mystery of the missing heart. Along the way, she unexpectedly solves another mystery, the mystery of her own heart.

ISBN 978-1-61929-017-4
eISBN 978-1-61929-018-1

The Chameleon
by Brenda Adcock

Six years ago Detective Christine Shaw left her happy life and a good job in Texas to follow her libido to New York City. She's still a cop, but her stewardess girlfriend has flown the coop and Chris hasn't been able to fill the void. Everything in her life begins to change when she and her partner are assigned to a high profile case.

The murder of Broadway star Elaine Barrie propels Chris into a whole new world. A fan of the murdered actress since she was a teenager, Chris isn't prepared for the secrets she uncovers during their investigation, including her attraction to the daughter of her number one suspect.

Was the victim any of the personalities witnesses describe, or was the real person a chameleon, satisfying the expectations of each person she met?

ISBN 978-1-61929-102-7
eISBN 978-1-61929-103-4

Now You See Me
by S. Y. Thompson

Corporate attorney Erin Donovan has nothing on her mind except representing her clients to the best of her abilities. One fateful day, she shows an irritating new client, Carson Tierney, around the tenth floor space of her own building and her life takes an unforeseen direction.

Carson is an awe-inspiring woman by anyone's standards. Possessing genius-level intelligence that has allowed her to become a self-made millionaire of a computer software company, Carson still has a dark secret that could be her undoing.

When the two are thrust together to escape a deadly killer in a high-rise office building while a blizzard rages outside, they have no one to count on but each other. So begins an unexpected yet tender romance. However, unchecked love and desire isn't in their future. The murderer is still out there and he's coming for them. Will Carson's street-wise skills protect them both as Erin attempts to discover the killer's identity just as relentlessly as he is seeking their demise?

ISBN 978-1-61929-112-6
eISBN 978-1-61929-113-3

OTHER QUEST PUBLICATIONS

Brenda Adcock	Pipeline	978-1-932300-64-2
Brenda Adcock	Redress of Grievances	978-1-932300-86-4
Brenda Adcock	Tunnel Vision	978-1-935053-19-4
Brenda Adcock	The Chameleon	978-1-61929-102-7
Sharon G. Clark	Into the Mist	978-1-935053-34-7
Michele Coffman	Veiled Conspiracy	978-1-935053-38-5
Cleo Dare	Cognate	978-1-935053-25-5
Cleo Dare	Faultless	978-1-61929-064-8
Cleo Dare	Hanging Offense	978-1-935053-11-8
Dakota Hudson	White Roses Calling	978-1-61929-170-6
Helen M. Macpherson	Colder Than Ice	1-932300-29-5
Linda Morganstein	Harpies' Feast	978-1-935053-43-9
Linda Morganstein	On A Silver Platter	978-1-935053-51-4
Linda Morganstein	Ordinary Furies	978-1-935053-47-7
Andi Marquette	Land of Entrapment	978-1-935053-02-6
Andi Marquette	State of Denial	978-1-935053-09-5
Andi Marquette	The Ties That Bind	978-1-935053-23-1
Andi Marquette	Day of the Dead	978-1-61929-146-1
Kate McLachlan	Hearts, Dead and Alive	978-1-61929-017-4
Kate McLachlan	Murder and the Hurdy Gurdy Girl	978-1-61929-126-3
Kate McLachlan	Rescue At Inspiration Point	978-1-61929-005-1
Kate McLachlan	Rip Van Dyke	978-1-935053-29-3
Damian Serbu	Secrets In the Attic	978-1-935053-33-0
Damian Serbu	The Vampire's Angel	978-1-935053-22-4
Damian Serbu	The Vampire's Quest	978-1-61929-013-6
Damian Serbu	The Vampire's Witch	978-1-61929-104-1
S. Y. Thompson	Now You See Me	978-1-61929-112-6
Mary Vermillion	Death By Discount	978-1-61929-047-1
Mary Vermillion	Murder By Mascot	978-1-61929-048-8
Mary Vermillion	Seminal Murder	978-1-61929-049-5

About the Author

Dakota Hudson is a self-described "cop with an overactive imagination." She has over 20 years with the Los Angeles Police Department, spending the majority of that time in front line crime fighting operations. Added to this is twelve years of military experience, including combat tours in Iraq and worldwide counter-terrorism operations, providing her with a wealth of experiences upon which to base her writings. This is her first publication and she is currently at work on its sequel. D.H. lives in the Los Angeles area with her wife and their four furry, four-legged children.

VISIT US ONLINE AT
www.regalcrest.biz

At the Regal Crest Website You'll Find

- The latest news about forthcoming titles and new releases

- Our complete backlist of romance, mystery, thriller and adventure titles

- Information about your favorite authors

- Current bestsellers

- Media tearsheets to print and take with you when you shop

- Which books are also available as eBooks.

Regal Crest print titles are available from all progressive booksellers including numerous sources online. Our distributors are Bella Distribution and Ingram.